NATALIE'S GOLD

A story of ultimate evil, love and revenge

BY:
DAVID W. DRAKE

Savanat Press

Natalie's Gold

Author's Photo by Jane Chouteau
        jane@janechouteau.com
        www.janechouteau.com

Book edited by Carol O'Donnell

Published by Savanat Press
http:// www.savanatpress.com
Published in the United States of America

ISBN: 978-1-7336163-5-5

Table of Contents

CHAPTER ONE

DR. WURZBURGERSTRASSE 12
BAYREUTH, DEUTSCHLAND
20 AUGUST 1907

The rays of the brutal summer sun beat down on the old German gardener and he was perspiring freely, saturating the rough woolen cloth of his shirt and causing it to cling to his back. He paused for a moment in his task of shoveling manure into a battered wheelbarrow, took off his wide-brimmed hat and wiped the sweat off his brow with the arm of his shirt. Though tall and very slender, he was stooped from years of labor in the sun and his hands were gnarled and calloused. His hair had gone all gray but there were still hints in his lined face that he had been handsome in his youth. Once he had hoped to marry and have children, but his timid and reticent personality had condemned him to the life of a bachelor. He now thought it was for the best as he was at heart a gentle soul, happiest when he was left alone with his trees and plants.

He glanced up at the late afternoon sun. It must be thirty-five degrees Celsius now, he thought. But it wasn't the heat so much as the high humidity. The spot beside the manure pile felt like a steam bath.

Friedrich Faber was chief gardener, and right now the only gardener, on the palatial estate of Doktor Kurt Wolf. There had been an assistant gardener to help him until late last year but then the frivolous young man had up and run off to Munich. The doktor had promised to hire a replacement but somehow had never gotten around to it. Friedrich dare not remind him. His employer had a mercurial temper and one never knew how he would react to things.

Doktor Kurt Wolf was a wealthy man, owning thousands of hectares of farmland near Bayreuth. He rented out the land to tenant farmers. Friedrich could only guess at the size of the pile of golden marks he amassed every year from rents. The doktor was also an important man politically. He represented Bayreuth in the Reichstag, the German national assembly. Everywhere he went in town, people would doff their hats and give him deference. Friedrich was proud to be a gardener for such an important, lofty man.

With all things considered, the gardener was content with his lot. He was provided with decent, abundant food with the other servants in the kitchen. Every evening he would climb the cramped staircase at the back of the house to his little room under the rafters in the attic. It was cozy and dry. To have adequate food and a safe place to sleep; what more could a man ask for? It was a lot better than many other Germans got.

He also loved his job and could lose himself in working with plants and trees. Having a knack for growing things, he could tell at a glance whether a plant was healthy or sick and knew just what to do to restore the ones that needed care. The shrubbery and trees on the Wolf estate were in top condition and Friedrich would beam with pride when the doktor would, on occasion, complement him.

Still, he was beginning to worry that the size of the estate grounds, Five hectares were getting to be too much for him to handle at his age. He was grateful that the land behind the house, most of the estate, had been left as virgin woods with paths cleared for walking which, therefore, needed minimal attention. Friedrich had just passed his fiftieth birthday, a good five years past the average German's life expectancy. Longevity ran in his family. His father and grandfather had lived into their early sixties so Friedrich was confident he had years more to live. But his body didn't perform like it did when he was young. He tired easily and didn't have the physical strength he once had. He anticipated that soon he would have to tell the doktor he needed help with the gardening. He dreaded the prospect.

To add to his problems with the heat and a worn out body, for the past week he had been tormented by two young boys dressed up as American red Indians. They would pop up out of nowhere whooping and shooting arrows at him. The arrows did no damage as they were blunt tipped, but the attacks would startle him and make his old heart race. It was frustrating that there was nothing he could do about it. One of the boys was the master's only son, the heir to the estate and Wolf fortune. Friedrich dare not rebuke him.

Ten meters away, nine-year-old Erich Wolf peered from behind a bush at Friedrich who was standing beside his wheelbarrow. Erich's skinny boy's body was clad in a fringed buckskin shirt and trousers with moccasins and a feathered bonnet on his head, all bought by mail order from Dusseldorf. His face was streaked in war paint borrowed from his mother's dressing table. Beside him, ten-year-old Herschel Stein was also dressed as an American Indian but much less elaborately. His chest was bare but he was wearing decidedly non-Indian short pants and sturdy shoes. He had a headband with a single feather stuck in the top at the back of his head. He also wore war paint. In both boys' hands were short bows with arrows nocked and ready to shoot.

§

Erich's fascination for American Indians started when his father had taken him by train last year to Dresden to see a performance of Buffalo Bill's Wild West Show. On its second tour of Europe, the show had generated tremendous excitement among the German public, and Erich beheld a large crowd clamoring for tickets when he and his father arrived at the entrance gate. During the show, he watched with wide eyes an attack on a stagecoach and the reenactment of some blue coated cavalrymen being massacred by Indians. He fidgeted in his seat with excitement. He had to pee but he dared not leave the stands even for a minute for fear of missing something.

It was when a group of Lakota Sioux warriors rode by close to where he was sitting that the eight-year-old became enthralled. They wore their traditional attire of buckskin and feathered headdresses and their faces and ponies were painted for war. In his mind's eye, Erich imagined the warriors roaming free on the vast American plains. Hunting and eating wild animals, they could do as they wished and didn't have to depend on others. They didn't have to wash before dinner or say, "bitte," and "danke," have good table manners or do anything else their parents told them to do.

Back home in Bayreuth, the boy began needling his Father for Indian accoutrements. Kurt Wolf indulged him, as fathers of only sons are wont to do. Kurt thought the childhood fantasy would quickly fade. It didn't. A year later his son was still roaming Bayreuth, playing at being a savage.

In mid-August, 1907, the famous Bayreuth Music Festival was in full swing. Inaugurated in the 1850s by the composer Richard Wagner to showcase his music, the annual month long festival now attracted huge crowds from around the world. The hotels and restaurants were packed with visitors to the town.

The crowds and excitement were like a candle to a moth for young Erich. He exchanged his Indian outfit for lederhosen and hung around the center of town, eating ice cream and watching the well-dressed people bustle by on the sidewalk.

One day near the opera house, a family walked past him. There were a man, his wife and two sons, one being about Erich's age. They caught his attention because they were speaking American English. Erich didn't understand the language but knew it when he heard it. The American family entered a restaurant for lunch and Erich hung around outside.

An hour later, the boy in the American family closest to Erich's age came out of the restaurant ahead of his parents. Young Wolf walked up to him.

"Are you American?" he asked in German.

"Ja, I am," replied the boy, also in German, proudly puffing out his chest.

"Do you know any Indians?"

The boy laughed, "We live in Chicago. There aren't any Indians around there anymore," When he saw the crestfallen look on Erich's face, he quickly added "but, west of Chicago in a place called the Dakota territory there are plenty of Indians."

Erich stuck out his hand. "I am Erich Wolf. I live here in Bayreuth."

"I am Herschel Stein."

The two boys shook hands. Erich noticed that Herschel wore a funny little round hat on the back of his head.

'Why are you wearing that little hat?"

"I must wear it for my religion."

Erich was about to ask what religion Herschel was when a motor car chugged past on the street and captured both boys' attention. It was dark green with yellow spoked wheels and lots of shiny brass and was spewing black smoke. Both boys followed it with their eyes until it was out of sight. The sight caused Erich to totally forget about his question about Herschel's religion.

For the next week, the boys were nearly inseparable, romping about the Wolf estate and nearby fields playing Indian and thoroughly enjoying themselves.

§

At a signal from Erich, the two fierce Indian braves burst from cover, each letting out a bloodthirsty whoop calculated to instill fear in the hearts of the enemies of the Lakota tribe. They ran in wide circles around the hapless gardener, shooting arrows at him as they ran. Friedrich, for his part was turning round and round and hopping about trying to dodge the arrows. His face was red and showed a very angry expression but he said nothing.

When all the arrows were expended, Friedrich pushed the wheelbarrow away cursing under his breath. The boys walked around retrieving the arrows. Erich looked up at the position of the sun and realized it was getting late. He must go inside and wash for the evening meal. His mother would be cross if he was late for dinner. He said goodbye to Herschel and took the path through the backyard woods and around the house to the front door.

He was confronted in the foyer by his father, who grabbed the boy by the arm, dragged him forcefully into his study and closed the door.

"Tell me," said a furious Kurt Wolf, "that you have not been cavorting all over Bayreuth in the company of a Jew."

"No, father, I don't understand," Erich truly didn't. The only Jews he had ever seen wore black suits, wide-brimmed black hats and long beards. A group of them had been pointed out to him as curiosities by his mother one day when he was accompanying her on an outing.

Kurt hauled back his right arm and slapped the boy on the cheek, hard, and Erich recoiled. He felt the sting of the blow, but the humiliation was worse, much worse. Kurt Wolf was a big bear of a man with a huge square head, loud voice and gave the impression of great power. He could be very intimidating to a small boy.

"That boy you have been playing with is the son of a German Jew who emigrated to America and got rich. He then has the gall to come back and pollute our festival and flaunt his wealth."

His father then grabbed Erich's shoulders and shouted in his face.

"Do you not realize my political position? I was only elected to the Reichstag last year. If this gets out it could damage my political career."

Erich started to cry. He didn't want to but he couldn't help himself.

"I didn't know he was a Jew. I am sorry," pleaded Erich his cheeks wet with tears.

"Sorry? Sorry? You must never say you are sorry for anything. Being sorry means you are weak and I won't abide by a weak son. Go to your room and don't come out until I say so."

Later in his bedroom Erich lay sprawled on his bed face down and weeping bitterly. The humiliation was more than he could bear. He should have known that Herschel was a Jew. Everyone knew Jews were sneaky, evil people. He lay there crushed by sadness for some time. Then his sadness gradually turned to anger. And then he found an outlet for his anger.

It was all the fault of that Jew Herschel. He had tricked him and was probably laughing about it with his Jew father. Rage built within him. He vowed never again to let anyone, especially a Jew, trick him. He would be strong, hard as steel like his father wanted him to be. The next morning when Herschel showed up to play, Erich chased him away with harsh words spoken in white-hot anger. Afterward, he took all his American Indian things and burned them in the incinerator behind the house.

CHAPTER TWO

GIEBELSTRASSE
JUDISCHES VIERTEL
KASSEL, DEUTSCHLAND
21 MAI 1908

G iebelstrasse was a typical street in the Jewish quarter of the city of Kassel in the region of Hesse, Imperial German Empire, in the first quarter of the twentieth century. It was narrower and more winding and the shops lining it were smaller and shabbier than in the Gentile areas of the city. Almost all the buildings facing the street were of two stories, shops on the ground floor with living quarters above. Each small establishment had a Jewish surname on a sign above the door and displayed the best of its wares in a modest window beside the entrance. All the crafts were represented, here a tailor, there a shoemaker, with a goldsmith in between.

There had been Jews in Kassel since the late eleventh century. After the black death swept through the region in 1350, Kassel's Jewish inhabitants were blamed for the calamity and slaughtered by hostile Germans in pogroms. The community was wiped out. In dribs and drabs over the centuries, however, other Jews emigrated there and now, in 1908, the Jewish population of Kassel exceeded twenty-four hundred souls.

It had been a fine spring day in May. The late afternoon sun shone brightly and a balmy breeze ruffled the geraniums in the window box on an upper window of Klein's Apothecary at

Giebelstrasse 44. The quarter's people were out and about enjoying the fine weather. Their dress varied according to the branch of Judaism they followed.

About half of the Jews in Kassel were Orthodox. The men of this faction wore black suits and wide-brimmed black hats and sported beards. Some of the wealthier Orthodox Jews had fur on their collars and the rims of their hats. Their young sons wore curled strands of hair called "Payot" dangling down in front of their ears and skullcaps called "kippot" in Hebrew and "yarmulkes" in Yiddish on the back of their heads.

The rest of the men, who didn't take their religion quite so seriously, wore ordinary German suits and workman's clothing with only kippots perched on the crowns of their heads as a concession to Judaism. All the women, young and old, were dressed similarly in modest, full-length dresses of earthy colors, many with shawls draped over their shoulders despite the warm weather. The married women all wore tichels, a type of scarf that was worn draped over their heads and tied at the back. In all factions of Judaism, a married woman must cover her hair in public.

The Jews of Kassel walked with a peculiar, head down, submissive gait that they had learned over the centuries gave the least offense to the hostile Gentiles around them. It was so ingrained in them that they walked this way even when there were no Christians around.

Not that they were sad on this day. It is difficult to suppress the human spirit. People everywhere have an inborn desire to enjoy themselves, no matter the circumstances of their existence. The fine weather, with a little help from the aroma of mandelbrot and rugelach being baked in Nussbaum's bakery down the street, had livened the residents and visitors to Giebelstrasse. Soon it would be time to go to their homes for the evening meal but, in the meantime, they were enjoying the beautiful afternoon.

The men stood in groups discussing the topics of the day with index fingers pointed at the sky, trying to impress each other with their arguments. An old man with a long gray beard had a gaggle of squealing children surrounding him. He pulled handfuls of sweets from his pockets and distributed them to the children, then protested that he had no more. The children weren't convinced and their cries rose in volume. The old man acted surprised as he pulled another handful of candy from his coat. The mothers of the children looked on with amusement. It was a little game the old man often acted out.

Just then a tall, powerful looking young man appeared striding purposely down the middle of the cobbled street. He didn't walk like a Jew. When the people saw the grim set of his jaw and the angry expression on his face, they parted swiftly to allow him to pass. He wore none of the outward trappings of Judaism. Drab, rough clothing that matched that of the German working class adorned his body. The sleeves of his shirt were rolled up almost to his elbows exposing sinewy forearms. His broad shoulders were thrown back with his head held high and his level gaze straight ahead. The young man's face was square and angular, the hard planes of which were softened by a wild unruly mop of dark brown hair.

One man in a group of Orthodox Jews nearby recognized the young man as Erhard Weiss, son of Abraham the shoemaker. The man told his companions and the group turned their backs on the young man. They strongly disapproved of the Weiss family. Had they not abandoned their faith and become assimilated Jews? They didn't respect Shabbat, keep kosher or even wear the yarmulke.

Others among the people on the street weren't as unforgiving. The Weiss father and son were hardworking and more than willing to aid others in times of distress. They were very good at their craft, turning out some of the best shoes and boots in Kassel. The family's women were modest and kind and well regarded. What was not to like? But more than a few in the crowd of the more tolerant Jews wondered what had made Erhard so angry.

Erhard was both angry and annoyed. He was annoyed that he was late for the monthly meeting of the Zionist club. There was supposed to be a Jew from Palestine speaking at the meeting and he was anxious to hear what he had to say. The reason he was late was also the reason he was angry. He had just had another argument with his father over Zionism.

"This Zionist nonsense will only anger the Gentile Germans!" Abraham Weiss had shouted. "It will only bring more trouble down on our heads."

Erhard replied hotly that it was high time for the Jews to give up on Germany and emigrate to Palestine.

"Give up our life here?" asked Abraham "Our family has been in Kassel for many generations. We should leave our home and live in squalor in a desert? Live on charity? No, we must stay and endure. The hatred of the Germans will pass. Better times will come."

Erhard's anger boiled over. "Why," he retorted, "does the Imperial constitution say Jews are citizens guaranteed equal rights, but we are systematically denied those rights in reality? Why do we subject ourselves to insults and physical danger from people who hate us? The goy newspapers are full of lies and hatred of our people. They call us a 'polluting alien race.' At any moment a mob of Jew haters could come storming down the street and kill us all and no one would do anything about it."

The young man had rushed out of his father's shop, seething with anger. His attitude was typical of the younger generation of German Jews since the rise of the Zionist movement. Theodor Herzl, a Hungarian Jew, had started the movement around the turn of the twentieth century. He argued that Jews would never be welcome in Europe but would always be subject to periodic episodes of violence by Gentiles. He went on to advocate that the Jews should return to their ancient home of Palestine and establish a state of their own. The movement had spread like wildfire and Zionist clubs and organizations had sprung up all over Europe. With the zeal of the young, Erhard Weiss had embraced the movement.

When he walked in the door of the rented hall the meeting was already in progress and the man from Palestine was speaking. Erhard scanned the room looking for an empty chair. Spying one near the back of the room, he made his way over to it and sat down. There were about thirty young people listening to the speaker rattle on in bad German. The man was tall and gaunt, wearing an ill-fitting suit, standing at a lectern. He was cleanly shaven with uncombed long hair that hung to his shoulders. Weiss settled himself in the hard chair and began to concentrate on his words.

"...comrades lived in tents until barracks were built. Today we live in modern buildings with plenty of heat in winter. There is ample delicious food. The climate is delightful, fresh air and sunshine the year round. We each do our share of the work and receive our share of the food..."

Erhard heard a chuckle coming from the person seated behind him and then a sarcastic comment, "Oh, I'm sure it's just so," said a female voice. He was annoyed but turned his attention back to the speaker.

"... benefactors, great men like the Rothschilds, buy the land from absentee Arab landowners. They also provide the materials for construction of our communal dwellings..."

There was another chuckle behind Erhard and another sarcastic comment: "I bet they do, and out of their care and concern for their fellow Jews, such compassion."

Weiss indignantly swung around to confront the person. He found himself nose to nose with a girl who had been leaning forward when he turned. She had an oval face and a smile on her lips, but Erhard only noticed her eyes. They were big and dark brown, but in the irises surrounding the pupil were little flecks of bright green. The eyes had a strange effect on him. His breath came quicker and he had a funny feeling in the pit of his stomach. Erhard's annoyance evaporated and he swiftly swung back around.

The speaker droned on but Erhard didn't hear a word. All he could think about were those amazing eyes. When the speaker finished talking there was enthusiastic applause in which Erhard joined. He walked away from his chair, carefully avoiding looking at the girl sitting behind him.

The club had provided a samovar of tea, cups and platters of pastries as refreshments. They were located on a folding table in a corner of the hall. Erhard stood beside the table with a cup of tea in his hand. He surreptitiously scanned the room for the strange girl. He spotted her talking to Naomi Schwartz but didn't recognize her. The Kassel Jewish community was small and everyone knew everyone else so the girl must be visiting from somewhere else.

She was a little taller than average and she wasn't wearing a tichel so he knew she was unmarried. Her dark hair was pulled back from her face and rolled into a tight bun behind her head. She was dressed in a floor-length brown dress with a bodice that buttoned all the way up to her chin. Though she was slim, she had larger than normal breasts. Her face looked very beautiful to Erhard. He felt a stirring in his loins. Suddenly, the strange girl turned and looked in his direction and he looked quickly away. A few seconds later he glanced back and saw the girl wending her way toward him. His mouth was dry so he swallowed as she approached and stuck out her right hand.

"I am Natalie Lapinsky and I wish to apologize. I seem to have offended you."

She had a smug smile on her face and was looking directly into his eyes. Erhard took her hand and blurted out a response without thinking.

"You need not apologize to me. But you should apologize to the

Zionist cause."

He knew immediately how pompous he sounded and mentally kicked himself for his stupid response. A touch of color appeared on Natalie's cheeks and her expression changed to one of annoyance.

"Apologize to them?" she retorted while pointing at the wild-haired speaker from Palestine. "Let me tell you. A cousin of mine listened to one of these people and emigrated to Palestine. He was lured there by wonderful promises like we heard here tonight. Do you know what he found there? The only land the Arabs will sell to Jews is swampland or desert with no water source. My cousin spent his days draining swamps in the blazing sun with clouds of mosquitoes hovering around him. The Arabs hate Jews so much that they have to travel in groups for safety. Do you know they raise pigs there? Imagine, Jews raising pigs. They hide them when the rich Jews that finance them come around. The whole idea of emigrating to Palestine is a fool's errand. I only came here tonight because Naomi didn't want to come alone."

Erhard was shocked at the outburst. He tried to think of something to say in return but his tongue wouldn't work correctly. It kept getting in the way as he tried to talk. He sputtered and fumed. The girl was infuriating. All he could do was stare into her amazing, angry eyes. Abruptly, Natalie turned in a huff and strode out of the hall, her head held high.

Before he left the meeting himself Erhard cornered Naomi Schwartz's brother Avi and asked him about the infuriating girl. He learned that her name was Natania Lapinski, but the girl refused to use her first name, preferring the Christian name, "Natalie," instead. She was the eldest daughter of a shoemaker in the village of Vellmar, eight kilometers north of Kassel. Avi also said that she had a reputation for being difficult and contrary with the opposite sex, and was good friends with his sister. Erhard was still smarting from the impertinent manner in which Natalie had treated him. He decided that she was just a rude girl. It was best to just go home and forget

NATALIE'S GOLD | **18**

the incident.

Erhard had a nightmare about Natalie that night. He dreamed that he was in a room crowded with people and he suddenly found himself naked. As he tried to cover himself, Natalie was suddenly there. She was laughing and pointing at his groin. He awoke with a start and couldn't get back to sleep for an hour.

The next day he couldn't get the strange, feisty girl out of his thoughts. He was irritable and snapped at his sister and mother. This was out of character for Erhard. He loved his family more than anything in the world.

When he was a young man about Erhard's age, Abraham Weiss had a voluble disagreement with his father. The family were Orthodox Ashkenazi Jews and considered themselves culturally superior to the Sephardic Jewish immigrants then pouring in from Poland. Abraham and his father had a violent disagreement about this discrimination because Abraham had it in his mind to marry a Sephardic girl. The old man had ordered him out of the house, never to return. Abraham had abandoned Judaism and never talked with his father again.

As a result of his father's decision, Erhard had grown up with over half his Jewish neighbors not speaking to him. Consequently, the young man felt no loyalty to his hostile Jewish neighbors and certainly none to the Gentiles in Kassel. That left his family as his anchor in life. He would do anything for his father, his mother Anna and his slightly older sister Gerta. So, it came as a shock when Erhard snapped at his sister at the evening meal the day after the Zionist meeting. Later that night, before she dropped off to sleep, Anna broached the subject of Erhard's strange new mood to her husband.

"I am worried about Erhard. Something is bothering him."

Abraham took her hand in his and reassured her. "I wouldn't

worry about him. I think the root of his problem is probably a young woman. Do you remember how crazy I was when I was courting you?"

Days went by and Erhard thought about Natalie constantly. The more he tried to get her out of his mind the stronger she would come back into his thoughts. He was morose and depressed and had trouble concentrating at the workbench. One day his knife slipped and he ruined an almost completed pair of boots and he cursed himself.

His anger at Natalie built as the weeks went by. As the date for the monthly Zionist meeting approached, Erhard wondered if the obstinate girl would show up there again. If she did, this time he would set her straight. He thought up witty comebacks to her arguments against Zionism and rehearsed them over and over in his mind. He would show her.

The evening of the meeting, Erhard took special care with his appearance. He took a bath, something he only usually did once a week. He dressed in his best clothes and even made an attempt to tame his wild hair with a comb. It didn't go well. The hair would spring back to its original chaos as soon as the comb had passed through. His sister Gerta, hearing him curse through the wall of her room next door, wondering what was wrong with him. Erhard finally threw down the comb and admitted defeat.

The June meeting of the Zionist club was held in the salon of a well-to-do doctor whose son was a member. When Erhard entered the home he saw about twenty young people standing around in groups talking and waiting for the meeting to begin. He looked around and didn't see Natalie. He was surprised to feel a big letdown. Then he saw her enter the room accompanied by Naomi. Erhard, so sad the moment before, was suddenly happy and his spirits soared, but then he brutally suppressed the feeling. He noticed that Natalie was more finely dressed than at the last meeting. She must be wearing her best clothes too, he thought. Erhard studiously avoided looking at her again.

The meeting was called to order. The first item of discussion was a proposal to send representatives to attend other Zionist meetings in Frankfurt and Leipzig. Erhard was called upon for his opinion. He rose and said that he thought the expense would be too much for the limited resources of the club. He was still talking when Natalie jumped to her feet and interrupted him.

"I think sending representatives is a fine idea. It is always good to expand our horizons."

Erhard looked at her with annoyance. How dare she speak. This was only the second time she had attended a meeting! He was reminded of one of the things he didn't like about the Zionist club. It had a socialist bent and considered females to be equal members. They often spoke their mind.

"And where are we going to get the money to send people all over the country?" asked Erhard haughtily.

Natalie jumped up again and looked over at him. Her brows were knit together and color flashed up her cheeks. Erhard thought she was the most beautiful girl he had ever seen. His annoyance evaporated and was replaced by desire.

"Take up a collection. I'm sure the expense will not be too great," said Natalie and sat back down.

The back and forth went on for some time to the amusement of the other club members.

All the clever responses and witty comebacks that Erhard had rehearsed were forgotten and he sputtered and stammered his replies during the rest of the meeting. He mentally fumed because he sounded like a fool.

He was thoroughly miserable as he walked home. The girl was

exasperating. Women weren't supposed to act this way. Why had she taken such a dislike to him?

The months rolled by and Erhard was no less miserable. The girl continued to consume his thoughts. At every Zionist meeting, she would make it a point to contradict him and make him look foolish. But he no longer cared about that. By September he had to admit to himself that he was desperately in love with Natalie Lapinsky, but what could he do about it? Should he go to her and declare his love? What if she laughed at him? What if she called him a fool? By the evening of the September Zionist meeting, he had decided to take the plunge and talk to Natalie. If she scorned him he would just emigrate to Palestine and go on with his life.

Erhard sat through the meeting without saying anything. Several times he glanced at Natalie and saw that she was looking at him. After the meeting adjourned, with a rapidly beating heart and sweaty palms, he approached her outside on the street.

"Miss Lapinsky, might I have a word with you?"

She turned and lifted her head. He almost gasped, she was so beautiful. Erhard lowered his gaze and stared at the ground as he spoke.

"I feel compelled to tell you that I think I have fallen in love with you, but I am sure you don't share the feeling. I am awkward and unworthy of your affection…."

He felt her hand on his arm and looked up into those beautiful eyes.

"Of course I love you, you big dumb ox. Why do you think I came to all those stupid meetings?" she asked quietly. Her eyes were shining and her beautiful lips were slightly apart.

In spite of being in a crowd and on a public street, Erhard took Natalie in his arms and kissed her. Her lips were soft and yielding.

Erhard's heart soared. He never again talked about emigrating to Palestine.

CHAPTER THREE

KANALSTRASSE UNT WOLFSTRASSE
BAYREUTH, DEUTSCHLAND
30 JULI 1914

The military band of the 1st Royal Bavarian Division, Imperial German Army, marched up Kanalstrasse past cheering spectators playing the Deutsche Art Marsch, their polished instruments gleaming in the bright sun of the warm July day. Their uniforms were elegant, with gold braid and piping, much fancier than the uniforms of the regular soldiers marching behind them.

In company-sized formations, the infantry followed the band. Ten abreast, they marched, and each group was led by two officers in impeccably tailored uniforms riding splendid horses. The ordinary soldiers wore gray-green uniforms with brass buttons and red piping around the collars, cuffs and down the front of their tunics. Each soldier also wore a Pickelhaube helmet. It was circular, made out of varnished leather and had a spike protruding from the crown. The helmets were covered in the same gray-green cloth as their uniforms with the number "1" stenciled on the front in white. Buckled around each waist was a black leather cartridge belt containing ammunition and a bayonet for the model 1898 Mauser rifles carried on their shoulders.

The soldiers, most of whom were shockingly young, were smiling. They were enjoying the cheers from the crowd lining the parade route. Some of the young soldiers had flowers or miniature Imperial flags stuck on various parts of their uniforms, put there by adoring young women.

Kurt Wolf was in the crowd watching the parade. Beside him was his son, Erich, a gangly boy with pimples about to turn sixteen years old. At the moment, the boy was not happy.

"Why do you want me to learn French and English? Those countries are our enemies."

Kurt shushed Erich as the national flag went by and put his hat over his heart. When the flag had passed, he turned and answered his son.

"That is precisely why I want you to learn those languages. Because they are our enemies. We are about to conquer them as we did the French in 1871. Maybe this time we will occupy their territory and rule them. There will be many opportunities in the occupied countries for a young man from good Aryan stock whose father is a member of the Reichstag."

The formations of soldiers came to an end. Many of the spectators fell in behind them and followed, still cheering. Wolf and his son stayed where they were.

Kurt was proud of Germany and of his Aryan race. When the English, French and Russians got a taste of German steel, they would rue the day they provoked a war with the Fatherland. Since the declaration of war, a wave of patriotic sentiment had swept the country. It was followed by a surge of anger at the British for instituting a tight naval blockade of German ports. Since Germany relied heavily on imports, especially food imports, the people looked on the blockade as a war crime against innocent civilians. But most of the German public was optimistic that the hostilities would be over before any shortages were felt.

Kurt wasn't angry at the British. Why be angry over an action that you would take yourself if you had the means. It further reinforced his belief that the ordinary Germans were childlike and needed men such as himself to rule them.

Kurt was very aware of his place in German society. He was of the ruling class, which consisted of the nobility, industrialists and wealthy landowners like himself. Germany had a rigid class system. Everyone knew their place within society and this was generally accepted by everyone. There was very little mobility between these classes. If a man was born poor, it was a good bet that he would die poor. A woman of the middle class through cunning or good looks might marry into the ruling class, but this didn't hold true for a man. Wealth alone didn't assure entry into the elite class. If a man didn't have the right pedigree, he would be shunned.

There was also a strict moral code, especially regarding sexual relations. Violators would find themselves as pariahs in society. In certain situations having sexual intercourse with someone outside one's class could land one in prison. Kurt didn't know it at that time, but the war he was so eager for would sweep away the system he so loved and defended.

He took the arm of his sulking son and walked toward his motor car parked across the street. It was a Benz 10/30 touring car painted bright yellow. The sight of Friedrich, his elderly gardener, holding open the rear door reminded him of his one pressing problem.

Kurt's groom, motor car driver, second gardener and butler had all been called into the army. His one remaining male servant was Friedrich. In his late fifties, the gardener was a nervous man who only wanted to be left alone with his rose bushes and azaleas. Wolf had pressed him into service as a motor car driver. A man in his position couldn't drive himself. Friedrich was deathly afraid of the big car. He compensated for his fear by driving very slowly. Kurt would have switched to a carriage but Friedrich was more frightened of horses than motor cars.

The trip back to the Wolf estate took an eternity. Kurt thought that he could have made it quicker aboard an ambling cow. To further test his patience, his wife Ailse was waiting for him in the entry hall.

"My dear, what is it?" he asked testily.

"Your son." Kurt groaned inwardly. When she said, 'your son' and not, 'our son,' it meant the boy had done something serious. "Your son has been carrying on a dalliance with his sister Hilda's maid, Maria. Imagine, in our Christian home. But that is not all. The girl is with child. She confided in the cook who came to me with the story."

"How do we know the brat is Erich's?" asked Wolf.

"Unfortunately, I am convinced that it is. The maid is barely sixteen. I questioned the other staff and they confirmed the affair. Oh, Kurt, I feel sorry for the girl. Her parents are staunch Catholics. They will disown her."

"You are not to concern yourself with this matter any further, I will handle it. Tell Erich I want to see him."

"Ja, Kurt," said Ailse. She always deferred to her husband's wishes.

Kurt sat in his overstuffed chair and waited until his teenaged son walked into the room. He gave Erich a stormy look he usually reserved for Social Democrats in the Reichstag.

"Do you understand my position in this community and nation?" Kurt asked his son.

'Ja, father."

"Then why did you have relations with your sister's maid and get her with child?"

Kurt watched Erich's expression change from curiosity to shock. He went pale. Then his expression hardened into one of defiance.

"I admit it. She was always smiling and flirting with me. She was the instigator, father. I did what any man would do with such temptation."

Kurt smiled inwardly at his son referring to himself as a man.

"I am a member of the Reichstag. This could create a scandal that would jeopardize my position there. In the future, you will keep your reproductive member inside your trousers, at least around the domestic help. Is that clear?"

"Ja, Father," said Erich with a stone face.

"That will be all."

Erich turned to leave. As he neared the door, Kurt called a question to him.

"Was she any good?"

"I don't know father. She was my first," said Erich with a smile.

A week later Kurt called Maria into his study. Her face appeared to be very young and it was framed by blond pigtails that fell to her shoulders on each side of her head. Even though she wore a shapeless smock, Wolf could tell she had a woman's body. In Kurt's presence, she was staring at the floor.

"You sent for me, Herr Doktor?" Her voice was barely audible.

"Yes, Maria, because you have been so careless as to get yourself in the family way, your services will no longer be required in my home."

Maria looked up in shock, "But Herr Doktor, he forced me to do it. He said I would lose my job if I didn't."

Wolf held up a hand stopping her. "That is immaterial," but then he smiled.

"But I am not unkind. I have arranged for you to enter a convent in Nuremberg. There you will be able to deliver your baby discreetly. In addition, I have an envelope here with one hundred marks in it. This will enable you to start a new life with your child." Kurt's face hardened. "But if you choose to cause trouble, I will destroy you and your family."

Maria stared at Kurt, as tears rolled down her cheeks. Finally, seeing no way out, she picked up the envelope and walked out with her head down. An hour later, Kurt watched from the study window as Maria trudged down the driveway toward the street. She was clad in a shabby dress and carried a bundle across her shoulder. When she reached the street, she looked back at the house. He was a considerable distance away but he could still clearly see the look of utter devastation on her face.

Kurt felt a twinge of guilt, then dismissed it. The whole thing was unfair. But the strong were always unfair to the weak. He was protecting his family and reputation. If he had to sacrifice a hundred maids to maintain his power and position, he would do it. But then Kurt Wolf felt an even stronger jolt of conscience. *Who am I kidding? This is not honorable.*

"Verdammt!" he shouted.

He sent Friedrich huffing and puffing after Maria with an envelope containing an extra five hundred marks.

In the ensuing months, Ailse never asked Kurt how he had handled the problem with Maria and he never told her. A new maid was hired for Hilda, an ugly one, and soon Kurt's memory of the incident faded.

CHAPTER FOUR

BANHOF
KASSEL, DEUTSCHLAND
21 OKTOBER 1919

L eutnant Erhard Weiss, late of the Imperial German army, wearily left the train. In four years of war, he had risen in rank from regular soldier to Leutnant. He often thought that the chief reason was that he had managed to remain alive through years of war and was not killed or maimed for life like so many others. When they came to put the officer's shoulder boards on him, he hadn't found a good enough place to hide.

He looked extremely thin and gaunt. Years of near starvation rations had taken their toll. His shabby enlisted man's uniform contrasted unfavorably with the smartly tailored uniforms of other Imperial Army officers on the train. The only indication he was an officer was the Leutnant's shoulder boards he wore on the otherwise standard enlisted men's uniform he wore. Unlike those other officers, however, his tattered uniform was adorned with two Iron Crosses bestowed for valor on the field of battle. Civilians could be forgiven for not appreciating what they meant but other soldiers knew exactly what they signified. One splendidly uniformed officer, a Hauptmann with the weary eyes of a veteran, upon encountering Erhard on the train had come to attention, clicked his heels, and saluted. He was sending an unspoken message of respect.

Erhard's Iron Cross Second Class had been earned for shooting a high ranking French officer during his short stint as a sniper. The Iron Cross First Class had been awarded for an action during the battle of Passchendaele in Belgium in October 1917. Erhard Weiss was commanding a platoon of men during a furious British attack. There were so many English Tommies advancing on the German trench line that the platoons on either side of Erhard's had started to crumble. The soldiers began to abandon the trench and flee for their lives. Erhard through threats, encouragement, example and true leadership had kept his men fighting. Just when it looked like his platoon would be overrun, a German counterattack had swept in from both sides and forced the British back. When the action was over Erhard had seven men still able to fight out of the twenty-eight he started the day with.

He looked around the station platform for Natalie. He didn't see her but was not surprised. Erhard had only been discharged a week ago and had written Natalie that he was coming home. But the mails were slow since the end of the war and he hadn't had money for a telegram.

Erhard began the walk toward the Jewish quarter of Kassel and his shoemaker shop. In times past it had seemed an easy stroll. Now, thanks to a scarred over wound in his right leg, courtesy of a French machine gun bullet, he walked with a noticeable limp and constant pain. The wound hadn't healed properly and the military doctors had said he would limp the rest of his life.

Walking the familiar streets of his home city, Erhard thought he should feel elation that he was almost home but all he felt were profound exhaustion and a sense of futility. The war, with all its blood and misery, had been for nothing. Germany was much worse off than when the war started. Weiss had been skeptical when a republic had been proclaimed after the Kaiser abdicated. Like most Germans, he favored order. He liked the stability that the Kaiser provided. Now there was chaos on the streets of the country. communists battled right-wing private armies. Several coup attempts by Communists had been suppressed, with many dead. A lot of Germans had returned to their old blame game against the Jews. All anyone could talk about was the war and the injustice of the Versailles Treaty that had brought it to an end.

§

By early November 1918, the German Army was just holding on, exhausted. The men were starving. Anyone with half a brain could see that defeat was near. Then rumors flew through the trenches that the Kaiser had abdicated his throne and a new democratic government was suing for peace. Erhard told his men not to get their hopes up. A few days later official word had come down that an armistice, to take effect on 11 November, had been negotiated with the Allies.

Erhard canceled all patrols and allowed no more sniper missions in his sector. As the day of the armistice approached, he and his men hunkered down deep in their dugouts, while the artillery of both sides continued to furiously shell the opposing trenches.

At 1100 hrs. on 11 November the artillery fell silent. Erhard and his men cautiously emerged from their dugouts and studied the enemy trenches through periscopes. Finally, one brave soul on the German side scaled a trench ladder and emerged topside. He waved his arms and cheering soldiers began pouring from the trenches on both sides. Unarmed, they met in the middle of no man's land and hugged, wore each other's caps and traded for tobacco and spirits. The British soldiers willingly shared their rations with the starving Germans.

The German Army trekked east a few days after the armistice, evacuating allied territory and setting up temporary camps just inside the German border. In late June, word came that a peace treaty formally ending the war had been signed at Versailles. Two days later Erhard led his company to a large field. In the presence of

British officers, they stacked their weapons in huge piles and joined the long snaky ranks of soldiers marching back to Germany. This time, the officers walked with their men. All the fancy horses they had ridden to war on in 1914 had either been killed by artillery or slaughtered for food. When Erhard's unit reached the 25th Division headquarters in Darmstadt they were quickly discharged and sent home.

§

Now as Erhard walked the familiar streets of his hometown, he began to perk up a little. A cold wind blew that caused his nose to run, but the sun was shining and it livened his spirits a bit. He would soon hold Natalie in his arms again. He noticed a crowd up ahead. They were gathered around a man holding on to a lamppost and making a speech. When Erhard got closer he began to make out the words.

"Comrades! We must unite in the struggle against the capitalists and Jew bankers that profited by the war. The Jews sent your sons off to die in a capitalist war but didn't go themselves. They kept their sons at home to help count the gold they made off the war…"

Erhard turned away in disgust and walked on. A few blocks further on he encountered another crowd and another shouting speaker. This crowd and speaker were better dressed than the other one.

"…German culture. The communists and the Jews want to turn Germany into a mongrel state. They want to destroy our beloved German Volk. For the sake of Germany, for the sake of your families, we must stop the Jews…"

Erhard couldn't believe what he was hearing. Both ends of the political spectrum were blaming the Jews for Germany's misfortune. The incongruity of this suddenly struck him as funny and he began to laugh out loud. Those crazy capitalist, communist Jews had been busy corrupting Germany. Some in the crowd gave him angry looks. Erhard ignored them and walked on, shaking his head.

As he neared the shop he quickened his pace as much as he could with his bad leg. It had been throbbing for many blocks. His heart began to beat faster in anticipation. The sign on the shop that read: "Weiss and Son, fine shoes and boots'" was almost illegible from peeling paint. He opened the door and went in.

Natalie had her back to him and was sweeping the floor. "I will be right with you," she said, obviously thinking he was a customer. She turned and gasped when she saw Erhard.

Her thin face went white with shock. She recovered immediately and leaped into his arms. Erhard Weiss braced himself or the two would have fallen to the floor. Pushing Natalie out to arm's length, he looked at her. She was painfully thin with dark circles under her eyes and looked very tired, but her eyes still held that mischievous spark that he loved so much. Erhard pulled her back into his arms.

Erhard knew peace and contentment for the first time in four years as they clung to each other. After a while she made tea and they sat across the kitchen table and held each other's gaze, both accustoming themselves to their long-awaited reunion. Natalie looked adoringly at him with huge eyes, watery with tears. They held hands and talked about a mundane thing just to have something to say to fill the awkward silences.

Then Natalie lowered her eyes and said she had some bad news. She said that Erhard's mother Anna, had died two weeks ago. She had forgone eating many days so that young Itzhak would have more food and she became weak. Then a virulent strain of influenza roared through the city and Anna caught it. She died after four days. Many people in the city had also died and still more were getting sick every day.

Erhard's joy at his homecoming was shattered. Memories from his childhood came to him. Anna at the big wood stove. Anna kissing him as he left for school. Anna with a look of care and concern when he left to go to war. Tears ran down his face and Natalie squeezed and kissed his hands. After all the horrors he had seen in the war, he had thought that he was hardened to the specter of death. The fact that it was his mother who had died had allowed the sorrow to penetrate his emotional armor.

While they were talking, Itzhak came home from school. He was eight now and he appeared thin but healthy. He greeted Erhard and hugged him, but in a reserved way. As Itzhak hugged his mother in turn, Erhard could see the love in Natalie's eyes for him.

That night, after the boy was tucked into bed, Erhard slipped into the bed he hadn't occupied for four years. He groaned with pleasure at the comfort. He was so tired that he was actually debating whether he wanted sex or sleep. That was until Natalie emerged from the small dressing alcove.

She stood proudly before him in the nude. Her body was thin but still able to drive him wild. She came to him and was the aggressor, urging him to faster and faster exertions. She cried out when she achieved orgasm. This was something she had never done before, always fearing that Itzhak would hear. Afterward, they lay spent in each other's arms. A quarter hour later, his soldier stood to attention again and they repeated the performance. At last, completely exhausted, Erhard settled down to sleep. But sleep wouldn't come. Seeing his old surroundings had brought back memories. He didn't think about the war with its unspeakable horrors. He purposely suppressed those memories. His mind went back to before the war, to happier times.

§

He remembered the evening he had told Natalie that he loved her and the joy he had felt when he learned his love was returned. They didn't get married right away but decided to wait until Erhard had completed his compulsory two-year military service.

And so, he had gone to Darmstadt and the headquarters of the 25th Hessian Division to learn how to be a soldier. Erhard hated it at first but then gradually began to enjoy soldiering. He liked the camaraderie with the other young soldiers and being part of a group dedicated to a single purpose: winning battles. Having never had a gun in his hands before, Erhard had developed a surprising ability at rifle marksmanship.

About midway through his second year of service Weiss had received a letter from his mother informing him that his sister Gerta had died. A sudden respiratory illness had felled her in a week. Since deaths such as this were very common in Germany at the time, the army didn't consider it a reason to grant leave. Erhard had sat on his bunk and cried and was consoled by his bunk mates.

About four months later he received a telegram from Natalie. It was more devastating news. Erhard's father Abraham, consumed with grief over Gerta's death, had gone to sleep one night and never wakened. Natalie said that she had moved into the shop with Erhard's mother to help run the business until he finished with the Army. Erhard's grief was deep. He loved his family more than anything and now he had lost two members of that family in the space of four months. For two days he stumbled through his duties like a zombie.

He received a summons from his company Commander, Hauptmann Miller, on the third day after getting the telegram. Officers in the Imperial Army tended to be aloof beings who almost never spoke to enlisted men so Weiss was fearful as he reported to the Company office. As he stood rigidly at attention in front of the officer, Erhard was surprised to see kindness in Hauptmann Miller's eyes.

"Weiss, I have heard about the unfortunate deaths in your family. You have done well here. Your Sergeant says you are a fine soldier. Good. Germany may need good soldiers very soon. I have arranged for you to be discharged early. Go home, Weiss. Take care of your family."

So Erhard had gone home to be met at the station in Kassel by Natalie and his mother. It was a joyous reunion. The two people still alive that he cared for the most were standing there. They went home to a special dinner prepared by Erhard's mother and a little too much wine in celebration. Late that night, after Anna was fast asleep, Natalie and Erhard became lovers. They were married a week later in a civil ceremony. Erhard and Natalie took over the running of the shoemaker shop and Anna attended to the domestic duties.

Their marriage got off to a surprisingly rocky start. Erhard Weiss was a very conservative man when it came to relationships. He preferred things as they had always been and didn't like change. When Erhard was growing up, his Mother had been submissive and deferential to his father. Abraham ruled the household as something of a benevolent tyrant. He had the final say in everything. Erhard had naturally assumed that he would have a similar arrangement with Natalie. But he stirred up a hornet's nest the first time he tried to assert his male authority.

Not only wasn't Natalie submissive, but she also declared that she wanted to be an equal partner in the marriage and the shoemaking business. Being the eldest daughter of a shoemaker, who had trained her well, she was a superb craftswoman. They had shouting rows and she wouldn't back down a centimeter. Poor Anna was forced to witness the arguments. She would stand by wringing her hands with a look of horror on her face. What made the situation more maddening for Erhard was that when it came to the business, Natalie's ideas usually turned out to be right. Gradually, he came to depend on the good sense of his feisty wife when it came to the running of their shop, although he sometimes chided himself for becoming a gelding.

Almost six months after their marriage Natalie announced that she was with child. Everyone was joyous. This was the first of what Natalie hoped would be many children. As the months passed she got bigger and bigger. She would negotiate the aisles in the workroom tripping over things because she couldn't see her feet. At last in July 1911 the day came for her to deliver.Everything had seemed normal at first. Then the midwife had frowned. She was seeing too much blood. It had been the bane of womankind's existence since time immemorial, bleeding to death during childbirth. The midwife had ordered Erhard to go get a doctor. Natalie was in labor for a day and a half. The doctor was able to staunch the flow of blood and she finally delivered a healthy baby boy. They named him Itzhak. Fearing that he would be totally ostracized by the community if he didn't, Erhard had his son circumcised on the eighth day.

Natalie recovered slowly but gradually the family resumed their old routine. Erhard and Natalie worked in the shop while Anna cared for the baby. When Itzhak cried with hunger, Natalie would drop what she was doing to nurse him.

After three months the couple resumed having sex. Erhard was particularly eager after the long abstinence. Natalie expected that she would be pregnant again quickly but it didn't happen. When six months passed and she still wasn't pregnant, Natalie became concerned. She went to the doctor who had delivered Itzhak. He examined her and gave her the bad news. Itzhak's delivery had damaged her womb. She would have no more children.

She was downcast and depressed for weeks. Finally, Erhard saw that she was perking up a little. She told him that since she was now barren, she would pour all the love she had reserved for her other children into little Itzhak. No matter what she would have to do, he would never want for anything.

Erhard remembered the time after Itzhak's birth as a happy time. The shop was doing well and the little family was happy. Then on 28 July 1914 a deranged Serbian Nationalist assassinated the Austrian Arch Duke Ferdinand and his wife Sophie in Sarajevo and plunged the world into war.

§

Erhard Weiss thought on these things as he lay in bed beside the warm naked body of his wife. Perhaps with the horror of the war behind them a new happy time will start for my family, he thought. He had hopeful feelings as he finally drifted off to sleep.

The air reeked of the strong chemical smell of exploding shells. Erhard heard the shrieks and felt the detonations as the shells landed. In the distance, he could see British troops with bloody bayonets converging on him. As they advanced, the Tommies were plunging their bayonets into the German wounded on the ground. Erhard wanted to flee but his legs wouldn't move. At last, he forced a step and then another. He was suddenly stopped short by a hand that gripped his ankle. Erhard looked down and saw Bruno Adelmann, a squad mate, his body gone below the chest, looking at him with pleading eyes." Help me," he croaked. Erhard saw that the enemy troops were getting closer. He tried to free his leg from Bruno's grasp but couldn't. A deep terror gripped him. A British soldier ran at him, hate on his face, raised his rifle with the bayonet aimed for Erhard's belly. He thrust....

Erhard shot up in bed and gulped for air. He threw the blankets off, ready to run. Then he realized that it was a nightmare. He had been plagued with them since the armistice, some nights getting almost no sleep. He was covered in sweat even though the room was cold. Natalie's warm body was suddenly beside him and her arms enfolded him. She talked soothingly and rubbed his forehead until he went back to sleep.

The next day Erhard got back to work. He made repairs to the shop and business started to pick up. Once again he and Natalie worked as a team in the shoe shop. The nightmares gradually ceased. The public's antagonism against the Jews continued unabated. Erhard tried to ignore it and go about his life.

Only one problem marred the family's happiness. Erhard and Natalie disagreed about discipline for Itzhak. The boy was headstrong and sullen and would throw tantrums if he didn't get his way. On the few occasions that Erhard tried to correct the boy, an argument would ensue with Natalie. She refused to see any faults in Itzhak. She was so smart and so practical but had a blind spot when it came to her son.

CHAPTER FIVE

VILLA WAHNFRED
BAYREUTH, DEUTSCHLAND
21 JULI 1923

It was a beautiful summer evening. Winifred Wagner, the daughter in law of the famous but now deceased composer Richard Wagner, was giving a dinner party for the social elite of Bayreuth. It would be considered a social blunder to ignore an invitation such as this from the town's most prominent citizen.

The Bayreuth Music Festival, the annual event that had made the town world famous, hadn't been held since the start of the great war. Richard Wagner's son Siegfried was touring the continent soliciting funds to start it up again in 1924. The local economy had suffered without the yearly infusion of tourist's gold, so everyone in town wished Siegfried well.

When Kurt Wolf and his son Erich arrived at the Wagner villa, their driver joined a long line of luxury automobiles waiting to drop off their wealthy, well-dressed passengers. When it was Wolf's turn, a liveried footman held the car door and they stepped out.

Kurt and Erich were both dressed in white tie and tails. Kurt, who never set off clothes to advantage, looked like a walrus. His huge belly was hard to disguise. His son Erich, by contrast, looked magnificent. At twenty-four, he had the slim body and handsome face that women loved. He looked so good that people ignored that he walked with a limp thanks to a British bombing raid in the war. Whenever he would think about that awful day, his palms would sweat and a deep feeling of fear would seize him.

§

In August 1917, Erich, full of romantic notions about the glory of war, had prevailed on his father to get him a commission in the army. Kurt had gone to a certain officer on the General Staff and asked for his son to be commissioned and sent to a place out of the fighting. He felt Erich was too valuable to risk his life like a common soldier. The General Staff officer was agreeable. He got many requests like this from wealthy, influential people. Eighteen-year-old Erich was duly commissioned and sent to a hurried officers training course. He was posted to Staden, Belgium, as a junior staff officer to the headquarters of General Der Infantry, Ferdinand Von Quast, commander of the German Sixth Army. The headquarters was in a luxurious estate thirty-one kilometers behind the front.

Upon arrival in Belgium, Erich hitched a ride to the front to see what it was like. What he found there appalled him. The soldiers lived in filthy, muddy trenches under constant shelling. They ate slop for food. The heavy disgusting smell of decaying bodies was everywhere. The infantrymen were dirty and covered with lice. While he was there, Erich endured an artillery barrage while sheltering in a dugout. When it was over, he fled back to the headquarters vowing never to return. He was grateful that he was who he was and not some poor bastard in those trenches. He slept each night between crisp, white sheets and dined at a table with a clean, white tablecloth and silver service. He was waited on by enlisted men, waiters with white towels draped over their arms, and spent his weekends chasing women in Antwerp.

One day he was walking across the courtyard of the

headquarters when he heard a peculiar droning sound. He looked off in the distance and saw a line of specks in the sky. As the objects became larger, the droning got louder. Erich suddenly realized that they were aeroplanes, but whose were they? A few moments later, someone shouted they were British bombers and for everyone to take cover.

In a panic, Erich sprinted across the courtyard and onto the lawn at the side of the main house, frantically looking for somewhere to hide. He saw a drainage culvert that emerged into a shallow ditch nearby. An enlisted man was trying to crawl into the narrow opening. Erich grabbed the man by his belt and hauled him out, his fear giving him great strength. The young soldier jumped up, looked at Erich in terror, and ran away. Just then the first bomb detonated sixty meters away. Erich fell flat and frantically began to slither into the culvert. He got his head and shoulders inside as more bombs detonated. Then he got stuck, his holstered pistol caught on the lip of the culvert preventing him from entering any further. As he struggled, he heard more bombs detonate. The concussions squeezed his insides and jarred his teeth.

Suddenly, he felt something hit the back of his left leg with the force of a kick from a mule. Another bomb detonated, this one very close. The concussion knocked him out. When he came to, all was quiet. He backed out of the culvert and saw the area was wreathed in thick smoke. He tried to stand but found his left leg was numb and wouldn't support his weight. He looked down and saw blood oozing from a long gash in the back of his leg, running down his boot and pooling on the ground. His surroundings started to spin and he fainted.

He awoke in a hospital bed. An orderly nearby saw that he was awake and went to get a doctor, who soon came to speak to him. He was tall, dressed in a white smock and was smoking a cigarette.

"You must lie still Herr Leutnant. You have suffered a serious injury and have lost a lot of blood. You are lucky to still have your leg. If the injury was any more severe we would have had to amputate. I regret to inform you that your soldiering days are over."

Five days later Erich was in his bed gritting his teeth against the pain when an Oberst in a magnificent uniform from the Headquarters came to see him. In an impromptu ceremony, he presented Wolf with the Iron Cross Second Class. Erich later learned that the Generals and Obersts at the headquarters had gone into a frenzy awarding each other medals for the bombing raid. Because Erich had been wounded, he was included.

Erich Wolf had recovered from his wound. It had taken a long time but the injury had left him with a slight limp. Actually, the limp hadn't turned out to be such a bad thing. It reminded people that he was a decorated hero of the war. Erich basked in the glory. He suspected that most war heroes were frauds like him.

§

Erich scanned the front of the Wagner villa. It looked like it had been constructed by piling huge blocks on top of one another. The tan and buff stone contrasted well with the greenery surrounding the building. Carved over the grand entrance was the villa's name: WAHNFRED. In the courtyard surrounded by a hedge was a bronze bust of the great Wagner on a granite pillar.

Once inside, the Wolfs waited in a line to be received by Winifred Wagner. She extended her hand to Kurt first and then Erich. Erich bowed, clicked his heels and kissed the back of her hand. Erich's gallantry drew a brief smile from Winifred. She was a somewhat stout woman in her late twenties. Her light brown hair was worn short and Erich could see dandruff flakes on her shoulders. The dark blue dress she wore was all wrong for her coloring and she had the appearance of dressing carelessly. It was a subtle statement.

She was implying that her social station was so much higher than others that she didn't have to dress well to impress them.

"I am so sorry that dear Ailse could not attend," said Wagner to Kurt.

"She is a little under the weather," replied Kurt.

Erich's mother Ailse had chosen not to attend. She had met Winifred at previous social functions and the two women had developed an intense dislike for one another. Winifred thought Ailse was vapid. Ailse, in turn, said that Winifred was too conniving for her own good.

"I am so sorry to hear that," said Wagner.

Kurt waited for a bolt of lightning to strike her dead for lying.

Winifred's face became animated. "Doktor Wolf, there is a man here tonight who you must meet. I will introduce him to you later. His name is Adolf Hitler."

"It would be a pleasure, Frau Wagner."

The great room was dominated by a huge crystal chandelier. Well-dressed people stood around in groups talking. Erich left his father and began to mingle with the other guests. He had known most of these people since he was a child and felt comfortable with them. One of the other guests asked him how he was progressing in his law studies. Erich replied that he had finished his university studies and had passed his first state exam. He was in the practical application phase now and would take the final state exam next year. When he passed that, he would be entitled to practice law.

Dinner was announced. Erich rejoined his father for the procession into the dining room. Erich noticed that Winifred had a strange looking man escorting her. He wasn't dressed for dinner but wore a somewhat ill-fitting, double-breasted, pinstriped suit. His hair was cut short in the military style but it was the mustache that set him off as peculiar. It looked like he had pasted a black postage stamp on his upper lip. Winifred positioned the man Hitler, he believed she had said his name was, to her right at the head of the table in the place of honor.

After an unremarkable dinner, overdone venison, the guests drifted back into the great room for after dinner drinks. They again split into groups. Erich was standing with his father in a group of their close neighbors, drinking brandy and smoking a cigar. Wagner approached with Hitler. A man walked behind them who looked like an oversized dwarf. He had a deformed foot and walked with a strange gait.

"Doktor Kurt Wolf, member of the Reichstag, I would like to present to you Herr Adolf Hitler, leader of the National Socialist German Workers Party."

Both men bowed and shook hands. Kurt turned to his son.

"Herr Hitler, I would like to present my son, Erich, late of the Imperial Army and holder of the Iron Cross for gallantry in action."

Hitler shook Erich's hand and smiled.

"I am proud to meet you, young man. The Fatherland will need such men as you in the future."

Erich was strangely moved by the compliment. Hitler had looked in his eyes when he spoke and his sincerity was obvious. Hitler had piercing eyes the color of a mountain lake.

"Gentlemen, may I introduce my associate, Dr. Joseph Goebbels." The little man only nodded and did not offer his hand.

Winifred Wagner cleared her throat. "Herr Hitler, how would you characterize the situation in Germany today."

"Our Fatherland is in a time of great peril. Our nation was on the verge of a great victory in the late war when we were betrayed by subversive elements within our own government. They were in league with international Jewish bankers. Our brave soldiers were betrayed and all the bloodshed was for nothing. The ruling Social Democrats are secretly taking bribes from the Jews. We must cleanse our great nation from this Jewish menace. Only then can we take our rightful place as the supreme nation in the world."

Erich was mesmerized by Hitler's words. He was saying the same things Erich had thought many times to himself. What was more important was that Hitler was saying these things from obvious conviction. He was not like a typical politician.

Hitler continued. "Our brave, long patient Volk are suffering. Communist and Jewish rowdies are making our streets unsafe, especially for Aryan women. Dishonest Jewish businessmen are cheating us. What are we to do about this situation? I will tell you. We need order in our society. We need people in power who will protect our brethren. We need to rise up and say, NO MORE!"

Hitler's voice rose at the end to where he was almost shouting. His voice echoed around the large room. When he stopped speaking the people in the room broke into applause.

On the drive home, Erich asked his father, who was thinking of giving up his seat in the Reichstag, about Hitler.

"He gives a good speech but he will probably be a flash in the pan. There are dozens of these small parties but the Social Democrats are just too strong," said Kurt.

"I am not so sure," replied Erich.

The next day, Erich Wolf took a train to Munich and joined the Nazi party.

CHAPTER SIX

BREMERSTRASSE 45
KASSEL, DEUTSCHLAND
12 SEPTEMBER 1925

There was a decidedly cool atmosphere at breakfast this morning. Erhard Weiss sighed and looked over at Natalie's stony face. Her eyes were downcast as she stirred her porridge. They had had a tremendous argument the day before that lasted into the night.

The dispute had its origins a few months before. Natalie had gotten hold of a Paris fashion magazine from somewhere. Inside were photographs and drawings of extremely skinny women in bone cracking poses wearing the latest "flapper" style dresses. Natalie poured over the magazine for days studying the shoes the models were wearing. She sequestered herself for many evenings in Gerta's old room drawing pictures of shoes on pieces of cardboard. Erhard was mystified. To his queries, she would only respond with a cryptic, "you will see."

Natalie ordered small amounts of various colored leather dyes from their supplier. She set up a small work area in the rear of the shop and spent her evenings there for a month. She would sometimes work far into the night. Erhard humored her. She was in an unusually happy mood so he let her be.

Yesterday she had summoned him to her area at the rear of the shop. There, lined up on a bench were six pairs of women's shoes, unlike anything Erhard had ever seen. They were all little wispy things with medium heels and multiple straps. Some had three straps, some had four. Some straps went straight across, some were diagonal. One pair had little bows sewn to the toes. Instead of honest black and brown, these shoes were a riot of solid and pastel colors.

Natalie looked at him expectantly, "What do you think?"

"What are they for?" Erhard asked back.

"I want to make and sell these shoes. They have style and grace. They are not like the clunky women's shoes that we make now."

"I don't think the hausfraus of Kassel would be interested in these. Such flimsy straps. They would break within six months."

Now Natalie was getting annoyed. "I intend to put my new shoes in the display window."

Erhard then made a strategic mistake. He responded with his 'I am the master of this family' shtick.

"I forbid it. You are being foolish."

It was a terrible row, each of them saying things that weren't very nice. Now, with the morning sun streaming in through the window, Erhard looked across the table at his wife. He was feeling guilty for some of the things he had said in anger. He decided to give her what she wanted. He always did. He couldn't resist her for long. The smile on her face when she won an argument was reward enough. Her project was sure to fail and she would see that he was right. Then they could forget about this nonsense. He cleared his throat and Natalie looked up at him.

"Will you need all the display space?"

Natalie came and sat on his lap and kissed him. She was happy again. Erhard much preferred it when she was happy. It bothered him when she was angry with him.

"No, only half," she replied.

That night they had sex. It was always really good after a fight. Natalie did something that shocked, then delighted him, but left him wondering what other French magazines she was reading.

§

One day about two months later, Erhard stood at the front counter and wrote up his fifth sale of Natalie's shoes for the day. The woman buying them was a stout practical looking hausfrau who was thrilled with her purchase. She had been measured and ordered the shoes a month ago. It had taken this long to make them because the demand was so high for Natalie's new shoes.

Eight other women were crowded around the display of women's shoes waiting to be measured. They all seemed to be talking at the same time. The women were all dressed in low waisted, short dresses and had bobbed hair. To Erhard, some of them looked patently ridiculous. At least two in the group weighed over eighty kilos!

Natalie emerged with a customer from a curtained-off booth. She handed the woman a claim ticket and called for the next in line. One of the women detached herself from the group standing around the shoe display and Natalie escorted her into the booth. Just as she was entering, she looked at Erhard and flashed him her "I told you so" smile.

Almost from the day Natalie's shoes went on display they had been popular with the women of the city. Through word of mouth, women began flocking to the shop. Even though it was in the Jewish quarter, it didn't seem to matter. Erhard was happy to admit he had been wrong. He learned an important lesson. With women, style will trump practicality any day.

What made Erhard the happiest was the hoard of golden Marks piling up in his hidden strongbox. It couldn't have come at a better time. After the war, the Weimar government had tried to meet the reparation payments imposed by the Treaty of Versailles. It had printed and circulated huge amounts of paper marks. By the early twenties, the paper Mark was almost worthless. Unless he didn't want to be ruined, Erhard had to begin to demand pre-war gold and silver coins as payment for his merchandise. He had no choice; his suppliers were doing the same.

When he started refusing to accept paper marks, some of his Gentile customers became angry and called him things like "dirty Jew" and "shifty kike". Erhard endured the abuse because he had no other recourse.

Erhard had pity for the ordinary German worker who worked for wages. They suffered terribly. With inflation, they fell further and further behind. They cast around looking for someone to blame settling their eye on their old enemies, the Jews. Anti-Semitism was everywhere. In newspapers and fiery speeches, Jews were accused of causing financial troubles. In Catholic circles, the old blood libel was dredged up again.

As a youth, Erhard had resented the anti-Semitism all around him and had been ready to fight for his rights. As an adult, after his experiences in the war, he didn't want conflict with anyone. He just wanted to be left alone.

CHAPTER SEVEN

DUSSELDORF HAUPTBANHOF
DUSSELDORF, DEUTSCHLAND
3 JUNI ,1926

At 7:30 in the morning, a fireman was busily oiling the many bearings on a giant locomotive within the cavernous Dusseldorf train station. He was interrupted in his task by a young lady who walked past where he was working. She was pretty and the fireman watched her jiggling bottom through her thin dress until she was out of sight. He returned to his task not realizing that the distraction had caused him to skip oiling a crucial bearing on one of the huge drive wheels of the big locomotive.

A few minutes later passengers began to board the train anticipating it's 8:00 a.m. departure. As the train pulled out of the station bound for Leipzig with no stops scheduled, it was anticipated that the trip would take just shy of five hours.

In one of the first class compartments, a woman sat and talked to her German traveling companion and interpreter. She was a tall, dignified woman of fifty. Her hair was worn in a short but stylish cut. She was perfectly groomed and her clothing was of the latest Paris fashion, expensive and superbly cut.

To the casual observer, she might appear to be a member of the minor nobility or the wife of a wealthy businessman. The observer would be wrong. The lady's name was Madame Marie LeClerc. Born into poverty, she had risen from seamstress to be the owner of a fashion empire. Along with Jeanne Lanvin, Coco Chanel and Jean Patou, LeClerc had revolutionized Paris fashions in the early 1920s. She was a shrewd, ruthless businesswoman who had reached the top of her profession by a combination of intelligence, a sense of timing and an iron will.

Her main business was the LeClerc fashion house. She also made and sold perfume, owned a fabric mill and invested in dozens of ventures throughout the Paris metropolitan area. She was rich and could have retired to a life of ease years ago but she loved the world of business. Le Clerc was a risk taker and was prepared to gamble everything on a new venture if she believed it would succeed. Every successful country produces people like her, but too rarely.

She was traveling with her friend and employee, Elizabeth Von Reitberg, an impoverished German countess. She served as LeClerc's German interpreter. Marie spoke German fluently but found it useful when dealing with Germans to pretend that she didn't. In negotiations, they sometimes let slip little tidbits of information because they thought that she didn't understand them.

She had just concluded negotiations with a company in Dusseldorf to supply dye to her fabric mill. She was on her way to Leipzig to interview a perfumer who said he had developed a new scent that would revolutionize the world of perfumes. We shall see, thought LeClerc.

About two hours into the trip, Marie was getting drowsy. Her companion was prattling on about a Polish count in Paris that was caught ducking into a cab with a prostitute. The train started to slow. Within five minutes it had slowed to a crawl and was pulling onto a siding off the main track.

There was a knock on the compartment door. The first class attendant, a little man in a green uniform, bowed obsequiously to LeClerc.

"I am so sorry madame, but the train has experienced mechanical difficulties. The conductor estimates the repairs will take three hours."

Marie looked out of the window. "What is this place?"

"It is Kassel, madame."

Marie gave the little man a withering look. He bowed again and backed out of the compartment saying, "I am so sorry Madame."

"This will play hell with our timetable," said Le Clerc, and Liz nodded.

"Oh, well, let's find a hotel or restaurant and eat a decent lunch. That is if this place has a decent restaurant."

The two ladies bustled off the train and found a taxi waiting for a fare in front of the station. Marie asked the driver of the location of the best restaurant in town. The driver recommended the Restaurant Spitzkuche in the older section of Kassel and away they went.

They drove about three kilometers then turned down a street lined with shops. About midway down the first block, a flash of color caught Marie's eye. She told the driver to stop and back up. When he did, Le Clerc saw a shoe shop with a collection of brightly colored women's shoes in the front window. She got out of the taxi and walked up to the window.

Marie went from pair to pair and minutely examined the shoes through the glass. They were unlike any she had ever seen. They looked durable but light and very stylish. Marie felt the beginnings of the excitement that welled up in her when she got a new idea. There were possibilities here. She turned to walk into the shop.

"Do not go in there Marie. It is a Jewish shop," said Liz.

Le Clerc fixed her with a disapproving glare. "I don't care if it is an Eskimo shop. I want to meet the person responsible for these shoes." Marie couldn't understand the German's obsession with Jews. As far as she could see, they were industrious people who were never a burden on society. How many times in her life had she seen prejudice blind people to great opportunity?

Le Clerc entered the shop and was greeted by a tall somewhat handsome man with a mop of unruly hair wearing a leather apron. "How may I be of assistance?" he asked.

"Are you the person responsible for those shoes in the window?"

"No, they were designed by my wife. I will summon her. "

The man disappeared through a curtained-off doorway. In a short while, a woman in her early thirties emerged. She was attractive in a dark sort of way but Marie looked past that. She looked at her eyes. The woman looked at her with a direct gaze and Marie saw intelligence and spirit there. Liz was standing next to Marie with her arms folded and a hostile expression on her face. Marie told her to wait in the taxi and she left.

Marie turned back to the woman," I would like to examine the workmanship of your shoes." The woman nodded.

LeClerc picked up the first shoe in the line of models. Taking a pair of spectacles from her bag she minutely examined each shoe in turn. The quality was amazing. The stitching was first rate. What impressed her more, however, was the design. They were light and would be comfortable to wear. Their style was subtly different from other shoes on sale in Paris. The colors complemented the design and were not an afterthought as was too often the case. The examination took thirty minutes. As she set the last shoe down, she made her decision. Now the hard part, Marie thought: the negotiation.

Le Clerc extended her hand, "My name is Marie Le Clerc and I have a fashion house in Paris."

"I am Natalie Weiss."

"I have a business proposition. Is there somewhere we can talk?"

Natalie led her to a shabby kitchen. She made tea and the two women sat opposite each other at a scratched wooden table. The negotiations lasted longer than Marie anticipated. She initially offered to set Natalie up in business in Paris in return for fifty percent of the profits. Marie expected Natalie to jump at the offer but she didn't and they haggled back and forth.

About twenty minutes into the conversation, Marie realized she was dealing with no fool. Natalie was a tough, resourceful negotiator and her eyes lit up with the excitement of the haggling. Marie recognized a kindred spirit in Natalie and began to like her immensely. The bargain they finally agreed to was this: The Weiss family would move to Paris. With Marie's backing, they would set up a shoe store. Marie would provide referrals to Natalie's store from her enterprises. LeClerc would also sponsor them as immigrants to the French republic, all this in return for thirty percent of the net profits. The deal was predicated on the approval of Natalie's husband.

LeClerc barely made it back to the station to catch her train. She had lunch brought to her compartment. She insisted that it be complementary after all the inconvenience the railroad had put her through. As the train chugged out of Kassel, Marie LeClerc sat back in her seat and smiled. If her instincts were right, this trip would pay off handsomely.

CHAPTER EIGHT

BREMERSTRASSE 45
KASSEL DEUTSCHLAND
10 JUNI 1926

Erhard Weiss sat at the kitchen table. It was after midnight and the living quarters above the shop were quiet except for the creaking of the old building. He stared at his hands, then formed them into fists and brought them down heavily onto the tabletop. He couldn't make up his mind. Should the family stay in Kassel or emigrate to Paris? His mind was a jumble of conflicting thoughts.

He was by nature a simple man and usually had no problem resolving issues. He had a strong sense of right and wrong and would follow his gut feeling as to what was right. His overriding concern was what was best for his family. To Erhard Weiss, his family, Natalie, and Itzhak, were the only really important thing in his life. The decision that Natalie had left up to him to make was the hardest he had ever faced. It was like asking him to move to Mars and start a colony.

He decided to list in his mind the pros and cons of staying in Germany. First, Erhard looked upon himself as a German. He was born here. Through years of trial and error, he had adapted to the conservative culture in Kassel.

He remembered as a child the smell of freshly tanned leather mixed with the aroma of his mother's cooking and the feeling of well-being it generated. Kassel was where he had met and married Natalie, the best thing that had ever happened to him. He thought of the friends who he would never see again if he left. The familiar streets and hangouts that held so many childhood memories that he would never look upon again.

And what about moving to a country with different customs and a different language? Would they be able to adapt? He had spent four years fighting French and British young men, looking upon them as his enemies. Could he now go live among them? Would they accept him if they knew?

He had about talked himself into staying in Kassel when he began to think of the negative things. He thought of the day as a small boy when he was caught daydreaming in school. The teacher had caned him severely and called him a "dirty Jew." He remembered his father being humiliated in public by a policeman for no reason except that he was Jewish. The Germans hated the Jews and were always saying they wanted them gone. He remembered defending Germany for four years in the Great War and coming home to vilification as a Jew. Erhard still couldn't decide. He was back where he started.

Then he thought of Natalie. She wanted to grab the opportunity and go. He had come to rely on the good sense of his headstrong wife. In the end, all the reasons for going and staying didn't matter. Natalie wanted to go and that was good enough for him. After sixteen years of marriage, he loved her more now than the day of the wedding. He could deny her nothing.

Erhard got up from the table and turned down the kerosene lamp. He undressed and put on his nightshirt. Slipping quietly into bed beside Natalie, he whispered in her ear. "We go."

Natalie, who hadn't been asleep, replied, "Oh Erhard, I am so glad."

The next morning, Natalie sent a telegram to Madame LeClerc, who got busy. A month later Erhard received a letter from the French Government approving their application to emigrate to France.

They sold the shop with all its tools and stock to Natalie's nephew who had just wed and wanted to break away from his father. Erhard took the proceeds from the sale and the strong box with his gold coins to a bank in Kassel. He converted everything into British pounds and put it on deposit. When he got to France he could have the money transferred to a Paris bank. This was preferable to trying to smuggle the gold into France.

Natalie and Erhard, with Itzhak, attended a going away party at her father's shop in Vellmar. Her parents cried and were sad to see them go. Natalie had fun talking to and playing with her young nephews and nieces, not knowing that by a decade and a half later they would all have died in the ghetto at Riga or at Auschwitz. None of the Lipinski family would survive the Holocaust.

In late October, Erhard Weiss escorted his family aboard a train headed west. As the train pulled out of the station, Erhard looked at the familiar landscape and felt sad that he was leaving the city of his birth, never to return. Mingled with the sadness was a rising excitement. A new life awaited them and it could be good or bad. It was up to them. Erhard resolved to not let his usual negative attitude hold them back. Whatever happened, the three of them would face the future together.

At the French border, the train halted. The Weiss family waited in their seats until a French official in a blue uniform approached them. The official looked over their immigration papers and asked how much money they were carrying. Erhard replied that he had only a few hundred marks. The official then came to attention, saluted them, and smiled.

"Bienvenue en France."

A young woman who worked for Madame LeClerc met them at the Paris Gare du Nord station. She said that Mme. Le Clerc had taken the liberty of renting them an apartment on Rue De Vaugirard in the sixth arrondissement. If they liked it, there was an option to buy.

The apartment was on the fourth floor of an older building. The upper floors were served by an ancient, rickety cage elevator. The apartment was small, just five rooms, with a salon, two tiny bedrooms, a bath and an even tinier kitchen. The furnishings were showing signs of wear but they were of obvious quality. There were huge windows in the salon that flooded the room with light.

Natalie took one look at the flat and cried. This was so much grander than their rooms over the shop in Kassel. She busily went about moving the furniture around to suit her taste.

Madame LeClerc showed up the next day and she and Natalie went off to look at prospective sites for their business. Erhard was a little miffed that he wasn't invited along. He was pretty sure that Madame Le Clerc thought he was a dolt.

After a few days, they found a suitable location. It was on Rue Anjou near Rue Lavoisier in the eighth arrondissement. Erhard and Natalie spent the next month interviewing prospective employees through an interpreter. They had their first argument in Paris. Erhard wanted to hire competent shoemakers and pay the prevailing wage. Natalie disagreed. She wanted to pay above the usual wage to attract highly skilled craftsmen. What good was it, she argued, to have a good design if it wasn't executed properly. Erhard gave in, as usual. They purchased the necessary materials, machines and tools. Madame LeClerc was as good as her word. She paid for everything.

Just after the start of the new year of 1926, the store opened for business. The sign on the front was in art deco style letters. It read: "LE CHAUSSURES PAR NATALIE."

CHAPTER NINE

DER BAMBERGER DOM
BAMBERG, DEUTSCHLAND
13 AUGUST 1927

The Bamberg Cathedral was founded by Holy Roman Emperor Henry II in 1002. No one living in the twentieth century had any inkling what it looked like for the first two hundred years. In the thirteenth century it was rebuilt in the gothic style, with pointed Gothic arches soaring eighty meters high. It made the people sitting in the rows of oak pews feel very small. Tombs of medieval Teutonic knights lined the sides of the nave, which today was decorated with a fortune in flowers. Their riotous color was a fine backdrop to the bishop who stood in front of the altar in his golden miter and gold trimmed white cape.

Erich Wolf accompanied by his father, mother Ailse and sister Hilda, sat in the front row of those pews on the right side. Behind them sat some four hundred friends and family of the bride and groom.

It was Erich's sister Marta's wedding day. Marta was known around Bayreuth as the "skinny" Wolf daughter. Her sister Hilda was enormously fat. Erich looked down the pew at her. She was wearing a flower print dress with the volume of a circus tent. Kurt Wolf leaned close to Erich's ear and began to whisper.

"Finally I am getting one of the girls married off, though Marta is the easy one. Her sister will be much more difficult. I have to find a man who has a cargo van to haul her around in."

Father and son chuckled together at the joke. Neither man saw the look of pain on Hilda's face, for her father had whispered too loudly. A tear rolled down her cheek, which she quickly brushed away.

The men in the Wolf family were nominal Roman Catholics. However, they were not very good Catholics. Any church teaching that conflicted with their world view was dismissed out of hand. Biblical passages that enjoined the faithful to turn the other cheek when wronged or that the meek would inherit the earth were as incomprehensible to Kurt and Erich Wolf as Nordic runes. Kurt had a special aversion to confession. He had once remarked to Erich that "If I want God to know about the things I do, I will tell him directly and not some fool priest who will blab it all over the vestry."

At last, the organ began to play and the audience stood. Marta, and her groom, Gerhard Drescher, walked side by side, down the aisle from the rear. Marta wore a flowing white gown with a veil and a long train. Drescher wore the smart black uniform of an Untersturmfuhrer in the Schutzstaffel. Known by the initials SS, it was an elite part of the SA Storm Trooper organization. Its sole purpose was to provide a guard for Adolf Hitler and the other leaders of the up and coming National Socialist Party that was becoming very popular in Bavaria.

When the couple reached the nave, they knelt before the bishop. Vows were exchanged and a ring put on Marta's finger. The bishop then said the high mass in Latin. This lasted quite some time. He droned on and on in Latin reciting words that few if any in the room understood. Kurt Wolf, who was fifty-seven years old, fidgeted like a small schoolboy. Then at last, it was over.

In a typical Bavarian wedding, the reception would be held in a Biergarten, with the men in lederhosen and the women in folk dresses. But this wasn't a typical wedding. Because of the Wolf's wealth and position, the reception was held in the ballroom of the Hotel Residenschloss. Guests drank French champagne, dined on pheasant and roast venison and danced to the music of a full orchestra. Many of the groom's friends wore the striking, black SS uniform and flirted shamelessly with the young women.

The next day most of the family drove the sixty-four kilometers back to Bayreuth. Erich remained behind. He spent four days with a woman who lived nearby. She had been widowed at thirty-eight and inherited a tidy fortune from her late husband. If she remarried, according to German law, she would have to hand over all that wonderful money to her new husband. That was something she was not prepared to do, so she had affairs. Erich was amazed at her sexual appetite. On the minus side, the woman wouldn't shut up. She babbled endlessly about everything and nothing. After four days, Erich was exhausted both physically and mentally.

On Thursday, 18 August he bid farewell to the widow and climbed into his beautiful, red, 1927 Mercedes Benz, S class, sport touring car. Its engine developed 180 horsepower and the car could do 200 kph on the right road. It had silver exhaust pipes that jutted out from each side of the bonnet. Bright wire wheels and a spare tire mounted on the left front fender completed the picture. Erich loved the car. He also loved the attention it drew from other drivers.

When he started the car, the engine responded with a satisfying roar. He set out for Nuremberg and the 1927 Nazi party rally. Erich had been a member for four years. He had thought about abandoning the party when Hitler had attempted a coup in Munich in 1923 and was sent to prison but had held on. Now Hitler was out of prison and the party was growing fast. Erich had high hopes for its future. Up to this point, all he had done for the Nazis was some volunteer legal work.

While driving with the wind blowing his hair around, Erich thought about his personal life. He was twenty-eight, well past the age when most Germans marry. He just couldn't imagine confining himself to one woman for the rest of his life. The few women that he had more than a brief relationship with had proven to be disappointments. After a time, they had begun to make demands on his time and wanted to know where he had been and who he had seen. They wanted a commitment that he was unprepared to give. Each of these relationships had ended in an ugly scene.

He pondered what to do. He could marry for a home and children and have affairs on the side or he could remain single. The thought of sneaking around and lying to a wife tipped the scales in the direction of remaining single, at least for the time being. Besides, he was having fun. He was wealthy so he didn't have to work. He was licensed to practice law but rarely did any legal work. His passions were fast cars, drinking and sex.

As he entered the city of Nuremberg, he noticed that every open field held a sea of tents. Convoys of open trucks jammed the streets, with youthful Brownshirts, each wearing a Swastika armband, crammed in the back. The young men were enthusiastically waving to crowds lining the streets. Nazi swastika flags were everywhere. The atmosphere was like a carnival.

Erich inched his way through the heavy traffic to the Hotel Agneshof. Getting a room had been hard because all the hotels were full of Nazi supporters. Luckily, Erich had made reservations months ago. Even so, he could only get a small room on the top floor.

Friday was filled with parades. Sturmabteilung units from all over Germany, each with their own band, marched in their brown uniforms through the streets past crowded sidewalks filled with cheering people. Erich enjoyed the upbeat spirit of the people.

The next day, Saturday, was the main event, held in the Culture Union building. The three-thousand-seat hall was filled to bursting with party delegates and prominent people who supported the party. Erich had a seat on the main floor about halfway down from the stage. He had his Nazi party badge with its coveted low number prominently displayed on his lapel. The hall was decorated with swastika banners and smaller flags. Above the stage was a huge swastika emblem.

The festivities began with some preliminary short speeches by party leaders while the audience fidgeted, waiting in anxious excitement for the Fuhrer to speak. Then Adolf Hitler walked to the podium. He was dressed in full Brown Shirt uniform with a swastika armband. To a person, the audience hushed and leaned forward in anticipation so as not to miss a single word.

The speech wasn't long, only about twenty-five minutes. Hitler began to speak in a calm voice. His words weren't that remarkable. He had used the same themes in hundreds of stump speeches since becoming the leader of the Nazi party. His power dwelt in the way he delivered those words. He emanated power and sincerity and each rapt member of his audience felt as if he was speaking directly to him or her alone. He started his speech by stating that Germany had a need for more space for its people and pledged that the lands taken from her after the great war would be recovered. As he spoke on this subject, his eyes seemed to glow. He discussed the Great War itself. He said it was the most glorious war in the nation's history because they were fighting for the soul of the nation. Hitler said that Germany had not been defeated on the battlefield but had been sold out by weak democratic leaders.

The Fuhrer said that national power was needed. He asserted that true power comes from blood. The intrinsic power of a nation's race, the German race, was capable of producing the minds necessary to solve problems crying out for solutions. Democracy had failed to take into account the challenges of the age. What the fatherland needed were strong leaders, who could show the people the way forward to restoring Germany as the most powerful nation in the world. Hitler called for a renewal of the nation. This renewal would need a symbol. He pointed to the swastika flag.

"Our goal is for this flag to lose its character as a party flag and grow to be the German national flag of the future. We see this flag as inextricably bound to the renewal of the nation. May these colors be a witness of how the German people broke their chains of slavery and won their freedom. On that day this will be the national flag."

Hitler's voice rose in intensity until he was shouting. His eyes seemed to burn with passion and sincerity and a feeling of raw power and emotion radiated from him and further inflamed the crowd.

"Today, we see thousands behind this flag. Seven years ago there were none at all. All the people marched past us yesterday under this flag with enthusiasm and glowing eyes because they see in this flag the struggle for freedom of a people."

Hitler stood back from the podium and looked at the floor as the hall erupted in applause and cheers. Then a chant began in the back and swept throughout the room.

"Sieg Heil! Sieg Heil! Sieg Heil!"

Three thousand people stood with their right arms out in the Nazi salute.

"Sieg Heil! Sieg Heil! Sieg Heil!"

Erich Wolf was among them. The speech had had a profound effect on him. Tears rolled down his cheeks. He had seen a vision of the future. A strong united Germany as the premier nation in the world, beholden to no one. The Jews and vindictive foreign nations wouldn't be able to kick Germany around anymore. Then and there Erich pledged his loyalty and absolute obedience to Adolf Hitler. Erich Wolf, the wealthy and cynical playboy, had been transformed. He had found his cause and leader.

CHAPTER TEN

The decade of the 1920s in Paris was an exciting time. In art, music and literature it was the place to be. In the Montparnasse District on the left bank of the Seine, young artists developed a movement they called the "School of Paris." Young artists including Modigliani, Soutine and Chagall lived a hand to mouth existence and often peddled their paintings for a few Francs in the bars and bistros of the district.

A revolutionary movement in art and literature called Surrealism was also born in Paris in the decade. In literature, as well as art, it sought the depiction of true thought without a rigid structure.

Gertrude Stein, a wealthy American writer, opened her home at 27 Rue de Fleurus to gatherings of young American expatriate writers, with some European painters thrown in for seasoning. Writers like Ernest Hemingway, Sinclair Lewis and F. Scott Fitzgerald, and painters such as Henri Matisse and Pablo Picasso visited regularly. The guests would share their works with the group, honing their skills for the future. Stein's guests would one day dominate the worlds of art and literature.

Over at the Folies Bergere, black American dancers like Florence Mills and Josephine Baker performed with breasts bared to cheering crowds. American jazz also flourished as black artists fled discrimination in America for the more tolerant Paris. It was said that although jazz was born in America, it got its soul in Paris in the twenties.

In all these areas, new ground was being broken constantly. All this was possible because of the tolerant attitude of the Parisians. People could do pretty much anything they wanted to do if it didn't hurt someone else. The people of Paris had thrown off the pre-Great War yoke of morality and decorum. After the war years of horror and shortages, they just wanted to have fun. But this explosion of creativity and culture was lost on German immigrant, Erhard Weiss.

RUE D' ANJOU
PARIS, FRANCE
28 MAI, 1928

Clad in a stylish, smartly tailored single breasted suit of dark green wool with a straw boater on his head, Erhard Weiss strolled (if a person with a bullet savaged leg and a pronounced limp can be said to stroll) along the Rue d' Anjou. He might have been described as dashing, but at forty, he was a little old for the descriptive. His face had deeper lines than when he was a young man and the belt size he required was larger. He wore his hair much shorter now and expertly cut. But it made no difference, long or short, his hair had a mind of its own. He looked every inch the picture of an upper middle class Parisian.

It was cloudy but warm with a smell in the air that promised rain. A stiff breeze ruffled the skirts of passing women. After two years in the city, Erhard was still shocked at the clothing women wore on the streets of Paris. Thin, short dresses with the jiggling of their breasts under the fabric indicating they had nothing on underneath. See-through blouses were popular this year and Erhard had been treated to some angry comments for staring too long and hard.

And it wasn't just the clothing. The people of Paris appeared to be on one long hedonistic binge. Wine, women and song was the order of the day. Erhard had heard of one nightclub where the waitresses wore a bow in their hair and high heeled shoes, with nothing in between. In the evenings, drunken revelers filled the streets. With his conservative Jewish-German background, Erhard didn't approve of the loose morals in the city. He felt like a fish out of water.

The sidewalk was crowded and a woman bumped into him. "Pardon madame," he said in his atrocious French. The woman gave Erhard a suspicious look. When the family had first come to Paris Natalie had engaged a tutor, Madame Marguerite, to teach the family French. Natalie and Itzhak progressed well. Erhard didn't and after some months Madame Marguerite pronounced him hopeless and quit. He figured would forever sound to the French like a sinister villain in a spy cinema.

Erhard looked up and saw the sign over the front door of the family business in the next block. He had come to refer to it in his mind as Natalie's store. He was listed as the owner in government documents but in truth, the business was Natalie's. She ran it and ran it well. With the tutelage of Madame LeClerc, her business acumen had exploded. At the occasional lunch when he was included, the two women would talk in terms that might as well have been Swahili to Erhard. To top it off, Madame LeClerc's opinion of him hadn't changed. She still thought him an imbecile.

Not that he hadn't resisted being frozen out. In the beginning, he had insisted on being consulted on all major business decisions. Gradually, however, he had come to realize that he was about as necessary to the running of the store as a wart on an Alsatian hound's ass. Erhard had backed off, given Natalie the reins and was bored out of his mind.

As far as money went, things were wonderful. LES CHAUSSURES PAR NATALIE had been successful from the start. The family had a hefty balance in a Paris bank in case of an emergency. They lived frugally for the most part, though Natalie had taken to buying high fashion clothing of late. She was after him to purchase an automobile. So far he had resisted; it didn't make sense with the Metro so close and so cheap.

Erhard entered the door of Natalie's store. Inside it was all Art Deco design in glass and chrome. Annett, the pretty cashier, smiled sweetly at him and pushed out her breasts. She always flirted shamelessly with him. Two pairs of rich American women were gathered around a display talking excitedly about Natalie's shoes. Rich Americans were the majority of the customers of the store. Erhard wondered how so many could afford the steep prices. America must be a fabulous place with money just laying around, he thought.

He was looking for his wife. He found her in the workshop instructing a craftsman on the construction of a shoe from the new line she had just introduced. She hadn't seen him yet and he just stood and looked at her.

She was thirty-nine now but one would never know it. To Erhard, she looked young and sexy and was the most beautiful woman in Paris. Today she was wearing a low waisted, knee-length dress of light green material with little cream colored tassels sewn all over it that swayed when she moved. Her dark hair was styled into a bob cut. She dyed it of course, to cover the gray. All the women did.

Erhard felt a rush of desire for her but suppressed it. It would be many hours before there was the possibility of sex with her, especially with where he had to go and what he had to do after talking to her. He caught her eye and she came toward him with a slightly annoyed expression.

"I must talk to you. It is about Itzhak," said Erhard.

"Is he all right?" Her face went white and her hand flew to her mouth. Erhard held up his hand and rushed to reassure her.

"Yes, he is fine. The headmaster at his school telephoned me an hour ago. He was caught with a naked girl in his room. They were in the act of sex when the house governor walked in on them. Itzhak threw a tantrum and cursed the man. He has been expelled and I must leave now to go collect him."

Though relieved, Natalie was still upset. "Maybe it is not so bad. Maybe you can talk to the headmaster and smooth things over. He is a good boy."

"Not this time. the headmaster said the Itzhak is a troublemaker and a bad influence on the other boys. We will need to find somewhere else that will take him. I have to go, I have a train to catch," said Erhard.

"Be kind to him. He is sensitive and people don't understand him," said Natalie.

Erhard kissed both of her cheeks, and as he did so he thought to himself, oh I understand him all right. We have created a spoiled, obnoxious brat. The boy must be taken in hand or he will turn out to be a wastrel all his life.

Erhard splurged and took a taxi to the Gare de Lyon station. He bought a one-way ticket to Chavanges, two hundred kilometers away. He traveled second class. The huge fare they demanded for first class was outrageous. Settling himself on a padded bench seat, he adjusted his bad leg where it hurt the least and settled down for the two-and-a-half-hour ride.

Erhard was feeling glum, and a little sorry for himself. He had a worthless son and he was rarely able to spend time with his wife. They hadn't had sex in over a week-and-a-half. A typical Frenchman in his situation would go out and find himself a mistress. But Erhard thought that doing so would be a betrayal of his family, something he would never do. On top of everything, he had nothing productive to do with his days. He had taken to wandering around Paris and had seen all the famous buildings and monuments, the Eiffel Tower, the Louvre, Notre Dame Cathedral, Le Marais and the Palais Garnier. He had explored the Champ-Elysees and walked by the Arc de Triomphe. The monuments were impressive and the museums were interesting but he didn't need to see them a second time. Then he found a place that made him a little less lonely.

One day he was walking along the Rue de la Harpe in the Latin Quarter when he chanced upon Bistro Schwartz. It was a small cafe, only six tables, that specialized in German-Jewish dishes. Erhard was delighted and often went there. He spent hours talking to the proprietor in German and eating food remembered from his youth. It was owned by a German-Jewish immigrant named Abe Schwartz. He and Erhard became very chummy. It was a good place but he ended up drinking a lot of alcohol there. He had been concerned lately that because of boredom he was drinking too much and maybe turning into an alcoholic.

Erhard had dozed off in his seat and was awoken by the conductor announcing Chavanges as the next station. When the train stopped, he made his way onto the platform and continued into the small waiting room. There he saw his son with his luggage piled around him sitting dejectedly on a wooden bench and staring at the floor. The seventeen-year-old was thin and gangly, in the middle of a growth spurt.

Erhard looked at his watch and then at the train schedule posted on the wall. He saw that there was a train back to Paris that left in fifteen minutes. He bought two tickets and went to confront his son.

"Well, Itzhak, what is your excuse this time?" When he spoke, his son looked up with defiance in his face.

"About what father? The school? They are a bunch of provincial bumpkins. I didn't like it there anyway," said the boy flippantly. His face wore a haughty expression. It was all Erhard could do not to slap him.

"Do you know what sending you to that school cost?"

"It's all about money with you, isn't it father? don't you realize how those people humiliated me? I will talk to mother, she will understand."

"Bring your things to the platform. Our train leaves in a few minutes."

"Call a porter for my luggage."

'No, my son. It will do you good to carry your own luggage."

Erhard walked to the train, Itzhak following him with a suitcase under each arm and dragging a trunk. They started to board when the boy piped up again.

"Second class? Do you expect me to ride all the way to Paris with smelly workmen?"

"Yes Itzhak, that is exactly what I expect you to do."

The ride to Paris was a silent one. Itzhak sat in the corner of his seat and sulked the whole way. Weiss further angered the boy by refusing to hire a taxi at the Paris station. They rode home on the metro.

It was about eight in the evening when they arrived back at the apartment and Natalie was anxiously awaiting them. Itzhak stood silently inside the door. His mother rushed to him and held him.

"It wasn't my fault mother," said Itzhak in a whiny voice. This angered Erhard.

"Not your fault? Who is responsible then, the girl?"

He was going to say more when he saw the cold look in Natalie's eyes. He turned and left the room for the kitchen where he kept his bottle of single malt scotch whiskey.

CHAPTER ELEVEN

64 RUE DE VAUGIRARD
PARIS, FRANCE
29 OCTOBRE, 1929

H e was red and wrinkled and his toothless mouth was open in outrage. He had been perfectly content in the warm cozy place with no sound except the reassuring beating of his mother's heart. Then he had been jostled, pressed and pushed through a narrow opening into a cold bright world filled with frightening sounds. No, he didn't like it at all. To let the world know that he was not pleased, he let out an angry wail of protest.

The cool hands of Natalie Weiss reached for him where he lay nestled in the crook of his mother's arm and picked him up gently. Natalie enfolded the babe in her arms and brought his face close to hers, which was wet from tears of joy. The newborn looked at this strange apparition and somehow felt comforted. He stopped crying and listened as Natalie cooed softly to him. It could have been the warm blanket or the firm grip of her arms that made him feel secure or it could also have been the love flowing from Natalie's eyes into his. In any event, he soon dozed off and was still except for small pursing motions of his lips.

Erhard Weiss looked at his wife's face. She was in ecstasy. To have another child to love was making her face glow. For his part, Erhard felt his own outpouring of love and gratitude. This was his grandson. Another member of his family to care for and protect.

"What is he to be called?" asked Erhard to his son Itzhak, who was standing beside the bed in the room he shared with his wife Rachel.

"He will be called Adrien," replied Itzhak, looking every inch the proud papa. Erhard congratulated his son as well as his daughter in law, who was on the bed looking exhausted.

A grandchild was the last thing the Weiss family expected seven months ago. Out of the blue, Erhard had received a message from Nathan Rothstein, a wealthy art dealer, requesting that he meet him at Rothstein's gallery as soon as possible to discuss an urgent matter. Erhard was curious. What could a man like Rothstein want with him? Erhard took the metro to the gallery the next day.

When Erhard arrived at the gallery on Rue De Plessy, Rothstein saw him right away. He was ushered into an opulent office furnished with antique furniture and with valuable paintings on the walls. Rothstein, a large florid-faced man in an expensive Saville Row suit, didn't look happy. He didn't offer his guest any refreshment. After shaking Erhard's hand, he got right to the point.

"My youngest daughter Rachel is with child and your son Itzhak is the father."

'Are you sure?" asked Erhard without thinking. He was thunderstruck.

"Am I sure? Yes, I am sure. I guess I should be grateful it wasn't a taxi driver or a hotel waiter. Rachel has always been a willful child. The question is now, what are we going to do about it? I will not abide by destroying the unborn child. After all, it is not the baby's fault."

Erhard thought a moment. "They must be married, and soon," he replied.

'I think that is the only viable solution. Look here Weiss, I don't blame your son for all of this. It takes two to make a baby."

The two men shook hands. Erhard took a taxi to the apartment. He roused his son who was still in bed, even though it was past eleven am. They had a dreadful row. Erhard spoke to him like one of his soldiers during the Great War. For once Itzhak came around. He agreed to the wedding, possibly because Erhard threatened to beat the living shit out of him if he didn't.

Erhard took another taxi to the store. He cornered Natalie and told her about the pregnancy and the proposed wedding. At first, she was dubious.

"Isn't there some other solution? If she would sleep with Itzhak before marriage, she is not good enough for our son."

"What other solution? Do you want our grandchild to be called a bastard? That would be dishonorable."

The wedding was hastily arranged and took place without the usual fanfare. There was no scandal because, after all, this was Paris. Rachel moved into the Weiss home. But from the start there was friction between Natalie and Rachel. The apartment was small and they were thrown together constantly. For the first couple of months, Rachel was very lonely.

Then a peculiar thing happened. As Rachel's pregnancy began to show, the two women began to warm up to each other. They had the same aggressive practicality and the same sense of humor. The two would laugh together at things that would leave others in the room scratching their heads. As the time approached for Rachel's delivery they were thick as thieves. They shopped for baby clothes and equipment together and ignored the men.

In the meantime, Erhard put Itzhak to work at the store. Now that he was going to be a father, Erhard demanded that he grow up and assume responsibility for his family. His childhood was over. To his credit, Itzhak buckled down and was stable for the first time in his life. Erhard warned him that if he as much as looked at pretty Annett, the cashier, he would pull out his fingernails one by one.

Now the wonderful day had arrived. Erhard was a grandfather. The baby had fine blonde hair and blue-grey eyes. But, he told himself, you couldn't tell about eye color at birth. It would change over time.

Erhard felt he owed himself a treat to celebrate. He headed toward the kitchen and the bottle of scotch. He had promised himself to cut back on his alcohol consumption but on this day he put those cares aside and indulged himself, getting pleasantly drunk.

§

The joyous family was understandably not paying attention on this day to what was going on in the world. Across the Atlantic in New York, the stock market was in free fall. Sixteen million shares flooded the market amid panic selling. Known henceforth as Black Tuesday, this day would see the culmination of the ruin of a market that had been teetering for months. Banks began to fail and close their doors.

Millions of people from all social classes lost everything. Many people it seemed had been "playing the market," often with borrowed money. In the following months, businesses large and small went bankrupt. Millions were out of work. The panic spread to Europe. Germany was hit particularly hard. This was to have profound future consequences for the Weiss family.

CHAPTER TWELVE

GOETHESTRASSE 41
MUNCHEN, DEUTSCHLAND
30 JUNI, 1934

A little after nine p.m., a long black Mercedes sedan roared through the quiet streets of Munich. Clinging to the running boards and sitting in the front passenger seat were six SS troopers. An SS-Scharfuhrer, a non-commissioned officer, was driving and seated on the rear seat was SS-Untersturmfuhrer Erich Wolf. He was dressed in his black SS uniform with a red and black Swastika armband and silver deaths head badge above the brim of his hat, as were his men. Erich had been an officer in the SS since 1932.

The Wolf family had hosted a New Year's family gathering at the estate in Bayreuth. After dinner, Erich's brother in law, Gerhard Drescher had casually asked him about joining the SS. Erich had replied that he was probably too old and that he walked with a limp. Gerhard had replied that with Erich's war medal, low Nazi party number and long Aryan bloodline he stood a good chance of being accepted.

So in January 1932, Erich had applied. He was surprised at how easy it was. He was interviewed by a panel of high ranking SS officers and had to submit proof of Aryan blood. A month later he was commissioned an SS-Untersturmfuhrer, the lowest officer rank.

Since that time, Adolf Hitler and the Nazi party had seized

uncontested power in Germany. All other political parties were banned and dissidents were either driven out of the country or put in concentration camps. Erich was excited to be a part of the Nazi movement and the SS.

These were exciting times to be a German. The Fuhrer had brought pride back into the German soul. Everywhere Erich went, he felt a new spirit in the people. The universal greeting was the Nazi salute. For the first time, the Jews were being taught a lesson. They weren't able to get by with their tricks anymore.

Erich was proud of the mission he was on tonight. He was on his way to arrest a traitor to the Fuhrer. The truck slid to a stop in front of Goethestrasse 41. Erich and his men piled out of the lorry. All across Germany similar teams were on similar missions. Erich had a warrant in his tunic pocket for the arrest of SA-Standartenfuhrer Franz Neurath.

The Sturmabteilung, or SA for short, was known informally as the Brown Shirts. They were arguably the most powerful organization in Germany. Tonight that would change.

The leadership of the SA organization was accused of plotting to overthrow the Fuhrer.

"Take two men and cover the back. Take care he doesn't escape," said Erich to the Scharfuhrer. The man saluted and ran off toward the rear of the building. Wolf looked at the house. It had two stories and appeared to be the home of an upper middleclass family. It was neat and tidy and showed signs of a recent painting.

Erich and three troopers approached the front door. Erich drew his pistol from its holster and a photograph of Neurath from a pocket. He knocked forcefully on the door. The man who answered was a short stocky bulldog of a man. A coarse face and close-cropped hair didn't fit with the dressing gown and slippers he was wearing. The man had a confused expression on his face.

Erich shoved the muzzle of the pistol into his gut and forced him back.

"SA-Standartenfuhrer Franz Neurath, you are under arrest in the name of the Fuhrer."

The short man sputtered with anger. "What is this outrage?"

"You and other SA schwein are accused of plotting to overthrow the Fuhrer."

"Overthrow the Fuhrer?" Neurath thundered, then red-faced, he pushed forward toward Erich who was surprised by his aggression and fired his pistol into the man's face. The nine-millimeter bullet struck him in the right eye, and he toppled backward.

Suddenly a door at the side of the room flew open and a shape entered. Erich turned and fired two shots instinctively. One of the bullets struck the shape that Erich, a moment later, saw to his horror was a blond woman. She fell to the floor with a cry and there was a spreading red stain on the chest of her robe. One of the troopers bent down and checked her neck for a pulse. He rose.

"She is dead, Herr Untersturmfuhrer."

Erich stood transfixed. What have I done? he thought. He heard a scraping noise through the door that the woman had come through. He rushed through the door and saw a staircase. He looked up the stairs. On the first landing stood a girl of about seven with her fist in her mouth and a boy of about five holding a stuffed bear. The girl started to scream. Erich stumbled backward. He passed a room with the door ajar. It was the loo. Erich rushed inside and vomited.

Known henceforth as the Night of the Long Knives, this evening shattered the power of the SA forever. From this day until May 1945, Heinrich Himmler and his SS would be the power behind Hitler's throne.

By the third day after the shootings, Erich was feeling better about his actions. The man he shot was a traitor to the Fuhrer so the shooting was justified. The woman being shot was just a regrettable accident. Who knows, her husband had been a traitor; maybe she was a traitor too. His superiors weren't concerned at all.

When replaying the action in his mind, Erich was surprised how easy it had been for him to kill. He had always thought it would be difficult but it had been easy, just the flick of a finger.

CHAPTER THIRTEEN

22 RUE MOLITOR
PARIS, FRANCE
17 SEPTEMBRE, 1935

The automobile was waiting for Erhard Weiss when he descended the stairs from the front door of his home. It was a 1934 Daimler, Double-Six, sleeve valve V12. The automobile was about a block long with shiny green coachwork and silver wire wheels. Holding the door open was the family chauffeur, Pascal, a young man from French Morocco. Pascal was dressed in a dove grey uniform complete with a cap that Natalie had insisted upon.

Weiss entered the passenger compartment and sat on the butter soft leather seat. He felt patently ridiculous. The car and the house were too ostentatious for a man like him, a German immigrant who had entered France with just a few British pounds in the bank. The car was purchased at Natalie's insistence, as well as the fancy house on Rue Molitor. The house was big and luxurious but Erhard felt like a stranger inside. When he walked through it, his footsteps would echo through the cavernous rooms. It was like living in a museum and he couldn't relax there. He always felt as if someone was about to tap him on the shoulder and tell him it was closing time. The servants were another problem. Their fawning over him made him nervous and forced him to lock himself in his study. But he didn't have a bottle of whiskey stashed anywhere. He hadn't had a drink in four years. His difficulty in getting off the stuff had shown him that he had a problem with alcohol.

The family was richer now than he had ever dreamed possible. The worldwide economic depression had confirmed to Erhard the wisdom of moving to France when they did. The United States and Germany had been hit hard, but France largely escaped with unemployment that peaked at around five percent. France was more self-sufficient and relied less on foreign imports. Industrial output, however, had dropped twenty percent.

When the world economy went really bad in early 1930, Erhard had been worried about the family business. Rich, foreign women, mainly Americans were the majority of their customers. He need not have worried. Sales tapered off for a few months but then picked up again. A steady stream of wealthy women and those who wanted to appear wealthy continued to buy Natalie's shoes.

In June of 1931, Erhard heard about a shoe manufacturer who had a factory in Pontoise, northeast of Paris, who had gone bankrupt. The company had specialized in poor quality imitations of Paris fashion shoes for the export market. When the economic downturn occurred, the company's foreign markets dried up. The owners then made some bad business decisions and the company failed. Erhard made inquiries at the bank that now owned the property. The factory could be purchased for forty percent of its value before the economic panic. On a whim, he drove out to Pontoise and inspected the building and equipment. He came back to Paris and told Natalie about the property. Erhard found himself downplaying the possibilities of such a big purchase. It was as if he was talking himself out of the idea. He was torn. He was afraid of the risk but, on the other hand, saw it as a chance for him to have a real job and contribute to the family.

Natalie wanted to investigate further. She went to her friend Madame LeClerc and the two started digging into the property history and equipment values and the feasibility of making a going concern out of the failed business.

Two weeks after he had first told Natalie about the factory, Erhard, Natalie, and Madame LeClerc lunched at a sidewalk café and discussed the opportunity. Erhard spoke first. He advised caution. It was a huge risk. It would take all their savings and then some to buy the factory and start the company. They were doing well now. Why risk everything? Erhard looked at Natalie for her opinion.

Natalie didn't speak. Instead, she turned to LeClerc and nodded. The woman was showing her age now. She was over sixty but her mind was still as sharp as a tack. LeClerc spoke directly to Natalie. It confirmed his suspicions that the old woman knew where the brains were in the Weiss family.

"Mes chers, this is a great opportunity for you but also a great risk. You must not be frightened by the risk. You must embrace it. Any great reward involves the element of great risk. All those years ago in Germany I recognized you as a potentially great businesswoman. What do you feel in your gut? If you feel excitement at the prospect then you must seize the opportunity."

Natalie stared down at the tablecloth for a full minute. When she looked up her eyes were flashing.

"Alright, we will start the Weiss and Son shoe manufactory. Sears and Roebuck, you'd better watch out," said Natalie laughing.

"I want in for twenty percent of the company in exchange for twenty percent of the start up money," said Le Clerc immediately.

"Twenty percent of the company in exchange for thirty percent of the start-up," replied Natalie.

"Done," said LeClerc, and the two women shook hands.

Erhard sat across the table with his mouth open in disbelief. He protested.

"Aren't we being a little hasty? Maybe we should think about this a little more."

The two women stared at him. Le Clerc gave him a look similar to one a mother would give a small boy who had just announced he had pissed his pants. There was silence until Erhard threw up his hands and surrendered. The decision had been made.

The next week they struck a deal with the bank and bought the factory. Erhard through his lawyer filed the necessary government papers for founding Weiss Et Chaussures Fils Et Cie.

Erhard hired back most of the old factory workforce and allowed them to form a union.

After all, this was France. He paid them a little more than they had gotten before and lent a sympathetic ear to complaints about working conditions.

On the day the factory reopened Erhard addressed the entire workforce on the factory floor. He told them that under the previous owner they were making shoddy shoes as fast as possible. From now on there would be an emphasis on quality over speed. He asked for their cooperation and the employees, thrilled to have their jobs back, responded.

The first products from Weiss Et Chaussures Fils Et Cie were a line of working men's shoes. They were made of sturdy leather and would last a long time. A simplified design allowed them to be made and sold at a reduced cost. From the first, they sold well as people recognized their value. More stores began carrying the product because people asked for them. Weiss talked over all his business decisions with Natalie. He had swallowed his ego. He realized she had a better business mind than he did. He ended his first year in business in the black.

Natalie suggested that the company start a line of women's shoes. They would be simplified versions of her designs. The target customers of these shoes would be the shop girls of France. They would be able to buy stylish, quality shoes for a price they could afford. This new line was also a great success. Erhard had to expand the factory and hire extra people to keep up with the demand. The Weiss family was suddenly not just well off, but rich. They had millions of francs pouring in.

Erhard thought of his good fortune as he rode in the Daimler. Only two things cast a pall on his outlook. The first was his son Itzhak. He was twenty-four now and in charge of production at the factory. Erhard had heard complaints that he was rude and overbearing to the workers, especially the female office staff. At least two women had quit their jobs because of his abuse. Others complained that he fondled them inappropriately. Erhard mentioned it to Natalie but she rebuffed him. She refused to believe anything bad about her son.

The second thing that was troubling Erhard was the situation in Germany. They had been trying to persuade Natalie's family to get out. Her parents and sisters had so far refused saying that they thought that conditions would get better.

Just this morning Erhard had bought a German newspaper and read about the new Nuremberg laws that were announced by Herr Hitler at the annual Nazi party rally. Jews in Germany could no longer be German citizens. Jews could not marry Aryans or have sexual relations with them. Jews could not employ Aryan domestic help under the age of forty-five. Jews could not display the German flag or medals earned in wartime service.

The law defined a Jew as a person having three or more Jewish grandparents. A person who had one or two Jewish grandparents would be classified as a "mischling," or cross breed.

Erhard was so angry that he had crushed the paper into a ball and thrown it away.

Erhard believed he had survived the Great War because of a sixth sense he had on the battlefield. He remembered many times in

Belgium when he got a sudden feeling he should duck or take cover. He always obeyed these impulses and more than a few times narrowly missed being shot or blown apart by artillery shells. This sixth sense was screaming at him now but he didn't know how to react to it.

The Daimler slowed and stopped in front of Natalie's store. Erhard looked out the window and saw Natalie on the sidewalk holding the hand of six-year-old Adrien. He was tall for his age. The boy's blonde hair and blue eyes contrasted sharply with Natalie's dark features. Erhard often wondered about this. Was it possible that he wasn't really his grandson? Could Rachel have been involved with someone else and just said the child was Itzhak's? He had gotten to know Rachel pretty well and couldn't see her being that deceitful. But in the end, it didn't matter. He loved the boy as Natalie did, with all his heart. It was probably a trick of heredity. Maybe in the dim past, some Viking raider had had his way with a Jewish maiden and planted his characteristics in the bloodline, then many generations later they resurfaced.

Pascal popped out and opened the rear door. Adrien leaped through the door and onto his grandfather's lap.

"Grandfather, I am so excited. We are going to the zoo today," said Adrien as he squirmed into Erhard's arms.

"The zoo? I was under the impression that we were going to look at new machines for the factory," said Erhard with a straight face.

Adrien's eyes widened and he swiveled his gaze to Natalie, who smiled.

'He is just teasing you, mon cherie," said Natalie, with love in her eyes.

It took thirty minutes to get to the zoo. During the ride, they had a spirited conversation about little boy things. As a game, Adrien spoke to Erhard in perfect German with a Hessian accent. He would switch to impeccable Parisian French when talking to Natalie. The ease with which the boy switched back and forth between the two languages astounded Erhard. He complimented the boy.

"I am learning Polish, too, from Miss Walenska." Miss Walenska was a Polish immigrant who had been his nanny since he was two.

The three spent a wonderful afternoon at the Parc Zoologique de Paris looking at lions, tigers and zebras. Adrien's enthusiasm rubbed off on Erhard and he thoroughly enjoyed the day.

CHAPTER FOURTEEN

22 RUE MOLITOR
PARIS, FRANCE
21 AVRIL,1938

Five months ago Natalie Weiss had noticed a lump on her right breast while bathing. Not saying anything to her family, she went to her doctor. The doctor used a long needle and painfully extracted fluid from the lump. It was cloudy with little flecks of blood in it. He sent it away to be analyzed.

Two weeks later, Dr. Gold came to her home to give Natalie devastating news. It was breast cancer and he recommended surgery to remove the breast as soon as possible. She finally told Erhard about it and he was angry that she hadn't told him before. When he calmed down, she saw the look of worry and concern on his face.

Natalie had surgery the next week. Before going into the operating room, Erhard held her hand and spoke with great emotion.

"You must get well my liebchen. I cannot face life without you. You mean everything to me."

Afterward, the surgeon came and told Erhard that the operation was a success and Natalie would likely make a full recovery. After two weeks in bed, she rose, dressed, stuck a pad in her bra and went back to work. For the next month, she felt like she was slowly gaining back her vitality. She was very self-conscious about her missing breast. When she made love to Erhard she left her bra on.

A few months later when she developed a dry cough, Natalie dismissed it. She thought she was getting a cold. The cough persisted and one day she coughed and there was blood on her handkerchief. Natalie rushed back to the doctor and he immediately hospitalized her.

The look on the surgeon's face after exploratory surgery told the awful tale. With sadness and pity, the surgeon said that she had inoperable, terminal cancer. She had only a few months at most to live. Cancer had spread to her lungs and other internal organs. She would need morphine in increasing doses because the pain would be horrendous.

Natalie elected to go home and spend her remaining time with her family and Erhard hired round the clock nursing care. In the first few weeks after going home, there were some good times when the pain wasn't so bad. After that, Natalie was semi-comatose a large part of the time from the effects of the morphine.

Now her life was coming to an end. She could sense it. Her once vital body had shrunken with the brutal disease. She looked like a very old woman. Even though she was in great pain, Natalie refused more morphine so she could talk to Erhard one last time. He was sitting beside her bed and crying over her hand.

"Oh, Natalie, my liebchen, my life," his body was wracked with the sobs of terrible sorrow.

Natalie grimaced with the pain and looked up at her husband, the love of her life.

"My darling, I have loved you since the minute I first saw you at that stupid Zionist meeting. I was attracted by your wild hair and your passion. You have been a good husband to me. I wouldn't trade our time together for anything. Promise me to take care of Itzhak and Adrien. Itzhak is a good man at heart. Promise me!"

"Ja liebchen, I will do it."

Natalie gripped his arm.

"Erhard, oh my Erhard, I am afraid to die!"

Erhard watched the light leave her eyes and she was still.

The nurse who had been standing behind Erhard gently pulled the sheet up over Natalie's face. Erhard balled his fists and wanted to scream at the injustice of it all. Natalie was his anchor in life. They had come so far and built so much. It was tragic to have her end up like this. He didn't know if he could go on. How could he face the empty life ahead?

After a while, he stood and opened the door to the sitting room. Itzhak and Rachel were on a divan with Adrien in a chair nearby. Itzhak had a look of anguish on his face. He read Erhard's expression and wept into his hands.

"Mein mama. How can I go on without mein mama?"

Adrien rushed to Itzhak's side and tried to comfort him.

"It will be alright, Papa."

Itzhak roughly shoved him away and Erhard saw the look of shock on the boy's face. He picked Adrien up in his arms and they cried together for a long time.

The family decided to have a secular service. It didn't make any sense to bring religion into it at the end of Natalie's life when it hadn't played a role in the life she led. The Paris fashion elite attended, including a weeping Madame Le Clerc. The mourners shook Erhard's hand and murmured words of sympathy. He was in a daze throughout the service. He kept remembering Natalie's smile and the feel of her hand on his cheek.

In the days after burying his wife, Erhard's nightmares came back with a vengeance. There was a change, however. Instead of Bruno Adelmann crawling to him on the battlefield, it was Natalie with sunken eyes, pleading with him to help her.

Erhard started drinking again, trying to numb the pain with alcohol. He also began to make bad business decisions and Itzhak had to step in and stop him several times. Erhard turned the running of the factory over to Itzhak temporarily. Strangely, Erhard turned to nine-year-old Adrien for comfort. The two would sit for hours and talk about Natalie. Adrien was having a hard time too. His grandmother had been a huge part of his life.

Six months after Natalie's death, Erhard began to think straight again. At the same time, he realized he couldn't run Natalie's store without her. It required a woman's touch. He sold the business to Madam Le Clerc at a fair price and kept the proceeds as his personal fortune, separate from the family. He then concentrated on the factory, immersing himself in the business, spending sixteen hour days at his office. He often forgot to eat and still drank heavily. It was only a matter of time before it caught up to him.

One day in November 1938 Erhard was pouring over a batch of production reports and drinking Scotch whiskey. His jaw and chin started to ache. A strange pain radiated between his chest and chin. He sat down heavily in his chair. A dull dirty pain developed in the center of his chest. Erhard felt an overwhelming tiredness wash over him. He was barely able to flip the lever to the intercom before passing out.

When Erhard opened his eyes, he was disoriented for a moment. Then he realized he was in a hospital. Everything was painted white. A nurse was leaning over beside his bed taking his blood pressure.

"What has happened to me?" he croaked.

"You have had a heart seizure, Monsieur Weiss. Please do not move or exert yourself. I will summon the doctor," the nurse said as she breezed out of the room.

A tall man with long black hair wearing a white coat and

smoking a cigarette entered the room.

"I am Doctor Marceau. Are you in pain, Monsieur Weiss?"

Erhard shook his head, but asked, "What happened?"

"You had a heart seizure. I can tell you your condition was serious for a while. But, now I think you will be alright. You will have to take it easy from now on. Your heart is not strong enough to withstand another such episode."

Erhard nodded.

"Your family is outside. You may see them for a moment, but only a moment. Then you must rest.

Adrien burst through the door and rushed to hug him. Erhard felt a surge of love for the boy. I have to live he told himself, if only for Adrien's sake. Itzhak and Rachel made a less dramatic entrance. Concern was written on their faces. They chatted for a while and then left. Erhard was alone in the room. Quietly he whispered to Natalie.

"Mein Liebe, I forgot my promise so soon. I will not forget it again."

CHAPTER FIFTEEN

SS MUNCHEN HAUPTSITZ
WAGMULLERSTRASSE 16
MUNCHEN, DEUTSCHLAND
15 NOVEMBER 1938

SS-Hauptsturmfuhrer Erich Wolf sat at his desk and fumed. He was sitting in a huge room with sixty other desks identical to his, all occupied by uniformed SS officers like himself. He was assigned to Hauptamt SS-Gericht (SS Main Court Office) and served as judge jury, and prosecutor of minor crimes committed by SS enlisted men. Members of the SS were not subject to German law. They could only be brought to account for misdeeds by the SS itself. Erich hated his new job.

Up until July 1937, he was considered a rising star in the SS. Erich thought there was no limit to how high he could advance in the organization. His low Nazi party number and enthusiasm for the SS had come to the attention of his superiors. He was working as a Munich deputy to SS-Obergruppenfuhrer Kurt Delange, chief of the Ordungspolizei (Order Police). Erich was in charge of a large portion of Munich's uniformed police.

Then a misunderstanding had occurred. In July 1937 Erich took leave and returned home to Bayreuth. It was during the annual music festival which had now been turned into a garish Nazi party event. Swastika flags were everywhere and a considerable part of the Nazi leadership was there. It was an attempt to demonstrate to the world that Germany's leaders were men of culture.

Erich and his father Kurt were invited to another reception at Winifred Wagner's villa in honor of Adolf Hitler. Kurt wore white tie and tails and Erich his finest black SS dress uniform. When they arrived this time, the entire villa was ringed by SS troopers in shiny black helmets with SS lightning bolts on the sides and white gloves. It demonstrated how much more powerful Hitler had become since 1923.

Inside, they discovered that almost all of Hitler's deputies were also there, including the enormously fat Herman Goering and Heinrich Himmler, chief of the SS.

During the evening, Winifred brought Hitler to the group that included the Wolfs. After some small talk, Hitler remarked that he remembered Erich from his last visit to the villa in 1923. It was all very innocent.

Erich learned later that Heinrich Himmler was watching from across the room. He saw Hitler talking to Erich and asked an aide who he was. His aide told him that Erich was the son of a wealthy Bayreuth landowner and worked in the SS for Kurt Delange.

There was no more paranoid person in the fatherland than Heinrich Himmler. He was convinced, with some justification, that other members of the Nazi leadership were plotting to topple him from power. Himmler had been behind the purge of the SA "Brown Shirts" to get rid of his nominal boss, Ernst Rohm. He suspected that Goering and Heidrich, his own deputy, were plotting to do the same to him. By the end of the evening, Himmler had convinced himself that Erich Wolf was a spy within the SS working for his enemies in the Nazi leadership.

A few weeks after the reception, Erich was transferred from the police to his present assignment at the SS-Main Court Office. Erich soon discovered it was boring, mind-numbing work. Momentous events were happening in Germany while he was stuck punishing minor crimes committed by SS troopers. He had tried to find out why he was demoted and had asked around at SS headquarters. Finally, his brother in law, who was privy to gossip within the SS leadership, had told him what had happened and to keep his mouth shut if he didn't want to end up in a basement interrogation cell.

Erich snorted and picked up the day's newspaper, the Suddeutsche Zeitung. The main story was about a Jewish immigrant to France, Herschel Grynspan, who had assassinated a German diplomat in Paris. In a front page editorial, the newspaper called for revenge against German Jews. The name of the Jew reminded Erich of Herschel Stein, the Jew who had humiliated him as a child. Even after all the years, he still felt the anger return.

Erich put the paper aside and looked at his schedule for the day. He had two "trials" this morning, the first at 9:45 a.m. Erich looked at his watch, 10:07 a.m. Good, he thought, I have kept the guilty swine waiting for over twenty minutes. He rose and walked upstairs to one of six interview rooms. It was simply a bare room with a table and one chair.

Erich sat down and called through the door for SS-Rottenfuhrer Schiller. A coarse barrel-chested man entered the room and stood to attention. His face showed no intelligence at all.

"Schiller, you are charged with getting drunk and running your hand up the dress of a waitress at the Briarhof Biergarten. What do you have to say?"

"I was drunk, Herr Hauptsturmfuhrer. I didn't know what I was doing."

"Loss of pay for one month. Dismissed," Schiller turned to go.

"Oh, and send in the other idiot waiting outside."

SS-Sturmann Niemann marched in noisily. He was fat with

double chins and a mouth containing only three or four teeth,. Erich groaned.

"You are charged with beating up a shopkeeper. What do you have to say?"

'Herr Hauptsturmfuhrer, I entered the shop, gave the party salute and said, 'Heil Hitler.' The shopkeeper said to me, 'Yes, yes, what can I do for you?' I took it as an insult to the Fuhrer and taught him a lesson."

Erich buried his face in his hands.

"Although your motives were proper, you can't go around beating up people any time you feel like it. If you want to beat someone up, go find a Jew. Forfeiture of one month's pay. Dismissed."

It was the same all day, every day. It was the same all week. Erich felt that he would go out of his mind if he had to do this job much longer.

He spent the weekend roaring about the countryside in his Mercedes, seducing a widow in Bad Tolz and getting blind drunk. When he returned to his desk on Monday, he received a copy of a memorandum to all SS personnel from Reichfuhrer Himmler. It stated that in response to the murder of the German diplomat in Paris, there would be a spontaneous demonstration of rage by the public against German Jews on 9 November,. SS units were instructed to not interfere with this demonstration unless Aryan shops and stores were threatened.

At 9 p.m. on 9 November, Erich left the suite he maintained in the Hotel Torbraeu. He was immaculately clad in his tailored black SS uniform. Strolling along the streets of Munich, he didn't know that this night was destined to be historic. Henceforth this evening would be known as "Kristallnacht" (the night of broken glass). He passed groups of grinning toughs, their arms were laden with pilfered goods. Other groups hunted for Jews, carrying clubs and other makeshift weapons. They paid him no mind. Wolf saw the sky glowing to the west and knew a large building was on fire.

Erich walked past the mouth of a street of small mixed Aryan and Jewish shops. The street was deserted. Broken glass littered the pavement in front of several of the small stores. As he turned and walked down the street, pieces of broken glass crunched beneath the soles of his boots.

Erich heard a noise from within one of the looted shops and turned in that direction. The sign over the door of the destroyed shop was marred by Nazi graffiti but Erich could make out "COHEN, FINE MEN'S WEAR." The interior of the shop had also been wrecked and looted and pieces of torn clothing littered the doorway.

A man staggered out of the door. He had blood on his face and the suit he was wearing had been ripped down the front and hung in tatters. Then Erich saw the skullcap on the back of his head.

The man looked at Erich and asked in a plaintive voice, "why?"

Erich looked at the Jew in the dim light. He was already frustrated with being sidelined in the SS. Suddenly an image of Herschel Stein flashed across his mind. He got angry. The thought of the crime of the Jew in Paris put him over the edge into white hot rage. Without consciously willing it, he drew his pistol and leveled it at the injured man who was hanging on to the doorframe for support. Erich fired two shots, both of which hit the man in his chest.

The man looked at Erich Wolf in shock and then his eyes rolled back into his head and he fell to the pavement. Erich walked over to the fallen man. This Jew was the third person he had personally killed. Standing over the body, his rage gradually subsided and he coldly analyzed his feelings. He felt...nothing.

CHAPTER SIXTEEN

22 RUE MOLITOR
PARIS, FRANCE
1 SEPTEMBRE 1939

In the magnificent Weiss home at 22 Rue Molitor in the fashionable sixteenth arrondissement of Paris, ten-year-old Adrien Weiss was weeping in his bedroom. He was having a terrible day. His best friend at school, Marcel, along with some others of his classmates had ganged up on him on the playground after school. Marcel hit Adrien in the face and bloodied his nose. As Adrien cringed on the stone pavement, Marcel yelled at him.

"My father says we will have war with Germany because of you Jews. My father says France would be better off without all you kikes."

The other boys then chimed in, saying the same sort of things. Adrien was bewildered. He played football every day with these boys and thought they were his friends. He had jumped to his feet and fled leaving his book bag and its contents strewn across the paving stones. He ran as fast as he could to the front of the school where he saw Pascal in his chauffeur's uniform standing beside the Daimler waiting to pick him up from school.

When Pascal saw him he opened the boot of the huge car and retrieved a towel. He used it to clean the blood off Adrien's face. Bundling the boy into the back of the automobile, Pascal drove him directly home. Adrien went straight to his room and threw himself on the bed sobbing. He couldn't understand why the boys at school had turned against him. How could he start a war? He was only ten. His family owned a factory that made boots for the French army. How was that bad? It was all so confusing.

Through the wall, Adrien heard the sound of someone entering his mother's bedroom which was next door to his own. Angry, shouting voices carried clearly through the wall. Adrien recognized the voices as those of his parents.

"If you must keep that woman as a mistress at least you could be discreet," said his mother.

"What do you mean keep? Sophie is my secretary. I have a business to run. I must spend time with my secretary."

"Spending time with her at your office is one thing, but late night suppers and expensive gifts are another."

"What are you talking about, Rachel? You are talking nonsense."

"Cartier's delivered a package here by mistake. It was supposed to go to Sophie's flat. A pair of gold earrings were inside with a card that read, 'To Sophie with love, Itzhak.'"

There was silence for a while then he heard his father's voice, dripping with venom.

"And what about you, acting so pure? Are you seriously going to tell me that Adrien is my son? Look at him. Does anyone in either of our families have blonde hair?"

"Itzhak, what a horrible thing to say."

Listening through the wall, Adrien was stunned. He had overheard them argue many times before but never had his father said anything like this. Could it be true? Was he a bastard? When he was little, his mother had often called him her little goyim. Was he not Jewish? The implications of what he heard cast a terrible hurt across his young soul. If Itzhak Weiss wasn't his father, who was?

Adrien heard his mother's voice. "I was going to tell you that I am pregnant again. Is this one a bastard too? Get out of my room, you filth."

The boy heard the sound of a slap, then a slamming door. There was silence except for his mother crying softly. Adrien buried his head in his pillow and felt like his whole world was crashing down around him.

A little later he heard muffled voices in his mother's room. Then his own door opened. He looked up and saw his grandfather standing just inside the door. Adrien rose from the bed and rushed into his arms where he sobbed uncontrollably.

"What is all this? Tell me what has upset you," said Erhard Weiss, as he gently moved the boy over to the bed and the two sat. In a gush of words, Adrien told him what had happened at school and what his father had said during the argument. When Erhard heard what his son had said, his eyes went cold with anger and his mouth set in a hard line.

"Your father said those words in anger. He didn't really mean them. We all say things when we are angry that we later regret. When your father says things that are unkind, you must forgive him because he is part of your family. Adrien, your family is the most important thing in your life. You may love your country and want to defend her, but that isn't your first obligation. You may love your friends but, again, they are not your first obligation. Your first obligation is to your family. Your family gave you life."

"As to the incident at school, the French people are worried about there being another war. They are afraid and are looking around for someone to blame for their situation. Some are choosing the Jews. People have been blaming Jews for their troubles for a thousand years. I wouldn't worry about it."

As Erhard spoke, the boy looked up at his grandfather. His sobs receded and he felt better. Then he remembered something his mother had said during the argument.

"When they were fighting, mama told papa that she was going to have another baby,"

His grandfather smiled broadly, "That is good news. That is good news indeed! Now get yourself cleaned up. It is almost time for dinner"

§

The Weiss family sat around the big mahogany table in the dining room. Itzhak sat at the head of the table. At twenty-eight years old, he was twenty kilos overweight and as a consequence, had a double chin and bulging waistline. His dark hair was slicked back with pomade.

Sitting on his right was his wife Rachel. She was one year older than Itzhak, tall and thin with dark Semitic features. Her hair was cut short in the latest fashion. She wore stylish clothes and her hands and throat were adorned with expensive diamond jewelry.

Across from Itzhak sat Erhard. He was close to fifty now and his hair and mustache were streaked with white. His lined face bespoke a life not a little afflicted with pain and hardship.

Adrien filled the remaining chair. His blonde hair and blue eyes were a marked contrast to the other three. Those eyes were downcast. He still wasn't over the emotional trauma that this day had brought.

To maintain their home, the Weiss family had six servants, a chauffeur, a butler, a housekeeper, two maids and a cook. One of the maids was now serving their dinner. They had a hard time keeping household staff, especially maids, because of Itzhak's overbearing demeanor. While slicing into his roast chicken, he was the first to speak.

"Well, father, are we going to have a war? If we do, it might be very good for our business."

"It certainly looks that way. France and England are treaty-bound to defend Poland.

When the Germans invaded they almost guaranteed a war. The problem is that Poland was gobbled up so fast. There is no way now to drive the Germans out, at least for a while."

"Don't you see an opportunity for negotiations?" asked Rachel.

Erhard started to answer but Itzhak interrupted him. "Negotiate with Hitler? We tried that at Munich and look how it turned out. No, we must be strong and confront Hitler. The French army is the finest army in Europe. We must attack him. "

"What if he attacks us first?" asked Erhard.

"He dare not attack us. Our magnificent Maginot line of fortifications are impregnable," replied Itzhak.

"I'm not so sure. I was a military man. I know that fixed fortifications are usually useless. The enemy simply goes around them," said Erhard.

"Nonsense, we are secure behind the mighty French army," said Itzhak.

"I am worried. The German army is formidable. Maybe we should take precautions and move some money to the United States. We could take shelter there if the worst happens. We don't want to fall into the hands of Hitler and the Nazis."

Itzhak's voice rose in exasperation. "Father, you are being an alarmist. Nothing like that is going to happen. We will be fine."

The butler entered the room and approached Itzhak.

"Excuse me, Monsieur Weiss. Monsieur Lavelle is here to see you."

"Show him in"

A harried-looking Louis Lavelle entered the room carrying his hat in his hand. He was a tall man who had a florid, heavy-featured face with a weak chin. He was the production manager at the shoe factory.

"You sent for me Monsieur Weiss?"

Itzhak turned toward him and leaned back in his chair. He then spoke to Lavelle in a clipped, rude manner.

"I have read the production reports for the month of August. Production is down seven percent. Because of your incompetence we are losing money."

"But Monsieur Weiss, we had three stitching machines break down last month. Don't you remember? They took longer than anticipated to repair," said Lavelle in a pleading voice.

"Excuses. All I get from you is excuses. If you can't do the job I require, then I will get someone else."

Erhard felt embarrassed for Lavelle. He was ashamed of his son for his rude manner. He didn't say anything though but only looked down at his plate. His son was a bully. He bullied everyone at the factory and everyone but him in the family. He had been spoiled and pampered his whole life and this was the result. Erhard was disgusted.

When he had finished dressing down Lavelle and the man was

backing out of the room. Itzhak called him back.

"Oh, Lavelle, I want you to discharge Michelle from the office staff. I said hello to her the other day and she ignored my greeting. See to it."

The next day Erhard went to his bank and made arrangements for a money transfer. He then boarded a train to Basel Switzerland. He went to the offices of the bankers, Bueche & Cie and he met with an employee of the bank, Monsieur Lazar. Weiss transferred funds from his bank in Paris, converted it to United States currency in the amount of one million, two hundred thousand dollars and deposited it in an account with the Bueche & Cie Bank. The sum was almost all of the money in his personal fortune. Lazar asked him to write down a code phrase that had to be used along with the account number to withdraw the money. Erhard remembered when he and Natalie were living in Kassel. She always referred to their cash savings in the strongbox as "Erhard's gold." Because most of the money he was depositing came from the proceeds of the sale of Natalie's shoe store, he wrote "Natalie's gold" as the code phrase on the bank form and went home to Paris.

CHAPTER SEVENTEEN

SCHELLING STRASSE 50
MUNCHEN DEUTSCHLAND
AUGUST 1939

In August 1939 Hauptsturmfuhrer Erich Wolf was officially notified that he would soon be transferred out of AMT-1of the SS-Main Court Office and that orders detailing his new assignment would come shortly. Erich was ecstatic. His mind-numbing interactions with SS enlisted men were about to cease. He hoped that somehow he was again in favor with the SS leadership. There was a war coming; he could feel it. Erich knew that his war injury would keep him out of the Waffen SS: his bad leg, as well as his age, made him unfit for front line combat. He hoped, however, that they would send him somewhere in the police organization, either the Gestapo or the Order Police.

His hopes were dashed. Instead of something exciting, he was ordered to the SS-Main Economic and Administrative Department in Berlin. He was given three weeks to settle his affairs in Bavaria, establish residence in Berlin and report for duty. Erich was dismayed. He was forty years old. He had been a party member since 1923 and an SS member since 1932, and he was still only a Hauptsturmfuher. Others who had joined the SS after he did enjoyed much higher rank.

Erich packed his belongings and arranged for them to be transported to the Hotel Adlon in Berlin. After much haggling over the telephone, he had obtained a suite on a continuing basis at the posh hotel, although he winced when he heard the cost.

Erich then got in his new automobile. It was a Mercedes 540K roadster and was painted silver grey. Its powerful engine roared as Erich pushed the car to its limits. It was rumored that the government would soon set a national speed limit at 80 kilometers per hour so Erich decided to have as much fun as he could while he could. It was 585 kilometers from Munich to Berlin and some of the distance was over the new autobahn. He made the trip in well under a day and settled into his suite at the Adlon Hotel. He spent a few days enjoying the nightlife of the city and reported to the SS offices at Schellingstrasse 50 at the appointed time.

The SS-Main Economic and Administrative department, SS-WVHA for short, was mainly responsible for keeping track of funds generated when the SS rented out slave labor to private German companies. These companies included Thyssen, Krupp, I G Farben, Siemens, Fordwerke (a subsidiary of the American Ford Motor Company), Adam Opel Ag. (a subsidiary of the American General Motors Corporation) and many others.

The SS offered these companies a good deal. The SS supplied the venue, a factory building near a concentration camp often built by the inmates themselves. They also supplied the workforce, slave labor from the camps, as well as an SS guard detachment to keep the workers in line. All this for one reasonable fee. The companies involved need only to supply specialized machinery and company employees to supervise the work. SS-WVHA also kept track of dozens of shell companies that were secretly owned by the SS.

Hauptsturmfuhrer Erich Wolf was assigned to section AMT W of the WVHA. He met his immediate superior; a short, fat, bespectacled SS-Sturmbannfuhrer named Oskar Prich. The two men immediately got off on the wrong foot. Prich was a nit-picking accountant type who had grown up poor. He resented Erich's wealth and social position and the fact that he was tall and handsome. He also knew that Erich was out of favor with the SS leadership. Wolf for his part saw Prich as a malignant little pencil pusher.

As a result of this animosity, Erich was assigned the least desirable job that Prich could find. Erich found himself writing and reviewing sales contracts for the German Earth and Stoneworks Company. Founded in 1938, the company supplied bricks and cut granite to the German market. It was an open secret that it was owned by the SS. The company maintained brickyards near Sachsenhausen and Buchenwald concentration camps and stone quarries near Flossenburg and Mauthausen. Using slave labor from the camps to make the bricks and cut the stone, they were able to significantly undercut the bids of their competition. Any of those competitors who complained were likely to receive a midnight visit from the Gestapo and a one-way trip to oblivion.

Erich had thought his last assignment was boring. This was torture. Day after day he sat at a desk and shuffled paper from one stack to another. He did learn one interesting piece of information. Adolf Hitler personally received twenty-five percent of German Earth and Stone's net profit and SS head, Heinrich Himmler, twenty percent. If the same held true for the rest of the SS shell companies, the Fuhrer and Himmler were on the way to being fabulously wealthy.

Erich spent his evenings and weekends enjoying the Berlin social scene. He became a regular at posh nightclubs and at parties. There was no lack of female companionship. He had relations with many women but decided that he preferred widows. They were broken in sexually and they were not as demanding as young, unmarried women.

On 1 September, Erich thrilled to the news that Germany had invaded Poland. At last the nation was on its way to expanding its borders to give the German people more territorial room to fulfill their destiny. But the news also made him a little sad. He felt events were passing him by. Now that the nation would almost certainly be at war with the French and the British, he longed for a position where he could make a real contribution.

On 3 September, France and Great Britain declared war on Germany. That day Heinrich Himmler decreed that the SS, for the duration of the war, would pack away their black SS uniforms and wear specially designed field-gray uniforms out of solidarity with the Wehrmacht. Wolf scrambled to find a tailor to make new feldgrau uniforms. Good tailors were in short supply due to the purge of the Jews from the profession.

Two weeks after the war started, Erich was called into Sturmbannfuhrer Prich's office. The little man spoke to Erich in a condescending voice.

"I have a special assignment for you. In Poland, or in what used to be Poland, in the city of Lodz, there is a Gutenberg Bible. It is in the former home of a Jew named Izrael Kalmanowitz. Herr Kalmanowitz is now our guest in the Lodz ghetto. Reichsfuhrer Himmler wishes to present the Fuhrer with this bible on his next birthday. You will travel to Lodz, retrieve the Bible and return here. I will then convey it to the Reichsfuhrer. Are my instructions clear?" He handed Erich an envelope containing written orders.

"Ja, Herr Sturmbannfuhrer."

Erich left the office elated. He would be able to get away from his boring job and see occupied Poland. He went home and carefully packed his uniforms and things he would need on the trip. On a whim, he took along his 16mm motion picture camera. It was a Siemens model C with twelve Agfa film cartridges. The next morning he picked up his travel orders from the SS office and boarded a train headed east.

Erich arrived in Lodz in the late afternoon. He showed his

orders at the control point at the station and was directed to the Hotel Lodz, where German officers were billeted. He had his things put in his room and set off to find Izrael Kalmanowiczs former residence. He had worried that it would be hard to find. It turned out that it was easy. Everyone in town it seemed to know where it was. It was huge and grand.

He introduced himself to the Wehrmacht sergeant commanding the guard detail at the place. He presented his orders from Reichfuhrer Himmler. The sergeant ran to find an officer. It went smoothly from there and within an hour he had the rare bible in its special protective metal case under his arm. Erich returned to the hotel and had the case put in the hotel safe.

That evening in the hotel bar he struck up a conversation with a fellow SS officer. His name was Otto Neumann and he was a Hauptsturmfuhrer like Erich. Over a few drinks, the two became friendly. He was younger than Erich with sandy brown hair and regular features and was the son of a baker from Dusseldorf. They had dinner together in the hotel dining room. After dinner over coffee, Neumann explained that he commanded a thirty-man Einsatzkommando (special action group). Erich had never heard of them or what they did. Neumann explained that his job in Poland was to liquidate Polish nobles, teachers, intellectuals and clergy. But, he said, he had a different assignment the next day.

"The occupation government here is forcing all the Jews into the Lodz ghetto. They intend to put them to work for the German war effort. But there is a village of Jews about twenty kilometers from here. They are dirt farmer Jews. My superiors have determined that they are beyond teaching a skill. My task tomorrow is to liquidate them. I will be using a new technique, suggested by a high officer at headquarters in Berlin. There are supposed to be only about eight hundred of them. Would you like to come along and watch?"

"That might be interesting," replied Wolf. At the same time, he was thinking, liquidate? Did that mean to kill them? Eight hundred people?

"Be in front of the hotel at six in the morning if you want to come," were Neumann's parting words.

Over the rest of the evening, Erich considered whether to accept the invitation. The thought of watching a mass execution both appalled him and aroused his curiosity. In the end, his curiosity outweighed his squeamishness.

The next morning Erich, in full SS uniform, was standing in front of the hotel at the appointed time. A Kublewagon driven by an SS trooper with Neumann in the back, stopped at the curb in front of him. Behind the Kublewagon was a line of Mercedes and Opel trucks loaded with soldiers. Erich got in the rear seat with Neumann and they set out.

On the drive out of town, Hauptsturmfuhrer Neumann explained that they would be using the services of two Wehrmacht, (regular German Army) platoons to assist in the operation. Their job would be to surround the village and prevent anyone from escaping.

After about thirty minutes driving, the convoy left the main paved road and followed a bumpy dirt track for three or four kilometers. They were surrounded by farmlands. Finally they topped a little hill and the village lay before them. It was a collection of ramshackle houses with thatched roofs. Erich could see people walking around near the houses.

The trucks containing the Wehrmacht troops roared ahead. They stopped beyond the houses and the soldiers jumped from the trucks and formed a cordon around the village. The lorries containing the SS Troopers moved into a clearing in the center of the houses and parked.

The SS men then jumped down from the trucks. At a hand gesture from Neumann, they began fanning out through the village and rousting out the people from the houses. The Jews were herded into a large dirt area in the center of the village. The people were all dressed in ragged clothing and were obviously dirt poor. When everyone had gathered they were told to sit down on the ground.

The SS men entered the houses and ransacked them for valuables. Very little was found, the villagers were too poor. Some live chickens were confiscated and put in the back of one of the trucks.

The villagers were ordered to stand and move as a group to a large plowed field about one hundred meters away. They shuffled off obediently, their eyes downcast, mothers holding babies and the hands of small children. SS troopers set fire to every house in the village. The thatched roofs igniting with a whoosh.

Neumann then signaled Erich to get in the Kublewagon with him. They drove away from the village on a dirt track different from the one they had come in on. Neumann seemed to be looking for something. At the base of a small hill, the Hauptsturmfuhrer got out of the vehicle. Natural erosion had formed a ravine on the side of the hill. It was five meters wide, three deep and one hundred long.

Neumann ordered his driver to return to the village and have one hundred of the strongest looking Jews brought to the ravine with shovels. Wolf and Neumann remained where they were, smoking cigarettes and drinking coffee from a thermos.

Presently a hundred Jews arrived guarded by SS men. Neumann ordered them to deepen and widen the ravine. The SS Schutzes stood around shouting insults at the Jews and smoking. Two hours later Neumann seemed satisfied with the trench the Jews had dug. He sent them back to the village.

The Hauptsturmfuhrer explained to Erich what would happen next. The male Jews would be separated from the women. The men would be marched toward the trench first. In a field just down the track from the ravine, they would be told to undress. Then the Jewish men would be brought to the trench in groups of twenty to be executed. After finishing with the men, the women and children would be next. Wolf and Neumann stood talking. Erich realized that his palms were sweating and his heart rate had gone up. The anticipation of what was about to happen both appalled and fascinated him.

Neumann then called a group of twenty men from his unit to attention. He spoke to them in a calm voice.

"Men, sometimes our duty compels us to do things that in peacetime would seem distasteful, even barbaric. Believe me when I tell you that what we do here today is necessary. The Jews are our enemy just as much as are the French and British soldiers. Be strong and trust in the wisdom of our Fuhrer."

The twenty SS troopers lined one edge of the trench, their rifles at the ready. Erich caught movement to his right. He looked and saw twenty naked men come running toward the trench, whipped along by an SS-Unteroffizier. They ranged in age from boys in their early teens to old men. Many wore beards. Their naked bodies were very white. Each had his hands covering his genitals. Erich was amazed at how docile they were as they lined up in the bottom of the ravine and turned their backs on the SS men above.

The SS troopers then fired down at the naked men. Blood spurted from the front of their bodies as the high-velocity rifle bullets bored through them. They fell to the ground and an SS non-commissioned officer went into the trench and shot any still moving in the head with a pistol. The members of the SS unit not in the shooting line went down into the trench and spread a thin coating of dirt on the bodies with shovels and climbed back out.

To Erich it was surreal. He knew it was actually happening but it seemed somehow unreal. He began to feel a little queasy in his stomach and stepped back out of the way and took several deep breaths.

Another group of twenty came running and the same procedure followed. The SS men moved up and down the trench before shooting so as to fill the bottom evenly.

Suddenly Erich remembered that he had his camera along. He retrieved it from the bag on his shoulder, set the speed at 16 frames a second, wound it up and began filming.

After about two and a half hours, they had shot all the men and were starting on the women and children.

Neumann sent one of his men to summon one of the Wehrmacht platoons to the trench. His men were exhausted, their shoulders bruised from the recoil of their rifles. He wanted the regular army soldiers to take over for a while.

A few minutes later a Wehrmacht Leutnant at the head of thirty men approached Neumann.

"Leutnant Von Bader reporting, Herr Hauptsturmfuhrer," said the young Leutnant and saluted.

"Yes Lieutenant, my men are tired. I wish for your men to take over the shooting for a while," said Neumann.

The Leutnant didn't answer at first. He seemed to be debating with himself. Then he nodded his head and said, "I am sorry Herr Hauptsturmfuhrer, but my honor will not allow me to obey that order." He turned and said to his sergeant, "turn the men around, we are leaving. "

Newmann reacted angrily. "What? I am your superior officer. You will do as I say."

The Leutnant turned back to Neumann. "My men and I are soldiers. We fight armed enemy soldiers in battle. Shooting down naked women and children is not honorable. I will not do it."

"I am also a soldier." said Neumann menacingly.

The young officer turned his back on Neumann. He then marched his men back the way he had come.

"You will regret this," Neumann called after him.

The SS officer then summoned the other Wehrmacht platoon leader. When Neumann told him what he wanted, he only shrugged and his soldiers replaced the SS on the shooting line.

The execution of the women and children was hard for Erich as he watched it through the viewfinder of the camera. One particular woman would haunt him for weeks. She was young and pregnant and leading a four-year-old boy by the hand. Instead of turning away from the soldiers, she faced them with a look of defiant hate on her face. A bullet struck her in the belly and she crumpled. The Wehrmacht soldier who shot her joked about getting two Jews with one shot, and the others laughed.

That evening Erich did not have an appetite and skipped dinner. He caught the first train in the morning for Berlin. Back at his desk at SS-WVHA, he mulled over the executions in his mind. After a few days, he began to rationalize them. Such incidents were brutal and distasteful but necessary in the country's war against the Jews. To have a Jew-free Europe, many things would need to be done that would shock a normal person. He decided to put his trust in the Fuhrer to make hard decisions and not to question his methods.

CHAPTER EIGHTEEN

22 RUE MOLITOR
PARIS FRANCE
21 MAI 1940

After six hours of labor, Rachel Weiss delivered a daughter. She was small and delicate, but her mother could tell that she would be beautiful one day. All the family members gathered around the bed after the birth were joyous except for one. Eleven-year-old Adrien was not happy at all. His father and mother barely gave him any attention as it was; now he would have to share his parents with a new baby sister. He stood there with a dejected look. Adrien's father said they would call the baby Gabrielle.

After a while, Adrien and the two men left Rachel's bedroom so she could rest. The baby was entrusted to a nurse and the rest of the family went into the salon and sat in front of the fire. A maid brought a bottle of champagne and glasses. Adrien's father and grandfather toasted the new baby. He wasn't offered any champagne. They still considered him a child and it piqued him a little.

"What are we going to do about the company?" asked his grandfather.

"I think I have a solution," replied Itzhak, "but I don't want to implement it until we are sure that the Germans are really going to win."

"Itzhak, the French line was breached on 15 May. The British are bottled up with their backs to the Channel. There is nothing between the Germans and Paris. The war is lost. We know what the Nazis did to Jewish businesses in Czechoslovakia and Poland. They confiscated them. We must get the company in the hands of someone that we can trust and get out of France to England or the United States and we must do it quickly."

"Father, I think you are overdramatizing the situation. Life under the Germans may not be so bad. After all, they are a civilized people. In any case, I have decided to transfer the ownership of the company to Louis Lavell temporarily."

"Louis Lavell? Your browbeaten assistant? Do you think that wise? Why not Madame Leclerc?" asked Erhard. Adrien's father was getting testy with the questioning.

"I trust Lavell more than Leclerc. In fact, I would rather give the business away than trust that pushy old woman."

Now Adrien's grandfather was getting angry. "Why? She gave us more than a fair price for Natalie's shoe business after she died."

"I just don't like that arrogant old woman."

"Alright. What about getting out of France? We must proceed quickly," said Erhard with forced calmness.

"We must stay and look after our interests. We just have to stay out of the Germans way."

§

Erhard stood and left the room, shaking his head in exasperation. True to his word, a few days later Itzhak signed over ownership of their company to Louis Lavell for a pittance. They drew up an agreement, with only two copies, that stipulated that the arrangement was temporary.

Later that week, Nathan Rothstein, Itzhak's father in law, and his wife visited the Weiss home. They were fleeing to London and possibly on to the United States. They wanted Itzhak to bring his family and come too. When he rebuffed them, they begged Rachel to come with the children. She thought it over for a few minutes, then said she would stay with her husband.

On 10 June the Germans entered Paris. A column of goose-stepping Wehrmacht soldiers, four abreast, marched under the Arc de Triomphe and through the boulevards of Paris. Before long the streets were flooded with German troops. The Weiss family stayed out of sight in their house.

Two weeks later a young German Leutnant, wearing the eagle insignia of the Luftwaffe on his blue-gray uniform, walked into the Weiss home without knocking. Erhard and Itzhak confronted him in the entry hall. The officer addressed them in French.

"This house has been commandeered by the German Luftwaffe. You have fifteen minutes to pack and leave. You may take one suitcase each." The family scrambled to pack. Under Erhard's direction, they took as many things of value as they could cram into the four suitcases. Necessary things for the baby filled the other case.

Their fine automobile had also been taken by the Germans so they hailed a taxi and piled in with their luggage. The Germans, possibly because they were Luftwaffe troops, had neglected to search their suitcases before they left. If they had they would have found Erhard's hoard of gold coins that he kept for emergencies.

The taxi took them to the apartment on Rue De Vaugirard where the family had lived when they first came to Paris. Erhard had kept it all these years out of sentiment. He and Natalie had been very happy there.

The place was dusty and the furniture was covered in white sheets. It was also smaller than they were used to. There were only two bedrooms. Isaac, Rachel and the baby moved into the larger one and Erhard and Adrien took the other. They settled in to ride out the German occupation.

When Hitler invaded France in May 1940, he didn't expect to conquer the country in six weeks. The lightening conquest presented problems. He didn't have enough troops to garrison the whole country and still mount Operation Sea Lion, his anticipated invasion of England. He decided to occupy the northern half of France which included Paris and all the northern ports. In the southern half, he set up a puppet regime under a French Great War hero, Marshal Petain.

In the occupied zone the Germans tried to accomplish their aims by working through the French officials. This wasn't Poland where they could do all kinds of things out of the prying eye of world opinion. This was Paris where mass murders of Jews and other undesirables would cause a world uproar.

The French officials through whom the Germans wanted to work, had a unique attitude regarding the Jews in their midst. Jews with French citizenship were regarded as Frenchmen and they resisted molesting them. However, their attitude toward Jews who were not citizens, mainly refugees from Germany and the countries the Germans had conquered, was different. The officials regarded them with indifference. As a result French Jews enjoyed a level of protection unknown in other German-occupied countries, but their fellow religionists who were not citizens were not so lucky.

Life under the occupation was hard not just for the Jews but for most French men and women. There was a curfew between the hours of 10 p.m. and 5 a.m. Anyone caught out during those hours would be arrested unless they had a special pass. The Germans took 80 percent of French food production and sent it back to Germany. This caused shortages of food, prompting officials to institute rationing. The authorities allowed for only 1800 calories per person per day. A black market sprung up. If one had money, one could still eat well.

There were also the daily humiliations of dealing with the arrogant, rude German soldiers. They jammed the cafes, bars and hotels and filled the nightclubs. Edith Piaf sang to rooms filled with German uniforms.

The Weiss family was lucky. Thanks to Erhard, they had sufficient money to buy extra food on the black market. The main problem was boredom. They read a lot and played games. Itzhak was the most affected by the inactivity. He roamed the apartment like a caged animal, making surly comments to everyone. He howled in frustration when he heard that the Germans had seized all Jews' bank accounts. He seemed to live for the weekly visits of Louis Lavell, his former employee. Itzhak would browbeat the man and closely question him about production at the factory. It was making boots for the German army now.

During the first year in the apartment, Adrien discovered a new delight, baby Gabriella. One day when she was about six months old, he was walking past the bed where she was playing. She looked up at him and smiled ear to ear. Adrien, who had been indifferent to her until now, smiled back. He sat on the edge of the bed and played with her.

Now, every time Adrien entered the room she would perk up, follow him with her eyes and smile. It was impossible for him not to love her. She was a beautiful child with huge brown eyes and a doll's mouth. The two developed an almost mystical relationship. He was able to soothe her when she was cross better than anyone else in the family. As she grew and became a toddler the family started to call her "Gabbi." It was clear that she thought Adrien was the most wonderful person in the world.

On 3 October 1940, the French government passed the "Statut

des Juifs" under pressure from the occupiers. Jewish businesses that hadn't already been looted by the Germans were confiscated by the French government. Jews were forbidden to use public parks and cinemas. They were only allowed to shop for food in the late afternoon hours after everything was gone. Jews were required to provide their names and addresses and get special ration cards.

When the Weiss family heard about the new law they debated their response to it late into the night. Itzhak wanted to obey the law and register. He thought that if they broke the law it would go much harder on them later on. Erhard argued that to give the French their names and address would be the same as giving it to the Germans. Who knew what future schemes the Germans had for dealing with the Jews. In the end, the family decided to follow Erhard's advice. He calculated that they had enough gold and other valuables to allow them to exist on black market food for three years if the prices didn't rise too much.

At Erhard's urging, the family members became very cautious when they went outside for exercise. They stayed on the residential streets around the apartment and far from where German soldiers congregated. By the close of 1941, the family was still existing. They didn't live, they existed.

CHAPTER NINETEEN

O
n the western edge of Berlin, on the shore of Lake Wannsee, stood the Villa Minoux. The Nazis had confiscated the palatial estate from its Jewish owner in 1938 and had used it since as a guesthouse for the Security Police and the Security Service.

On 20 January 1942 a conference was held at the villa. It was chaired by SS-Obergruppenfuhrer Reinhard Heydrich, chief of the Reich Main Security Office, his deputy and assistant Obersturmfuhrer Adolf Eichmann was by his side. Heydrich was tall and blond with small eyes. Eichmann was smaller in stature and very ordinary looking.

The conference was called in response to a written directive from Hermann Goring, dated 31 July 1941, ordering Heydrich to submit a plan for the "final solution of the Jewish question." In attendance were representatives from the Ministry of Justice, State Security, the Foreign Ministry, Secretary of State, Nazi Party and the courts and many high SS officials.

Heydrich opened the discussion by stating that there were eleven million Jews in Europe including in England, Wales, Scotland, Ireland and the former Soviet Union, areas the Reich expected to conquer. He invited suggestions as to how to make these areas Jew-free.

One of those present suggested mass expulsion. They discussed it and decided that expulsion was impractical. It had been tried before on a smaller scale and the rest of the world refused to accept the Jews. Besides, there was a war going on. How would they find the means of transporting that many Jews out of Reich territory?

The next suggestion was mass sterilization. At first glance it looked promising, but several problems soon became apparent. The Jews were sly and cunning and some would find ways to avoid sterilization. Also, the Reich would have to put up with Jews living among them for sixty years until they all died off.

Heydrich then proposed, shocking some at the conclave, that the only way to make Europe Jew-free was to kill them all. There were immediate objections to this, particularly from the representatives from the Secretary of State, Foreign Ministry and the courts. However, they soon came around after little private talks with Heydrich during breaks and some veiled threats delivered in a cold voice.

That settled, the discussion turned to methods. The SS commander of a special action group said that they had disposed of thousands of Jews by shooting. It was costly in terms of ammunition and it lowered the morale of the troops to shoot women and children.

Mobile vans with the exhaust from the engine diverted into the rear sealed compartment had been tried but were too cumbersome and slow.

Eichmann opined that poison gas was the most humane, efficient method and suggested setting up special camps where the extermination could be carried out in a systematic, efficient manner. After some discussion the participants, one by one, nodded their heads to the proposal. Heydrich congratulated the conference participants on their hard work.

They then adjourned to the next room and had a nice lunch.

Adolf Eichmann had a talent for organization. After the

conference he got to work. He drew up plans for implementing the decisions made at the conference. He proposed that the first Jews to be liquidated would be the two million living in ghettos in the General Government of Poland. When Germany gobbled up the western half of Poland in 1939, it annexed huge areas of the former country and made them part of Greater Germany. The part they didn't annex they called the General Government of Poland.

Eichmann named his proposal Operation Rheinhard. As a start, three special death camps would be quickly constructed in the territory of the General Government. Belzec, Sobibor and Treblinka would not be work camps. They would be designed for one purpose only, mass extermination on an industrial scale.

By the spring of 1942 all three camps were up and running.

DR. WURZBURGER STRASSE 12
BAYREUTH, DEUTSCHLAND
17 APRIL 1942.

Kurt Wolf was a very old man now. He was 72, well past the average German life expectancy. He was totally bald except for a small fringe of hair just above his ears. He had lost most of his fat over the years as his appetite declined, but his doctor still railed at him on each visit to lose more weight. Kurt wished the meddling busybody would mind his own business. He would live like he wanted to live and that would be that. He wasn't as mobile as he used to be and used a cane now to get around.

Now that there was another war, he had all female servants again. Old Friedrich, his gardener, had died in 1922. Being served by women didn't seem to bother him as much as it did in the Great War. I mean, who gives a shit what the bushes look like at my age, he thought.

Ailse had died in 1921. His daughter Hilda's extreme weight

caught up with her and she did not survive a heart attack a year later. Kurt was alone in the huge rambling house except for the female servants. A few times a year Marta would visit with his grandchildren. Although Kurt loved them, he was usually glad to see them go. The children were noisy and had disgusting habits like picking their noses and running around barefoot.

He rarely went out now but when he did one of the maids drove him in his car. He didn't care how it looked to the people in town. Mostly he just stayed at home. A maid would read to him in the evenings while he sat in his favorite chair with his eyes closed.

Physically, he was winding down. Mentally though, he was still sharp. He kept up on the news. Distrustful of the information from German stations, when atmospherics permitted he listened to the BBC German language broadcasts on a short wave radio hidden in his bedroom. He knew that if the authorities found out about it he would be in trouble so he kept the radio under lock and key.

When Germany invaded the Soviet Union in 1941, Kurt was furious with Hitler. Why open up a second front while England was still unconquered? It made no sense.

Then in early December of 1941, Hitler declared war on the United States following the Japanese attack on Pearl Harbor. To Wolf this was idiocy. Germany now had most of the world arrayed against her. He feared that they would lose the war, with disastrous consequences for the German people.

There was one bright spot on Kurt's horizon. His son Erich was coming home on leave. He hadn't seen him for a year. Kurt rubbed his hands together as he sat in his study and contemplated a long conversation with his son. He was anxious to hear Erich's views on the war.

Kurt Wolf was standing on his front porch when his son drove up in his sports car. Erich hopped out and the two embraced. They went inside while one of the maids ran to the car to get Erich's luggage. Erich was wearing his Feldgrau SS uniform. Later, father and son sat in Kurt's study. Each had a glass of brandy in his hand.

"Tell me what you are doing now and how you have been faring," said Kurt.

"I'm fine, father. I am still with the SS-Main Economic and Administrative Department. I deal with the economic issues of the concentration camp system."

Kurt noticed that his son was aging. He was 43 now and his once handsome face was starting to look dissipated and his hairline was receding.

"Concentration camps? Couldn't you find anything better than that?" asked the old man.

"The work that I do there is vital to the war effort. The Reich has enemies that have to be dealt with appropriately."

"What are your views on the conduct of the war?" asked Kurt.

"The Fuhrer is brilliant. We are advancing on all fronts. Our armored spearheads are about to break through in southern Russia. We will soon invade England."

Kurt could tell that his son actually believed the propaganda put out by the government.

"I think it was a mistake to invade Russia before dealing with England."

Erich got defensive. "I will not listen to any criticisms of the Fuhrer's decisions. Such talk is defeatist."

"I meant no disrespect to Herr Hitler," said Kurt, backing down.

Later at dinner, Kurt Wolf kept the subject of the war out of their conversation. He concentrated on the food. The roast beef was cooked just right. At the end of the meal, Erich said he had some films he wanted to show him.

He set up a 16mm projector in the study. Erich produced one big reel that he threaded into the projector. Turning off the lights he said, "This is how we dealt with the Fuhrer's enemies in Poland when I was there early in the war."

Kurt settled back in his chair as the black and white images flickered onto the screen. Kurt saw a line of naked men running toward the camera at the bottom of a trench. Soldiers with rifles were standing over them outside the trench on piles of dirt. The naked men stopped and turned away from the soldiers who raised their rifles and fired into them. Kurt saw the bullets strike them and pass through with spurts of blood. He was appalled. No, a better word was outraged. He gasped for breath. Was this what Germany had come to? Cold blooded murder of naked human beings. Like his father before him, he had always detested Jews, but he looked upon them as political enemies to be defeated politically. He was hostile to them but never meant for them to be killed like cattle in a slaughterhouse.

As he watched the film, Kurt had a disturbing thought. Did he, by the things he had said publicly against the Jews, contribute to this atrocity? Was all that nonsense about racial superiority that he had spewed out to get votes coming back to haunt him?

Kurt was in for another shock when the women with babies began to appear on the screen. Line after line of naked women appeared, some leading or carrying children and were shot before his eyes. Two little girls were particularly sad. They looked like his daughters Marta and Hilda had looked at four years of age. Tears began to roll down his cheeks.

"Does this happen often?" asked Kurt, his voice betraying his anger.

"This was just the beginning. I shot this film in 1939. Now the SS has special extermination camps in Poland where they kill thousands each day. Other camps are under construction including a huge one at Auschwitz where the SS will be able to kill tens of thousands each day," replied Erich.

With surprising speed for one his age, Kurt Wolf jumped up and snapped on the light. He swung his arm and swept the projector onto the floor and faced his son.

"Do you approve of this wholesale murder of women and children?" he asked in a furious voice.

Erich appeared shocked by his father's outburst. Then his expression turned angry. "This is necessary. We must defend German blood against our enemies the Jews. They are subhuman vermin who pollute our race and we must wipe them off the face of Europe and later the world," Erich shouted.

"Get out of my house!" roared Kurt.

Erich stomped out of the room. A short time later Kurt heard the sound of his car starting and roaring away. The old man sat in his study and cried openly, his mind reeling. Germany was committing a terrible sin. We deserve to lose this war. "May God forgive us," he whispered.

CHAPTER TWENTY

56 RUE VAUGIRARD
PARIS FRANCE
16 JUILLET 1942

By June 1942, the Weiss family had been sequestered in the apartment for almost two years trying to remain out of the notice of the French and German authorities. The ordeal had taken a toll on all of them. They spent only limited time outside because of the risk of a confrontation with a policeman. All three of the adults had visibly aged. Erhard's hair was completely gray now and his lined face and sallow color gave him the appearance of an old man. Itzhak too had changed. All his excess fat was gone along with his bravado. Only Gabbi and Adrien seemed normal, although thin. The uncertainty and the constant strain of so many people living in a small area led to arguments and recriminations. Adrien's mother blamed her husband for their plight and rarely hesitated to tell him so. More worrisome, the gold coins in Erhard's hoard had dwindled rapidly.

One evening the Weiss family listened to the nightly radio news broadcast. The announcer droned on about mighty battles where the German army was victorious. Near the end of the broadcast, the announcer said the French authorities had decreed that all Jews would henceforth have to wear a yellow Star of David with the word "Juif" written on it when they went out in public.

Adrien sat quietly while his parents and grandfather talked about this. It was Itzhak's view that they comply. Adrien's mother shouted at him, "Don't be an ass. Don't you see what this means? They could snatch us off the street any time they wanted." Adrien's grandfather agreed. He said that no one would now go out except to buy food. The discussion turned to who would be the one to venture out.

Erhard said that Itzhak and Rachel would not be considered. They looked too Jewish. Erhard added that he could pass as a gentile Frenchman, but the minute he opened his mouth his heavily accented French would arouse suspicion. Reluctantly and with great sadness, it was decided that thirteen-year-old Adrien was the only real choice. With his blonde hair and blue eyes, he looked anything but Jewish. The Germans or the FLICs, the French Policemen, would need to lower his trousers and see his circumcised penis to identify him as Jewish. Still, it was very dangerous. Those who engaged in the black market, both sellers and buyers, risked years in prison or death.

So Adrien found himself in the center of Paris on this beautiful July day. He wasn't wearing a Star of David on his shirt. He was walking down Rue Saint Honore toward the Louvre Museum on his way to a shop on Rue Vauvilliers where he had heard he might be able to get some meat. The man he had bought bread from this morning had given him the tip. The street was crowded with people.

Adrien looked at the front of the Louvre as he passed. A huge banner hung on the front of the building, "Free admission to German soldiers," it read. There was also a draped Nazi flag. In fact, there were Nazi flags and banners everywhere. German soldiers were also everywhere, mingled with Parisians. They strolled in groups looking at their German army supplied maps of Paris. Adrien had learned to distinguish between the different service branches. The Navy wore dark blue. The Army wore gray-green that they called Feldgrau. The SS also wore gray-green but of a slightly different shade. The Air force wore blue-gray.

Suddenly two blue police vans passed him with their sing-song sirens blaring. They pulled up and stopped about fifty meters ahead of him. Blue-uniformed French policemen jumped out and formed a cordon across the street, blocking both vehicular traffic and pedestrians. Alarmed, Adrien turned and began to walk rapidly the other way. He had taken only two steps when he saw two similar vans pull up and block the street in that direction. He was trapped! Fighting his panic Adrien stopped and watched the scene unfold. French policemen moved among the crowds of people, lining them up on the sidewalk.

The police set up two checkpoints, one at each end of the street, and began moving the people through them. Each time they encountered someone wearing a yellow star, they roughly pulled the person out of line and hustled them into the back of one of the vans. Adrien was terrified as he moved closer to the head of the line. Could they tell he was Jewish? Were they going to pull down his pants? Finally, his turn came. A tall policeman looked him up and down and then perfunctorily waved him through. Adrien was weak with relief as he made his way home.

Similar raids were happening all over Paris. Although the French police tried to keep it secret, news of the mass raid netting thousands of Jews raced through the city. The police were finally going after Jews with French citizenship. In addition to street roundups, they also raided Jews at home - the ones that had registered with the police.

Safely at home, Adrien told the story to his family. His mother cried and hugged him. His father went very pale and sat down. His grandfather just looked angry.

The Weiss family had bread and cheese at their evening meal and no one complained.

After eating, they gathered around the radio and listened to the BBC French language broadcast from London. The news was bleak. The announcer said that all Soviet resistance had ceased in the Crimea. The Germans were driving toward Stalingrad.

The next evening Monsieur Lavell came for his weekly visit with Itzhak. More and more Itzhak had been taking out his frustrations on Lavell. He waved a sheaf of papers under Lavell's nose and said, "Production was down twenty percent last month. You are destroying my business, you incompetent fool." Lavell just hung his head.

Summer turned to fall and Adrien managed to find enough food to keep them alive. The tension became almost unbearable because they couldn't go outside. Adrien's father spent most of his time in silent depression. His mother was little better. His grandfather drank heavily when Adrien could find alcohol.

The two most cheerful people in the family were Adrien and Gabbi. They spent hours together playing childish games and laughing. She was a little over two now and growing fast. She had started to talk. She called her parents, "mama" and "papa." She called her grandfather " pere-pere," and Adrien "Arien." Gabbi's favorite game was hide and seek. She would hide in obvious places and Adrien would pretend to search for her. She would then pop up and he would pretend to be surprised. Gabbi would laugh and clap her little hands.

CHAPTER TWENTY-ONE

UNTER DEN LINDEN 77
BERLIN, DEUTSCHLAND
10 DEZEMBER, 1942

The hotel Adlon was built in 1907 and was famous throughout the world for its luxury. In the 1920s it attracted such important guests as Franklin Roosevelt, Mary Pickford, Louise Brooks and Charlie Chaplain. Its location on Unter Den Linden was in close proximity to the German government complex. Among its attractions was a luxury bomb shelter in the basement where guests could ride out bombing raids in comfort.

SS-Hauptsturnfuhrer Eric Wolf sat in the sitting room of his small suite at the Adlon. Drinking a glass of mediocre wine, he was contemplating the falling out he had had with his father. When Erich had left Bayreuth, he was furious. At first, he had thought to turn his father in to the Gestapo for treason. When he calmed down, of course, he decided against doing so. His father was an old man and one had to make concessions for age and the loss of mental faculties. It was a shame, felt Erich, that the old man couldn't understand that what the SS was doing in Poland was vital to the defense of the German race. He doubted that the Jews, were they to gain the upper hand, would treat the Germans any different.

The village he had seen liquidated in Poland convinced Erich that the Jews were indeed sub-human. Dirty, lice-ridden, living in squalor, obviously carrying untreated diseases, they were a threat to public health. The Jews, the Gypsies and most of the Slavs would have to go. The generations of the future would thank Germany for what they were now doing.

He had by this point resigned himself to the fact that he would never have a glamorous position within the SS or be promoted. He had made peace with the situation. He felt that what he was doing now was important to the war effort.

By mid-1942, because of the war, civilian building projects in Germany petered out and then almost ceased altogether. As a result, the German Earth and Stone Works Company did less and less business. Erich would have had nothing to do had not SS-WVHA been handed a new responsibility.

With the advent of the extermination camps, the SS had come into possession of the property of the people they disposed of. Currency, gold and silver jewelry and other valuable items fell into SS hands. To keep these valuables from being stolen, an accounting system was established. Foreign currency, gold, including gold from the exterminated Jews' teeth were shipped to the SS-WVHA in Berlin. It was one of Wolf's responsibilities to see that it was carefully weighed, and then sent under guard to a foundry where it was melted down and cast into ingots. This was then added to the nation's gold reserves. The same procedure was done with silver, diamonds and other precious metals like platinum. Wolf was aware that a certain percentage was diverted to the private vaults of the Fuhrer and Himmler. He didn't know the percentages and didn't want to know. He kept quiet about it.

A treasure trove of vital commodities followed. Watches, fountain pens and other personal items were collected and distributed to the troops of the German army. Clothing and eyeglasses were distributed to the German public. An unexpected resource proved to be the hair that was shorn from the heads of the

Jewish women before they were gassed. It was sold to German mattress makers by the SS. Erich thought it was a well-run system, as were the death camps. Everything was done with maximum efficiency.

He looked out his window at nighttime Berlin. The city lights glittered. There had been no air raids for most of 1942, only some false alarms, so the authorities had relaxed blackout regulations. Erich hated air raids. He remembered the first British raid on Berlin.

It was in the middle of a night in August of 1940. Erich awoke to the sound of sirens. He rose from his bed and looked outside. The city was in darkness and searchlights stabbed the sky. Then he heard the first crunches as bombs hit the ground and exploded. Harking back to his experience in the last war, Erich was seized with panic. His suite was on the fourth floor and he pounded down the stairway in his robe and slippers. On his way he knocked an elderly woman down, such was his panic. He sat in the luxuriously appointed Adlon bomb shelter, where a waiter served him brandy after brandy on a silver tray. He emerged long after the all clear sounded.

Erich thought the act of bombing German cities was an outrage. In his view, captured airmen should be lined up against a wall and shot. He didn't stop to think that the citizens of London, Coventry and Rotterdam felt the same way about the Luftwaffe.

He dreaded what was to come. In April hundreds of British bombers had devastated Hamburg. In Cologne 900 British bombers had raided the city center causing widespread damage. It was only a matter of time before it was Berlin's turn.

CHAPTER TWENTY-TWO

56 RUE DE VAUGIRARD
PARIS, FRANCE
21 JANVIER 1943

A t eleven in the morning, the Weiss family was all in the apartment. Erhard was sitting in a chair reading. Itzhak was in his bedroom taking a nap. Rachel was in the kitchen preparing lunch for Gabbi, and Adrien was preparing to go out in search of food. It was cold in the apartment. They were all wearing extra clothing to ward off the January chill.

There was a loud knock on the door. Erhard looked at the door with an expression of dread but remained in the chair. Rachel walked in from the kitchen. Suddenly the door flew open and splinters of wood from the jam flew across the floor.

A tall, beefy French policeman in a blue uniform with two white stripes on his collar strode in followed by two other gendarmes holding machine pistols.

"Stand and put your hands up," he said, as the two other policemen brushed past him and went into the bedrooms. Itzhak stumbled into the room followed by one of the policemen poking him in the back with his weapon. Shortly, the whole family was standing in the salon of the apartment with their hands up. One of the policemen came out of a bedroom carrying Erhard's remaining three gold coins and showed them to his leader, who grinned.

"One for each of us. Put them in your pocket. We will divide them later."

The French policeman leader announced. "You are all under arrest for failing to register as Jews." As he said this another person entered the door behind him. Itzhak gasped as Louis Lavell walked in with a malevolent grin. Lavell handed the policeman some folded money and the gendarme quickly put it in his pocket.

Itzhak's face was filled with rage as he started toward Lavell. The policeman produced a pistol, pointed it at Itzhak's face and forced him back.

"I have put up with your abuse for years, you filthy Jew. But now the tables have turned. Now I own the company and you are going to prison," said Lavell, with a satisfied smirk.

Itzhak was going to respond but the policeman cut him short and began to herd the family out into the corridor and down the stairs and onto the street. As they were leaving the apartment, Adrien glanced back and saw Louis Lavell coming out of a bedroom holding a piece of paper in his hand. Gabbi became frightened by the shouting and started to cry.

The tall policeman told Rachel to shut her brat up. They were all roughly forced into the back of a blue police van and the doors were shut and locked. Gabbi began to cry harder.

They rode in the back of the van for forty-five minutes through the streets of Paris. Then the doors opened and they got their first look at Drancy Internment Camp. It was a large U-shaped, multi-storied building surrounded by barbed wire. As they were herded toward the gate, Erhard didn't see a single German uniform; only the blue uniforms of the French police. He couldn't believe that Frenchmen would treat their fellow countrymen in this way. Once inside the gate, they were assigned to a room. It was about fifteen meters square and was crowded with multi-tiered bunks with thin mattresses shared by seventy other people.

The family sidestepped through the narrow aisles looking for empty beds. All they could find were two empty bunks together. They settled down in the limited space.

Itzhak looked at Erhard and said, "father, I have been a fool. We should have left France before the Germans got to Paris."

"Nothing can be done about it now. Concentrate on surviving," replied Erhard in a sad voice.

The Drancy Internment Camp was built in the late 1930s as high rise residential towers in the Drancy suburb of Paris. It was intended for middle-class French families. It was built to hold 700 people but held ten times that number as a way station for French Jews being sent east for "resettlement."

In 1940, the complex was confiscated by the Germans and used for a while as a police barracks. Then it was turned over to the French police to be used as a detention center for Jews and other undesirables.

The Weiss family reluctantly submitted themselves to the routine of Drancy. At six a.m. they would descend to the huge courtyard between the wings of the building for roll call. They would stand there for two hours. It was in the January cold and they breathed out clouds of steam. Thank heaven the family had been dressed in their coats in the cold apartment when they were arrested. Other people among the prisoners weren't so lucky. They stood in thin shirts and blouses, shivering from the cold.

After roll call they would return to their rooms and a watery soup would be served in huge tin pots. Served in a tin bowl with no spoon, this was all they ate, morning and late afternoon. Water was available for a few hours each day from a leaking tap in the room.

After roll call, the French guards made the inmates sweep out their rooms. Then they were left alone until evening roll call at six p.m. Toilet facilities for the whole complex were located in the courtyard. Called the "Red Palace," there were 60 stalls for seven thousand people. Dysentery was endemic and people had to wait in line for the toilets. Many couldn't wait and the courtyard near the toilets was slick with filth and littered with feces. This, added to the fact there were no bathing facilities, made the complex reek with a horrible stench.

The gendarme guards at Drancy were usually surly and did not hesitate to use their truncheons on anyone they took a dislike to. They would plunder prisoners packages sent in by relatives and friends and would take all the food and cigarettes out of the packages and keep it for themselves. They did this in full view of the prisoners.

Then a peculiar thing happened. Gabbi, for some reason, took a liking to a particular guard. When he would pass in the corridor she would give him a big smile and wave at him. At first, he just scowled, but gradually he warmed up to her. One day he waved back. Soon he was smiling and talking to her. She would return his conversation with mostly gibberish. It only made the guard smile more.

One day this guard, who said his name was Marcel Lefevre, came to the room and took Gabbi and Adrien to the guard room on that floor. He gave the children bread and cheese and a little milk. To the Weiss family's surprise and gratitude, he did this at least four times a week for the whole time they were at Drancy.

Their stay in the building dragged on. They had been there a little over two months when Marcel the guard took Adrien aside while Gabbi was drinking milk he had brought for her. He said that the Weiss family would be transported to the east very soon. He gave Adrien two one-liter bottles with stoppers, a length of sturdy string and a bag of almonds.

"Tie the string between the necks of the full water bottles and hang them over your neck under your coat. Hide the almonds in your pocket. This is for Gabbi on the train journey. Do not tell anyone except your parents."

When Adrien returned to the room he told his grandfather what the guard had said. Erhard told the others and they wondered where they were going. Sure enough, two days later the family's names were called out at a roll call along with about a thousand others. French policemen marched them through the gate to a nearby railroad siding where a locomotive and twenty railroad cars waited. They were loaded on the train, fifty people per car, and the doors were slid shut and locked.

The journey seemed endless. On the second day the train was parked on a siding for twelve hours without moving and the people in the car drank up all the water in the two pails that had been in the car when they boarded. Adrien took care of Gabbi. When she would say "firsty Arien," he would sneak her a drink from one of the hidden bottles. When she was hungry he would give her some almonds. The rest of the family didn't share this little hoard. By mutual consent, they saved it for Gabbi.

There was only one bucket to use as a latrine in the car. With fifty people it was soon overflowing and the car stank. With such close quarters, arguments and fights broke out. Every lurch of the train brought moans and cries of pain. It was cold in the car but the people were so tightly packed together, that they were reasonably warm.

By the beginning of the fourth day, most of the people around the Weiss family were raving mad with thirst. A woman near Adrien saw him give Gabbi a drink from one of his hidden bottles. The woman made a grab for the bottle. Adrien's protective instinct rose up in him and he pushed her away savagely.

Gabbi, amazingly, was in good spirits during the whole trip. She would smile at everyone and peek through her fingers at Adrien and then pull them away pretending to be surprised. She had recently learned to count to five. Over and over she would count and wait for Adrien to clap.

Adrien was worried. The water in the bottles was almost gone. His throat was so parched that it hurt to swallow,. He didn't know how much longer they would last in the train car without food and water. If they were treated this way for the journey, what awaited them in the east?

CHAPTER TWENTY-THREE

UNTER DEN EICHEN 126
BERLIN, DEUTSCHLAND
5 APRIL 1943.

Erich Wolf was tired, had a hangover and was sad this Monday morning. He was tired and hungover because he had stayed up too late and drank too much. He was sad because he didn't know how to deal with the estrangement from his father. He had attended a party at the home of a high official in the foreign ministry on Saturday night. It was a gay party with plenty of available females but the problem with his father put a damper on his enthusiasm. He went home alone and spent Sunday drinking and feeling sorry for himself.

Kurt refused to take Erich's telephone calls and his letters to him went unanswered. Marta had written to him and said that his father had become very religious. He attended mass and took communion daily. Marta also said that Kurt had told her that everyone in Germany was going to hell for the things the SS was doing in Poland and Russia. Such talk was dangerous. It could land the person saying it in a concentration camp. Erich wondered what to do about it. He decided to let some time pass and then attempt a reconciliation.

Erich put his thoughts aside and reached for the stack of papers in his in-tray. They were reports on the proceeds of commodities from the extermination camps for the month of March. He scanned the columns of figures. Page after page went into his out tray. All seemed to be in order.

Oh, ho, what's this? he thought when scanning a particular report. The amount of gold received from Sobibor extermination camp was only half of that received in February. Erich checked another list and saw that the number of Jews gassed had not declined. Also, the other commodities (human hair, shoes and clothing) were nearly the same as the prior months. Wolf circled the Sobibor entry on the gold list in red pencil and went to see his superior.

Erich entered Sturmbannfuhrer Prich's outer office and spoke with his secretary, Frau Glick. She was a pretty woman in her mid-thirties whose husband was away in the army guarding the Atlantic Wall. Erich had slept with her several times. He asked her for a moment of Prich's time and was soon standing before his superior. Erich showed him the discrepancy. Prich looked at the paper and frowned.

"We must find out about this. If someone is pilfering gold from the Reich, it must be stopped." He fixed his beady little eyes on Erich.

"You must go to Sobibor immediately and investigate this. Do not tell them you are coming."

Prich called in Frau Glick and ordered her to draft orders and travel documents for the trip. Erich went home to pack.

The Fuhrer had abolished luxury train travel throughout the Reich at the start of the war. Erich, however, knew that depositing a few marks in the right hands would guarantee a higher level of comfort on the train. Sure enough, after the exchange of a ten-mark note, he was escorted to a formerly first class car for the journey east.

The seats were plush and comfortable and there were only three other occupants in the compartment, a German businessman with business in Warsaw and two engineers from Siemens who supervised work at a factory in a satellite camp at Auschwitz.

The train part of his journey lasted but a day and a half. The food in the dining car was surprisingly good, particularly a dinner of roast chicken. He spent his time reading or chatting with the other passengers. The only sour note was having to sleep in his seat. Erich was philosophical about this. Everyone must make sacrifices in wartime.

He got off the train in Brest-Litovsk on the Bug River. There was no passenger service south from there except for Jews of course, and that was only one way. Erich smiled at his little joke. Brest-Litovsk was one of the first cities conquered by the Wehrmacht when Germany attacked the Soviet Union in 1941. Erich could see signs of combat in its shell-pocked buildings. At the station, he passed hollow-eyed children with distended bellies on his way to the central SS headquarters. He showed his orders and was given the loan of a Kublewagon and SS driver for the 76 km drive to Sobibor.

The drive was uneventful though the road was bad. Numerous ruts and rough patches made for a jarring ride. The territory he passed was heavily wooded with occasional clearings along the way. The early spring weather was good but there was still a little chill in the air.

At last the Kublewagon entered a clearing and there was Sobibor. The camp was in the middle of the clearing and the woods were about two hundred meters from the barbed wire fences on all sides. He could see smoke billowing up in the northern part of the camp. His driver drove over some railroad tracks and they approached the main gate of the camp.

Standing beside a lift gate barrier was a soldier in a black uniform and cloth cap with a silver deaths head badge looking bored. Wolf knew that he was an SS Ukrainian auxiliary. They were mostly ethnic Germans who had lived in Ukraine before the war and captured Soviet soldiers who had turned coat. As Erich's vehicle approached, another Ukrainian came out of a guard shelter and held up his right hand in a gesture to stop.

Erich asked the second soldier to fetch an officer and the man scurried away inside the camp. A few minutes later an SS officer appeared. He was the same rank as Erich, Hauptsturmfuhrer, but here the similarity ended. The officer was overweight, bordering upon obese, with the dissipated face of a chronic alcoholic. The officer gave Wolf the Nazi salute and he returned it.

"I am SS-Hauptsturmfuhrer Franz Reichleitner and I am the Commandant of Sobibor. How may I help you?"

Erich got out of the Kublewagon, introduced himself, and showed his orders to Reichleitner. The fat officer's face took on a concerned expression and he became very eager to please.

"I am sure that this is just a misunderstanding and will be cleared up shortly. Please come to my quarters and get some refreshment. You must be tired after your journey."

Erich followed Reichleitner into the camp. As he walked, he noticed the stench. It was of decaying bodies and burned flesh and was strong enough to trigger his gag reflex. He saw prisoners dressed in pajama-like suits with vertical stripes alternating black and grey trotting around, each intent on some task. They were all just skin and bones. None of the prisoners walked. They all ran. Apparently only the SS walked in Sobibor.

The Commandant's quarters turned out to be a spacious, two-story house painted dark blue with white shutters. Inside it was furnished in a neat, homey fashion. He was shown into the Commandant's office and a prisoner brought him a glass of brandy. The Commandant excused himself to get the pertinent records and left the room.

Reichleitner returned a few minutes later with a file that he showed to Erich.

"Just as I have told you, it was a misunderstanding. During the month of March, we were 'processing' ghetto Jews from Lithuania. They have been in those ghettos since 1939. They have long since sold what valuables they had for money to buy food. Some of them had even pulled out their own gold teeth."

Erich looked at the camp records and satisfied himself that what Reichleitner said was true. It was a perfectly logical explanation and he told the Commandant so. Reichleitner sagged in relief.

"Please stay for lunch. Afterward, I will show you around the camp and explain our operation here if you like."

Erich agreed, and they had what he thought was an excellent lunch of roast beef and boiled potatoes. During the meal, he chatted with the Commandant and began to warm up to him. He was a gracious host and kept refilling Erich's wine glass.

After the meal, feeling quite tipsy, he followed Reichleitner out of the house to the east to the railroad platform which bordered the edge of the camp and was oriented north and south. It was about a hundred meters long and ten meters wide.

The Commandant stood with his back to the tracks and pointed his finger to the west.

"We have three lagers in the camp. Lager one is straight ahead beyond the guard compound. There we house our Jewish workforce that we need to run the camp. We use the workers until they are too weak to work and then we gas them and get new ones off the trains. Some of the skilled workers, particularly tailors, shoemakers and jewelers we keep long term."

Reichleitner then pointed northwest.

"Next is lager two. It contains the undressing station and sorting barracks for the Jew's belongings."

The commandant pointed further north.

"Next is lager three. It contains the gas chambers and the area where we burn the bodies."

Reichleitner then pointed to some narrow gauge railroad tracks that paralleled the main tracks.

"Some of the Jews that arrive can't walk or are unconscious. They are loaded on trolleys and wheeled by prisoners to the "hospital" where they are shot and taken to the cremation area. Now, if you will follow me I will walk you through the process."

The Commandant turned to the right and walked north on the platform. Several SS enlisted men walked with them on the tour.

"The train pulls in and the doors are opened. We get the Jews out and make them form two lines, men in one and women and children in the other. The Ukrainian guards bully them into line."

"Next, one of my deputy commandants, either Oberscharfuhrer Wagner or Oberscharfuhrer Frenzel, makes selections for workers for the camp. We segregate them into a group by themselves back at the end of the platform.

"We march the rest of the Jews, women and children first, north on the platform. If you will follow me."

Erich followed and they made a left turn and walked through a gate with a sign above it that read, "Sondrcommando Sobibor." There was a pathway that led straight ahead with high barbed wire fences on both sides. Flowers had been planted on the other side of the fences. The commandant said this was to allay the Jew's fears as to what was going to happen to them. Erich wondered what the Jews would be thinking. There was no way to disguise the stench of death that filled the air.

The path led to a long, wooden pass-through building with

counters on both sides.

"This is where the Jews are told to deposit their luggage. We even give them a claim check, though for some reason they never come back to claim their luggage." This was spoken to gales of laughter from the SS enlisted men accompanying them.

The path led on and opened up into a large open-air area. On both sides, there were walls under short roofs with a series of windows that looked like teller cages in a bank.

"This is where we tell the Jews that they are going to be put to work in Ukraine but first they must undergo a delousing shower. We tell them to undress but maintain the trick by telling them to remember where they put their clothes. We also tell them that for security reasons they must turn in their valuables to the clerks behind the counters. This they dutifully do."

"Next, we march the women and children first into the 'tube'." This was another barbed wire fenced path; this one had barbed wire strung over its top also.

Reichleitner walked on, followed by Erich. They came to another pass through building with numerous benches arrayed down the center.

"This is where inmate workers cut off the women's hair, gather it up and compress it into bales for shipment to Germany."

The group continued walking and came to a large rectangular building. There was a central aisle with three doors on each side.

"These are the gas chambers. Each one will hold a maximum of three hundred people. We gas them using the exhaust of captured Russian gasoline tank engines. It usually takes about thirty minutes."

Erich glanced inside one of the gas chambers. It appeared to be just a large empty room with no windows. A closer look, however, revealed that the wooden walls were covered for much of their height with scratch marks where the Jews had apparently tried to claw their way away from the gas.

The commandant walked through the building's main hallway and out a door into the open air.

"Each of the gas chambers has a large door at the back leading to the outside. After everyone inside is dead, worker Jews drag the bodies out with meat hooks and put them on carts and haul them to the cremation area. We burn the bodies using timber cut from the surrounding forest as fuel. The process takes much longer that the gassing. A trainload of Jews can take three days to burn."

"Most of the Jewish workers in Sobibor are woodcutters, to fuel the cremation pyres. The Jews who work here in Lager three never leave. Every month or so we shoot or gas all of them and get replacements from the trains. Some of these workers we call dentists. Their job is to pull gold teeth from the mouths of the corpses."

Erich looked in the distance and saw a huge pile of naked bodies waiting to be burned. As he watched, prisoners laid a row of logs on the ground. A layer of bodies was then placed on the logs, then another layer of logs. It continued like this, alternating bodies and logs until the pyre was about five meters tall. A prisoner then scaled the stack with a small can of liquid, which he poured on the pyre. An SS man then threw in a flaming wad and the pyre ignited with a woosh. Wolf could see five more pyres, burning in the open field. The stench was horrible. The scene was surreal, like a scene from Dante's Inferno. Erich was both horrified and fascinated by the spectacle.

The tour was over and the commandant walked back to his quarters taking another route through the camp. He paused outside the blue house.

"Well, that is our little operation. There is only one thing more I have to do each time a train arrives. When we pick workers for the camp from those arriving on the trains, I usually do something to shock and terrorize them. I have only about twenty SS men and eighty to a hundred Ukrainians to guard this camp. It fluctuates because the Ukrainian swine are always deserting. We use nearly seven hundred workers. It is necessary to scare the shit out of them from the beginning to keep them in line. There is a train scheduled in about an hour full of French Jews. I don't speak French. I don't know how I will communicate with them."

"I speak French. May I offer my assistance? I would be happy to make a speech and provide a demonstration," said Erich. Maybe it was the alcohol but, for some reason, he wanted to impress the commandant and the other SS guards. He wanted to prove to them that he was not just a desk worker but just as ruthless as they were.

"Very well," said Reichleitner skeptically, "but carefully arrange with my men what you are going to do."

CHAPTER TWENTY-FOUR

SS-SONDERCOMMANDO SOBIBOR
SOBIBOR, POLEN
7 APRIL 1943.

The train came to a complete stop, then started forward again very slowly. After a minute or so, it stopped again. Adrien heard shouts outside and the door on the train car was slid open. On the platform beside the train, dozens of black-uniformed men were shouting into the train cars in Polish.

"Z pociagu juz teraz! Juz teraz!"

Someone in the car asked, "What do they want? I don't understand."

Adrien stood up and shouted, "They want us out of the train."

The people in the car began to jump down onto the platform as quickly as they could. Everyone had wobbly legs from the confinement of the journey. The shouting continued from the guards but only Adrien understood what they were saying.

"Twerza dwie linie. Mczczyni w jednym. Dubiety w drugiej."

As the people emerged from the car, the black uniformed men grabbed them and roughly shoved them into two parallel lines. Confusion still reigned. The smell inside the railcar had been foul, stinking of feces and unwashed bodies, but to Adrien the air outside was worse. It smelled like rotten meat with an added sharp tang of burning hair.

A shot rang out and everyone on the platform froze. Gabbi started to cry along with several other children. Everyone looked in the direction from which the shot had come and saw an SS enlisted man with his pistol out and pointed into the air. The SS man then addressed them in bad, German-accented French.

"Everyone two lines. Women small children one, men other. Do quickly, I shoot."

All the Jews on the platform scrambled to comply. Soon they were in orderly lines with their luggage beside them. Adrien saw that everyone had yellow stars of David sewn on their clothes except for the Weiss family.

There were many people who couldn't walk or who had passed out. Prisoners in striped suits loaded them on flat bedded carts that ran on narrow railroad tracks at the edge of the platform. The prisoners then pushed the carts along the tracks and into the camp. One of the SS men on the platform called in German, "We are taking them to the hospital," he said with a smile.

Adrien looked beyond the platform and saw a high barbed wire fence into which tree branches had been woven. He couldn't see what was happening on the other side.

The same SS enlisted man who had fired his pistol in the air began walking down the line of men and picking out the strongest looking among them. At the same time, he was calling out in bad French for carpenters, plumbers, electricians and mechanics. Some of the Jews raised their hands in response and the SS man motioned them to assemble in a group at the end of the platform with the men he had already picked. He did this all the way to the front of the train and then came walking back.

A tall, slim SS officer, older than the other SS men and who walked with a slight limp, appeared and began walking between the two lines of people. His uniform appeared to be of better quality than the other SS men. The officer seemed to be searching for something. He came to where Rachel was standing, holding Gabbi, and stopped. Gabbi smiled at him, having recovered from her earlier upset. The officer spoke to Rachel in good French.

"How many members in your family?"

Rachel replied that there were five.

"You and the rest of your family, follow me. "

The officer began walking down the platform toward the group of men that had been picked for workers for the camp. Rachel followed and the Weiss men, having heard the conversation, fell in line behind her.

The SS officer directed them to stand just in front of the group of selected camp workers. They stood and watched as the SS marched the rest of the Jews, women, and children first, north on the platform and then turned left into the camp through an opening in the barbed wire fence.

When the rest of the Jews from the train were out of sight, the SS officer with the limp walked back to the front of the group containing the Weiss family and the Jews selected to work in the camp. This time he was flanked by two burly men in black uniforms, each carrying a meter-long bar of thick, construction steel. The SS officer put his hands on his hips and spoke loud enough for everyone to hear.

"You Jews will have the privilege of laboring for the Third Reich. Any breaking of camp rules will result in immediate execution. You must labor diligently and obey all orders of the camp guards. You have no rights."

Surveying the group, the officer's eyes settled on Adrien's mother who had set Gabbi down and was holding her by the hand. The officer walked toward her and bent down.

"What an enchanting child, so beautiful," he said.

The officer reached out his hand to Gabbi and she trustingly put the hand not held by her mother in his. He started to lead her away. Adrien's mother held on to Gabbi, a look of fear on her face. The officer looked at her and smiled and she let go, but there was a wild look in her eyes.

The SS officer led Gabbi to a spot about seven meters in front of the group. He looked down at the toddler. She was wearing a blue dress with white kittens embroidered on it that flared out from her little body.

"You are so pretty. Would you like a sweet?"

Gabbi smiled and nodded her head up and down.

"Open your mouth wide and close your eyes," said the SS officer.

Smiling, Gabbi did as he asked, tilting her head up toward the German.

In one motion the SS officer pulled his pistol from its holster on his belt and shot Gabbi through the mouth. Adrien watched in disbelief as her little body crumpled to the pavement, a look of surprise and pain on her small face. Everyone on the platform was frozen for two or three heartbeats.

Adrien's mother screamed and started forward followed by his father. Adrien also made to move but was stopped by the vise-like grip of his grandfather's hands on his shoulders.

Adrien's mother and father were intercepted by the two men in the black uniforms. His mother was struck across the mouth by an iron bar swung full force and went down. His father was battered to the ground immediately after.

Adrien's grandfather swung him around away from the savagery. Adrien was in shock.

Everything seemed like it was happening in a fog. He couldn't grasp what was occurring. He felt light-headed and sick. His grandfather slapped his face hard, then spoke urgently to him for about a minute. He then shoved him back toward the crowd of men behind them. Adrien made his way into the middle of the crowd of taller men.

The two men in black continued to beat Adrien's parent's obviously dead bodies with the iron bars. After two or three minutes they were unrecognizable as human. Their skulls and bones were crushed and blood was everywhere. The two men in black were spattered with it from head to foot.

"Swine! Murdering scum," shouted Erhard Weiss in German. "I was a Leutnant in the great war and won two Iron Crosses. You disgrace the uniform you wear." He began advancing on the SS officer in a rage, his fists opening and closing.

The SS officer was taken aback by this outburst. His mouth hung open and his face showed shock and then fear. He stepped back a few steps. He raised the pistol he had used to shoot Gabbi and began firing point blank at Adrien's grandfather. The officer fired six shots, emptying the magazine. One of the shots went wild, one struck one of the Jews in the crowd behind, but four struck Erhard Weiss. He staggered and fell to the pavement. One of the bullet holes was on his forehead just above his right eye.

The SS officer stood there. He had a murderous expression on his red face. He started to say something, then shut his mouth and stomped away. The SS enlisted man who had originally picked the group of men as camp workers now reappeared in front of them. He was muscular and exuded vitality.

"Alright you fucking Jews, run!" He pointed west toward the camp.

The group ran across the railroad tracks. A camouflaged gate in the barbed wire fence swung open and they ran through it and crossed a large open area. One of the Jews had apparently sprained an ankle crossing the railroad tracks. He was struggling to keep up with the group but lagging several meters behind. The SS man ran up beside him and shot him in the head. The group ran on, leaving the body sprawled on the packed earth. The running group entered a second gate and pounded across an open area bordered by buildings. They were called to a halt near a building on the far side.

The SS man, not winded at all, spoke again in German. "Form a line. Get in there and change into camp uniforms." The prisoners, some of whom spoke German, hurried to obey and began to file into the building. Suddenly Adrien was jerked from the line by the German.

"Who are you? I don't remember selecting you," the SS man said as he reached for the flap of his holster.

In later years Adrien Weiss would often wonder how he had found the words to respond to the German. He was in a fog. Everything seemed to be happening in slow motion. His mind couldn't register what had occurred within the space of the last few minutes. Perhaps his unconscious mind in an act of self-preservation had taken over. In any event, he heard himself speak.

"Herr Offizier, I speak three languages, French, German and Polish."

The SS man paused, brought his left hand to his chin and studied Adrien.

"What is your name?"

"Adrien Weiss, Herr Offizier."

"Well, Adrien Weiss, I have decided to let you live for now. I don't think you are a Jew anyway. With that blonde hair and those blue eyes, you look like you could be on a poster for the Hitler Youth. Perhaps you are an Aryan who was kidnapped by Jews as a child. Get back in line."

CHAPTER TWENTY-FIVE

IN TRANSIT
OSTPREUBEN, DEUTCHLAND
9 APRIL 1943

The Prussian countryside was coming alive with the advent of spring, but Hauptsturmfuhrer Erich Wolf didn't really see it as he stared through the window of the moving train. He was still fuming, even after two days. He sat on the comfortable seat resplendent in his SS uniform and accused himself. The Iron Cross hanging at his neck bespoke a warrior. Erich felt he had shown himself anything but.

The old Jew had ruined everything. Erich had hastily planned his little drama in the hour before the train carrying the French Jews arrived. He decided to make a speech in French exhorting the Jews to work hard and obey the SS, then pick a family with a small child and place them with the selected workers for the camp. He would shoot the child, prompting the parents to rush forward. Two SS guards would then beat them to a pulp with iron bars. Erich would then shoot the remaining members of the family.

The trouble with the plan started right away. The SS guards refused to do the killing with the iron bars. They didn't want to ruin their uniforms with spatters of blood. He was forced to recruit two Ukrainian guards, little better than animals, for the task.

It went well at first. He made his speech and then he lured the child out in front of the group and shot her. The parents reacted as expected and were beaten down. But then the old Jew had shouted insults at him. To his shame, Erich had reacted with fear and retreated before coming to himself and shooting the Jew.

The intended effect of the performance was shattered. He was made to look like a fool. After shooting the old Jew he had looked at Oberscharfuhrer Gustav Wagner, the deputy Commandant, who was standing nearby. Wagner was laughing at him. Wolf felt humiliated and ashamed. He had gotten out of the camp as fast as he could and went back to Brest-Lovitsk.

He felt no sympathy for the family he had wiped out. After all, they were just Jews and would have been gassed anyway. He just hoped no report of the incident reached SS headquarters. He couldn't stand the thought of being laughed at behind his back.

When Wolf had boarded the train to Berlin and entered his assigned compartment, he had noticed a Wehrmacht Hauptmann slumped in one corner sound asleep. As the train was approaching Poznan the officer came awake. The Hauptmann opened his eyes, looked around and saw Erich. He reached inside his tunic and produced a silver flask. He saluted Wolf with the flask and took a long swallow. After wiping his mouth with the back of his right hand, he put the flask back inside his tunic.

Erich saw that the Hauptmann looked exhausted. He was very pale, had dark circles under his eyes and stress lines around his mouth. He uniform was disheveled and threadbare.

"You look like you have been through a battle Herr Hauptmann," said Wolf.

"I have been through more than one battle, thank you. I have seen more carnage than a man should see in a hundred lifetimes." His words were slurred and Erich could tell that he was mildly drunk.

"Are you on leave from the Eastern Front?"

The officer nodded, "I have been in six months of constant combat. I now have two weeks, two glorious weeks of leave to go see my Maria. After that, I will go back to Russia and die."

"Come, come, my friend. It can't be as bad as all that. Germany is winning in the east."

"Winning? Let me tell you how it is on the Eastern Front. We are constantly short of ammunition and benzene. The front line troops exist on horse meat and black bread. The Russians keep attacking. We kill thousands of them. Bodies pile up in front of our positions two meters high but still thousands of Russians keep attacking. Our tanks and other equipment are worn out, as well as the men. That is how it is in Russia."

"I have been told by competent authority that it is only a matter of time before we crush the Russians," said Erich.

"Let me introduce myself. I am Hauptmann Franz Miller of the Tenth Panzer," Miller stretched out his hand to Erich and they shook.

"Hauptsturmfuhrer Erich Wolf," Erich didn't tell him what his present assignment was. He was too ashamed.

"Well, Wolf, did you know that on 2 February, Field Marshall von Paulus surrendered the entire Sixth Army to the Russians at Stalingrad. Ninety-one thousand men were taken prisoner."

Miller gestured to Erich's SS uniform.

"Do you know what the Russians did to SS enlisted men they captured? They shot them on the spot. The SS officers were taken behind the lines. I don't know what happened to them then, but I have a feeling they probably ended up wishing they had been shot with their men. My advice to you if you are about to be captured by the Russians is to take out your pistol and shoot yourself in the head. The things you SS did in the Ukraine and Western Russia have really made them angry."

Both officers jumped as loud gunfire could be heard.

"The train must be under air attack," shouted Miller. "That is the sound of firing from the flak car." Every train that moved in the Eastern part of Germany had a flak car attached to it. Mounted on the car were two four-barreled, twenty-millimeter anti-aircraft guns.

Wolf threw himself onto the floor of the compartment. He was in mortal terror. He heard something repeatedly strike the top of the car. There was an explosion directly above him. The firing continued for a couple of minutes more and then there was silence. The train continued to move as before. Wolf got to his knees and then resumed his seat. Miller was still sitting where he was before. He was looking at Erich with a look of mild contempt.

"Explosive cannon projectiles blew out the roof," said Miller and pointed at the ceiling. Wolf looked up and saw daylight through a jagged hole in the roof of the train car.

On the other side of Poznan, Miller fell asleep again. Wolf was a bundle of nerves, constantly looking out of the window trying to spot more Russian airplanes.

By the time he got off the train in Berlin he had calmed down. He hailed a taxi to take him to the Adlon. Once there, the desk clerk handed him a stack of letters. Leafing through them, he saw that one of the letters was from his sister Marta.

Later, relaxing in his suite he read what his sister had written. It was about his father. Kurt was becoming harsher in his comments to her about the Nazi government. He was calling the Fuhrer the anti-Christ. So far, he had not spoken out publicly but had confined his comments to a few relatives and friends.

Erich forgot all about his humiliation in Poland and his harrowing adventure on the train and concentrated on this new threat. Such disloyal talk could result in his father being shot as a defeatist. He suddenly realized that it could also affect him. Erich was already out of favor with the SS leadership. If his father was arrested for maligning the Fuhrer, Erich might find himself under suspicion by the Gestapo himself. All of the family money and lands would be confiscated.

The next morning, he reported to his job at SS-WVHA with a worried look on his face. He submitted his report on Sobibor to Sturmbannfuhrer Prich, omitting any reference to his taking part in activities there. Prich shrugged and seemed satisfied with the report. Before leaving his superior's office, Erich requested a week's leave to take care of family business.

Prich gave him a particularly hostile stare as he considered the request. Erich wondered if his boss had found out he was screwing his secretary. Finally, the Sturmbannfuhrer shrugged his shoulders again and granted his request.

Early the next morning Erich roared out of the hotel garage in his Mercedes. He got the early start because he wouldn't be able to exceed 80km per hour on the trip. The Fuhrer had ordered the reduced speed limit to save benzene. His 540K roadster performed flawlessly and in a little, over twelve hours he pulled into the driveway of the family estate.

An unsmiling maid answered the door. "Your father is in his study."

Erich walked across the entrance hall and knocked on the door to the study. When he heard a muffled "geben sie," he walked in.

Kurt Wolf was sitting in a large chair reading a book. Erich was shocked at his appearance. He looked like he had aged twenty years since he last saw him. His skin looked like parchment and his eyes were watery. Kurt lifted the book from his lap and put it on a table beside his chair. Erich saw the cover. It was the Bible.

"Hello Erich," he said calmly but there was no warmth in his voice.

"Father, I have been worried about you. You didn't take my calls or answer my letters."

"Those films hurt my soul. Erich. I couldn't talk to you for a while. I have been dealing with the guilt of being partly responsible for what is taking place in Poland and Russia."

"How could you be responsible? You have never been to Russia or Poland. What is happening there is official government policy. The Jews are our ..."

Kurt held up his hand to stop him.

"The Jews are being killed for being born Jews, not for anything they have done. For years I have preached this hatred of them. I stoked the flames of hatred. For that I am ashamed. I feel that my and my generation's reckless words have led to the wholesale murder of thousands, maybe millions of human beings. May God forgive us."

"Father, you must not openly criticize the Fuhrer. If the Gestapo gets wind of it, you and I could be arrested."

"Do you think I am an idiot? I am careful about what I say to people. I say things to Marta to blow off steam, but I know to keep my mouth shut around the servants and people with Nazi sympathies."

"Obviously, I don't agree with you on this subject, but you are my Father. You must be very careful about what you say to everyone.

Kurt nodded. "Shall we have dinner together, father and son?" asked Kurt. His expression revealed that, in spite of their disagreement, he still loved his son.

"Yes father, I would like that."

During dinner, Erich noticed another change in his father. He had always been rude and dismissive to the servants. Now he said bitte and danke and smiled at them pleasantly. When Bettina, the venerable Wolf cook, served the sauerbraten, Kurt asked her about her son serving on the eastern front. She replied that he was well. Erich could tell by the way she looked at his father that Bettina loved the old man.

Then Kurt dropped a bombshell. He said that he had sold all the family's stock in industries contributing to the German war effort. He had bought negotiable securities with the proceeds and had taken a train to Switzerland. Kurt told the inspector at the border that he was going to the Lenkerhof spa in Bern for his health. Instead, he went to the Schroeder & Co. Bank AG in Zurich. He cashed in the securities for American dollars and deposited the money in both their names. Kurt slid a slim folder across the table to Erich.

"Here are the account numbers and passwords. In case something happens to me, commit them to memory and destroy the papers and don't forget the gold hidden in the cellar."

"Father, you act as if you believe Germany will not win the war."

Kurt looked at Erich with a bleak expression.

"Germany will not win the war. God will not permit it."

CHAPTER TWENTY-SIX

SONDERCOMMANDO SOBIBOR
SOBIBOR, POLEN
13 OKTOBER 1943

A drien Weiss, sixteen days shy of his fourteenth birthday, stood in ranks with hundreds of other Jews for afternoon roll call. They were assembled in the large open area in the center of camp two. A kapo from each barracks called names from a list. Each prisoner answered "hier" when his name was called. Some of the prisoners' voices were weak. They were all stark, thin scarecrows. The daily ration was so little that they were all wasting away. They were also incredibly filthy. They were not allowed to wash regularly. Every three months inmates were allowed a brief dip in the drainage ditch behind the men's barracks. At the same time, they were issued new camp uniforms hastily sewn together in the tailor's shop. Very few inmates survived to get a change of uniform, especially the woodcutters. The combination of back-breaking labor and low caloric intake usually killed them off in a couple of months.

In front of the ranks of Jews stood two SS men. Behind them was a crude steel frame. It consisted of two uprights and a crossbar connecting them about three meters above the ground. Three Jewish prisoners were standing on wooden boxes underneath the crossbar with their hands tied behind their backs. Lengths of heavy wire were looped around their necks and connected to the crossbar. They were wearing the camp uniform of vertical striped pajama-like garments with a yellow Star of David sewn to the left breast.

When the roll call was finished, Oberscharfuhrer Karl Frenzel spoke.

"These three have been naughty Jews. Simon Avraham here," he pointed to the first of the Jews, "didn't avert his eyes when he spoke to an SS guard."

Frenzel kicked the box from under Avraham's feet. His body slumped as the wire became taut and cut into the skin on his neck. His face became red and then turned blue. The drop wasn't sufficient to break his neck so he slowly strangled.

"Salomon Zingel" Frenzel pointed to the man standing on the next box, "was caught walking in the compound." He kicked over the second box.

"Max Baum here didn't really do anything. We have just become tired of looking at his hooked nose." Oberscharfuhrer Beckmann, the other SS man, let out a loud guffaw. Frenzel kicked over the third box.

One might imagine that seeing this would cause horror in the heart of a thirteen-year-old boy. It didn't affect Adrien at all. He had been in the camp for six months. In that time, he had seen so many people die that he had become completely inured to death and suffering. Living in fear of a violent death that could come at any time, had worn him down to the point that he no longer feared death. The only things that kept him from completely giving up were the promise he made his grandfather to survive and his anger. He boiled with rage inside but carefully concealed it from the Nazis. When the three Jews stopped jerking and were still, Frenzel told the prisoners to go back to work.

Adrien remembered that his first night in the camp was the worst. He was alone for the first time in his life and he had hours earlier seen his entire family murdered in front of his eyes. The loneliness threatened to crush him. He had lain awake and cried softly most of the night. Prisoners slept in two huge barracks. There were floor to ceiling stacks of shelves like in a warehouse. Each prisoner was allotted a space half a meter wide and three-quarters of a meter tall. There was no bedding and no heat.

The next morning after a meal of watery soup with almost no nutritional value and a quarter slice of hard black bread, the newcomers were jogged to the camp administration building where they were given their work assignments.

Adrien was assigned to work in lager two in the clothing sorting barracks. His job was to gather up the Jews clothing they left in the undressing area before being gassed and carry it to the nearby sorting barracks. He would help sort the clothing according to gender and size and wrap it into bundles.

Adrien's secondary job was to act as interpreter between the SS men and the Jews on the work details. There were only about twenty SS men in the entire camp. Half of them could only speak German. When new workers were selected for the camp, Adrien would accompany them on their work details the first day. He would translate the German commands to them. Adrien made it clear to them that they must learn the commands that day because if they didn't know them the next day, they would probably be shot. This was done totally for the convenience of the SS and not to help the prisoners.

Some of the Jewish prisoners in the camp enjoyed a somewhat protected status. Jewelers, shoemakers and especially tailors were not regularly shot but were kept long term. The reason for this was that these people provided things the Germans wanted. The SS guards at Sobibor demanded new uniforms, boots and jewelry for their wives and girlfriends before going home on leave. The stench of the rotting corpses and the smoke from the burning bodies permeated the uniforms and the leather of the boots of the SS, and they would carry the stench of death with them when they went back to Germany. The captive tailors and boot makers were kept busy fulfilling these orders.

Because of Adrien's language skills, he was on the cusp of this protected group. He made life easier for the SS guards. He learned later that Gustav Wagner had told the other guards not to kill Adrien for fun or a minor offense but "if the little Jew gets uppity, shoot him."

Adrien thanked his lucky stars that he was not assigned to lager three where the gas chambers and crematory areas were. Once a Jew entered lager three, he never came out. The Germans gassed or shot the entire workforce in lager three every month or so and replaced them with fresh Jews from the trains.

It was in the sorting barracks that he met Yossi Hirsch. Yossi was a Polish Jew from Lublin who became his only friend in the camp and probably saved his life. The clothing sorting barracks was overseen by Oberscharfuhrer Rudolf Beckmann. He was lazy and stupid and addicted to nicotine. The Commandant had forbidden smoking in the barracks because of the risk of fire. Beckmann was constantly ducking out to smoke foul Polish cigarettes. This gave the prisoners inside a chance to talk.

On his first day in the barracks, Yossi had approached him while Beckmann was outside. Yossi was of medium height and very thin with prominent Jewish features.

"Hello, I am Yossi Hirsch. Are you new to the camp?"

Adrien had nodded.

"Listen to me and I will tell you what you need to know to stay alive a little bit longer."

Yossi told him how the camp was organized.

The Ukrainian guards were responsible for manning the guard

towers and the gates. They also guarded the newly arrived Jews from the time they got off the train until they were locked in the gas chambers. They usually didn't bother the prisoner workers much. There were about a hundred of them and they were very crude and uncultured.

On occasion, the SS would cull a group of young, pretty Jewish women and girls from the people getting off the trains and give them to the Ukrainians. These poor souls would be gang-raped again and again. When the Ukrainians were through with them, they were shot or strangled.

There were only about twenty uniformed SS guards in the camp and one-fifth of them was away on leave at any given time. They were not front line soldiers. Almost all of them had been working in the German T-4 euthanasia program before coming here. Most of them were stupid and one just had to stay out of their way. A few of them, however, were deadly.

Oberscharfuhrer Gustav Wagner was very dangerous. He was intelligent and very hard to fool. When Yossi described him, Adrien realized he was the same SS man who had spared his life. Yossi said that Wagner actually ran the camp. Reichleitner, the Commandant was a drunk who never left his quarters except when transports arrived.

Another one to give a wide berth to was Unterscharfuhrer Paul Bredow. He commanded the detail that took the invalids and unconscious people from the trains to the "hospital," where they were shot. Bredow boasted to the other guards when he first came to the camp that he would shoot fifty Jews a day with his pistol. If there weren't enough invalids, he would pull some Jews out of the line to the gas chamber, take them to the cremation pits and shoot them there. He particularly liked children's heads as targets.

Oberscharfuhrer Karl Frenzel loved killing. He derived almost sexual pleasure from watching people die. He would often stand at one of the small inspection ports on the gas chamber wall and watch the Jews writhing in agony.

Unterscharfuhrers Anton Novak and Adolf Muller had devised a sadistic little game. They would pick a prisoner at random and order him to kneel in front of them with his mouth open. They would then both piss in his mouth. If the prisoner gagged on the urine or spit it out, they would shoot him.

As if it wasn't enough to worry about the Germans and Ukrainians, some of the Jews were dangerous as well. Some of the kapos, or barracks heads, traded information to the SS in return for remaining alive. One particular collaborating kapo was known as the "Berliner." A lot of Jews had died because of his tip-offs to the SS.

Yossi Hirsch was a gold mine of information. He seemed to know everything that went on in the camp. Adrien told him what had happened to his family. Yossi sadly shook his head.

A few days after Adrien had entered the camp, Oberscharfuhrer Frenzel came into the sorting barracks to talk to Beckmann. They spoke in German, of course, and Adrien who was working nearby heard their conversation.

"Can you believe that prissy officer from Berlin thinking we would be impressed with him for shooting that little girl and beating her parents to death?" asked Frenzel.

Adrien's ears perked up.

"That old Jew scared the shit out of him," replied Beckmann and they both laughed.

"Who was he anyway?"

"He's an accountant type from headquarters in Berlin named Wolf. He's rich and has a big estate in Bayreuth, you know, where they have the music festival."

Adrien burned the information into his brain. I now have the first name, he told himself.

On some days Adrien would be called from the sorting barracks to the camp administration building for translation duties. The SS didn't want to stink up the interior with a Jew so he would be ordered to stand outside the door and wait. His position allowed him to look into the undressing area. He would watch as the Jews from the trains would undress and walk trustingly into the "tube" to the gas chambers. He wanted to shout to them what was going to happen to them. But he didn't. In the end, he chose self-preservation and remained silent.

One morning about three months after he arrived in the camp Adrien was standing by the door of the administration building. He heard the Ukrainian guards going through their roll call around the corner of the building. Taking a chance, he edged to the corner and looked around. A Ukrainian officer was calling out names. Adrien watched. Five minutes later he edged back beside the door. The names of the Ukrainians who beat his parents to death were Yovenko and Kostachuk.

When he went back to the sorting barracks, Adrien asked Yossi if he could find out the two Ukrainians first names. Yossi said he would try. Two days later the Polish Jew told him the names. They were Konstantyn Yovenko and Mykhaylo Kostachuk, both from Kiev. Adrien filed away the information in the back of his mind for future reference, if he had a future.

In September 1943 a train arrived carrying ghetto Jews and a hundred Russian Jewish prisoners of war. The Germans selected eighty of the Russians to work as woodcutters and gassed the rest. Throughout the month of September and into early October, Adrien would see some of these Russians and some of the Poles huddled together talking intently at night. One night he approached the group wanting to know what was going on. He was rebuffed, told to mind his own business and that if he told anyone about them he would get his throat cut.

On 14 October, the day after the three Jews were hung, Adrien arrived at the sorting barracks to find Yossi jittery and almost giddy with suppressed excitement. When Beckmann left the room, it all came tumbling out. Yossi said that the Commandant, Wagner and three other SS men were on leave. The resistance committee was going to stage a revolt and escape at evening roll call. Adrien was incredulous. He hadn't heard there was a resistance committee in the camp.

Yossi assured him that it was true. The SS guards would be lured into the workshops with the promise of new uniforms or boots and would be killed. All the prisoners would break out of the camp and run to the forest.

Could it be true? Adrien was filled with inexpressible joy. We may all be killed he told himself, but we will all die for sure if we stay here.

Beckman came back into the room and the two Jews bustled about doing their work. Beckmann was stupid so he didn't notice that Adrien and Yossi had a strange new spring in their step. Beckmann went out for another smoke about a half hour later. Yossi spoke urgently to Adrien.

"When we get out of the camp we will travel together. We must go northwest about sixty-five kilometers to the Parczew forest. I know the area. I am from Lublin. I heard two of the SS talking about there being Jewish partisans there, if they all haven't all been killed."

Adrien nodded his head. It was as good a plan as any.

At around 5:10 that afternoon the kapos began blowing the whistles for evening roll call. The "Berliner" was strangely absent. Adrien lined up beside Yossi. All seemed normal except there were no SS men in front of the formation. Then Adrien noticed that the Russian prisoners were all in the front rows. They were wearing coats and seemed to have objects concealed under them.

Suddenly shots rang out from the area of the Commandant's house. Oberscharfuhrer Bauer came running into view and was firing his pistol at something in the SS compound.

A tall man, one of the Russian prisoners of war, sprang out from the front row and raised a hand with a pistol in it. He turned toward the prisoners.

The commander of the Ukrainian guard appeared around a blind corner and walked toward the assembled prisoners unaware of his peril. Several men in the front row sprang on him and felled him with blows from axes. The tall Russian then shouted to the prisoners.

"Our day has come. Most of the Germans are dead. Let us die with honor. Remember, if anyone survives he must tell the world what happened here."

A Ukrainian guard in one of the towers figured out what was happening and opened up with a machine pistol on the prisoners. Everyone scattered. Adrien and Yossi ran toward the west fence. They had to leap over several bodies along the way. Adrien's heart was pounding in his chest.

When they got to the fence they discovered that a prisoner with an ax had already cut the barbed wire and people in striped camp garb were pouring through the hole. Adrien and Yossi ran past the fence into the field beyond. A woman running ahead of Adrien stepped on a mine and he saw her legs disintegrate. She collapsed in a heap. Adrien heard other mines explode on either side of him. He fixed his eyes on the woods two hundred meters ahead and ran as he had never run before.

About halfway across the field Adrien knew that he had cleared the minefield. A new hazard presented itself. He heard rifle and machine-gun fire behind him and heard the snap of the bullets going by. People around him were falling.

At last, he and Yossi made it into the shade of the trees. They kept running and stumbled to a stop a hundred meters inside the forest. Both bent over with their hands on their knees gulping air. After a minute or so, Yossi spoke.

"We must keep running. We head west. We must get as far from this place as we can. I don't know how long it will take the Germans to get organized but when they do, we had better be far from here."

Adrien nodded and they resumed running. It was an old growth forest here, so there wasn't much undergrowth. Still, Adrien fell several times as he tripped on roots.

§

It was now three days since their escape from the camp. Yossi reckoned that they had come a little over fifty kilometers. They were resting on a wooded hill. They could see the Parczew Forest from afar. Wooded ridges stretched off into the distance. Between them and the forest, however, was a kilometer wide clearing with a road running through it about fifty meters from where they were hiding.

It was too dangerous to cross in daylight. Since the escape, they had seen German observation planes circling overhead constantly. They decided to rest until nightfall. They had to be very careful.

On the second day after the escape, they had stumbled upon a berry patch and had gorged themselves on the not quite ripe berries. Since then they had eaten nothing. Adrien's stomach growled with hunger.

The terrain they had passed through was mainly dense woods with an occasional meadow or farm clearing. These they skirted. They stopped only when they were too exhausted to go on. Then after two or three hours sleep they were up and moving again.

Adrien was sleeping when Yossi roughly shook him awake and put his finger to his lips.

Adrien looked to his left and saw a German half-track creeping along the road keeping pace with a line of men that extended from the road into the woods on the same side as the two Jews. An SS officer was standing up in the half-track calling instructions to the troops on the ground. A second later, Adrien heard voices and the sound of people moving through the trees.

There was nowhere to run. They decided to hide. Jossi crawled under a bush and Adrien went behind a large tree. He jumped up and grabbed a low limb and levered himself up. He climbed about three meters up and hugged a limb.

Adrien was looking down from his perch and saw a Ukrainian in a black uniform came into view. Adrien realized that his path would take him directly to where Yossi was hiding. He could see the top of Yossi's head and mentally willed him to get further under the bush.

When the soldier was only two meters away, Yossi looked up and made eye contact with Adrien. Weiss realized later that Yossi was saying goodbye with the look. He suddenly sprang up and ran. The Ukrainian yelled and fired his rifle. He apparently missed because he worked the bolt on the rifle and ran after Yossi yelling in Russian.

Adrien clung to the branch as more men in black rushed by. About ten minutes later he heard five shots echo through the woods. Adrien hung his head and cried.

As soon as it was dark Adrien came down from the tree. The vehicle and troops were gone. He quickly crossed the clearing and the road, running low. About a kilometer into the woods he stopped and had four hours of fitful sleep.

Around noon of the next day, Adrien was crossing a stream when two men stepped out from behind trees. They were ragged and unkempt with scraggly beards and long hair. The two appeared very fierce looking and were dressed in filthy, ragged peasant clothes with bandoleers of ammunition strung across their chests. One carried a German rifle and the other a machine pistol. The one with the rifle approached Adrien and gestured with the rifle at the Star of David on his camp uniform.

"Juden?"

Adrien was crushed. To come all this way to be killed by anti-Semitic Poles was more than he could take. But he nodded his head, suddenly not caring anymore.

The man lowered the rifle and a big smile appeared on his face. He tapped his chest with a fist and said "Juden."

CHAPTER TWENTY-SEVEN

PARCZEW LAS
POLSKA
17 PAZDIERNIK 1943

A drien Weiss almost fainted with relief and joy. The partisan with the machine pistol asked, "Are you from Sobibor?"

Adrien nodded his head. He didn't trust himself to speak, he was so relieved.

"You are the third one from the camp that had made it here. Welcome to the Parczew forest and the Yehiel Grynzpan Jewish partisan unit. Did you kill any of those SS bastards?"

"No, sir," Adrien replied, his eyes on the ground.

"You don't have to say "sir" to me boy. Hold your head high. We aren't ghetto Jews cowering in fear. We are a new type of Jews with guns in our hands."

The other partisan interrupted his companion, "Oh, shut up, Benni. You stand here making speeches like some commissar. Can't you see the boy is starving? Send him on so he can eat and rest." It was said with a smile.

The one with the rifle told Adrien to continue north. He followed a barely discernable path through the woods for about a thousand steps. Two more partisans stepped out and directed him west.

The trail was more distinct here and Adrien had no trouble following it. He had walked perhaps another five hundred meters when a fourth partisan stepped out from behind a tree and held up his hand for Adrien to stop.

The man looked to be in his mid-twenties. He was cleanly shaven. He wore a brown tunic crisscrossed with bandoliers of rifle bullets over baggy brown trousers tucked into mid-calf length boots. He had on a brown visored cap with a red star on the front and red tabs on the collar points of his tunic. He was holding a pistol in his hand.

Behind him stood a woman with a rifle. She was wearing men's clothes and had her hair tucked under a cloth cap. Adrien stumbled to a stop and the male partisan spoke.

"Pull down your trousers and let me see your penis," he said in Polish.

A year ago if Adrien had been told to show his privates in the presence of a woman, he would have refused. After Sobibor, it didn't seem to matter. He pulled up his shirt and jerked down his prisoner pants.

"Alright, I guess you are a Jew then."

The woman was staring with a look of shock at Adrien. He could see tears in the corners of her eyes.

Adrien pulled up his trousers. He asked the partisan if any of the other Jews who had arrived from Sobibor was named Yossi Hirsch. The officer thought a moment, then shook his head. Adrien felt a stab of grief at the loss of his friend. And then something snapped in Adrien. Everyone he cared about ended up dying. He decided he wouldn't make any more friends. It hurt too bad when they died.

The man and woman led him into the partisan camp. It consisted of about fifty or so dugouts with log roofs spread over about a seventy-meter circle under the concealment of the trees. In the center of the huts was a crude kitchen with a woman tending a large kettle over a fire giving off very little smoke. The smell of the food almost drove Adrien wild. He began to salivate and some of it dribbled from the corners of his mouth.

Adrien sat beside a fire and the woman brought him a heaping wooden bowl of venison stew and a crude wooden spoon. Adrien ate ravenously. He had never tasted anything so good in his life.

The woman who had led him into the camp sat beside him. She had slung her rifle over her back and taken off her cap. Her long hair spread down her back. She cautioned Adrien, "Don't eat so fast, you will be sick."

Adrien saw that she was about twenty-five years old with dark eyes. Her other features were delicate but also dark. He thought she had a pretty face.

"I am Rivka Feldman," she told him.

Adrien had trouble finishing the bowl of food. His stomach had shrunk from not eating in so long. When he had eaten all he could, Rivka led him to one of the dugouts. She entered and emerged a minute later with an armload of clothing. She led Adrien back to the fire.

"Strip," she ordered. "Get rid of those Nazi clothes." Adrien pulled off his cap and shirt and pushed down his trousers.

"Burn them," she ordered.

Adrien tossed the Sobibor uniform onto the fire. He watched as the yellow Star of David curled and blackened in the flames. He looked up to see Rivka looking at him and smiling. She seemed fascinated by his blonde hair. Reaching up a hand, she ran her fingers through it.

Adrien pulled on the rough peasant clothing. There were a grey tunic, dark baggy trousers and black leather boots which were a little loose. He tied a length of rope around his waist to hold up the trousers. Last, Rivka handed him a brown cloth cap.

The partisan in the brown uniform returned. He faced Adrien and spoke, "You can sleep in Rivka's hut tonight. In the morning we will assign you a job."

Rivka led Adrien to her "hut." It was only a hole dug into the side of a hill that had been roofed over with logs. A blanket hung over the front for privacy. Inside there was room for two people to lie down. On the right side, a blanket had been spread over pine needles with another blanket to cover up with. Adrien lay down on the blanket. It felt better than any feather bed. He was almost instantly asleep. He dreamed about Sobibor.

Gustav Wagner was pointing his finger at him at evening roll call. "Weiss, you didn't look down at the ground quick enough. Come here." Adrien walked forward and Wagner put a wire noose around his head. "You didn't think you would live through this, did you?" asked Wagner, whispering in his ear.

Adrien shot up on the blanket. Sweat was pouring off him, and he was gripped by terror. When he realized it was just a dream, he lay back down.

He heard a noise outside, the blanket on the door parted and Rivka entered. She struck a match and lit a wick floating in a little bowl of oil. Ignoring Adrien, she moved to her side of the hut, unslung her rifle and leaned it against the wall. She pulled her tunic over her head and Adrien could see that she had nothing on underneath. Her breasts were full with dark nipples. Sitting down on her blanket, she removed her boots and struggled out of her trousers. She folded them and put them aside. Standing up, she turned to face Adrien naked. Adrien was no stranger to naked bodies. Day after day at Sobibor, he had watched naked Jewish women walk to their deaths in lager three. Rivka's body didn't arouse him.

"You look like my husband. His hair was dark, yours is blonde, but your faces are the same. He was killed by the Germans in 1939. I miss him so."

Adrien just stared at her.

Rivka lay down beside him and pulled the blanket over them both. She put her arms around Adien and began to cry.

"I miss my Reuben so much," she whispered between sobs.

After a while, she quieted down and told him her story. Adrien learned that she was the second daughter of a chemist in Lublin. When the Germans came and ordered all the Jews into a ghetto, her husband objected to a German officer and was shot. She ran away into the forest. Rivka learned later that her parents and all her brothers and sisters had perished in Auschwitz.

"I want to kill every German bastard on earth," she said.

They spent the night holding each other under the blankets, but there was no sex.

The next morning the officer in the brown uniform came to the dugout and told Adrien to follow him. He spoke as they walked.

"I am Jacob Ditkowicz. As you can see, I am a senior lieutenant in the Red Army. I command about one hundred Jewish fighters. My superior is Yehiel Grynzpan. He commands all Jewish fighters in the Lublin area."

"You are too young and scrawny yet for fighting. I am going to make you a forager." Adrien wondered what that meant but kept silent. They walked through the camp to the north edge and followed a path through the trees. About twenty meters in on the side of a hill were two more dugouts.

Sitting on a log nearby were two partisan fighters. Both were about forty, one short and stout, the other tall and powerful. They both stood as Ditkowicz and Adrien approached.

"Yakob, I have a new forager for you. Yakob Shapiro, Tovia Stein, this is Adrien Weiss." The short one was Yakob and the taller Tovia.

"You call it foraging. I call it stealing. Twenty years in prison I could get for what I do." said Yakob with a smile.

The officer left and the two men sat back down on the log. They invited Adrien to sit beside them. Yakob spoke.

"Our job is mostly to steal grain to make bread for the fighters in the camp. We also stalk and kill game for the pot. We prefer to do it stealthily but we kill for it if we have to. The first thing we must find out is how quietly you move through the woods. Follow me."

The short man led Adrien into the woods about fifty meters. He then walked back to the dugout and sat down on the ground with his back to Adrien. He called, "come to me as quietly as you can."

Adrien carefully made his way back being as quiet as he could. Yakob stood and shook his head.

"Could walk through these woods an elephant and be quieter than you. We have much work to do to teach you." It was not said unkindly and Yakob clapped Adrien on the back.

Around the fire that evening, Adrien learned that Yakob had been a gamekeeper on the estate of a Polish count. He knew everything there was to know about the woods. He was missing a front tooth. That and his shaggy appearance made him look like a pirate out of a children's book.

Tovia had been a Polish Army Sergeant and fled to the woods after the Germans defeated the Polish Army. Yakob told Adrien that he was one of the fiercest fighters in the camp. He was an expert with guns but preferred the knife. He had gotten tired of killing a few months ago and asked to be assigned to the foragers with his good friend Yakob. He was tall and muscular with enormous hands.

The two men were very good friends, almost as close as brothers and, like brothers, they bickered all the time. Tovia explained to Adrien the partisan's situation. Although he appeared to be a rough peasant, he was very articulate in his speech.

"Jews in this forest have three main enemies. The Ordungspolizei are German civilian policemen organized into military units and sent to fight partisans in Poland and Russia. They are not front line soldiers. They are mostly middle-aged men in bad physical condition. The Schutzmannschart are locally recruited collaborators. They have had very little military training. Both of these groups have little stomach for combat. They are deathly afraid of being surrounded in the forest and massacred. As a consequence, when you are in a fight with them if you send men around their flank, they will retreat."

"The third enemy is the Gentile partisans. We share the forests around Lublin with the Polish Peoples Guard. They are more numerous than us. We cooperate with them in fighting the Germans but most of them hate Jews. As a rule, if you encounter armed men in the forest, give them a wide berth. Every once in a while we do encounter small units of the SS. They can be very dangerous. Stay away from those bastards. Basically, the situation is this. If the Nazis ever get around to sending front line combat troops against us, we are dead."

Tovia got up from the log and entered his dugout. He emerged a few seconds later carrying a holstered pistol. He threw it to Adrien, who withdrew it from the holster. It was black and lethal looking.

"It is a P-38, nine millimeter. There are two extra magazines in a pouch on the belt. Now you are that most rare of things, an armed Jew."

CHAPTER
TWENTY-EIGHT

I n February of 1942, Arthur Harris was appointed as Chief of Bomber Command, of the British Royal Air Force. He was henceforth known to his peers as "Bomber" Harris. He addressed his new staff.

"The Germans entered this war under the rather childish delusion that they were going to bomb everyone else and nobody was going to bomb them. At Rotterdam, London, Warsaw and half a hundred other places, they put their rather naïve theory into operation. They sowed the wind and now they are going to reap the whirlwind."

First, Harris had to build up his bomber forces. By November 1943 he was ready.

§

UNTER DEN LINDEN 77
BERLIN, DEUTSCHLAND
22 NOVEMBER 1943

At 11:30 p.m., the quiet of the Berlin night was broken by the wail of air raid sirens. One by one, searchlights blinked on and stabbed the sky. SS-Hauptdturmfuhrer Erich Wolf's eyes snapped open in the bedroom of his suite at the Adlon and he felt terror grip him.

He jumped up out of bed, donned robe and slippers and bolted out his door. On his way down the stairwell, he was caught in the rush of other guests similarly attired in their bedclothes.

Only when he reached the shelter and the big steel door was shut did he begin to calm down. Erich found a seat on a sofa near the back of the shelter and ordered a double brandy from the waiter.

As he gulped the fiery liquid, he felt the first concussions of the bombs exploding. For the next hour, he would wince at every detonation. The people around him settled down and some went to sleep. A fat man with a Kaiser mustache began to snore loudly. Wolf was rigidly awake, fighting a growing panic. He tried thinking about other things.

A week ago the German government finally told the German people about the debacle at Stalingrad. Since then the Russians had pushed back Wehrmacht forces in Russia and into Poland at an alarming rate. When the announcement was made about Stalingrad, Erich wasn't shocked. Hauptmann Miller had told him about the defeat on the train in Prussia. Wolf began to worry though. He knew that the Americans and British were building up their forces in England for an invasion of France. If that happened, Germany would be squeezed from two sides.

Up to this time Erich had believed in an inevitable German victory in the war. Now, sitting in the bomb shelter listening to the crash of bombs, he began to have doubts.

What if Germany loses the war? What would the victorious allies think about what the SS had done in the places Germany had occupied? Would everyone in the SS be held responsible for the extermination campaign against the Jews?

Erich began to examine his own culpability. He had personally killed five people since joining the SS. The first two, the Brown Shirt and his wife, he was sure the Allies wouldn't care about. The killing of the Jew in the shop on Kristallnacht in Munich was unseen by anyone else. That only left the little girl and the old Jew at Sobibor. Erich was sure that most of the SS guards would not remember him. If they did, they wouldn't know who he was. Still, it was his one vulnerability. He resolved to have the record of his trip to Sobibor purged from the SS files. Perhaps he could sweet talk Prich's secretary to do it for him.

Erich remained in the shelter all night. When the all clear sounded, the other guests went back to their rooms. The next morning, he returned to his desk. The bombers had done extensive damage to the residential areas west of the center of the city. Two thousand people were dead and 175,000 left homeless. There was catastrophic damage to the Tiergarten, Charlotsburg Palace and the Berlin Zoo.

During the next week at his desk in SS-WVHA, Wolf discovered that shipments of commodities from Treblinka, Belzec and Sobibor had trickled off to nothing. He surmised that the SS had closed the camps. Erich asked Sturmbannfuhrer Prich about this. The two of them had been getting along better recently.

It was then that Prich swore him to secrecy and told him about Sobibor. The Jewish camp workers had revolted on 13 October 1943. They had killed most of the SS guards and three hundred prisoners had escaped into the forest.

Back at his desk, Wolf began to worry. He had assumed that all the Jews who had witnessed his killing the little girl and the old Jew would end up dead. Now there were potential witnesses roaming the Polish forests who could tie him to the killings if they survived. He decided to move forward on his plan to erase from SS records his trip to Sobibor.

He went back to Sturmbannfuhrer Prich's office carrying a sheaf of papers in his hand. No one would ever question one's intentions around headquarters provided one carried papers and looked determined. Erich made a date for the next Saturday night with Frau Glick.

Erich took her to the famous Nollendorfplatz nightclub. They had an expensive though, by prewar standards, unappetizing dinner and danced afterward. Later, he took her to his suite at the Adlon and used all his sexual skills to please her in the bedroom. She had multiple orgasms which left her in a particularly compliant state.

It was then that he whispered his request in her ear. Implicit in his request was a promise of more nights of fine dining and lovemaking. Frau Glick said she would try.

A week later Erich was walking by Prich's office when Frau Glick motioned to him to come in. She smiled and said, "That problem you had with the Sobibor reports has been corrected. You should have no more trouble." Wolf thanked her and went back to his desk smiling.

On the night of 17 December 1943, the British bombers returned to Berlin causing extensive damage to the railway system. Erich spent another night in the bomb shelter at the Adlon. In the morning he made a request to the hotel manager to move a bed into the shelter for his use on the next air raid. The manager refused. Wolf railed at the man, creating a scene in the lobby. He threatened to move to another hotel. The manager smiled and told him that was his choice.

By March 1944 the British had made eleven raids on the Berlin area. During this time Erich Wolf became more and more jumpy and irritated. To make matters worse, the Americans had begun to bomb German cities in daylight. It was only a question of time before they came to Berlin and the building where he worked had no bomb shelter.

Erich began to scheme to get himself transferred out of Berlin.

CHAPTER TWENTY-NINE

DWADZIESCIA PIEC KILOMETRY
N/E LUBLIN, POLSKA
12 CZERWCA 1944

There was no sign of movement around the farmhouse. It was a rude affair made out of mud brick with a thatched roof. A ramshackle barn was behind the house. There were no farm animals visible, but then he didn't expect there to be. Adrien Weiss lay in the cover of brush at the edge of the tree line. The house was seventy-five meters away. Adrien had been watching it for quite some time. It was one of Yakob's first lessons to Adrien. Don't rush into things. Study the surroundings. If anything looks out of place, pull out and look somewhere else.

Adrien had been a partisan for almost seven months. He lived a rough existence, going without food for days at a time and in a filthy state. The living conditions were almost as bad as Sobibor with one important difference. Adrien was free and he had a pistol in his belt. The band of partisans was constantly on the move. Sometimes they stayed in one location for a week; sometimes just overnight. It depended on the aggressiveness of the German patrols. Weiss had been going alone on food raids for the past three months. He thought back to how noisy he was in the woods when Yakob first started teaching him.

§

Yakob had started by showing him how to walk in the forest without rustling leaves or snapping twigs, which was what city people did. Adrien learned to move slowly and bury the toe of his shoe under the leaves and debris on the forest floor before putting his weight on it.

Yakob lectured him about movement. The surest way to be caught by the Germans was to move at an inappropriate time. The human eye is very good at detecting movement. By using the right camouflage techniques and being still you could have the Germans walk right by you and never see you. "But," Yakob had stressed, "if the German has a dog, run like hell."

Adrien learned to use the natural folds of the earth for cover and the foliage for concealment. Never expose yourself on a ridgeline. Be attentive to smells as the Germans were fond of garlic laced sausages. You could sometimes smell them meters away.

Adrien learned these lessons and a hundred more. Yakob was a good teacher and Weiss was an apt pupil. Whenever Yakob wasn't on food raids, he spent a lot of time in the deep forest with Adrien teaching him the way of the woods. Adrien became comfortable in the forest and learned to become a part of its cycle instead of an alien presence. He learned that subtle changes in the behavior of the forest animals could alert him to the presence of a German patrol long before he actually heard them. Weiss took in all that Yakob taught him and added his own twist. He found that if he willed it, he could become a part of his surroundings. His heart rate and respiration slowed and he became still as death.

Then a surprising thing happened. After about three and a half months, the pupil started to eclipse the teacher. Adrien could move so silently that even Yakob, who had been a forester his whole life and thought he was the best there was in the woods, couldn't hear him.

One night Adrien had been on his pallet dropping off to sleep when he heard Yakob talking to Tovia outside the dugout.

"I swear to you Tovia, there is something supernatural about that boy. He can make himself disappear. One minute he is there and the next he is gone. A ghost maybe we are dealing with."

Tovia had laughed. "Just listen to yourself you fool. That boy is just smart and you are a good teacher. I'll admit that he seems to have a gift for being silent in the forest, but there is nothing supernatural about it." In the dugout, Adrien had smiled.

The day after this conversation Adrien left on his first foraging mission alone. He stole a large sack of wheat and was returning to the camp. He easily penetrated the camp perimeter security and approached his dugout as silently as a cat.

Yakob and Tovia were sitting near a fire and talking. Tovia was smoking his pipe. Weiss approached silently and waited for a moment when both were looking away. When the moment came he sat down on the log between them. Both turned to look at Adrien at the same time and jumped up in surprise.

"What did I tell you, Tovia, a ghost the boy is," said Yakob in surprise. Then all three began to laugh as Yakob patted him on the back.

At the same time that Yakob was teaching Adrien stealth, Tovia was teaching him how to kill, a useful skill if you are a Jew surrounded by enemies in a forest in Poland.

One day about a month after Adrien joined the partisans, Tovia went somewhere in the camp and came back with a German army bayonet, the blade honed to razor sharp. He handed it to Adrien. "Now, balance the bayonet on the side of your finger." Adrien complied. The center of balance on the blade was a few centimeters along the blade from the handle. "Now, put your thumb on the blade where your finger was and wrap your fingers around the handle. Now the blade is balanced in your hand. Hold it flat so the cutting edges are to the side. This is the correct way to hold a knife. Never hold the knife with the blade protruding from the back of your fist and do an overhand stab. If you do that in a knife fight, you will die."

"There are two basic movements in knife fighting, the slash and the stab. Many fighters slash with the knife back and forth. In my experience this is wrong. Slashing attacks produce mostly shallow cuts on your opponent. The best move is to get inside your enemy's guard and stab. Aim for the vital organs in the torso, just below the ribcage."

"To protect yourself, wrap a coat or sweater around the hand and arm not holding the knife. Use it as a shield to protect yourself from your opponent.

"If your intent is to cut someone's throat from behind, don't reach around and try to cut the front of the throat. If the person has fast reflexes, he can grab your hand and throw you over his shoulder. Approach from behind and plunge the blade, cutting edge out, into the side of the neck. Then slice forward. This will cut his arteries and windpipe at the same time and is done in one motion."

On and on it went. Every minute Adrien had that was not spent with Yakob was with Tovia practicing. Throughout the cold, snowy months, many of the other partisans would come and watch the skinny teen aged boy and the tall fierce soldier circle each other looking for an opening.

They would practice using sheathed blades to protect against an accidental cutting. Early on in his training, Adrien would leave each session with his chest covered by bruises where Tovia had penetrated his guard and struck him with the tip of his scabbard. As he progressed and his skill level improved, he got fewer and fewer bruises. Then one special day, Tovia walked away with a spreading bruise under his sternum.

In February Tovia, after one of their practice sessions, lowered his sheathed knife.

"I have taught you all I know. Now it is time to try it out on the Germans. On one of your missions if the offer presents itself, slit one of the bastard's throats." The big partisan stopped and thought for a moment. "Just a moment," he said and ducked into his dugout. He emerged after a few moments carrying what looked like a fat needle. He showed it to Adrien and placed it in his hands. It was an icepick. It had a thirty centimeter long, thin shaft of blued steel attached to a wooden handle which had the name of a Warsaw hotel stenciled on it.

"My present to you. This is one of the most effective killing weapons I know of. You sneak up on a German and ram this in his ear to the hilt, then jiggle it back and forth. He will drop like a stone."

Tovia then patted him on the back, sat down on the log and lit his pipe.

It was around this time that Adrien Weiss killed his first man. Ironically, it wasn't a German or even a Pole that he killed. It was a fellow Jew.

There was a group of young Jews in the camp that had banded together and given themselves the nickname of "The Meyer Otriad" after their leader, Moshe Meyer. Styling themselves as an elite group of fighters within the partisan band, they went around with red scarves tied around their necks. One of their number, a nineteen-year-old named Benny Friedman, took a dislike to Adrien. Benny was tall and muscular with long arms.

Maybe it was Adrien's blue eyes and blonde hair that made Benny so hostile to him, Weiss would never know. Friedman would push Adrien out of the food line and tell him to "go eat with the women." Friedman's companions would laugh. Another time Benny stuck out his leg and tripped Weiss as he was walking by carrying a big bundle of firewood. He made disparaging comments about Adrien at the cook tent in front of groups of the other partisans. "Hey little blond sissy boy, want us to find you an old woman's tit to suck on?"

It was a blustery, cold day in the camp. Adrien was carrying a bowl of stew across the camp toward his dugout. Friedman came up behind him and knocked the bowl of food out of Adrien's hand.

Adrien Weiss had reached the breaking point. First, his family was murdered by the Germans. Then he had been a slave in Sobibor. Next, he had to live like a hunted animal in the forest. Then to have a fellow Jew, a person supposed to be his ally, harass him like this was all too much for Weiss. He cocked back his arm and planted a punch on Friedman's nose.

Benny stepped back as a trickle of blood flowed from one of his nostrils. He looked behind him and saw his friends watching. He turned back to Weiss, his face a mask of malevolence.

"You will be sorry you did that, you little rat. I am going to cut off your little goy dick and stuff it in your mouth," said Friedman, as he pulled out a long knife and waved it at Adrien.

Adrien pulled his sharpened bayonet, shucked off his coat, and wound it around his left arm just as Tovia had taught him to do. He went in a crouch and balanced on the balls of his feet. He was ready when Benny rushed at him.

The fight lasted probably no more than a minute. It seemed like forever to Adrien. He dodged Friedman's initial slash by ducking his head and stepping to the side. The knife whistled by his head with a few centimeters to spare. Benny came at him again with wide slashes. He swung with such force that he was off balance for a split second after each slash. Adrien noticed this and danced away from Friedman's attacks.

The two circled each other. Friedman was getting frustrated that Weiss wouldn't stand still. He glanced behind him at his friends and Adrien took this opportunity to dart in close and jab at Friedman's midsection. The knife struck Benny's stomach, but only penetrated a millimeter or so, just enough to draw blood. Adrien danced back out of the reach of the bigger man.

Friedman put his hand to his stomach and it came away red with blood. His face showed a mixture of fear and confusion for a moment. Then rage took over and Benny yelled and charged with his knife reversed in his hand and held over his head. Weiss waited until his opponent was almost upon him and Benny's knife was slashing downward. Abruptly he sidestepped and as Friedman went by, Adrien's arm drove forward and buried the bayonet in Benny's gut up to the hilt. The big man staggered a few paces but was still on his feet.

Adrien retreated a couple of meters or so. He knew Benny was still dangerous. Tovia had taught him to remain wary until his opponent was on the ground and still. Suddenly, Friedman charged at him bellowing like an angry bull, but only managed a few steps before crashing to the ground. Benny looked up at Adrien one last time, trying to focus, then his head crashed into the dirt and he was still.

The crowd of partisans who had been watching the fight and shouting suddenly got very quiet. Adrien stood over the prostrate Friedman and gulped air, the bloody bayonet still in his hand. Friedman's friends wearing the red scarves began to grumble. Several pulled knives. A few drew their pistols. Almost as one, they began to advance on Adrien.

"EVERYONE STOP AND DO NOT MOVE." The shout came from behind Adrien. He turned to look and saw Yakob with a double-barreled shotgun and Tovia with a machine pistol standing side by side. The muzzles of their weapons were pointed at the partisans with the red bandannas.

"The boy only defended himself. He was attacked with a knife. Adrien, come and get behind us," said Tovia.

The three then backed out of the area and returned to their huts. Tovia told Adrien that he had made enemies that day and to be very careful when alone. Adrien now had to contend with the fact that not only did the Germans want to kill him but some of the Jews as well.

§

Adrien had still detected no movement around the farmhouse. He steeled himself to break from cover. This was the most critical time. If he was walking into a trap he would know it soon. He planned to skirt the house and go directly to the barn. Any grain would probably be hidden there. He was tensing his muscles to move when he detected a faint engine sound. He hunkered back down and waited as the sound grew louder.

A motorcycle with a sidecar driven by a German in uniform came into view. It was coming up the track to the farmhouse. In the sidecar there appeared to be a child. The motorcycle stopped in the farmyard and the German got off. Adrien recognized the feldgrau uniform as that of a German Army enlisted man. He had seen many of them in Paris. The soldier wore a silver plate around his neck signifying that he belonged to a police battalion. He had an MP38 machine pistol slung across his back. The German walked around the motorcycle and retrieved a bottle from the sidecar. Then the child seemed to fly out of the same sidecar. Adrien could see that it was a young girl about ten or eleven and she had a rope around her neck that the German was pulling. The soldier, with the girl in tow, kicked in the door to the farmhouse and pulled her in after him.

Adrien debated what to do. He should leave. The girl was not his responsibility. But some indescribable feeling kept him from stealing into the woods. He finally decided to have a look just to see what was going on. Breaking cover, he walked lightly to the corner of the house. He edged along the front of the building being as quiet as possible and peered in a dirty, fly-specked window. The girl was on her back on top of a table. The German was standing over her taking a long drink from the bottle. As Adrien watched, the soldier put the bottle down and unfastened the belt on his trousers. They fell to his knees. He leaned forward and began forcing the girl's legs apart.

Without consciously willing it, Adrien found himself moving silently through the door. Step by quiet step he drew closer to the German. Finally, he was directly behind the Nazi and he leaned over the soldier's shoulder and swiftly rammed the ice pick into his right ear. Adrien was surprised at what little resistance he encountered. When it was all the way in, he jiggled the handle back and forth, up and down. The German went rigid, arched his back, his eyes bugged out, and he collapsed in a heap, his trousers still around his ankles. Adrien removed the ice pick and wiped it on the dead man's uniform.

Adrien looked at the girl. She was staring at him with huge brown, frightened eyes. Her short blonde hair was dirty and disheveled. Painfully thin, almost emaciated, she was wearing a thin, ragged shift that was as filthy as her hair.

"Juden?" he asked her. She shook her head.

He turned away from her and bent down beside the German. He found the man's pay book and wallet and took the few marks of General Government currency he found inside. He slipped the sling of the machine pistol from the German's shoulder and put it over his own. The soldier also had a pistol and magazines that Adrien took.

Outside in the sidecar, Adrien found some boxes of nine-millimeter bullets, a pouch containing extra magazines for the machine pistol, and a sack of canned food. Heavily laden, he walked across the farmyard toward the forest without looking back. He entered the trees and walked another fifty meters. He could hear the girl noisily following him through the woods. Adrien walked back to her.

"Do you have parents to go home to?"

The girl shook her head, silently staring at his face with her huge, pleading eyes.

"Do you have any relatives that are alive?"

She shook her head again.

Adrien Weiss wasn't a normal human being. What he had been through had changed him. He was hardened to the sight of death and suffering in all its forms. He had promised himself he would form no new attachments. But when he looked into the young girl's eyes, he felt a little flame of compassion stirring. It wasn't much but was proof that the Nazis hadn't totally stripped him of his humanity. She is like me, he thought, with no one living that she calls family. An orphan that nobody wants. He reluctantly decided to help her. Maybe, later on, he could find a safe place to drop her off.

"Would you like to come with me?"

She nodded her head but still refused to speak.

"Well, come on then. We have to get away from here."

Back at the partisan camp, Adrien told Yakob what had happened and the partisan busied himself finding a bowl of food for the girl. She was starving and attacked the food like a hungry puppy. After hearing the story, Yakob advised Adrien not to tell others in the camp that she wasn't Jewish. They might not let her stay.

Word went around the camp about the new arrival. Some of the partisan women came to take the girl to stay with them. She would have none of it. She clung to Adrien and shook her head vehemently when the women asked her to accompany them. That night sitting next to the fire, after another meal and kind word and actions by Yakob and Tovia, the girl finally told them her name. In a small voice, almost a whisper, she said her name was Aleska.

CHAPTER THIRTY

FRIEDRICHSTRASSE 56
BERLIN, DEUTSCHLAND
22 JULI 1944

E rich Wolf and the three SS enlisted men approached the house on Friedrichstrasse cautiously. They didn't want to be overly anxious and warn their target of their approach. Their mission was to arrest Oberst Karl Gutmann for treason against the German Reich.

Erich foreswore the bell and knocked politely on the front door. A few moments later the door swung open to reveal a grey-haired dignified lady in her fifties. Wolf strode boldly into the room, brushing her aside.

"I have a warrant for the arrest of Oberst Karl Gutmann. Where is he?"

"He is not here," said the woman. Her face showed that she was in the grip of mounting terror. Erich looked beyond her at a doorway with a set of closed sliding doors off the entryway. He started toward the doors. The woman rushed to block his way.

"Please, I told you he was not here."

From behind the doors, Erich heard a gunshot and the woman collapsed to the floor sobbing. Erich slid open the doors and saw Oberst Gutmann in full Wehrmacht uniform slumped in a chair. There was a smoking hole in the side of his head and a Mauser pistol was still grasped in his right hand. Erich went back to the woman and helped her to her feet.

"My apologies, Madame, for this unpleasantness."

Hauptsturmfuhrer Erich Wolf had been at his desk on 20 July when all hell broke loose. Word traveled through the government offices like wildfire. Elements within the military had tried to assassinate the Fuhrer at his command post in Rastenburg in Prussia. The traitors had also staged a coup and tried to take over the German government. The whole thing fell apart when the word was flashed to Berlin that Hitler had survived.

Heinrich Himmler's Gestapo and security services swung immediately into action. Almost immediately it became apparent that the leader of the plot was Oberst Count Claus Von Stauffenberg, an aristocratic officer attached to the general staff. Many other high ranking German officers were implicated in the plot.

Every available SS officer, including Erich, was pressed into service to round up the plotters. Wolf had been assigned four people to arrest today. One had been taken without incident; the other three had been suicides.

During the next few weeks, Wolf arrested or verified the suicide of nineteen German officers. He tried to appear zealous when making these arrests. A witch hunt mentality had set in within the Gestapo and the Nazi leadership. No longer would one have to be guilty of a crime. Just the suspicion that one might harbor disloyal thoughts was enough for an arrest and an interrogation.

Erich worried constantly about his father. If the old man slipped and made a comment about Hitler to the wrong person, there would be hell to pay. He desperately sought a way to contact Kurt and tell him to be extra careful. He couldn't use the telephone Since the attempted coup the operators had been instructed to listen in on calls and report any disloyalty. It was the same with the mail. There was no way to guarantee that a letter would not be read by the censors. He decided to try to wrangle some leave time to go home and warn his father.

Erich was now convinced that Germany was losing the war. Hitler had taken on too many enemies at once. Erich's father had been right. They should have conquered England first before attacking the Russians. The Third Reich was starting to crumble. The Allies had landed in France in early June. After a dogged struggle, German forces tried to organize an orderly retreat but were encircled and slaughtered in the Falaise pocket. The Russians had not only taken back all their own territory originally conquered by the Germans but were now smashing through Poland. Air attacks on German cities were intensifying. Wolf knew in his gut that it was just a matter of time before the Thousand Year Reich would come crashing down.

He had been desperately trying to get transferred out of Berlin. Stories had been circulating that the Russians were summarily shooting all the SS men they captured. Erich didn't want to be around when they conquered Berlin, but every trick he had tried had failed. Prich had denied his going anywhere. The fat little toad just smiled as he tore up the requests in front of Erich's eyes.

Erich's only option was to flee, to desert his post. But that was very dangerous also. If the SS caught him he would be immediately shot. So it was a choice, either be shot by the Russians or the SS. He decided to hang on a little while longer and hope he wasn't killed by a British bomb. Maybe a solution would present itself.

CHAPTER THIRTY-ONE

PARCZEW LAS
POLSKA
1 KWIECIEN, 1945

The young doe was peacefully feeding on the grass poking up out of the snow. She was grazing in a small clearing amid tall pine trees. Her head suddenly snapped up. Sensing danger, she sniffed the air. The animal remained absolutely still. At any sign of a predator, she would bound into the tall trees in an instant. After a while, apparently mollified, she resumed feeding.

Adrien Weiss, twenty meters away, aimed the Mauser rifle at the deer. He had used all his skill to get this near without alerting the animal, approaching her from downwind and inching forward using only his elbows and toes. The stealthy approach was necessary because Adrien was a poor shot with the rifle. Also, he was running low on ammunition and had to make every shot count. He eased back the trigger and the rifle recoiled against his shoulder. The doe, hit where her neck met her shoulder by the high-velocity bullet, collapsed, rolled over on her side and was still. Adrien walked to where beautiful, graceful animal lay. He picked up the carcass, hoisted it on top of his shoulders, and ducked into the cover of the trees. Even though there were no Germans hunting him, old habits die hard. The shot might attract attention and notice by anyone was the last thing Adrien wanted. Once out of the immediate area of the kill, he began the long walk back to the cave.

§

In late June 1944, masses of German soldiers had appeared in the Lublin area. They were retreating before the Red Army advance. Long lines of tanks, trucks, and marching men entered the area from the east. Tovia's nightmare came true. The Germans began to aggressively patrol the Parczew forest with combat troops.

The partisan bands had to abandon their camps and flee for their lives. Adrien's group decided to split up into small units of two to five people, to better evade the soldiers. Adrien found himself with Tovia, Yakob, and Aleska, trying to stay alive.

Adrien recalled a particularly narrow escape from this time. Every time he remembered the incident, his palms would sweat and he would involuntarily shiver with fear. The four partisans had fled to a remote, rugged part of the forest to avoid detection. Ancient seismic activity had formed the area's terrain into a jumble of ridges, ravines and huge rocks. It was hard going for the partisans.

On that day, they had climbed down a steep ridge toward an overhanging boulder, intending to shelter under its overhang during the night. On the way down the slope Tovia slipped and sprained his ankle badly. The rest helped him to the shelter of the boulder and Adrien went a little way back the way they had come to stand guard. He picked a good position in a clump of brush between two trees that overlooked the track and had a good view across an open area they had recently traversed. He checked that he had a full magazine in his MP-38 machine pistol and settled down to watch.

He hadn't been there long when he saw a German patrol emerge into view about eighty meters away on the track he and his friends had traversed. Adrien recognized the uniforms. They were SS paratroopers! And there were five of them. Each trooper wore a camouflaged smock over his feldgrau uniform and wore a diminutive paratroop helmet. But what caused Adrien's pulse to race was the presence of a large leashed dog and dog handler with the German patrol. The dog was sniffing the ground and straining at his leash following the partisan's scent. The dog handler wore a regular Wehrmacht uniform, not SS. Two of the SS carried machine pistols and the others had rifles.

Adrien had a decision to make. If he did nothing, the patrol would be upon him in no time. Aleska and the rest would be caught. The patrol was too spread out to be effectively ambushed. Adrien had few options. He broke cover and showed himself, then raced into the open area. There was a shout from the Germans and one fired a burst from his machine pistol. But, by the time the German fired, Adrien had darted into the trees at the edge of the clearing, running perpendicular to the German's advance. He ran for all he was worth fifty meters into the forest, then veered to his right. Up and down rises in the ground, Adrien ran, knowing the Germans would have to follow him much more cautiously, fearing an ambush.

Adrien's only hope was to confuse the dog. He had to circle back around the Germans and cross the trail he had come in on with the other partisans. Hopefully, the dog would become confused by the scent going off in two directions. Yakob had taught him the trick but this was the first time he had had to use it. He took advantage of all his skill to minimize the noise of his passage through the trees. Emerging on the original track behind the Germans, he could hear the dog's excited barking. The patrol was following him around in a circle. Adrien ran twenty meters back down the track and darted off again into the woods. He scaled a rocky, brush-covered outcrop that overlooked the track and concealed himself. His position allowed him to look back down the trail the way the Germans had come. He breathed a sigh of relief when he realized the SS patrol was alone and not the lead elements of a larger force.

The Germans emerged into his view. When they reached where Adrien had intersected his old trail, the dog began turning in circles and barking, confused and unsure of which scent to follow.

Then Adrien smiled. The SS was making a huge mistake. Spread out when he first saw them, now all six of the Germans were bunched up around the dog and the SS patrol leader was shouting at the dog handler angrily. The handler was trying to control the dog and answer back at the same time. Adrien stealthily made his way closer to the milling group of Germans, using all his skill at being quiet. When he was ten meters away, he pulled a German stick grenade from his belt. After unscrewing the cap, he yanked on the little porcelain ball in the wooden base, waited for a two count, stood up and threw.

The grenade exploded in the center of the group of Germans, about a meter above the ground. The blast sent white-hot bits of steel in all directions, mowing down the soldiers. A second or two later, two of the six Germans started to get shakily to their feet. Adrien rushed them and emptied the magazine of his machine pistol into them.

Adrien stood over the bodies. The dog and five of the Germans were dead. The sixth, one of the SS men, was still alive. He had a bad stomach wound from the grenade. The SS trooper looked up at Adrien with shocked, pleading eyes. "bitte," he said. His face was young with Nordic features. Adrien took his ice pick from his waistband and plunged it through the SS man's right eye into his brain and the German quickly stopped breathing. Adrien was in no mood to be compassionate, not to anyone wearing an SS uniform.

Adrien heard a noise behind him and whirled. He saw Yakob approaching him carrying a rifle. The partisan looked at the bodies and then at Adrien.

"It seems that Tovia has taught you well," he said and smiled.

Adrien and Yakob collected the Germans weapons, then cut off each German's genitals and stuffed them in his mouth. The Germans routinely mutilated the bodies of partisans they killed and displayed the bodies in nearby villages as a warning. The partisans had taken to returning the favor. Such was the savagery of the war in the Parczew forest.

For almost a month Adrien's small group were like hunter's prey, scurrying from one close call to another, one step ahead of the Nazis. They sometimes went without eating for days at a time. Throughout it all, Aleska refused to leave Adrien's side. Then on 22 July, the Soviet advance rolled past the Parczew forest. The German troops in the area made a mad dash to the west. They wanted to get across the Vistula River before they were encircled.

The Jewish partisan band reunited in one of their previous camps. There were barely thirty of them left. The rest had been caught by the Germans and shot. They licked their wounds and rested.

In early August 1944, a group of Soviet officers entered the camp. Gathering everyone together, they called them "Comrades" and said that all the partisan fighters would be inducted into the Red Army and would have the privilege of fighting the fascists. Anyone who refused to join, and the women and children unsuitable for fighting, would be interned in the former Nazi concentration camp at Majdanek near Lublin. They gave the partisans twenty-four hours to report for duty. That night around the fire, the little group of Yakob, Tovia, and Adrien discussed what to do. Aleska was silent as usual.

Tovia was the first to make a decision. "I will go with the Red Army and kill more Nazi bastards."

Yakob sighed, "I will go with him. Without me, Tovia would be lost. Who would do his thinking for him?" Tovia reached over and knocked the burning wad of tobacco out of his pipe onto Yakob's lap. Yakob yelped, jumped up and patted his burning trousers.

Adrien Weiss looked into the fire and took stock of his situation. He knew that he had to get the hell out of the continent of Europe. It hadn't been nor ever would be a healthy place for Jews to live. The Russians were almost as anti-Semitic as the Germans had been before the war. He thought about his relatives. He had to assume that all of them who had lived in Kassel were now dead. That left his grandparents on his mother's side, Nathan and Julia Rothstein, and two aunts. They had fled France in 1940 to England with the intention of going on to the United States. If Adrien and Aleska could make it west to where the American troops were, he could contact his grandfather and get out of Europe. First, though, he and Aleska would have to hunker down and wait until the fighting was over.

One might think that this was surprisingly adult thinking for a fifteen-year-old boy. It was, but the circumstances of the past two years had forced him to grow up before his time. There is nothing like having people trying to kill you to sharpen your cunning and quest for survival.

A bond had formed between Adrien and Aleska that was growing stronger every day. Adrien now looked upon her as his family. He had adopted her as his sister and transferred all the love and protective instincts he had felt for Gabbi to her. For her part, she never left his side. Beyond her name, she still had not spoken. She appeared to have absolute trust in him. He could not see leaving and abandoning her to Majdanek.

"I am not going," said Adrien finally.

"Where will you go?" asked Tovia.

"We will hide in the forest, then head west. Maybe someday Aleska and I can get to America."

It was the last time he would see Tovia and Yakob. He had been through many hardships with them and probably owed them for his survival. Still, parting with them wasn't hard. Adrien had put up an emotional wall. Ever since Yossi was killed, he hadn't wanted any close friends that he would have to mourn for if they died. Aleska was different, she was now his family.

Before dawn the next morning, Aleska and Adrien gathered provisions. He took Tovia's Mauser rifle and ammunition, leaving his MP38 in its place. Tovia wouldn't mind. He could kill more Germans with it than with the rifle. Laden with coats, blankets and enough food for a week, they slipped into the forest.

Throughout the rest of the summer and autumn, they wandered from temporary camp to temporary camp. Adrien went on food raids to the villages on the edge of the forest. He also went into Lublin several times disguised as a Gentile to get salt and other things they needed that couldn't be obtained in the woods. When it started dipping below freezing at night, Adrien knew they would have to find proper winter shelter soon.

On a hunting stalk in November he discovered a cave. On a rocky outcrop, the entrance was concealed by pine branches. He explored inside. It was about four meters deep and three wide. The floor was more or less flat. The next day he and Aleska moved in. Adrien knew that if this was 1943 and the Germans were hunting them, the cave would be a death trap. There was only one way in or out. But, since the Germans were gone and the Russians and Poles had better things to do than hunt Jews, they were reasonably safe.

In December there was a horrible snowstorm. They were confined to the cave for three days. During this time Aleska finally started to speak.

Adrien had just returned from the small fire pit he had made near the entrance to the cave. He had a piece of smoked venison in his hand. He sat down, looked at Aleska across the cave and saw tears rolling down her cheeks. He got up, sat down beside her and held her. After a while, she started talking in a barely audible voice.

"My family name is Pisarski. My father was a baker in Lublin. I lived over the bakery with my parents, grandfather and two sisters. I was the youngest child. When the Germans came, we were not molested at first, not being Jewish. Then one day, two drunken German soldiers were stabbed to death in an alley in Lublin. They took my parents and grandfather and shot them as a reprisal along with many of our neighbors. My sisters and I were alone. The four of us kept the bakery going. A year later some other Germans came for my sisters. They said my sisters would be used to entertain the German troops. I was only seven. The Germans didn't want me and chased me away. I wandered around Lublin begging for food. A kindly farmer and his wife took me in for two years. Then they too were shot by the Germans for hoarding. I was on my own again, begging and stealing food. Then one day a German soldier on a motorcycle forced me to go with him. He put a rope on my neck and drove with me out of town. The rest you know."

Aleska sobbed. More tears rolled down her cheeks. Adrien held her and stroked her forehead.

§

Adrien pondered all this as he neared the cave. Carrying the doe over his shoulder, he paused before going near the entrance. He looked for anything that wasn't as it should be. When he was sure that it was safe, he approached and gutted and dressed the deer. He cut the meat into long strips for smoking as Tovia had taught him to do. At a built up fire in a pit by the cave entrance, he put the strips of meat on sticks to cook. Aleska appeared from deeper in the cave. Her hair was long and shaggy and blew into her face from the breeze at the cave mouth.

"Why are you cooking it that way?" she asked.

"For our journey, the meat will stay edible for a month this way," Adrien replied.

"So, we are going soon?"

"Yes."

All of their conversations were like this. Short, to the point and without excess verbiage. They communicated in other ways. When they sat around the fire or slept on the rude bed of pine needles, Adrien had his arms around the girl. They were outcasts whom nobody wanted, at least in Europe, and they clung together and took comfort from each other.

On the day before they set out, Adrien took Aleska to a place about a kilometer from the cave. Several boulders had formed a natural dam on a stream creating a small pool about a meter deep. They stripped and washed their clothes as best as they could. They spread them on rocks to dry and then bathed together without shame. Afterward Aleska sat on the rocks nearby, naked, combing out her long hair with a crude comb Adrien had painstakingly made during the winter from beech wood. Later, back at the cave, they packed their meager belongings and the meat and then slept. They would begin their trip to the American zone in the morning.

CHAPTER THIRTY–TWO

358TH BOMBARDMENT SQUADRON
303RD BOMB GROUP
8TH U.S. AIR FORCE
RAF FIELD MOLESWORTH
MOLESWORTH, ENGLAND
APRIL 8, 1945

A t 6:45 am, First Lieutenant Eddie Baxter, USAAF, walked out of the mess hall shaking his head. Watery powdered eggs and half cooked bacon again. Worse than the food was the insolent look of the moron PFC with his cap worn cocked to the side who served it to him with a big spoon. Baxter wished the Germans would finally give up so he could get back home to some decent food. If it hadn't been for the war, Baxter would now probably be eating his mom's pancakes and working as an apprentice plumber at his father's business instead of preparing to drop lethal ordinance on a town in Germany.

Eddie Baxter had just turned twenty-two years old and was a Bombardier in B-17G, "Sassy Sally." He had completed twelve missions over Germany. The airman wasn't very tall, only five foot nine, which was good. The bombardier compartment on a B-17 was incredibly cramped. He had sandy brown hair, green eyes, a wide mouth that was prone to grin at inappropriate times and he shuffled instead of walked, demonstrating that the army had failed in its efforts to make him into a military man. He hurried over to the briefing building. The Colonel would chew his ass if he was late.

The Wing Commander, a Brigadier General in his early thirties, described the mission for today to the huge room of assembled air crews: Bayreuth Germany. Eddie didn't know where that was and didn't care; that was the Navigator's job. When the briefing got down to the information that concerned him, Baxter paid attention and took notes on his clipboard.

After the briefing, the ten member crew of the "Sassy Sally" piled aboard one jeep and headed to the flight line. The vehicle was so overloaded that Eddie imagined it looked like a group of ants attacking a beetle. The jeep stopped beside a huge silver bomber. The B-17 bristled with fifty caliber machine guns. Baxter had heard that earlier in the war the bombers were painted olive drab green. Then some bright boy staff officer in the Pentagon had realized that the weight of all that paint and the drag it caused was slowing down the airspeed of the bombers. The brass took his suggestion to heart and then probably transferred the bright boy to a weather station in the Aleutians. It wouldn't do to have people around who were smarter than the Generals.

Eddie swung himself up into the plane through a hatch under the nose. He was wearing two layers of long underwear and socks, two layers of wool pants and shirts, an A2 leather jacket and fleece lined boots. Some others in the crew, the gunners mostly, wore a heavier, very thick, fleece-lined coat, Baxter couldn't wear it because it was too bulky and he needed a certain freedom of movement to do his job. The B-17 was not pressurized like the newer B-29 and the temperature at bombing altitude was around thirty below zero.

Eddie wriggled into the nose, which was his position in the aircraft as bombardier. He sat in his cramped seat. One by one the engines began to fire up. Clouds of blue smoke enveloped the plane. After revving the engines for a minute or so, a flare arced across the sky, the pilot released the brakes, and the aircraft began to roll, joining others on the taxiway. It was a bumpy ride to the runway threshold. The B-17 wasn't designed for comfort.

When the runway cleared ahead, the pilot gunned the engines and the big bomber gradually gathered speed. The jarring rumble suddenly stopped and they were in the air. The plane circled the field, and then in an intricate series of precision turns joined up with the other ships in their squadron. Their squadron, in turn, joined up with their wing and with other squadrons and wings to form a mighty force headed east, leaving hundreds of white vapor trails in the thin air of the morning sky.

§

GESTAPO HAUPTSITZ
SCHLOSS DONNDORF
ECKERSDORF, DEUTSCHLAND
8 APRIL 1945.

At around 11 am, Gestapo Kriminalkommisar Oskar Renke was going through a stack of papers directed to him by his subordinates for his attention. He was a small man and very unimposing to look at. The power he wielded though was enough to make him seem like a giant to those who had the misfortune to meet him in an official capacity. The Gestapo had a fearsome reputation. The ordinary Germans thought they were being continually watched by this all-knowing, all-seeing organization. The truth was much different. The Gestapo was a huge bureaucracy and suffered from the same weaknesses of all large organizations. Senior members seemed to care more about building individual fiefdoms than doing the actual work. Petty infighting and squabbles over jurisdiction were common. Very little actual detective work was done. Instead, the

Gestapo relied heavily on informers.

There were three types of informers. The first was the patriotic German who was shocked and appalled to learn that his neighbor was secretly listening to the BBC or participating in the black market. The second type were people who wanted to settle old scores with their enemies. The third type wanted something in return for their information.

Most of the papers in the stack on Kriminalkommisar's desk dealt with mundane reports on the black market and hoarding. In his district, those were his main concerns. Midway through the stack was a letter that promised to be more interesting. Renke adjusted his glasses and read it.

It was from a woman who said she had started a new job as a housemaid in Bayreuth in the home of Doktor Kurt Wolf. Renke recognized the name. Wolf was a rich man and a prominent citizen. Renke read on. On her first day of work, the new maid was cleaning Doctor Wolf's study. She saw a partially completed letter on the doctor's desk. It was to someone called Marta and it was full of vile slanders against the character of the Fuhrer. The housekeeper had caught the informant reading the letter and the woman had lost her job. She was making the report as a good German citizen should.

Renke sat back and pondered the letter. This might be an opportunity to pad his emergency fund. The Third Reich was kaput. Everyone knew it and were doing what they could to prepare for life under American occupation. Being a member of the Gestapo, Renke would have to lay low for a while after the Amis got here, so he needed money. Now he had a perfect excuse to squeeze some gold out of old Kurt Wolf.

For this reason, Renke decided to confront Doktor Wolf alone. If he took underlings with him, he would have to share what he pried out of the old man. He walked downstairs and got in his car. He drove the five kilometers to the Wolf estate. When he entered the driveway and saw how palatial the place was, he increased the amount of gold he intended to demand to dispose of this little matter of treason.

Parking in front of the ornate entrance, he walked to the door. A uniformed maid answered the bell. Renke flashed his Gestapo identification and the maid showed fear on her face. It was a standard reaction to him and Renke loved it. He followed her to a door off the entrance hall. When the door was opened, the Gestapo man saw a very old gentleman sitting in a chair looking at Renke with a surprised expression.

"Are you Doktor Kurt Wolf?"

"I am."

"I am Kriminalkommisar Renke of the Gestapo. You may be in a lot of trouble."

To his surprise, Wolf didn't react in the usual frightened way. Most people turned white, some shit their pants.

"What kind of trouble would that be?" asked Kurt Wolf.

"An employee saw a letter you wrote to someone called Marta. In this letter, you slander the Fuhrer and disparage the Nazi party."

"Do you mean my calling Hitler the Antichrist and the Nazis a bunch of murdering devils?" asked Wolf defiantly.

Renke was becoming a little unnerved. Wolf showed no fear. Usually by this time the suspect was pissing his pants.

"Let me come to the point. What you wrote in that letter was a crime." Renke put his hands behind his back and strolled about the room, turning his back on the old man. "Due to the circumstances and your advanced age we might be persuaded to forget all about this matter for a small consideration, say five thousand gold marks."

Renke turned back to Wolf and jerked his head up when he saw the small black pistol in the old man's hand. Just then the air raid sirens went off in the distance.

§

They were approaching the IP, about to start the bomb run. The bombers had picked up nine squadrons of P-51 fighters over the French coast. Called "little friends" by the bomber crews, there were reassuring swarms of them around the bombers. Baxter had heard horror stories about bombing Germany in 1943 and early 1944. The B-17's had flown missions far into Germany without fighter protection. The bomb groups suffered appalling losses, sometimes up to half the force. Since the introduction of the P-51 Mustang fighters which could escort the bombers all the way to the target and back, the bomber losses had plummeted. So far on this mission, they had encountered no flak or fighter opposition. The pilot spoke over the intercom.

"Pilot to crew. We are about to make our bomb run. Look alive for fighters. Just because we haven't seen them yet doesn't mean we won't."

Eddie laughed at the pilot trying to be so stern. George Wilson was twenty-one years old, a year younger than Baxter. He acted the way he thought a stern commanding officer should act. He wanted the enlisted men in the crew to call him "Skipper," like in some Hollywood movie. Every person on the plane was barely out of his teens. For the umpteenth time, Eddie questioned the wisdom of entrusting a multi-million-dollar airplane loaded with lethal ordinance to a bunch of kids. He shook his head and cracked a grin.

Eddie went on his knees in front of his Norden bombsight. It was a complex mechanical device that used gyroscopes and gears to calculate when to drop bombs. On this mission, the bombardier in the lead ship would do that. Eddie only had to fly a precise course and drop his bombs manually when he saw the lead ship drop hers. The pilot's voice came over the intercom again.

"Bombardier, we are at the IP, starting bomb run now."

Eddie answered, now all business. He flipped a lever with a black Bakelite knob down by his left leg.

"Bomb bay doors opening."

"Pilot to bombardier, it's your airplane."

The Norden bombsight had a unique design feature that allowed the bombardier to steer the plane during the bomb run. He could make small lateral adjustments to the bomber's heading.

He put his eye to the eyepiece. The target was coming up. He made a small course correction to the right and put the crosshairs right where they should be. He kept an eye on the lead ship of the formation. When he saw them drop their bombs, he would too.

Bombs emerged from the belly of the lead plane in the formation. Eddie toggled the manual bomb release on the Bombardier's left panel and nothing happened. He flipped it again and still nothing. He punched the panel with his gloved fist and finally got a green light. The bomber surged upward with the release of the bombs. The pilot instantly brought it back under control.

"Bombs away," called Eddie over the intercom. "Closing bomb bay doors."

The delay with the switch had meant that the "Sassy Sally" had dropped its bombs three seconds after the rest of the formation. They missed the target completely, detonating in the residential districts to the east of the town of Bayreuth. Baxter wasn't concerned. They probably only killed some cows in a pasture but if they blew up some Kraut civilians, so what? They should have thought about that before they started the war. Eddie settled back in his seat for the long flight back to England.

§

Kriminalkommisar Oskar Renke was shocked to see the gun in Wolf's hand.

"Doctor Wolf, there is no need for this."

"No need? You people have been bullying people for years. God is going to bring retribution down on you Nazis for your many sins." Both men heard the sound of explosions that progressively got nearer. The house shook with each detonation. Renke looked up at the ceiling. In a turnabout to the usual situation, it was his face that showed fear.

A 500 pound AN-M64 general demolition bomb crashed through the roof of Wolf's house. It was painted olive drab with yellow rings around the nose and the tail. About five meters over the heads of Wolf and Renke, 262 pounds of TNT exploded, vaporizing the two men, three female servants, a neighbor's dog named Heinz who had been begging at the back door and the house. Shattered boards and chunks of concrete soared a hundred feet in the air.

Old Kurt Wolf had been correct. God did bring retribution down on Kriminalkommissar Oskar Renke for his many sins, but he used First Lieutenant Eddie Baxter, USAAF, of Stockton, California, as his instrument.

CHAPTER THIRTY-THREE

OBRZACH LUBLINA
POLSKA
10 APRIL 1945

leska Pisarski and Adrien Weiss came down out of the
forest carrying bundles over their shoulders. They were
both lean and hard from years of subsisting on a diet of
mostly animal protein and they were burned bronze by the sun. The
mismatched clothing they wore looked like it had come from a rag
picker's bag. Aleska's long hair was gathered and tied by a strip of
cloth behind her shoulders. Adrien's blonde hair was shoulder length,
loose and scraggly. At first glance, Adrien at sixteen and Aleska at
thirteen looked about as non-threatening as anyone could get. If one
looked closer though, especially into Adrien's eyes, one would see
that they weren't the eyes of a typical teenager. They were hard and
dangerous and world-wise beyond his years. He wasn't a typical
teenager inside either.

Yakob had taught him to be able to move as stealthily as a zephyr
over a mountain meadow. Tovia had taught him how to kill in
multiple ways. The Nazis had crushed the humanity out of him.
They had stolen that feeling of loyalty to community, nation and
mankind in general as well as shared morality common in a normal
person. Adrien Weiss didn't fear death and didn't care at all about

anyone in the world except the slim girl who walked beside him. But what made him really dangerous was his utter ruthlessness. He was prepared to kill without hesitation or remorse anyone who got in his way or threatened Aleska .

Trading his rifle to a farmer for a sack of cornmeal, Adrien had kept his pistol. He carried it tucked into his waistband in the small of his back. His ice pick was slipped up the sleeve of his coat.

From conversations with Yakob and Tovia, Adrien had learned about the geography of this part of Europe. Adrien gave a lot of thought to their route to the west. The war was still going on in the heart of Germany so it was too dangerous to head directly west. He decided to head south into Slovakia and them swing west. He asked Aleska what she thought. She just looked at him with her big brown eyes and shrugged.

The main road southwest from Lublin was lined on each side with a stream of humanity. Most were afoot, though here and there the two teenagers encountered a pushcart or horse-drawn wagon containing the owner's few possessions. The people on the roads were mainly forced laborers of the Nazis returning to their homes in the west mixed in with ethnic Germans from Ukraine who had been forcibly evicted by the Russians.

Adrien and Aleska joined the stream of people. On the road, they kept to themselves. They camped in the woods beside the road and bathed in streams when they felt they needed to. In six days they reached Rzeszow, Poland, and continued through the town and camped on the other side. The next morning, they set out for Kostice, Slovakia, 200 km away. They got an early start, leaving before dawn. Because if the early start they had the road to themselves for a change.

About ten km outside of Rzeszow as they approached a bridge over a stream, four Polish peasant youths climbed out from under the bridge and blocked their way. They all appeared to be in their late teens or early twenties and were armed with clubs, except for the leader who carried a rusty German rifle. Adrien and Aleska stopped in their tracks and the leader of the group approached Adrien and leveled the rifle at him.

"What have you got in those sacks?"

Adrien looked at the Pole with a wary expression and didn't answer. The peasant patted the stock of the rifle with a smug expression on his face.

"We are going to have what is in those sacks. After we deal with you, we are going to have some fun with her," said the Pole, gesturing at Aleska.

Adrien cringed away, pretending to be frightened and the peasant made a huge mistake. He swaggered closer, dropping the muzzle of the rifle and got within the reach of Adrien's arms. As quick as a striking cobra, Adrien plunged the ice pick up under the peasant's chin and into his brain. His eyes bulged, he fell over backward and the rifle clattered to the dirt of the road.

Adrien whirled to his right. Another of the peasants rushed him with a wooden club in his hands. The Pole made a wild swing at Adrien, who ducked under the swinging club and stabbed the ice pick into the man's stomach. The young man dropped the club, sat down on the road and held his midsection.

The other two peasants, frightened by the violence, fled after seeing their companions so easily vanquished. Adrien watched them until they were out of sight. He walked to the wounded man who was groaning and looking at the blood seeping between his fingers. Without hesitation, Adrien plunged the ice pick into his right ear. The peasant teetered, then fell over on his side. Weiss searched the pockets of the dead men. He found enough silver coins to purchase food for a month. He put it in his pocket. He left the rifle where it had fallen.

Adrien took Aleska's hand and they darted about seventy-five meters into the woods beside the road. They hid where Adrien could see the bridge with the bodies lying on it but not be seen.

About a half hour later, a wagon pulled by a scrawny horse arrived at the bridge. The wagon had old automobile rubber tires instead of regular wagon wheels. In the back were six peasants. They appeared older than the first four and two of them carried rifles.

Two people got out of the back of the wagon. Adrien recognized them as the men who had run away after the fight. Everyone in the group was shouting at each other but Weiss was too far away to understand what was being said.

The men in the group picked up the two bodies as well as the rifle and loaded them in the back of the wagon. The group climbed back on the wagon and it clopped off to the southwest. Adrien was patient. The wagon came by several more times in the next two hours searching for them as the verges of the road swelled again with miserable people trudging west. Adrien stayed under cover all day, holding Aleska's hand while she slept. When it was full dark, they broke cover and walked all night to the southwest.

Aleska showed no emotion to Adrien killing the two men. In truth, she was just as inured to violence and death as he was.

§

On 28 July 1945 Adrien and Aleska stumbled into Nuremberg, Germany. They were more dead than alive. They had traveled over 1300 kilometers in three-and-a-half months, all on foot. Arriving late in the day, all they could think about was finding someplace to sleep. They were exhausted and hadn't eaten in two days. Walking through the city, they passed block after block of bombed out, gutted buildings. Not finding a suitable place, they finally lay down in the still standing doorway of a destroyed building that would provide shelter from the rain. They were instantly asleep.

They were so exhausted that they didn't hear a vehicle approach and stop beside them. A hand shook Adrien's shoulder. He came groggily awake. A split-second later, he stiffened and prepared to fight. Adrien opened his eyes to see two soldiers in green uniforms with strange looking helmets. They wore armbands with the letters "MP" on them.

"Joe, look, it's a couple a kids. They look starved. I got some chocolate in the jeep. Hand it to me willya."

Adrien didn't understand English so he didn't know what the soldier was saying. Aleska was now awake and clinging to his arm. One of the soldiers got something out of their vehicle and handed it to Adrien. It was covered in waxed paper. When he unwrapped the paper he discovered two chocolate bars. He handed one to Aleska and they attacked the chocolate like wolfhounds.

In all the world, the American soldier, the GI, was known as a fierce warrior when aroused. The Germans learned that lesson twice in a century. But the American soldier was also known throughout the world for his compassion, especially to children.

The two soldiers gently helped Adrien and Aleska into their jeep and drove them to their headquarters. In the mess tent, they were given huge portions of meat, potatoes and ice cream. Adrien was so overwhelmed with their generosity that he removed the German P-38 pistol from the back of his waistband and gave it to one of the Americans.

"Oh, jeez, is this for me? Thanks."

They were given the use of two cots for the night with clean, white sheets on them. Adrien hadn't slept between sheets since Paris.

The next morning, after a heaping breakfast of bacon and powdered eggs, a truck arrived and took them to the Liepheim Jewish displaced persons camp, 180 km away near Ulm. It was located on a former Luftwaffe base and was run by the United Nations Relief and Rehabilitation Administration. The place was spotlessly clean. After being allowed to shower and receiving an issue of clean clothes, Adrien was led to a real bed, again with crisp white sheets. The people there were kind and tolerant when Aleska refused to leave Adrien's side and sleep with the women. A nice lady who seemed to be in charge said in German to her staff, "Let her alone. We have no conception of what those two have been through."

Late that night Adrien lay in bed staring at the ceiling. The building was quiet. Aleska was sleeping soundly in the next bed. Without him bidding it, the voice of his grandfather on that terrible day at Sobibor began playing in his head.

His grandfather had forcibly turned Adrien around to face him as his parents were being beaten to death. Then he had slapped Adrien's face, hard.

"Listen to me. They intend to kill our whole family today. Our only hope is for you to mingle with the crowd behind us while I distract them. You must survive, Adrien. Do what you must to survive and grow up strong. One day when you have prepared, you must return and avenge your murdered family. Promise me, Adrien, that you will do as I say."

"Yes, grandfather, I promise I will do as you say," Adrien mumbled.

"Listen to me. In the Bueche & Cie bank in Basel, Switzerland, I have deposited one and a quarter million American dollars. You may get the money by giving them the account number 162465 and repeating two words: "Natalie's gold.""

Adrien looked at the ceiling as unbidden tears rolled down his cheeks. "I have done the first part grandfather, I have survived."

CHAPTER THIRTY-FOUR

THIRD US ARMY DETENTION CAMP FOR SUSPECTED
WAR CRIMINALS
DACHAU, GERMANY
18 DECEMBER 1945.

Erich Wolf screwed up his face in disgust as a fat former Rottenfuhrer walked by and farted in his face. It was outrageous. He was an officer and being quartered with enlisted men was against every tenet of proper military decorum. Erich considered the SS enlisted men beneath him and little better than swine. The men sensed this and went out of their way to make his life miserable. The situation was galling because, just a few months ago, these same men would have been bowing and scraping to Erich, trying to please him.

He was sitting dejectedly on the bottom bed of a three-tiered bunk. The huge room was crowded with former SS officers and other ranks. The room that had once held the tormented now held the tormentors. It was delicious irony and was deliberate on specific orders from the American Army. The living conditions were deplorable. There was only one thin blanket to ward off the December chill and no sheets. Before this, Erich had never in his life slept in a bed without sheets. The whole camp stank of human sweat, death and misery. As bad as the living quarters were, the food was unspeakable - overcooked meat and potatoes and canned vegetables that all tasted like cardboard. Wolf would sit and dream about the sumptuous meals that he once enjoyed. Then the realization would come to him that at least he was alive. He had not been captured by the Russians.

§

On 29 April 1945, Erich had arrived at the WVHA headquarters in a haggard state. The bombing had kept him awake all night. It was almost constant now. The British came by night and the Americans by day. During the past few months Erich had narrowly escaped death several times.

Today, Frau Glick was nearly hysterical. For months now she had been nervous and fearful. The reports of what the Russians were doing to German women in East Prussia had unnerved her. Today she was worse than usual. Wordlessly, she pointed to the open door of Sturmbannfuher Prich's office. Wolf looked inside. Papers were strewn across the floor and the door of the safe in the corner yawned open, its contents gone. It was clear that Prich had flown the coop.

Erich sat down to think. He had to get out of Berlin today. He had been trying to get a transfer for months but it was impossible. One had to be careful. Any sign of disloyalty to the Fuhrer was punished harshly, usually with a rope.

Suddenly Erich hit upon a plan. He steered Frau Glick into a chair and asked her to draw up official looking orders sending him on an urgent mission to Nuremberg. If he could get that far he was sure he could make it home to Bayreuth. Frau Glick calmed down fast. She agreed but only if Erich would take her with him and provide money for her to live on after the war. Wolf pondered the proposition. It might add to his cover if he had a secretary along on the trip.

Thirty minutes later the orders were complete including official seals and Prich's forged signature. Carrying only briefcases, they made their way through streets full of rubble to the Hotel Adlon where they retrieved Erich's car from the basement garage. As they emerged from the building onto Unter Den Linden the air raid sirens started to wail.

Erich drove like a mad man, dodging piles of debris from collapsed buildings. At Kreuzberg, they ran into their first checkpoint. A group of young SS fanatics had blocked the road with a large truck. Behind the group four bodies had been strung up. There were three German soldiers and a civilian. Each had a placard around his neck saying that the person was a deserter or a traitor.

Erich used his phony orders to bluff his way past. He put on quite an act with the Young SS men. He was aggressive and haughty and shouted a lot. Frau Glick kept quiet, sitting in the car with her knuckles white on her briefcase.

Near Templehof, American bombers droned overhead and bombs started exploding all around them. The smoke and dust were so thick that Erich made several wrong turns and had to backtrack. They passed another SS checkpoint, this one abandoned, and crossed into Potsdam. The devastation around them was almost total. Shells of buildings were all that remained. The capital of the Third Reich was dying and Wolf desperately wanted to get out while it was still possible.

He breathed a sigh of relief when he reached the open road south of Potsdam. The wide, paved road was crowded with German civilians and defeated looking German soldiers headed west toward the advancing Americans. Erich stood on the horn and bullied his way through them. Several of the soldiers tried to climb in his car. He backed them off with his pistol.

Thirty kilometers west of Potsdam, several specks appeared in the sky. As the objects got closer, it was apparent that they were airplanes. Jabbos! They were American P-47 and British Typhoon fighter bombers that shot up everything that moved on German roads. Erich saw they were coming fast.

The crowds on the sides of the road scattered and Wolf skidded the car to a stop. Jumping out, he ran for the ditch beside the road. Frau Glick, frozen by terror, stayed in the car. Reaching the ditch, Erich looked back to see a stream of bullets tear into his beautiful car followed immediately by the roar of an airplane passing low overhead. He ducked as the Jabbos made another pass, spewing bullets, and then flying off.

Erich emerged from the ditch and walked to his car. Frau Glick was still in the passenger seat, or what was left of her. A 20 mm cannon shell had decapitated her and there were blood and brains all over the dashboard. Another shell had hit the engine. The car was going nowhere. Erich abandoned it and Frau Glick's body and joined the crowds at the sides of the road walking west.

About two kilometers further on he saw another victim of the Jabbos. A large Opel Wehrmacht truck was resting on its side in the ditch beside the road. The bodies of five soldiers were scattered beside the truck. Wolf looked at the bodies. One of the soldiers, a Gefreiter, was about his size.

Erich stripped the body and exchanged his smart SS uniform for the torn and bloody enlisted man's uniform. He left his SS uniform stuffed under the truck and put his wallet in one of his boots. He started walking west. The picture on the Gefreiter's pay book in his breast pocket didn't look anything like Erich. He shrugged, you couldn't have everything.

The next day Erich reached the Elbe river at Magdeburg. At the highway bridge he saw his first American soldiers. They were in green uniforms and wore steel helmets. Each wore an armband bearing the initials, MP. A long line of German soldiers was waiting at a checkpoint manned by the Americans. Wolf joined the line. When it was Erich's turn to pass through the checkpoint, a young soldier with one stripe on his arm waved him through.

"Wait a minute," said an older sergeant with a cigarette dangling from his lips as he walked up to Erich.

"Kinda old to be a corporal ain't cha Fritz?" Take off your shirt."

Erich understood English but tried to play dumb.

"Was is loss?"

Another soldier then told him in bad German, "off, take shirt."

Erich knew he was caught then and took off his uniform tunic and undershirt. The Sergeant raised Erich's right arm and saw the SS blood group tattoo in the armpit.

"Just as I thought," he said, and punched Erich in the face. Erich found himself sitting on the ground.

"Take this SS asshole and put him with the others. There will be a truck here soon to take them to Dachau."

The soldiers took Erich to a bombed-out building where there were other SS men who had tried to use the same ruse. A few hours later a truck arrived and took them to Dachau. An American guard rode with them with the bolt snicked back on his submachine gun, ready to fire, which the look in his eyes told Wolf he was ready to do. When the truck first started to move, the young American spoke to his prisoners.

"Any of you beauties even twitch an eyebrow, you'll be off to hell. I saw what you did at Buchenwald."

§

A young American soldier came into the room and called Wolf's name loudly. Erich stood and raised his hand. The soldier then waved his arm in a come here motion and said, "Come on Fritz, the Colonel wants to see you," in English. This infuriated Erich. These American enlisted men didn't salute him or address him by rank as the men in the SS had. The American guards called the SS officers, Fritz, Heinie or Kraut; very undisciplined. Wolf followed the soldier to the camp headquarters where he was shown through a door.

It was a small room with just a desk and a chair. Sitting at the desk was an American officer. He was wearing silver oak leaves on the collar points of his shirt and a patch on his arm with a picture of a tank and the number "4." He was built like a prize fighter with muscular arms and a barrel chest and looked like he was in his late thirties. Erich could see that he was balding on top and was wearing glasses. The plaque on his desk read, "LIEUTENANT COLONEL MARX." The officer was looking down at some papers on his desk. Oh, no, a Jew thought Erich. The officer looked up at Erich.

"Wolf, is it? I have some questions for you," said the officer in perfect German.

Erich's frustration boiled over. For the first time, he let on that he spoke English.

"Colonel, I must protest. I am a German officer. I demand that you address me by my rank with respect. Also, the living conditions here are atrocious. Officers should not be held with enlisted men. The food is little better than slop."

"Are you through?"

"Ja,"

Colonel Marx carefully took off his glasses, folded the earpieces in and put them in a breast pocket of his uniform. He stood and walked around the desk. Out of nowhere, Marx unleashed a vicious uppercut to Wolf's jaw. Once again Erich found himself flat on his rear end in the presence of an American. What was with these Americans? Every time you tried to talk to them, they knocked you down.

The Colonel stood over Wolf and pointed a finger in his face.

"Listen, you Nazi son of a bitch, if I had my way all you SS bastards would be taken to Auschwitz and given a nose full of Zyklon-B. Stand up and answer my questions or I will kick the shit out of you."

Marx then reseated himself behind the desk, took his glasses from his pocket, unfolded the earpieces and put them back on. Erich got to his feet shakily, rubbing his jaw.

"It says here that you were a clerk in the Reich Main Economic Office. You coordinated shipments of things looted from the Jews your asshole Fuhrer gassed. Is this true.?"

'I was not a clerk but, yes, that was what I was under orders to do. I had no choice. It was orders."

"All you pricks say the same thing. Did you ever have occasion to visit a death camp and witness what went on there?"

"Nein"

"Alright, dismissed. We will notify you if you will be required to stand trial."

Erich fled the office and hurried back to the barracks holding his jaw. He thought one of his teeth was loose. Erich was very frightened of the prospect of a trial. If he was sent to prison, his lands and money could be taken away.

CHAPTER
THIRTY-FIVE

I n June 1942, President Franklin Roosevelt, in anticipation of a flood of refugees and displaced persons after the war in Europe ended, proposed a global effort in order to be ready to help these people.

On January 9, 1943, at a ceremony in the White House, forty-four nations signed an agreement creating the United Nations Relief and Rehabilitation Agency. The name was quite a mouthful. Most people ever after referred to it by the acronym UNRRA.

By early 1945 with the fighting still going on, the anticipated problem of displaced people was already occurring. In areas conquered from the Germans, Army civil affairs officers were overwhelmed by desperate, needy people.

The military, casting around for facilities to take care of these people, hit on former German military bases. These bases had the housing and food preparation facilities needed. Other facilities were used including hospitals, schools and even private homes.

Displaced persons' camps sprung up all over occupied Germany and Austria and were run by the American military. Each ethnic minority had their own camps. There were camps for Jews, camps for Poles, etc.

In July 1945, UNRRA took over the administration of these camps.

UNRRA LEIPHEIM
JEWISH DP CAMP
LEIPHEIM, GERMANY
18 JANUARY, 1946

Adrien Weiss and Aleska Pisarski sat at a long table in the huge dining hall ignoring the bedlam going on around them. Adults were shouting and children were running around screaming. Just another typical meal in the dining hall thought Adrien. Metal trays with ample portions of food sat in front of them. To look at them today, one would not recognize them as the emaciated scarecrows who had staggered into Nuremberg six months ago. Adrien had filled out and grown five centimeters. He exercised a lot and his muscles were showing definition.

It was Aleska, however, who had undergone the biggest transformation. She was fourteen now and well into the transformation to womanhood. With nutritious food and plenty of sleep, her body had repaired itself from the ravages of malnutrition. Her breasts had grown and her hips had widened. Some of the women in the camp had taken pity on her. They told her about women things like menstruation and having babies and showed her how to fix her hair to complement her face. She was turning into a great beauty. Some of the boys had begun to hang around and preen in front of her but she ignored them. Her gaze would always return to Adrien. She was still extremely shy and reticent around most adults.

Mrs. Morrison, an American UN worker assigned to take care of Adrien and Aleska, had also noticed the change in Aleska. She thought that it was time for her to move to a women's barracks. As diplomatically as she could, Morrison told Aleska that it wasn't proper for two unrelated, unmarried teenagers to live together.

Aleska had gone white and the terror and feral look in her eyes caused Morrison to relent. She assigned the pair to one of the small rooms intended for married couples.

Early in their stay at the camp, Adrien had gone to the Red Cross office in the administration building. He filled out paperwork to try to contact his grandfather in England or America, wherever he was. The woman there, a British lady named Steele, said that the inquiry could take some time.

Life in the camp was pretty dull. People organized theater groups, book clubs and musical groups. There were schools for younger children. Adrien and Aleska took no part in any of these activities. The one thing Adrien seemed to want to do was to play football. He was out on the field daily, running and kicking a soccer ball with the other teenaged boys, with Aleska sitting on the sidelines watching. Sited beside the Danube River, the countryside around the former Luftwaffe base was beautiful. The camp's gates had been removed so the people staying there could come and go as they pleased. If they chose, they could walk to the nearby villages of Gunzburg, Wasserburg or Bodenheim. Or they could stroll down to the shores of the wide river and watch the barges go by. Most chose not to venture outside the camp. They still distrusted the German people. Recently, this attitude was reinforced by reports of Jews being beaten up in the area.

Almost everyone in the camp was anticipating emigrating to Palestine in defiance of the British blockade. The word "Palestine" was on everyone's lips. They imagined it to be this far off magical place where all their troubles would be over.

Representatives of a secret Jewish organization called Mossad Aliyah Bet were in the camp organizing clandestine truck convoys of Jews going south to the Italian coast on the first leg of the journey to Palestine. These activities were not very secret. The administrators of the camp knew all about them and approved. Unfortunately, the British knew all about them too.

Adrien steered clear of the Jews from Palestine. He didn't want to go there. In his young life, he had spent six years avoiding being killed for being a Jew. His family was dead because they were Jews. He reasoned that any place where there was a large number of Jews would be unsafe because someone would come along and want to kill them. No, the United States would be safer.

One evening Adrien took Aleska to the camp's open-air theater to watch a film. Aleska was fascinated with films and American movie stars. On the day that a new film was to be shown, she could hardly contain her excitement. Because she enjoyed it so, Adrien escorted her.

The film was "The House on 92nd Street" with Lloyd Nolan and Signo Hasso. Before the film, there was a British PATHE newsreel over-dubbed in German. One of the segments covered a Soviet trial of Ukrainian traitors who had served in the SS. The camera panned the faces of a long line of young men standing against a wall.

Adrien had been half paying attention when he saw a face on the screen that he knew. Mykhaylo Kostachuk, the man who had beaten his father to death, was in the line of condemned men. Adrien watched as a Russian firing squad shot the men dead. Adrien had mixed emotions. He would have liked to have killed him himself but at least the bastard got what he deserved for his crimes.

Adrien finished his meal and took the empty tray to the pass-through window to the kitchen and put it with the other dirty ones. Aleska dutifully followed him. Adrien looked at her fondly. He wasn't blind. He could see that she was becoming a woman but he didn't think he had sexual feelings for her. What he had was a strong compulsion to protect her from harm. Weiss didn't know exactly what was going on behind those big brown eyes. The girl still talked little, but he knew she needed him and depended upon him. He had vowed long ago that what happened to his family would not happen to Aleska.

Before the teenagers left the dining hall, they donned their heavy coats and stocking caps. A blast of frigid wind greeted them when Adrien opened the outside door. Germany in January was not a balmy place. Holding hands, they ran to their barracks and the warmth of their little room. They were not there five minutes before a messenger knocked on the door and told Adrien that he was wanted in the Red Cross office.

Adrien was so excited that he ran the whole way to the office, arriving winded. For some reason, Aleska had stayed behind in their room. Mrs. Steele showed him to a chair in her office, then sat down behind her desk. The expression on her face wasn't a happy one and Adrien felt a lump of dread form in the pit of his stomach. She cleared her throat and picked up a paper. She began to read in stilted German.

"Your grandfather, grandmother, two aunts, the aunt's husbands and five children escaped from France and fled to England in May 1940. They stayed in England for five months. On 23 October 1940, they boarded a merchant ship, the Falstaff Star, in Southampton as passengers bound for New York. The ship was part of a westbound convoy. While passing the southern tip of Ireland, the ship was torpedoed by a U-Boat and sunk."

"I am so sorry to be the one to tell you this, but your relations did not survive."

Adrien was stunned, but only for a moment. He was used to bad news. The realization that he was truly alone now hit him. He would have to make his own way in life. He could expect no help from relatives because they were all dead. How would he get out of Europe now? Then he thought of something.

"Can I still go to the United States, even if I don't have relatives there?"

Mrs. Steele's face was sadder still. "You can talk to Mrs. Morrison about this but the United States has a very restrictive immigration policy. You could apply for entrance but the chances of being accepted are almost nil."

Adrien got up and walked dejectedly back to the barracks. He didn't feel the cold wind. What do I do now? He thought about the money on deposit in Switzerland. He could try to get it, but how would they get there? And if they somehow managed to get to Switzerland, the bank wouldn't hand over a million American dollars to a teen-aged boy. Down deep, he knew that he should be feeling grief at the loss of his grandparents and aunts, however, he just couldn't muster the emotional strength to feel emotion for anyone.

When he arrived back at the cubicle, Aleska rushed to him and clung to his torso. In a few words of Polish, he told her what the news was. To his astonishment, she seemed relieved and Adrien scolded her about it. Aleska began to cry and whispered to him.

"I was so afraid that you were going off to America and would leave me here."

Adrien hugged her tightly and stroked her hair.

"I will never leave you Aleska. Never! Don't ever think that I would abandon you. You are all I have left for a family. You are the only person in this world that I care about. Whatever the future holds, we will face it together."

The next day Adrien saw Eitan Zion, one of the Mossad agents, in the dining hall. He was a fit young man with nervous eyes and bushy eyebrows. Adrien approached him.

"How do I get signed up for one of your trips to Palestine?"

CHAPTER THIRTY-SIX

THIRD US ARMY DETENTION CAMP FOR SUSPECTED
WAR CRIMINALS
DACHAU, GERMANY
12 MARCH 1946

Former SS-Hauptsturmfuhrer Erich Wolf was once again summoned by Lieutenant Colonel Marx. Not wanting to be knocked down again, Wolf was the very picture of cooperation. He stood at attention a meter in front of the Colonel's desk. Marx looked up at him with disgust and read from a piece of paper he was holding.

"The legal staff of the War Crimes Tribunal has determined that you will not be prosecuted for your part in the mass murder of victims of the Nazi regime. You will be released."

Marx then laid the paper aside.

"Now I want to give you my opinion. If it was up to me, you would be hanging from some gallows in the courtyard. You and your kind are as guilty as the SS murderers in the death camps. You stood back and didn't get your hands dirty with the actual killing, but you supported the killers with material assistance. You helped make the killing possible. I know that the guilt of this will not affect you. Pricks like you have no honor. But someday I hope that retribution in some form will be visited on you. Now get out of here, you filthy bastard."

As Erich left the building and walked back to his barracks he had mixed emotions. The first was elation. He would be free. He could go back to Bayreuth and resume his life. On the other hand, the things that Jew had just said about him stung his pride. How dare he call me names and say I had no honor. The killing of the Jews had been done on Hitler's and Himmler's orders. A German officer had no choice but to obey the orders of his superiors. Anyway, if Germany had won the war no one would even know or care about what happened to the Jews.

It was all Hitler's fault for not winning the war. If he had finished off England before attacking the Russians, Germany night have won. And not only that, Hitler threw away the troops needed to keep the Russians at bay on his ridiculous Ardennes offensive.

Erich thought about his killing of the two Jews at Sobibor. Had any witnesses that could tie him to the incident survived? Erich figured the odds of that were so small as to be infinitesimal. And even if one should surface, thanks to Frau Glick, there was no official record that he had been anywhere near Sobibor. He could hire sharp lawyers to argue that it was a case of mistaken identity. Besides, who was going to worry about the deaths of a few Jews out of the millions killed. But Erich Wolf was very wrong. There was someone who cared about his murder of the two Jews in Sobibor. Someone who cared very deeply.

The next morning an America private came to the barracks and escorted Erich to the camp administration building. Wolf was required to sign a sheaf of papers. These included a promise, under pain of death, not to take up arms against the occupation authorities and a statement attesting to the fact that he had not been tortured or maltreated while in the custody of the Americans. Erichwas given a voucher for transportation by train to Bayreuth and escorted out the gate.

As he watched the countryside roll by from the hard bench seat in third class, Wolf was amazed by how normal the small villages along the route looked. Except for the presence of American soldiers and their vehicles, they looked untouched by the war.

When the train pulled into Nuremberg, however, everything changed. There was near total devastation. This had been Hitler's show city and massive Nazi rallies were held here. The Allies had responded by flattening it. Erich could see no habitable buildings. Weary-looking workmen were salvaging bricks from the rubble and making neat piles of them in the streets. A grey pall hung over the city and the few people he saw looked haggard and thin.

Bayreuth was a little better. The bombings of April 1945 that had killed Erich's father had also destroyed about a third of the town. As he walked the route to his father's ruined house, he saw whole sections that looked like they did when he was a boy. Other areas were flattened into piles of rubble.

After walking five kilometers, Erich reached his house, or what used to be a house. Debris was scattered over a wide area and lay where it had landed in a fan pattern. He trudged to where the house had stood. All that was left was some of the concrete foundations with a haphazard pile of broken boards piled on top. Climbing over the debris, Wolf spotted the stairway down to the basement.

The stairway had been partially cleared as far as the wine cellar door. Erich descended and forced open the creaky door. The wine cellar had been looted. Only a few dusty bottles remained. But he wasn't interested in wine. He made his way to the back wall on the lower right. There, hidden by the edge of one of the shelves was a recess just big enough to admit two fingers. Erich reached in the recess and pulled out a cord with his fingers. He gave it a jerk and a hidden panel swung open. Nestled inside were two leather bags. He opened the top of the first. Gold glinted back at him and Erich breathed a sigh of relief. Now he had money. Five thousand marks in gold coins. He could buy food and shelter.

Erich took two fistfuls of the coins and replaced the bag behind the hidden panel. He trudged the five kilometers back to the center of town. When he tried to rent a room for the night he came in for a shock. There wasn't a place to sleep to be had at any price.

The town of Bayreuth's population had swelled to over 55,000. The newcomers were mostly displaced persons and ethnic German refugees who had been forced out of their homes in the east by the Russians. Even the Festival restaurant next door to the Festival Hall was home to five-hundred people. Erich had to make other plans.

He asked around and bought a car. It was a battered, wheezing pre-war Opel. It was the best he could find and it was better than walking. For five freezing nights Erich slept in the cramped back seat of his Opel. On the sixth day he was able to find a small dingy hotel room at an outrageous price.

Having gold opened up many doors for Erich. There was a shortage of hard money. The Hitler era German paper marks were declared worthless by the Americans. They issued official occupation currency. The people, however, didn't trust it. Anyone who had prewar gold and silver coins was very lucky indeed.

During his first week back in Bayreuth, Erich drove his Opel to the American occupation headquarters and registered as a Bayreuth resident. The soldiers gave him a temporary identification card while the permanent one was processed. At the same time, Erich asked for permission to travel outside Germany. When they asked the purpose of his travel, he answered, "family business." The army clerk told him that the necessary travel permit and temporary passport would take about two weeks to a month to process.

After leaving the U.S. occupation headquarters, Erich went to a tailor's shop and bought two suits off the rack. Up to this time he had been wearing a German army uniform with no insignia, given to him at Dachau. At the shop, he changed into one of the suits and threw the uniform into the trash.

For the next few days, Erich drove around Bayreuth and talked to each of his tenant farmers. He suspected that they were sorry to see him return and would have preferred it if he had died in the war. He told them that they would have to start paying rent again, which they had neglected to do since Erich's father was killed.

When his papers came through from the Americans, Erich boarded a train to Zurich, Switzerland. He visited the Schroeder & Co Bank AG and returned to Bayreuth two days later with a briefcase full of American twenty dollar bills.

CHAPTER
THIRTY-SEVEN

ABORDO DEL VAPORE DOV HOS
HARBOR, LA SPEZIA
LA SPEZIA, ITALIA
8 MAGGIO, 1946

She was the Dov Hos, an aged, wood hulled steamer that had been built before the turn of the century. Her hull was rotten and eaten away by worms. About thirty-five meters long, she stank of olive oil, fish and corruption. Her worn out, rusty engine could barely propel her at five knots in a calm sea.

Until three weeks ago she was named the Fede. The steamer was culled from some Mediterranean backwater by the Jewish Mossad Aliyah Bet organization for the purpose of running the British blockade of Palestine. Crammed into every available space aboard the Dov Hos were 685 souls. 675 passengers and ten crew members.

The passengers and crew were all Jews. They were the survivors of the attempt of the Nazis to make Europe Jew-free. All carried emotional and physical scars from their ordeal. Many had tattooed numbers on their arms from the work camps. All had the beaten down look of weariness of spirit.

The passengers who lined the rail on this day though were jubilant. They were sailing to Palestine today. Near the prow of the ship, a young couple stood and hugged each other. Adrien Weiss and Aleska Pisarski were not cheering. Adrien had his characteristic somber expression and Aleska stared at him with a frown. Adrien was still wondering if this whole Palestine thing was a good idea.

§

After he had spoken to the Mossad man in the Leipheim camp, things had moved swiftly. Because Adrien and Aleska were teens they were given a priority for transport to Palestine. The Jews in Palestine needed fighters for the upcoming struggle with the Arabs. The two were the perfect age to be trained to defend the Jewish settlements.

The Mossad man, Eitan Zion, rapidly educated Adrien about the British blockade. After the war ended, thousands of Jews were trapped in Europe. They knew they were unwelcome there and sought to emigrate to Palestine, the site of the ancient land of Israel. The Arabs who occupied that land reacted violently to the thought of hordes of Jews coming to their shores.

The British government, who had ruled Palestine since the end of World War I under a mandate from the League of Nations, allied themselves with the Arabs. The Jews of Palestine were shocked. Had not the Palestinian Arabs sided with Nazi Germany in the war against the British? Hadn't the Grand Mufti of Jerusalem, Haj Amin al-Husseini, the leader of the Palestinian Arabs, spent the entire war in Berlin being feted by the Germans? The foreign office said yes, yes, they did but the Arabs have oil, vast seas of oil under their burning deserts that rich and important Britons are anxious to exploit. You Jews have no oil.

The Jews responded with a guerrilla war against the British army stationed in Palestine with the aim of driving them out. At the same time, other Jews began buying ships, loading them with Jewish survivors of the camps and landing them illegally on Palestinian shores.

The British reacted to these actions by cracking down on Jewish residents of Palestine, and the Royal Navy was ordered to stop the flow of refugees entering illegally. British secret agents fanned out all over Germany and Austria and began spying on the Jewish DP camps, trying to find out when convoys of refugees would leave for the Mediterranean coast.

On 7 March, 1946, a convoy of trucks left the Leipheim DP camp at two in the morning. The trucks were a hodgepodge of different types. The truck in which Adrien and Aleska rode was a 1943 Studebaker, two-and-one-half-ton, late of the American army. They were wearing heavy coats and gloves and were clutching bags of oranges and water bottles they had been given before climbing aboard. As the trucks left, a British agent watching the camp, saw them and relayed the information to MI6.

During a three-day journey, the convoy drove south through southern Germany and then across Austria, all the while taking little-traveled, rough roads. It was an uncomfortable ride for the refugees in the backs of the trucks. They started out happily talking and singing songs. Soon, however, most talking ceased.

On the second day, an overweight woman with a skinny boy beside her on Adrien's truck began to complain in a whiny voice about the jostling. She kept it up until Adrien wanted to strangle her. Finally, a man across from the woman threatened to throw her out if she didn't shut up. She was quiet after that.

As they entered the foothills of the Alps, the upgrade caused the drivers to have to switch to lower gears and the convoy slowed. It began to get very cold. Adrien and Aleska huddled together under a blanket, their breath turned to vapor when they spoke.

Twice a day the convoy would stop and the people in the trucks could stretch their legs and be fed. It was simple fare, a piece of fruit or bread and cheese. The only thing to drink was water.

The convoy was stopped at the Italian border. The British had bribed the Italian border guards to stop them from entering Italy. One of the Mossad men promptly trumped the British and re-bribed the guards again to let the convoy pass. The Italians were beaming with pleasure when the trucks rolled by, their pockets stuffed with cash.

At the foot of the Alps, the going once again got easier. Finally, the convoy entered Parma and stopped at a convent run by some sympathetic nuns. They joined other Jews from other convoys and they slept in the courtyard of the convent that night. The trucks turned around and started back to Germany.

Late the next afternoon 73 British Army lorries arrived, driven by members of the Jewish Brigade of the British Army and commanded by a Jew dressed in the uniform of a British Major. The trucks had been "borrowed" from their usual Rome to Bologna supply run. The refugees piled aboard. Their destination was a backwater Italian port called La Spezia on the Italian coast south of Genoa, 119 kilometers away.

Using forged papers, the "Major" bluffed his way past an American checkpoint along the way. It was very dark when the trucks pulled up in a huge field next to a dock in the harbor. The people jumped down stiffly and started to form lines to board two ships tied up at the dock. Mossad men with battery operated torches shouted to try to organize the crowd.

Suddenly, two searchlights from a British corvette in the harbor snapped on a hundred meters away. The dock was lit up like daylight. A loudspeaker blared.

"Stand where you are. This is the Royal Navy. You are all under arrest."

The sirens of approaching British vehicles could be heard. The Jews froze for a moment. Then as one, they made a dash for the first of the two steamers. There were bottlenecks at the two boarding ramps as the desperate people clawed their way aboard. But by the time the British ground forces arrived, all 1400 refugees were aboard the ship called the Fede and had barricaded the gangways. In the meantime, the phony Major and his men had melted away into the town.

A real British Colonel in a crisp uniform with a swagger stick under his arm arrived and took command of the situation. He addressed the refugees with a bullhorn.

"You are all in His Majesty's custody. Disembark and form orderly lines on the dock. If you refuse, we will use force. You Jews will do as I order."

The British officer had made a huge mistake. He used an overbearing, arrogant tone. The Jews got angry. Hitler had tried to kill them all and had succeeded in killing most of their families. They had been herded into DP camps and forgotten. Europe didn't want them; they could accept that. But now this pompous ass was trying to prevent them from leaving Europe. They yelled in anger at the British troops, calling them Nazis and Gestapo. One of the Mossad men used a bullhorn to tell the British that the ship was wired with explosives and they would be detonated if they tried to board using force.

On the other side of the Fede, the corvette lowered a cutter with a boarding party of Royal Marines. Cases of canned goods had been stacked on the deck of the Fede to feed the refugees on their voyage. When the cutter neared the steamer, the Marines were met with a shower of canned food. One of the marines took a hit in the head and fell overboard. The cutter beat a hasty retreat. The siege of La Spezia had begun.

Adrien Weiss was one of those throwing the canned goods at the cutter. He and others around him continued even after the boat was out of range. It felt good to be striking back at someone. One of the Mossad men ran up and stopped them. They would need that food.

Adrien and Aleska found space on the deck to lie down and were almost instantly asleep, exhausted from the journey and all the excitement.

Dawn brought an impressive display by the British. A destroyer had replaced the Corvette in the harbor, its guns ominously pointed at the Fede. Ashore, there was at least a battalion of British soldiers arrayed against the unarmed refugees. Adrien shared a can of peaches with Aleska as they watched armored cars augment the cordon of soldiers on the dock.

The toilet facilities on the Fede, rudimentary to begin with, were soon overwhelmed. The ship began to stink of feces and unwashed bodies. That morning at ten, the Mossad leaders declared a hunger strike. No more food would be distributed. Before the stocks of canned food were taken away, Adrien pilfered two cans of fruit and hid them under his coat.

The Italian authorities arrived but were ignored by both sides. After an hour of shouting and gesturing with their hands, the Italians left.

Late in the day, the first journalists arrived in La Spezia. Soon there were a hundred, representing newspapers around the world. The Jews on the steamer did everything they could to appear pitiful. Many staged acts of drama worthy of Sarah Bernhardt took place on the deck of the Fede.

A week later the British made a concession. Because of the risk to the health of the passengers from the overcrowding, half of them were allowed to disembark and board the other immigrant ship, the Phoenicia. When this was done, the Mossad played it for all it was worth to the press. They renamed the Fede, the Dov Hos. The Phoenicia was renamed, Eliahu Golomb. They were the names of dead Palestinian Jewish heroes. A new flag flew over both vessels. It was white with a blue Star of David.

One of the Mossad men told Adrien that the British were taking a beating in the world press over the siege. Crowds of hostile Italians mocked the British troops. On 7, May, the pressure became too great for the Labour government in London. The British capitulated and announced that the Jews on the two steamers would be allowed to enter Palestine. There was wild jubilation from the Jews, silence from the British ranks.

Adrien and Aleska stood at the rail near the prow of the steamer as they cleared the harbor. Thousands of well-wishing Italians lined the shore. The corvette escorted the two vessels all the way to the dock at Haifa, where Adrien Weiss and Aleska Pisarski walked down a gangplank onto the soil of Palestine.

Although Adrien didn't acknowledge it, and couldn't have cared less, this land was his ancestral home. Much blood had soaked into its rocky soil since Moses and Joshua led the Israelites here in the dim and distant past. Unfortunately, much more blood was destined to soak into its arid soil.

After the Romans destroyed their temple and exiled them from their land, the Israelites had wandered the continent of Europe as a despised alien race. They were always under suspicion by their Gentile neighbors, shut up in ghettos, unfairly taxed, blamed for every calamity, slaughtered in pogroms and exiled from country after country at the whim of ignorant rulers. Lastly, Hitler and the Nazis had tried to kill them all.

Now, the Israelites had had enough. They were abandoning Europe for their ancient homeland of Eretz Israel. They were going home and the British couldn't stop them. No force on earth could stop them.

CHAPTER
THIRTY-EIGHT

DR. WURZBERGERSTRASSE 12
BAYREUTH, DEUTSCHLAND
18 NOVEMBER 1947

Built in 1880, Erich's old family home had been in the neoclassical style, with four Greek columns framing a grand portico entrance. It was large with ten bedrooms, grand dining room and ballroom. In the early part of the century, the house had had to be retrofitted with modern plumbing and electrical service. As a result, many of the inside spaces had a makeshift, unplanned appearance.

Upon returning to Bayreuth, Erich Wolf had elected not to replace the bombed-out house with the old style. Instead, he had decided to break with tradition and the taste of his neighbors and build a modern house. The architect he chose was just twenty-seven years old. Wolf had interviewed seven other architects and was not satisfied with their presentations. They were all combinations of historic styles that didn't suit him.

When he met Peter Fischer, he was at first unimpressed. The young man had long, unruly dark hair and an air of nonchalance. He seemed unconcerned whether Erich hired him or not. When he saw Fischer's concept drawings, however, he was impressed. Fischer was a devotee of a more modern style of architecture-- form must follow function. Instead of a conventional house, Fischer envisioned a sprawling structure of beige sandstone and glass. A central block dominated and contained the core functions of the house, the kitchen, great room, dining room and two huge water closets for guests. one for females and one for males.

Radiating wings jutted out from three sides. One of the wings was for the master of the house and contained a bedchamber, sitting room, bathroom, and study all with generous proportions. The other two wings contained three guest bedrooms each. Every bedroom had an attached bath and sitting room but were smaller than the master's quarters.

Because it was a single story, the footprint of the house was much larger than the old one. Erich thought that was no problem as he had plenty of land. He was more concerned that it would look more like a wartime bunker than a house. After considering it carefully, Erich took a chance, hired Fischer, and construction began. Wolf deliberately kept away. He didn't want to see it built. He wanted to see it for the first time in a completed state. Then he could either move in or demolish it and start over. Erich was finally able to find decent accommodations. The housing shortage had gradually abated. He rented a suite in a good hotel and waited for his house to be built.

Today he would tour the house for the first time. He arrived in his new blue Mercedes 170v sedan and drove up the driveway of crushed white stone. The first sight of his new home enchanted him. The central block soared seven meters into the sky. On each side of the entrance, set into the limestone blocks, were huge walls of glass outlined in white. The structure was imposing. It gave the impression of solidity and permanence. It looked like it had always been there. There was no external decoration. It needed none.

Erich passed through the double entrance doors also painted plain white and four meters high. The great room was huge and flooded with light. The high ceiling was coffered into squares made of varnished beechwood. Plain furniture of white leather and tables with glass tops were arranged into many seating areas so his guests could gather and hold intimate conversations. The furniture contrasted favorably with the limestone interior walls. A massive stone fireplace dominated one end of the room.

Erich walked through every room, feeling increasingly pleased. Fischer took him through a wide door off the kitchen which led down into the basement, past the wine cellar to the equipment room. The house was heated with an oil fired furnace and something Erich had not expected. There was a refrigeration cooling system. Both heating and cooling were controlled by a thermostat, something Erich had never heard of before but was delighted with.

Erich walked outside after the tour and congratulated the young architect. It had cost a huge amount of money, but he felt it was worth it. He could well afford it. He had emerged from the war with his fortune intact, thanks to his father Kurt's decision to divest himself in war investments when he did. Most of his neighbors and friends were not so lucky. Many had lost everything when the Nazi regime collapsed.

The next day, Erich hired a butler and housekeeper. He put them in charge of hiring the rest of the staff. The servants' quarters were in a separate building a short walk through the woods behind the main house. Because of the design of the house, Wolf needed fewer servants than his father had employed.

When the house was properly staffed, Erich moved in. He felt he now needed a proper automobile. The Mercedes 170 v was adequate transportation, but the grand house called for a finer mode of transportation for its owner. Rolls Royce was making cars again, as was General Motors in America. He liked the looks of the Cadillac. He would decide in due time.

With his wealth in a country so devastated, Erich was inundated with people who wanted him to invest in their business ventures. He dismissed most out of hand. So far he had not found the right venture to back.

About two weeks after moving into his new house, Erich had an encounter that would directly affect his future. He was driving from his home to the center of town for lunch when he saw a car with a flat tire parked at the side of the road. It was an old battered Opel similar to the one he had when first released by the Americans. Standing beside the car looking frustrated, was an extraordinarily beautiful woman. She was tall and slim and bareheaded. Wisps of her blonde hair were being blown about by the breeze. Erich skidded to a stop, got out of his car and approached her. She had wide-set blue eyes, a perfect nose, and full lips. The woman was wearing a raincoat tied at the waist.

When she saw Erich come near, she smiled. Her face lit up with animation and dimples formed on her cheeks. Erich was enchanted. He felt a stirring in his loins. He smiled back. Up close he could see that she wasn't a girl but a woman in her mid-thirties. He was extremely attracted to her. He told himself he had to have this woman.

"May I be of assistance?" he asked gallantly.

"Oh yes, please. My stupid car has a flat tire. I would try to change it but I don't know how," she replied. Her voice was husky and very sexy.

"I will be honored to take you to a garage where we will find someone to take care of this problem. Let me introduce myself. I am Erich Wolf." He extended his hand. He was putting on all the charm he could muster.

The woman took his hand and they shook.

"I am Mina Schuster, and I would appreciate your assistance." Her smile widened. Wolf liked the way Mina looked him straight in the eye without any coyness.

Erich escorted her to his car and held the door for her to enter. On the way to the nearest garage, they talked about the weather and made other small talk. The garage attendant said that he could go and get the car, change the tire and have it ready at the garage in one hour.

Erich invited Mina to lunch and she accepted without any hesitation. He took her to the Festival restaurant, which had finally cleared out the displaced persons and reopened. It was a pleasant place with crisp white tablecloths and polite male waiters. They sat at a little table in the back. What was intended as a quick lunch turned into a two-hour meal.

Mina told Erich about herself. She was the widow of a Wehrmacht Hauptmann who was killed on the eastern front in 1944. They had no children. Before the war, she and her husband lived in the little village of Hanstedt, south of Hamberg, in northern Germany. It was a pleasant life. A Jewish family lived just down the way. Mina would nod and greet them on the street.

When the Nazis came to power, she and her husband were caught up in the patriotic fervor that swept the country. They believed that Hitler was a great leader who would lead Germany to greatness. In mid-1937 she began to have second thoughts. One day a truck with black-uniformed SS men pulled up in front of the home of the Jewish family. The SS dragged the whole family into the street and proceeded to beat them, even the children. Mina saw the elderly patriarch of the family dragged by his beard and thrown in the back of the truck with the rest of his family. She never saw them again.

When the war started, Mina's husband Albrecht fought first in France and then on the eastern front when Hitler attacked the Soviet Union. He came home on leave in November 1943 a disillusioned man. Albrecht told Mina about the atrocities he had witnessed by the SS and the regular German military against unarmed and defenseless Jews, Gypsies and ordinary Ukrainians. Waving goodbye to her at the train station when he returned to his unit was the last time she had seen him.

When the war ended and details started to surface about the scale of mass murder perpetrated by the SS, she had felt a deep shame. Mina felt that German honor would be stained for a hundred years by what the Nazis had done.

As she spoke, Erich began to fidget in his seat and look uncomfortable.

"My family is well off so I didn't need to work to support myself. I decided that I had to do something as personal atonement for not objecting publicly to what had been going on. I heard that UNRRA was accepting German women volunteers for their displaced persons camp system. I signed up and was sent to the UNRRA camp for displaced Ukrainians outside Bayreuth. Then one day I had a flat tire and a handsome gentleman gave me assistance and invited me to lunch. Alright, enough about me. Who are you?"

Erich told her about his early life growing up in Bayreuth, about his service in World War One and his Iron Cross medal. Mina seemed impressed with that. Erich told her about his becoming a lawyer and then he arrived at the tricky part.

"I, too, was taken in by the Nazis. I joined the party early and joined the SS in 1932."

When Erich said this, a coldness came into Mina's eyes and she began to gather her things to leave. He was desperate. He searched around for something to say that would mollify her. He placed his hand on top of hers, looked into her eyes and lied.

"Mina, look at me. I promise you that I had no hand in any atrocities. I am an honorable man. During the war, I served in the Waffen SS on the western front. All my battles were against armed soldiers in honorable combat."

Mina searched his face, looking to see if he was sincere. Erich gave nothing away; he was a good liar. Finally, she seemed to make a decision and spoke.

"Promise me that you had no hand in killing Jews."

"You have my word," said Erich, with as much feeling as he could summon.

"Alright," she said to him and smiled.

A week later, Erich picked Mina up at the DP camp and brought her to his home for dinner. She was very impressed with the house. She was dressed in a long, blue, flowing dress that emphasized her figure. Erich could see the impression of her nipples on the thin fabric and it drove him wild with desire.

After dinner they sat on one of the sofas in the great room before a roaring fire. Erich felt he had never met a woman such as this. He had slept with hundreds, maybe thousands, of women but never met one before that he liked to talk to. She was intelligent and had a good sense of humor. She also exuded sexuality.

Erich could stand it no longer. He slid over to Mina, took her in his arms and kissed her passionately. She responded. He put his hand on one of her breasts and gripped the nipple between his thumb and forefinger.

Mina stiffened and pulled away. She broke his grasp and stood.

"I am a virtuous woman. If you think I will just hop into bed with you, you are mistaken. Please take me back to the camp."

Erich was taken aback. He wasn't used to women resisting his advances. It made Mina all the more desirable to him. He groveled and apologized profusely. After a while, she relented and smiled but there was no more kissing.

Three months later they were married in a civil ceremony in Bayreuth.

CHAPTER THIRTY-NINE

KIBBUTZ STAR OF ZION
GALILEE REGION
STATE OF ISRAEL
19 MAY 1948

Sweat streamed off Adrien's bare back as he swung the pick into the rocky ground. Four other members of the kibbutz worked with him extending a defensive trench. Two other kibbutzniks, with rifles at the ready, stood guard over them a little distance away. The sun was blazing hot and Adrien cursed the kibbutz, the new Israeli government, the Arabs and the British. What a fool he had been to come to Palestine.

Across the fields, three kilometers away, Iraqi irregulars camped, preparing another attack on the settlement. Elsewhere, seven Arab armies were attacking the new country. Adrien looked over to where their defensive arms were stacked. His rifle was Czech on the Mauser pattern similar to the one he had had as a partisan. In addition to the rifle, Adrien had an ancient Webley pistol that dated from World War One. The Iraqi forces had airplanes and armored cars as well as infantry. How were the Jews expected to win against these odds? The kibbutz had been under sporadic attack for four days.

Even before the war had started with the Arabs, Adrien had hated the kibbutz. There was constant, back-breaking work in the hot sun with no reward at the end of the day except a bowl of beans and coarse bread. He decided he wasn't cut out for farm labor. But he had no choice. This was where the Jewish Agency had assigned him. He had nowhere else to go.

§

When he and Aleska had arrived in Haifa, the British authorities had issued them residence papers and passed them through a gate. They were met by Jewish Agency officials and directed to a line of trucks. A man with a clipboard told Adrien and Aleska to board a particular truck. Climbing aboard, they were scarcely seated before the vehicle began to roll, accompanied by two others.

They traveled east. Adrien wasn't impressed by Palestine. Haifa wasn't so bad but when they got out into the countryside they passed mud-brick huts with people living in obvious poverty. There were no trees and everything was brown. Was this the fabled land of Palestine? Why in the world were people fighting over this?

The trucks entered the good sized Arab town of Nazareth. As they passed an Arab coffee shop, a group of deeply tanned men wearing white flowing robes came out shaking their fists and throwing rocks at the vehicles.

Another hour on the dusty, bumpy roads brought them to their destination. It was a group of low buildings made out of brick with tin roofs, the home to four hundred plus people. Adrien looked around at the surrounding country. They were in a wide valley with the green of cultivated fields stretching away about a kilometer or so. At least it was greener here.

They drove through a gate in a barbed wire fence guarded by a sandbagged machine gun position and stopped in a dusty courtyard. Adrien and Aleska jumped down from the truck and joined a group of about twenty others from the three trucks. A tall balding man in his thirties, wearing sandals, blue shorts and a white open-collared shirt, came to greet them. He spoke to them in German.

"I am Dov Rosenbloom, the director here. Welcome to Kibbutz Star of Zion. We are a self-sufficient community. Everything we eat, we grow right here. You will all be assigned jobs in due course. Those who don't work don't eat. If you say you are too sick to work, a doctor will examine you. His decision will be final."

"Married people will be assigned cubicles. Single people will live together in barracks.

We all eat in the dining hall in shifts. We cannot accommodate special diets. We try to keep kosher as much as we can but we are not strict."

"A word about security. The Arabs in the surrounding countryside hate us. Do not leave the kibbutz for any reason without armed guards." Rosenbloom pointed to the east. "Trans-Jordan is only a few kilometers away across the Jordan river. Do not attempt to cross the river. The British have a Tagert fort a few kilometers away and are supposed to protect us. The commander, however, is an anti-Semite and does very little."

Adrien and Aleska were assigned to barracks. Aleska would have none of it. She could not bear sleeping in a different place than Adrien. Every night she would sneak out of the female barracks and be found in the morning curled up under Adrien's bunk. Finally, Dov Rosenbloom threw up his hands and gave up. With a wry smile, he assigned the two teenagers a small room meant for married couples just as the authorities in the displaced persons camp had.

Adrien was sent to work in the fields. Daily he would trudge off at dawn and spend his days hoeing crops, baling hay and doing other farm work. He hated every minute of it. He would come back in the evenings so tired he barely had the strength to eat before falling on his cot.

Aleska, by contrast, loved her job. She was assigned to work with other women taking care of and milking the kibbutz's cows and goats. She was still very reserved around people, rarely speaking, and went around with her eyes downcast. With her cows and goats, she was a different person. She talked kindly to them and gave each of them Polish names. As a result, the animals took to her. It was amusing to watch as she walked around the animal pens with two cows and a herd of goats following her everywhere she went.

Every few weeks a lookout would sound an alarm and the kibbutzniks would scurry around hiding their defensive arms. A British raiding party would come roaring into the kibbutz in jeeps and conduct a search for illegal weapons. The guns were hidden well and they never found any. Sometimes the commander of the local Tegart fort, Captain Nicholson, would accompany the soldiers. He made it very clear by his attitude and demeanor that he despised Jews.

Aleska was fifteen now. She had matured into a real beauty. The young men of the Kibbutz swarmed around her like flies but she would just lower her eyes and ignore them.

Aleska's beauty was causing a problem for Adrien. The room they shared was tiny. It had barely enough room for their bunks. During most of the year, the atmosphere at night was stifling, causing them to pant with the heat. Aleska would shed her clothing and lie on her bunk naked. Occasionally she would get up to get water from the flask in the corner. She had the body of a grown woman, and a very attractive one at that.

Adrien, in the other bunk, would look at her nude body and his own would respond. He would try to suppress the feeling but it was hopeless. He chided himself. What right did he have to be thinking those thoughts about Aleska? She deserved better than him. He had let his whole family be murdered in front of his eyes and done nothing about it. Usually, Adrien would turn toward the wall and discreetly do what every teenaged boy does to relieve the pressure.

Almost two years on the kibbutz had changed Adrien too. He was nineteen now and he had grown another five centimeters. The hard farm work had built up and hardened his muscles. The sun had turned his body a deep bronze which contrasted nicely with his blonde hair and blue eyes. The young girls at the settlement noticed. Adrien ignored them. In fact, he ignored most of the men too. He was known as a surly loner and after a while, the other men gave him a wide berth.

During his two years on the kibbutz, Adrien made a mighty effort to educate himself. When he wasn't too tired after work, he scoured the kibbutz library reading all he could about history, contemporary thought, geography, and politics. He also discovered the bible. He read it three times and gained insight about his Jewish heritage. He would have read the New Testament too, but the kibbutz didn't have a copy.

Likewise, Aleska got herself educated. She had never attended school and could neither read nor write in any language. She started at the beginning. She got permission to attend the afternoon classes given for the small children. She soaked up the instruction like a sponge. Aleska learned to read and write in Hebrew and English in the space of about six months. She also learned about history and geography and a little politics. The teachers saw how eager she was to learn and put in extra effort to help her.

Adrien's work crew consisted of castoffs from other crews. Difficult people that the other workers didn't want to be around were thrown together in the crew. The kibbutz administrators called it the "leper colony." It was just fine with Adrien; he didn't want to get chummy with anyone anyway. Another member of his work crew, Carl Greenspan, had just the opposite problem. He was put in the leper colony because he never shut up. He had been an international banker in Vienna before the Nazis and he regaled the others in excruciating detail on arcane banking rules of various countries, how banks influenced politics and how they shifted money around between them. Adrien didn't know it at the time but the information would be very useful to him in the future.

The kibbutz routine changed abruptly on 14 May 1948. That day David Ben Gurian declared the establishment of the State of Israel. The surrounding Arab populations responded with rage. Seven Arab armies began preparations to invade Israel and drive the Jews into the sea.

The settlement went on a defensive footing. All farming ceased. Everyone worked tirelessly to build up the settlement's defenses. No one in the kibbutz was a military man. When fortifying the kibbutz, they neglected to secure a low ridge four hundred meters outside the gates of the settlement. They didn't realize that someone on that ridge could shoot directly down into the kibbutz.

On 15 May, a soldier, Mordechai Asher, arrived with twenty Haganah soldiers. The Haganah had been the Jewish underground army while the British ruled Palestine. It was now the nucleus of the new Israeli army. Asher was a tight-lipped, red-faced man who didn't suffer fools gladly. In addition to rifles and Sten guns, he and his men brought with them two British Vickers .303 caliber machine guns and a 1930 vintage Italian anti-tank gun with seven shells.

On 15 May the Iraqis attacked with infantry and two armored cars. They ran into a wall of fire from the Jews. Adrien had been in a trench firing his Czech rifle, He didn't know if he hit anybody. He was a lousy shot with a rifle. When the Iraqis retreated, one of their armored cars was left on fire and Arab bodies littered the landscape. They came again daily after that but with much more tepid attacks.

The Iraqis then settled in for a siege. They placed a group of snipers on the low ridge near the settlement and began a harassing fire into the kibbutz. Few of the kibbutzniks were hit. Unfortunately for the Iraqis, one of those who was wounded was Aleska Pisarski.

§

Adrien returned to his room after digging the trench, about two hours before dark. He could hear rifle fire in the distance but none of the bullets came near him. He was just closing his door when the woman from the neighboring room called to him and said that Aleska had been wounded and was in the infirmary. Adrien went white and ran as fast as he could across the courtyard.

Aleska was on a cot with a bandaged arm in a state of panic. When she saw Adrien, she tried to rise but was restrained by Dr. Rosen who was treating her. Adrien sat down on the cot beside her and she hugged him fiercely and sobbed. Adrien talked to her soothingly and her sobs subsided.

Dr. Rosen said he had given Aleska a sedative and it would take effect at any time. She stopped crying and her eyes became droopy. A minute later, Adrien lay her back on the cot. She was asleep.

"It is a clean flesh wound to her right arm. She will recover fully. There is nothing to worry about," said Rosen. Then the doctor saw the look in Adrien's eyes and was taken aback. The young man's eyes were lit by a cold rage.

Adrien got up and left the infirmary. He strolled through the kitchen and emerged with a razor-sharp kitchen knife under his shirt. He walked to the perimeter trench closest to the ridge, sat down beside the on-duty guards, and waited for dark.

§

Mustafa Ben Aden worked the bolt of his Mauser rifle and rammed a fresh cartridge into the breach. He pointed the rifle in the general direction of the Jewish settlement and jerked the trigger. He was getting the hang of it now. Today was the first time he had fired his rifle and he had been surprised by the recoil when he first shot it. Mustafa pulled back the bolt and fed a fresh clip of cartridges into the magazine.

He was finally fighting the hated Jews. He imagined every one of his bullets striking a Jew and leaving him in a pool of blood. All the walking from his Iraqi village had been worth it. Soon they would overrun the settlement. Mustafa thought of the young Jewish women he would rape and the Jewish gold he would take. He would return home a hero to his village of Haqlaniyah.

Mustafa was a twenty-year-old farmer's son. All his life he had toiled in his father's field beside the Euphrates River. His younger brother worked with him while the eldest son and his father sat in a coffee house in Haditha. He was resentful of his brother and father.

So it was a welcome relief when Captain Hussein came to Haditha and summoned all young men from miles around for a jihad. Captain Hussein was clad in a splendid uniform with shiny brass buttons and military medals adorning the breast. The group of young men waited breathlessly for him to speak.

"Brothers, the detestable Jews have had the nerve to establish a state in Arab Palestine. They have stolen land from your brothers that live there. All Arab Muslims, even the Shia dogs from the south, have pledged armies to go to Palestine and drive the Jews into the sea."

"Come with me brothers. It is your obligation to Islam to wage jihad against the infidels. I promise you young Jewish maidens to ravish and Jewish possessions to plunder. Your tribal leaders have already consented to this jihad."

Mustafa had cheered with the others and signed up. He was given a uniform coat of khaki cloth with brass buttons, a new pair of shoes, and a fine rifle. Captain Hussein announced that they would be part of the Iraqi Liberation Army and henceforth would be called The Lions of Haditha.

Mustafa said goodbye to his family and the Lions, about a hundred strong, set out on foot for Palestine. After two days of walking, Mustafa's new shoes wore blisters on his feet. He threw them away and donned his sandals which were much better for walking. That night Captain Hussein was very angry with him and threatened to have him shot. Mustafa groveled at the officer's feet and Hussein spared him.

At last, trail weary and footsore, the Lions had arrived in Palestine. Uniting with other units of the Iraqi Liberation Army, they had marched into the Bet Shean Valley and attacked the Jewish settlement of Star of Zion. Mustafa learned that it was going to be tougher to conquer the Jews than originally thought. During the first attack, many of his fellow lions had died. He liked the present tactic of sniping much better.

It was getting dark and Captain Hussein came to the top of the ridge and told them to cease firing. He posted sentries and warned them to stay awake. The bulk of the Lions then went to their camp on the reverse slope of the ridge. After a dinner of flatbread and tea, Mustafa went to sleep under his thin blanket.

He was awaked at dawn by shouts in the camp. An early riser had gotten up and was searching for water to make tea when he discovered the body of one of their sentries. Mustafa joined the group of fellow Lions around the body. The man had not just had his throat cut, but it looked as if the whole front of his neck had been ripped out. Mustafa could see the white bones of his spine. Flies crawled on the wound and the blood had turned black.

One of the other Lions speculated that Jinn had done this. While they were talking, there were other shouts and word flew through the camp that five of the seven sentries had their throats ripped out in similar fashion. One young peasant said that at midnight he had looked up from his blanket and saw the unearthly image of a Jinn flying through the air.

The whole bunch of them were close to panic when Captain Hussein stepped in. "It was not Jinn, you illiterate fools. It was the Jews who did this. The sentries fell asleep and the filthy Jews murdered them. It will not happen again. Tonight we will be ready for them."

The Lions fired at the settlement all day. As dark approached, Captain Hussein personally posted sentries in pairs, to keep each other awake. He doubled the number of sentry posts and gave orders to shoot at anything that moved. He ordered fires to be lit and men to feed them, to illuminate the camp all night. He then retired to his tent, the only one in the camp. Mustafa had a hard time getting to sleep. A little after midnight he finally dropped off.

He was awakened for a second day by shouts. A crowd had gathered at the flap of Captain Hussein's tent. Mustafa wriggled forward through the crowd. The sight inside the tent horrified him. Captain Hussein was on his cot. His throat was slashed and his privates had been cut off and stuffed in his mouth.

Mustafa had had enough. He didn't want any part of conquering Palestine now. A man could not fight jinn. He backed away from the tent and started walking east toward home. He left his rifle and bedroll behind. As he walked, he shed his uniform coat and threw it to the side of the road. In twos and threes, with averted eyes and frightened looks, the rest of the Lions of Haditha followed him. After a while, it was silent on the ridge. The only sound to be heard was the buzzing of the flies feeding on Captain Hussein's corpse.

§

Mordechai Asher was checking the perimeter lines before dawn when he saw movement in front of him. He drew his pistol and challenged a shadowy figure. Adrien Weiss stopped walking. Mordechai flipped on his torch. Adrien was covered in blood and was holding a bloody knife.

"What the hell were you doing out there?" he asked he asked the bloody apparition.

Adrien dropped the knife at his feet.

"Go to the top of the ridge and see," he said, and walked away.

By nine a.m. there had been no shooting from the ridge. Asher sent ten of his toughest Haganah boys to the top of the ridge. They came back thirty minutes later and the patrol leader made his report. The Iraqi camp was deserted. Articles of equipment were strewn about, including about a hundred rifles and thirty crates of ammunition. There were also six dead bodies with their throats cut. One had his dick and balls cut off and stuffed in his mouth.

Asher sent a detail to retrieve the rifles and then went to the Kibbutz administration building. He entered the director's office and shut the door. He picked up the telephone and was surprised to get a dial tone. The wires hadn't been cut yet. Mordechai dialed a number in Tel Aviv. When the person answered he spoke.

"Gideon, this is Mordechai. Remember you told me to keep an eye out for people who would be of use to your group? Well, I think I have a candidate for you."

§

By 22 May, the Iraqis had withdrawn and life started to return to normal in the settlement. Aleska was on the mend but would wear a scar the rest of her life. She was glad to get back to her cows and goats. Adrien went back to the fields.

That day Adrien was called to the director's office. Upon arrival he was ushered into an office. Sitting behind the desk was a stranger. He was short, fat and bald and had a cigar between his lips. He was wearing the ubiquitous white open-collared shirt.

"Weiss, my name is Gideon Green. I run an organization out of the foreign ministry. We deal with enemies of Israel who operate overseas. I was wondering if you would be interested in a job. It would get you out of this dump and we will provide you with an apartment in Tel Aviv."

"Doing what?" asked Adrien.

"Israel has a lot of enemies. They stir up trouble for Jews in foreign countries. My organization neutralizes them."

"Do you mean you kill them?"

Gideon paused for a moment then nodded.

"Why not," said Adrien Weiss and smiled.

Green involuntarily shuddered. He held Adrian's gaze. The boy had the hardest eyes he had ever seen.

CHAPTER FORTY

DR. WURZBERGERSTRASSE 12
BAYREUTH, DEUTSCHLAND
12 AUGUST 1953

Her name was Adalie, but no one usually called her that unless she had done something particularly naughty. She was, "Addie," and at four-and-a-half years old was spoiled rotten. Erich Wolf at fifty-four years old was thoroughly enjoying fatherhood. Addie, with her big blue eyes and doll's lips, knew the expressions and gestures to use to manipulate her father into doing what she wanted, resulting in her nursery being piled high with toys.

For as young as she was, Addie was also a remarkable clothes horse. Her closet was stuffed with frilly dresses and dainty shoes. She didn't like to wear the same outfit twice and her millionaire father made sure she didn't have to.

This evening Addie was cross. Her parents were taking her to the opera. Her mother said it was to teach her culture, whatever that was. She had decided last year that she didn't like opera. The loud screeching and crashing music scared her and she couldn't get up to go pee when she wanted to. Also, she couldn't take Max along.

Max was a Giant Schnauzer who thought Addie smelled better than anyone else in the world. He was constantly at her side, allowing himself to be dressed in frilly bonnets and to be ridden like a horse.

Addie announced to her mother that she didn't want to go to the opera. Her mother, who wasn't the pushover that her father was, said that was just too bad, they were going. So, Addie punished her parents by sulking the whole evening.

§

In his dressing room in the master wing of the house, Erich Wolf finished tying his bow tie and preened in the full-length mirror. Not bad for fifty-four, he told himself. His formal attire was custom made to fit his frame and showed him off to advantage. His once abundant hair was now balding on the top and solid grey at the temples. Erich thought it gave him a distinguished look.

Mina walked into the room and came up behind him.

"Admiring yourself? Let me assure you darling that you look good enough to eat." She reached up and kissed him on the ear.

Wolf looked at his wife in the mirror. She was dressed in a full-length satin gown that clung to her and emphasized her still curvy figure. Her hair was shot through with grey, which she refused to dye. (Ach, such foolishness). Her beautiful face was still unlined and Erich felt a surge of desire for her. His physical attraction for her had not diminished in the five-plus years of their marriage. From the twinkle in her eye, he surmised that it was the same for her.

There wasn't a day that went by that Erich didn't thank whatever god was up there for meeting Mina. He was also thankful for the beautiful little girl that Mina gave him. But he was more thankful for the way his wife had changed the way he looked at the world.

In the early days of the marriage, they had many spirited discussions about the Jews. Erich would spew out his enmity and repeat some of the ancient accusations against them. Just as emphatically, Mina would respond.

"The Jews are just people. There are good and bad people Erich, but no good and bad races." She would then recite examples of Jewish philanthropy and great Jewish composers and scientists. Gradually her logic brought Erich around.

In one of their discussions, He had told her about Herschel Stein and his humiliation when he was nine. Mina had laughed, which made him angry. She looked in his eyes.

'Erich, you were both little boys playing at being Indians. Do you really think that a nine-year-old boy was capable of hatching a scheme to humiliate you for no reason? He just liked you and you shared an interest in the American West."

He was angry with her for days until he decided to look at it objectively and realized that she was right. All his old prejudices gradually toppled one by one. With this change came a huge weight of guilt about his part in the "final solution."

He tried to assuage his guilt by donations to Jewish causes, including underwriting most of the cost of an orphanage in Israel. He went from right to center-left in his politics, joining the Liberal Democratic Party. All this helped a little, but his conscience still bothered him. He was at that time still keeping what he had actually done in the SS a secret from Mina. This festering boil came to a head just before Addie's third birthday.

His daughter approached him when he came home from an errand. She stood at his feet and looked up at him and opened her mouth to speak. Erich had a sudden flashback to the little girl he had shot on the train platform at Sobibor. A vivid image of her small trusting face flashed onto his brain. He watched the bullet enter her mouth. Wolf felt faint and staggered back, overturning a table and lamp beside the door. Addie began to scream and Mina had come running.

Erich fell to his knees, put his arms around Mina's waist and sobbed. His wife stroked his head and kept asking what was wrong. After a while, Erich stood and led Mina by the hand to the sitting room in the master wing. He sat her down and told her everything he had done in the SS. He kept back nothing.

Mina didn't say anything for a long time. Erich sat on the sofa with his head in his hands. Finally, she spoke.

"It is a hard thing to find out that your husband, the man you make love to, was at one time an unspeakable monster. Erich, I forgive you for lying to me; that is of little consequence. But the things you did in the SS have to be atoned for. You must dedicate the rest of your life to helping people. You have a huge fortune. Use it for the betterment of mankind."

"As for me, I still love you. You are not the same man who did those terrible things. The way you have acted today proves it. I guess every man deserves a second chance."

Mina came and sat beside him and put her arms around him. The two had cried together.

Erich carried through on Mina's advice. He committed half his fortune, which was considerable, (having heavily invested in Volkswagen in 1949) and established a charitable foundation. The Adalie Wolf Foundation contributed to causes around the globe, from American civil rights organizations and helping southern Negros, to orphans in Brazil.

He also began to speak out and say that Germany needed to atone for its Nazi past and became a German champion of the State of Israel. Neither of these sentiments was popular in Bavaria in the early 1950s and Erich was invited to many fewer cocktail parties than before because of them.

erich went out to the garage to get the Cadillac. He didn't have a chauffeur anymore. He thought it was too presumptuous and besides he liked to drive. The Wolf family drove to the Festival Opera House and watched "Lohengrin," an opera by Richard Wagner first performed in 1850.

It was a ridiculous story about a stranger coming to the rescue of a damsel in distress in a boat pulled by swans. He would only consent to save the maiden if she didn't ask his name. Erich had grown up with the story and it was one of his favorite operas. The only one who did not enjoy the performance was Addie. She wet her pants halfway through the performance.

CHAPTER
FORTY-ONE

HELIOPOLIS AIRPORT
CAIRO EGYPT
23 MARCH 1955

The Egyptian customs official took the American passport from the young blonde man's hand and examined it.

"Timothy Miller is it? What is the purpose of your visit to Egypt?

"I am a graduate student at the University of Maryland studying archeology. I am here to examine some exhibits in the Cairo Museum related to my studies."

The inspector noted that the young man was not nervous and his blue eyes made eye contact. His clothing was what one would expect from a student, tan slacks and brown long sleeved shirt. The American was carrying a battered canvas covered suitcase.

"How long will you be staying."

"About a week. I don't have money for more." Miller smiled

when he said this.

The customs officer sighed. When solitary tourists from say, Denmark or Sweden arrived at the Heliopolis airport, the officials sometimes found a "discrepancy" in their papers and locked them in a room for two hours. By the time the officials returned to collect them, the tourists would be wild-eyed and desperate enough to pay a "special fee," before being allowed to proceed.

The customs officers, however, had orders not to harass Americans or Russians. These two countries didn't take kindly to anyone messing with their citizens. The Americans and the Russians were very powerful, and there was nothing the Arab mind respected more than power. Also, the American CIA and the Russian KGB were particularly nasty and vengeful when one of their agents was harassed, and one never knew which tourists were agents and which were not.

"Welcome to Egypt. Have a pleasant stay," said the official and handed back Miller's passport. Tim walked down the concourse, through the airport lobby and outside to the taxi stand. He entered the taxi at the head of the line and asked in English to be taken to the Benghazi Hotel.

The cab ride was harrowing. There seemed to be no traffic laws in Cairo. Miller's driver dodged in and out of traffic while blowing his horn and shouting at other drivers. It was enough to scare most Americans to death. They were used to orderly traffic flow back in the States.

Adrien Weiss sat back in the rear seat totally relaxed. During the wild cab ride, his heartbeat never topped sixty beats a minute. Though he was an Israeli agent in the middle of a hostile Arab capital, he didn't worry. He was carrying no weapons. His passport would pass every test because it was genuine. Adrien had applied for it himself in Dayton, Ohio, five years ago.

The Benghazi Hotel was a medium to budget priced tourist hotel that fit Adrien's cover. He dare not stay at the Windsor or the Mena lest someone in Egyptian Intelligence become suspicious. His room was small with a high ceiling and a motorized fan that ran lazily, not stirring up much air. The bed was lumpy and the towels were thin.

Timothy Miller had dinner at the hotel that night and visited the bar for a drink afterward. He went to bed early, tired from his journey.

§

Later that night in the hotel bar, the bartender opened the freezer to get ice to make a drink for a German tourist. He looked for his icepick to chip ice off the block inside but couldn't find it. He got down on his knees and looked under the freezer, but it wasn't there. The bartender was angry now. He called to his assistant barman and raged at him in Arabic. The assistant rushed to the storeroom to get a replacement icepick.

§

Adrien rose at seven ready to go to work. His target was a member of the Muslim Brotherhood named Hassan al-Aria. It had come to the attention of the Israeli Secret Service that al-Aria was recruiting young Egyptians as Fedayeen terrorists to attack Israeli settlements. One group al-Aria recruited had caught a young Jewish mother and her baby who had strayed too far from her kibbutz. She was found the next day. She had been gang-raped and her head was cut off as well as that of her baby. Al-Aria was also raising funds from wealthy Arabs to support the Muslim Brotherhood cause. Tel

Aviv had decided that he must be removed from the land of the living and they sent Adrien.

This was his fifth such assignment, about one a year. The other four had been concluded successfully. He was getting quite a reputation within his branch of the secretive organization. He specialized in killing effectively but making it look like an accident or natural causes and his superiors were very pleased with him.

§

The day after he had spoken to Gideon Green (Adrien learned later that that wasn't his real name) a car had arrived at the Kibbutz and taken him and Aleska to Tel Aviv. The driver was a tight-lipped man in his thirties who was silent most of the way. Adrien noticed two loaded Sten guns in the rear seat. He asked the driver about them and he replied that the war situation was fluid and they might encounter hostile Arabs.

The car stopped in front of a five-story apartment building on Shtand St. in Tel Aviv. The driver helped them carry their meager belongings to an apartment on the third floor. He handed Adrien a key and started to leave. Adrien stopped him.

"What happens next?" he asked the driver.

"This is your new home. The kitchen has been stocked with food. Get some rest. You are going to need it. Someone will come and get you at eight tomorrow morning. Beyond that, you don't need to know anything else. Good night."

After the driver had gone Adrien and Aleska toured their new apartment. It consisted of a large room about seven meters square with French doors leading to a shallow balcony. Weiss saw the blue of the sea in a gap between two other buildings across the street. The furniture wasn't new but looked comfortable. There was a tiny bathroom with a shower bath but no tub and a small bedroom with twin beds. The kitchen was smaller yet, barely an alcove.

Neither one of them had learned how to cook on a stove. Aleska fumbled around in the kitchen and managed to open a can of pea soup and warm it up in a saucepan over the gas burner. They ate in silence. Aleska seemed sad. Adrien asked what was wrong. She replied that she missed her animals. Weiss told her that he could arrange for her to live back at the kibbutz if she wanted to. A look of panic came into her eyes and she replied, "NO!'" She stopped eating and dropped her spoon into the half-eaten bowl of soup.

The next morning at eight a man, identifying himself as Alex, in a white open-neck shirt with a pistol stuffed in his waistband, came to get Adrien. Before he left with Alex, Adrien tried without success to calm an anxious Aleska who was worried about him leaving. When Adrien looked at her, as he was going out the door, she was wringing her hands. Adrien worried about her all day.

As it turned out, he needn't have worried. He was not gone ten minutes when Mrs. Sobieski from next door dropped in to meet the new neighbors. Mrs. Sobieski was also a Polish immigrant. She was a mountain of a woman in her early fifties. Aleska spoke English, German and Hebrew but Polish was her native tongue. When she heard Mrs. Sobieski speak in Polish she was so glad, she began to cry. Mrs. Sobieski, who had had a daughter Aleska's age who had been murdered by the Nazis, enfolded her in her huge arms and adopted her as her replacement daughter on the spot.

Alex drove Adrien across the city to a cluster of government buildings surrounded by barbed wire and sandbags. Adrien could see the snouts of several machine guns poking through openings in the sandbags. After passing a checkpoint at the compound gate, Alex parked and led Weiss into one of the buildings.

Adrien was ushered into a dingy room holding only a table and chairs. Sitting on one side of the table, facing Adrien, were three men. All were wearing the standard Israeli uniform of an open-necked white shirt. They were all in late middle age with hard eyes and tanned skin. They didn't identify themselves but the center man was Gideon Green. Green, apparently the one in charge of the others, invited Adrien to sit with a gesture of his right hand.

"Tell us the story of your life. We want to know everything," said the Israeli.

In as much detail as he could, Weiss told them about Paris, Sobibor, the forest, the trek to the American zone of occupation,and the immigrant ship. The only part he omitted was the words his grandfather had said to him on the Sobibor platform and the money in the Swiss bank. He did this purposefully; it was none of their business.

During his recital, Adrien mentioned his facility with languages. The man on the right, who wore a beard and was stroking it with his hand, interrupted him.

"How many languages do you speak?"

"I am fluent in French, German, Yiddish and Polish. I also speak Hebrew and English but not as well. Learning languages comes very easy for me."

Green cleared his throat and looked first at the man to his right. The man nodded. He then looked to his left and got the same nod of approval. He turned back to Weiss.

"We are prepared to offer you a job. You know what the job entails from our previous conversation. This will be your chance to show your patriotism and devotion to protecting the Jewish people. We are..."

Adrien held up his hand and stopped Green, who looked annoyed. Adrien coolly looked him in the eye.

"I am not doing this out of devotion to the Jewish people. Being a Jew has been a curse for me. It got my whole family murdered. I hold no special loyalty to Israel. I will do your dirty work for you because if the Arabs overrun Israel, Aleska will die. She is the only human being living on the face of the earth that I care about. I have some skills that you need. Let's just say that our relationship will be one of business. I expect enough of a salary to live a decent life in Tel Aviv. If you are worried that I will betray you for money or ideology, don't be. I don't love money like some and I have no ideology. So, that is my proposition. Take it or leave it."

Green was annoyed. Adrien had taken charge of the interview. Instead of Adrien getting their approval, he was testing them. He didn't like to take insolence from a kid like this. Still, he thought about the dead Arabs on the ridge and was intrigued. If he was as good as he suspected, they needed this boy.

"In the next several months you will be tested and your skills honed with specialized training. As to salary, I would offer this." He wrote a figure on a piece of paper and slid it over the table to Adrien, who looked at it and nodded.

During the next six months as the Israeli War of Independence raged on, Adrien trained. He spent hours with a linguist working on his English. Soon he could speak the language fluently with two accents. One was the British public school upper-class accent. The second was the flat vowels of the American midwest.

He also spent much time with a man named Jocko Clarke. Clarke had served in World War Two as a close combat instructor for the British Special Operations Executive. He had been a sergeant in the Royal Marines and was stationed in Palestine after the war. He had met and married a Jewish woman and stayed in Israel after the British left. He was an expert in unarmed combat, knife fighting, and pistol marksmanship.

On the day of their first training session, Jocko took Adrien down to the seashore. In the midst of some sand dunes he stopped and handed Adrien a Sykes-Fairburn commando dagger. It was a long thin stiletto with a double-edged blade.

"Alright, boy, stab me. Don't hold back. Try to kill me."

Adrien thought back to the lessons he had learned from Tovia in the forest. He went into a couch with the knife held in front of him with his thumb at the balance point of the blade. He circled Jocko. The Englishman seemed overconfident. Adrien darted in and feinted with the blade and immediately pulled it back. At the same time, he swept his left hand up towards Jocko's right shoulder as if to grab it. When he saw Jocko's eyes follow his left hand, he drove forward with the knife aiming for the gut. An instant before the knife would plunge into Jocko's midsection, Adrien felt an iron grip on his wrist and the instructor shoved him back, with a look of surprise on his face.

"You almost skewered me there boyo. Who taught you how to fight with a knife?"

"A Jewish partisan named Tovia in the Parczew forest in Poland."

"Well, your partisan friend was a shit good teacher. I still might be able to teach you a thing or two. From now on though, we will practice with the sheath on the knife."

Jocko was true to his word. He did teach Adrien some things with a knife. He also taught him about unarmed combat and pistol shooting. Jocko favored small pistols chambered for the .22 Long Rifle cartridge. While not as powerful as the larger calibers, the .22 had the advantage of less recoil leading to a faster second shot. It was also less noisy and therefore needed less bulky suppressers. Jocko taught the double tap method-- Two shots fired in quick succession to the head. Adrien spent many hours on a pistol range pumping the tiny bullets into paper targets. Pistol marksmanship is best learned by repetition. The more practice, the better the skill. With all the practice, Adrien became very good.

In unarmed combat, however, Adrien was a naïf. He had no experience. He hadn't needed it before. Only a foolish partisan would take on a German in a Polish forest without a weapon in his hands. Upon hearing this, Clarke had only shrugged.

"I could take a year and make you into a bonny boxer or judo killer but we don't have a year. So, we'll keep it simple."

Clarke led him to a crude, upright wood frame in the shape of a rectangle. Suspended in the frame was a rough approximation of a human body made from coils of old canvas firehose. Lengths of postal twine tenuously held the dummy in place. Adrien was amused to see that a crude face had been painted on the dummy's head with a Hitler hairdo and mustache.

"Most people when confronted with a madman rushing toward them intent on violence recoil and tilt their heads back instinctively to protect their face. You are going to use this natural instinct against them. I will demonstrate how on 'Adolf' here."

Jocko exploded into action, running full tilt at the dummy. When he came within arm's length, his right arm shot out and his fist landed squarely with a thud on the slim coil of canvas representing the throat of the enemy. The pieces of twine parted and the dummy fell to the ground with a loud plop. Jocko raised his right boot and brought it down with all his weight onto the dummy's groin. Adrien expected him to stop then but he didn't. Clarke stood beside the upper body of the dummy and gave three swift kicks to the side of its head. When he was done, Clarke turned to face Adrien with his hands on his hips.

"This maneuver depends on exercising immediate, overwhelming violence. If you dawdle and stand around for a bit looking at each other in the eyes like bloody lovers, it won't work. You have to be on him before he recovers from the shock of seeing you."

Jocko sauntered over and stood in front of a suddenly wary Adrien.

"A man facing you has three fatal vulnerabilities. The first is the eyes," said Clarke as he used the index and third fingers of his left hand to mimic poking out Adrien's eyes. "The second is the front of the throat. A hard blow here will crush his larynx and shut off his air, rendering him helpless." Clarke then rapped Adrien's groin with the back of His right hand causing Adrien to flinch away. "The third vulnerability is the gonads. A good kick in the 'jewels' and all the fight will leave the bugger. But, remember, everything depends on speed and overwhelming force. So, to recap, you put the bastard down by crushing his larynx and balls and then kill him with kicks to the head."

"What if there is more than one opponent? asked Adrien.

"Then use your fookin' knife or gun, and if you've forgotten to bring them to the parade, you deserve to die. Now help me string up 'Adolf' again and you have a try."

Adrien struggled with the heavy dummy. It must have weighed over thirty kilos. His arms began to tremble as he held it up while Jocko retied the twine. When 'Adolf' was once again strung up, Clarke told Adrien to have a go at him.

Adrien ran at the dummy as fast as he could and aimed a blow at the throat. His fist connected with the canvas and Weiss felt a jolt of pain from his hand and up his arm. The blow was much weaker than Clarke's and 'Adolf' teetered a moment before falling. Adrien snapped his foot down toward the dummy's groin but didn't hit it square. His shoe slid off the slippery canvas and he almost lost his balance. The three kicks to the dummy's head came off more or less without mishap. Adrien looked at Clarke. He was shaking his head from side to side with an expression on his face as if he smelled something rotten.

"That was shitty, if I may say so. From now on you will perform this little exercise ten times first thing every morning. If you don't improve, I will recommend that they send you back to the kibbutz to grow oranges."

In the evenings, Adrien would return to the apartment and Aleska. Mrs. Sobieski was trying to teach Aleska to cook. Some evenings her preparations were edible. On others, they were downright awful. On these occasions, after holding her while she cried, he would steer her to the small café on the corner where they would eat by candlelight.

Aleska seemed happier after the second month in Tel Aviv. She got a job working in an orphanage nursery taking care of small children. The children took to her much as the goats had. She was very animated with them, while still extremely shy around most adults.

There was one problem that caused Adrien some frustration. On weekends in the summer months, they were in the apartment all day together. Aleska would walk around the apartment without a stitch on. Adrien was a healthy young man and Aleska was a healthy young female of prime breeding age. Hormones were working overtime to get the two together. Adrian would grit his teeth and try to suppress his physical attraction. He loved her above everything but soon realized he was starting to love her in a different way, definitely not as a sister. He would condemn himself for this. He thought having sexual relations with her would be a violation of his promise to protect her. He was twenty years old and had never had sex with a woman, but would his first experience be to violate someone he had sworn to protect?

At the end of six months of training, Adrien had honed his killing skills to the point where Jocko pronounced him ready to proceed to the next phase of his preparation for fieldwork. Adrien was called back to the foreign ministry and into Green's private office.

"It is now time for you to start building up your legends." Gideon saw the confused look on Adrien's face. "A legend is a foreign identity. To operate in Arab countries, you can't use an Israeli passport so you have to get passports from foreign nations that the Arabs have relations with. Don't worry, it is usually very simple." Green then on to explain how easy it was.

A week later Adrien and Aleska flew to London carrying Israeli passports in the name of Harvey and Anna Silverman. From London, they took a TWA flight to New York. Then they took a train to Dayton Ohio where Adrien rented a post office box.

From Dayton, they took a local bus south and got off in the small town of Springboro. They chose the town because it was the county seat and the location of the county Hall of Records. They walked around the town until they found a graveyard. Walking through the headstones they found the grave of Timothy Miller. born June 12, 1929. He had died May 23, 1931, just shy of his second birthday. They walked back to the town hall and asked for a copy of Miller's birth certificate. After paying a two-dollar fee, they had the document in their hands. Adrien and Aleska rode a bus back to Dayton where he applied for a Social Security card, driver's license and passport in Miller's name. Adrien asked for the documents to be mailed to the post office box. In a month's time, he would return to the box and collect the documents.

Using the same technique, Adrien obtained another identity in the state of Indiana, two in California, one in England, one in Germany and one in Belgium. In only one place did he run into a snag. In Gary Indiana, a prune-faced clerk at the Motor Vehicles Department asked why he was just getting around to getting a driver's license, at his age. Adrien thought fast and told her in a midwestern twang that his parents were in the Air Force and he had lived abroad most of his life and now he wanted to live in the country of his birth, the best dang country in the world. It was a plausible lie and the clerk shrugged her shoulders and gave him the license.

On 21 October 1949, Adrien and Aleska returned to Israel. Aleska had a wonderful time traveling the world. She particularly liked the United States. The people there were friendly and trusting. Adrien commented that he agreed with her but that those traits would someday get the Americans in a lot of trouble.

§

Hailing a cab in front of the Hotel Benghazi, Adrien gave the driver an address on Port Said Street which was two blocks from Hassan al-Aria's house. Port Said St. bordered the famous Khan el-Khaliti, one of the major souks of Cairo. It was a wide busy road with shops and small cafes lining each side. The area was a major attraction for tourists so Adrien blended right in.

Adrien strolled by the target's house. He stopped to light a cigarette and got a good look at the building. The cigarette was just a prop, he didn't smoke. The house was of two stories with the only entrance that Adrien could see in the front. There was a sign over the door that read: "FRIENDS IN SOLIDARITY WITH PALESTINE" in big red letters, in English and Arabic. Two large Arabs in ill-fitting suits and fez hats guarded the front door. They looked bored and one was leaning against the wall.

Adrien found a sidewalk café with a view of the building, ordered coffee and watched the target's house. At 10:15 am exactly, al-Aria emerged and walked north on Port Said. He was an overweight, apple-cheeked man in a double-breasted suit and an Arab headdress. The two guards left the building and went with him. The target returned at exactly 11:15 and went back into the building and the guards took up their posts outside.

At 6:15 p.m. as the daylight was waning, the target reemerged and again walked north on Port Said, followed by his guards. A young woman wearing a hijab emerged from Al-Arian's home a few minutes later, locked the door and walked south on Port Said. At 8:15 pm the target returned followed by his guards. He unlocked the door with a personal key and went inside. The guards remained outside by the door. At 9:00 p.m. the sentries were replaced by the night shift and the day guards left.

Adrien watched the building for the next three days, not staying in any one spot too long to avoid arousing suspicion. He bought a straw hat and sunglasses. He used these items and changes of clothing to vary his appearance during his surveillance of the target's house. He felt that agents didn't need fake mustaches or makeup. These artificial devices sometimes aroused suspicion and got agents killed. The target's daily routine was the same and varied only by a very few minutes. Hassan al-Aria was a creature of habit.

On the fourth day, Adrien was watching the building waiting for an opportunity to get inside without being seen. At 10:22 a.m. the opportunity came.

Security regimes are hard to maintain. It takes a great deal of training and motivation to maintain vigilance. In the beginning, people are hyper-aware of their surroundings and adhere to the security plan closely. But when nothing happens for a long time, they tend to get sloppy and are not as vigilant. Compromises to the security arrangements are made, for convenience sake.

A few minutes after the target had left for his morning outing, the same young woman in the hijab emerged. She hurried north on Port Said and entered an Arab bakery a half block away. She didn't lock the door when she left. Perhaps she hadn't had time for breakfast and was hungry. Adrien didn't know. By the time she was ten steps from the door, he was moving.

He entered the building through the front door. He saw a large lobby with Anti-Israeli posters and maps, a long counter, and a doorway to the back. Adrien hurried through the doorway and down a hall, checking the rooms he passed, looking for living quarters. He went up a flight of stairs and found the target's bedroom. He quickly looked around. There was an elaborately furnished sitting room with a sofa and a bedchamber and bathroom accessible through two doors at the back of the room.

He looked for a place to hide. The house didn't have closets for some reason so Adrien was at first at a loss. Then he discovered an alcove in the bedroom containing pillows of various sizes stacked almost to the ceiling. Nestling himself out of sight among the pillows, he waited. He heard the door downstairs open and close, so he knew that the young woman had returned.

Adriensettled himself down to a long wait. He was good at it. It was one of the things he had learned from Yakob in the forest. He remained absolutely still and suppressed his breathing and heartbeat.

At 8:20 pm, by Adrien's watch, the door of the bedroom opened and he saw his target enter the room, retrieve something from a bureau, and walk back out of the room leaving the door open. He heard the water start to run in the tub in the bathroom next door. A little while later the water was turned off and Adrien heard a click, then Arabic music started to play. He waited ten more minutes.

He slowly extracted himself from the pile of baskets, careful to make no sound. The music from the bathroom was not loud. He could also hear splashing sounds like someone was bathing. He crept to the door and looked out into the sitting room. There was no one there. Silently he moved to the edge of the bathroom door and peered in through the crack on the hinge side of the door.

Hassan al-Aria was sitting in the tub with his back to the door. Adrien pulled the ice pick he had stolen from the hotel bar from inside his shirt and crept forward. He bent down next to the back of the target's head and whispered, "Vengeance from the Jews," Al-Aria jumped and started to turn his head. Adrien rammed the icepick into his right ear and shoved the handle upward and to the right, so the icepick shaft would tear into the brain stem. Al-Arian's eyes bugged out, his body stiffened, and his mouth flew open. Those were his last actions on earth.

Adrien removed the icepick. The target's death had been so quick, that there was only a tiny amount of blood in his ear. Weiss removed tissue from a box near the sink, wiped the blood out of al-Arian's ear and cleaned the shaft of the icepick. He rolled the tissue into a little ball and put it in his pocket.

The radio was sitting on a small table less than a meter from the tub. Arabic music was still playing. Adrien moved the table to the edge of the tub and tipped the radio into the bathwater. The room lights dimmed for a second and then brightened again.

Adrien switched off the light and moved to the only window in the bathroom. It was partially open to catch the evening breeze. It was dark outside except for a glow from the neon lights on the street to the left. Adrien steeled himself. This was the most dangerous part of the operation. If he was seen dropping from the window, he would be discovered, arrested and probably executed. He took a deep breath, and in one motion levered himself over the sill and dropped the four meters to the ground. He landed on the sandy soil, without spraining anything and without a lot of noise. All was quiet. Apparently, no one had seen him leap from the window. He breathed a sigh of relief and walked toward the street, watching where he stepped, to avoid making noise. At the front edge of the building, he paused before emerging. Seeing no policemen present and no one else looking in his direction, he joined the throng of tourists on the neon-lit sidewalk and was gone, headed back toward the hotel and an early morning departure from the airport. He ditched the icepick in a pile of rubble in a vacant lot. The guards standing in front of the building were talking to each other intently and hadn't noticed the shadowy figure emerge from the side of the house.

The next morning, the senior of al-Arian's bodyguards became concerned when his boss didn't come downstairs by nine a.m. He went up and discovered the body. The police were called. The Cairo police inspector assigned to the case was skeptical of the bodyguard's claim that the Jews had murdered al-Aria. Any fool could see that the idiot must have tipped the radio into the tub and electrocuted himself. But, just to be on the safe side, he ordered an autopsy on the body. As the ambulance attendants were carrying al-Aria out of his former house, Timothy Miller's plane was landing in Rome.

The next day, an autopsy was performed on the body of Hassan al-Aria. The medical examiner was an incompetent that had been appointed to his job because he was the area police commander's nephew. He had to kick back part of his salary to his uncle every month. In his report, the doctor said that it was his opinion that al-Aria died by electrocution. The Cairo police listed the death as a tragic accident.

CHAPTER FORTY-TWO

743 SHTAND STREET, APARTMENT 3C
TEL AVIV, ISRAEL
30 JULY 1956

Aleska Pisarski was twenty-three now and had grown to become a stunningly beautiful woman. She had a chance encounter on the street last month with a man who asked her if she would be interested in being a fashion model. He was impressed by her large eyes, high cheekbones and stately figure. Aleska brushed him off thinking he was just trying to pick her up, but took his card anyway.

The modeling agency turned out to be legitimate. She went to the agency and presented the card she had been given by the stranger. She was interviewed by several people and ended up across a desk from a short, fat bald man who was the owner of the agency. He spoke to her in English with a New York accent and rejected her as a fashion model.

"Your breasts are too big, sweetie. All the fashion models we represent are flat chested. Sorry. That's what the magazines want.

But, you could make some money posing nude for men's magazines if you wanted to."

Aleska had shaken her head, no.

"I didn't think you would," said the man and the interview was over.

Aleska should have been content with her life. Adrien made a good salary. Coupled with what she made at the orphanage, they had plenty to live on. Instead, she was miserable.

It was a normal evening in the apartment they shared. Adrien was sitting in his chair reading a book and twisting the hair of his right eyebrow with his fingers. For the ten millionth time, she looked at him with love and desire.

Back in Poland, after seeing her parents and grandfather shot by the SS, she watched her sisters get rounded up and taken away by a group of German soldiers. Later, when she was captured by the German on the motorcycle, she knew that she was in desperate trouble. In the farmhouse, seeing the evil in his eyes and smelling his foul breath, she had given up hope and was sure he was going to do to her what men did to women and then kill her.

Then Adrien had appeared and killed the German. It was a reprieve from death. Aleska had looked at his youthful face and cried with gratitude. She wondered if he was one of those blonde haired angels her mother had told her about when she was little. Whether he was supernatural or not, Adrien was the first person who had helped her since the farmer and his wife she was living with were shot. He had just rescued her from death. Still, she felt utterly alone. She had no one in the world who cared if she lived or died and nowhere to run. In those moments after the German was killed, Adrien became not just her savior but her lifeline, and she clung to him with an intensity born of desperation.

Aleska willingly shared the hardships and dangers of living

among the partisans and the trek to the American zone. During their stay in the DP camp and after arriving in Israel, Adrien had fiercely protected her, while treating her like a sister. During all this time she was terrified that Adrien would abandon her. Aleska thought back and decided that it was during the winter they spent in the cave in Poland that she had fallen hopelessly, irretrievably in love with him. From then on, he was her shining star.

A new terror had arisen when they arrived at the kibbutz. She saw the girls there flirt with Adrien while arching their backs and thrusting out their breasts as she stood by and stared daggers at them. Aleska was terrified that Adrien would have sex with one of them and marry her. That was when she started to walk around nude in front of him. She was trying to tempt him with her body, but it hadn't worked. Even as her body got more mature and they moved to Tel Aviv, it hadn't worked. He would only avert his eyes and act embarrassed. Tonight Aleska, staring at the man she loved, reached a tipping point.

She got up from the sofa and went into the bedroom where she carefully checked her appearance in a mirror. She thought she looked pretty good. She marched back into the living room and planted herself in front of his chair, and leaned forward.

"Adrien Weiss, look at me."

Weiss looked up at her with a quizzical expression.

"What is wrong with me?"

"Wrong with you? Nothing is wrong with you. You look nice," replied Adrien in a slightly exasperated tone.

"Then why don't you want me? Why don't you want to make love to me?"

He looked up at her with a shocked expression for a few moments before speaking.

"Aleska, are you saying that you want me to love you in a physical way? I would give my life to protect you, you know that. Are you saying you want me to be your lover?"

"That is exactly what I am saying. I want you to put your hands on me. I want you to make love to me. I want to be your wife and bear your children." Tears began to freely flow from her eyes as she said this.

Adrien looked up into her anxious eyes.

"Do you really feel this way? Do you truly want me to love you in that way? I cannot take advantage of you. I promised that I would protect you."

Aleska planted herself on his lap, forced up his face and kissed him on the lips. She felt him harden under her thighs and it excited her.

"Adrien, if you don't make love to me I will just die. I love you so. I want no other but you. If you reject me I will die a spinster."

Suddenly Adrien kissed her fiercely. The hard muscles of his arms encircled her. Aleska felt giddy and started to get very aroused. She was about to shed her clothing and drag him into the bedroom. Suddenly, he went still and his arms relaxed their fierce hold. She looked into his eyes, afraid.

"I will not make love to you until you are my wife. Doing otherwise would not be honorable."

Aleska laughed to herself. She had figured out what Adrien did for the Israeli government. He killed people. Yet he wouldn't sleep with her because it wouldn't be honorable! My, what a complex man I love, she thought.

"Does that mean that you want to marry me? Do you love me too?"

"Ja," Adrien looked up at her like a little boy with a guilty, sheepish look.

The blood rushed to Aleska's head and she saw little stars floating in front of her eyes. She couldn't say, "yes," fast enough.

"Before we are married I have a duty to perform. It is a promise I made to my grandfather."

"You are going to kill the people responsible for murdering your family, aren't you?"

"Ja, I would have done it before, but I wanted the bastards to get warm and comfortable in their lives. I wanted them to pat themselves on the back and think they had gotten away with their crimes before I brought hell down on them."

Aleska thought about the Germans that had murdered her parents and grandfather and probably her sisters also. She wished she was a man and had the skills Adrien had. She would love to track them down and kill them. As far as she was concerned, all the Nazis deserved to die. She wished she could go with Adrien and watch those evil men squirm, but she knew it was impossible.

"Perform your duty, Adrien and then come back to me. I will be waiting," said Aleska and laid her head on his shoulder.

CHAPTER
FORTY-THREE

24 NIEDERHOLZSTRASSE
BASEL, SUISSE
21 AOUT ,1956

The children, two boys ages ten and twelve, were arguing with each other and his wife looked annoyed when Peter Balthis came down to breakfast. He was a distinguished looking man in his late thirties with a hint of grey at the temples of his wavy brown hair. Wearing a dark, somber suit with matching waistcoat and conservative tie, he was the very picture of a conservative Swiss banker.

Running a little late, he bolted his food and fled the bedlam that was often his home life with two preteen boys. Although he was a high officer in the Bueche & Cie Bank and could afford a car and driver, he preferred to take the streetcar to a stop near the bank and walk the rest of the way.

There had been a rain shower during the night and this morning the air was fresh and clean as he approached the bank. If it wasn't for Senor Mendoza I would be a happy man, Peter sighed to himself.

The employees greeted him politely as he walked by their desks on the way to his office, which was big and ornate with dark heavy furniture and paintings of dead Swiss bankers on the walls. The decorating style was deliberate, meant to suggest stability, tradition and conservative values. Peter hung up his raincoat but not his suitcoat, seated himself behind his desk and began his day.

At a little after ten, Peter's assistant, Hans, knocked and entered his office.

"Pardon me, Monsieur Balthis, but there is a man out in the lobby who wants to make a substantial withdrawal of one and a quarter million American dollars."

Balthis cleared the top of his desk of papers and told Hans to show the gentleman in.

A taller than average, athletic-looking man with neat blonde hair and blue eyes, wearing a tan suit came in and Peter motioned him toward a chair. The man sat.

"Bonjour Monsieur," said Peter in French. Basel was nestled on the Swiss border, just where Germany and France came together. Most of Peter's clients spoke one of the two languages. He always started off speaking in French.

"How may I help you?"

The man replied, also in French.

"In September 1939, my Grandfather, Monsieur Erhard Weiss deposited one million, two hundred thousand American dollars in this bank. The account number is 162465. And the code phrase is "Natalie's gold." I wish to withdraw this sum and any interest that has accrued."

Balthis felt as if someone had punched him in the gut. This was one of the "special" accounts! Peter thought fast.

"The bank doesn't have that much American cash at the moment. Can you come back tomorrow? We should be able to get it by then. In the meantime, what is your name and where are you staying. The bank would be happy to pay for your room tonight."

"I am Adrien Weiss. I am staying at the Schweizerhof, and it will not be necessary for the bank to pay for the room."

Sweating, Peter shook hands with Monsieur Weiss and he left. As soon as he was out the door, Balthis picked up his phone and dialed. By the time the person he called answered, he was close to panic.

"I must see you today. Say, five o'clock at the usual place."

The rest of the day was torture for Peter. At four-thirty he rushed out of the bank and walked to a bar two blocks away, which was his usual meeting place with Mendoza the Spaniard.

Peter's association with Senor Mendoza dated from 1954. Peter was on a business trip to the South of France when he decided to swing by Monte Carlo for a day or two. Peter fancied himself an excellent baccarat player. He played for four hours the first day. He won at first, but a few hours later he was down three million francs and Peter was agitated. What would he tell his wife? Would the board members at the bank hear of this? Would he lose his position?

The next night he returned to the baccarat table determined to win his money back but there was a problem. The casino wouldn't advance him any more money. Peter was dejected and feeling very sorry for himself. He began to down drink after drink in the bar and was well on the way to getting drunk when Señor Mendoza appeared. He was a big muscular man in an impeccably tailored suit and sported a large gold ring in the shape of a bear's head on his right hand. The two struck up a conversation and became very friendly. After several drinks, Peter lost count. Mendoza offered to lend him some money to continue playing, persuading him his luck was about to change. Like a fool, he had accepted the offer. He returned to the tables and lost ten million francs of Mendoza's money.

At the end of the evening, Mendoza was no longer friendly. He wanted his money back, saying menacingly that he represented a powerful organization and hinted that Peter would be killed if he didn't come up with ten million francs. Peter cowered before the Spaniard. Mendoza then offered a way out. Close to a breakdown, Peter was eager to hear his offer.

Mendoza said that millions of Jews had died in the war. Some had accounts in banks like the one Peter worked for. Any Jews who were still alive would have retrieved their money by 1954. Therefore, the account holders who hadn't shown up were dead. Mendoza suggested that Peter take money from these accounts to pay back his organization.

"A perfect arrangement," said Mendoza. "The Jews are dead. They don't need the money. But we do."

Against his better judgment, Balthis had done what Mendoza wanted. It should have ended there, but it didn't. Mendoza had contacted him again wanting more money. He threatened to expose Peter as an embezzler if he didn't cooperate. Since then Peter had been owned by Mendoza's organization and a lot of money had been pilfered from dormant accounts with Jewish names. There had been no questions raised until today.

Sitting at a booth in the back of the dark bar, Peter told Mendoza about Weiss showing up for his grandfather's money. Mendoza's gold bear ring gleamed in the dim light.

"What is his name and where is he staying?"

Peter told him.

"Don't worry about this. I will take care of it," said Mendoza and left the bar.

Balthis went home in a highly agitated state. He snapped at his wife when she greeted him and ignored the boys. He sat in his study and drank until late. Add murder to my list of crimes, he thought.

The next morning, he left for the bank at the usual time. He was hungover and in an agitated state. He stopped and bought a newspaper from a kiosk. On the front page was the story he both hoped for and dreaded. A man's body had been found floating in the Rhine river near the old docks. It also said the body was missing a finger. That was curious, Peter wondered about that.

At 10: 45 Peter's female secretary said a man was outside asking for him. Hans was down in the vaults and unavailable. Peter was concerned it was Mendoza. It was insanity for him to come to the bank. The man who walked through his door, however, wasn't Mendoza. It was Adrien Weiss.

Adrien had a pleasant expression on his face. When the woman left and closed the door, Adrien threw an object onto Peter's desk blotter. The banker looked down and saw to his horror that it was Mendoza's gold bear ring and there was a finger still inside it! Peter went ashen with fear and looked up to Adrien's face.

"Let me tell you what you are going to do. I want one and one half million American dollars in a briefcase in one hour. I will wait for it. I don't care how you get it. Maybe you can rob some other Jew's accounts. If you don't do as I say I will expose you as an embezzler and you will be sent to prison. While you are there, I will kill your wife and children in a very gruesome and painful way. Do we have a deal?" asked Adrien and smiled pleasantly.

Peter Balthis was nearly hysterical. He kept nodding his head at Adrien but didn't move.

"You had better get moving. Two minutes of your hour has already expired."

Peter was galvanized into action. Within the allotted time Adrien walked out of the bank carrying a black leather briefcase. He didn't count the money, Balthis was too terrified to cheat him. Before leaving the banker's office, Adrien said one last thing to him.

"By the way, Mendoza was working alone. There was never any gang behind him."

§

Because of the gabby old banker at the kibbutz, Adrien knew what to do with the money. He took a train to Zurich and went to the offices of the Batliner & Cie bank. An account was opened and his newly acquired American dollars were deposited. The account was in the name of Adam Browne, an Englishman. When Adrien was traveling the world putting together his legends, he had gathered some that he didn't tell Mossad about. Adam Browne was one of these. He kept out fifteen thousand dollars in one hundred dollar bills, for the expenses he would incur in tracking down some murderers.

Adrien set up a system allowing him to access the rest of the money through bank transfers to any bank in the world that took wire transfers. He provided a long list of code phrases to be used in succession for each transfer. All Adrien would have to do would be to go to any good-sized bank in the world, provide the account number and the appropriate code phrase from the list and he could have access to his money.

The banker who helped Adrien set up the account assured him that because of Switzerland's banking laws, all transactions would remain forever secret.

CHAPTER
FORTY-FOUR

LAVELL, ET CIE. FACTORY
PONTOISE, FRANCE
2 SEPTEMBRE, 1956

Louis Lavell sat behind his desk, clasping and unclasping his hands. During the sixteen years, he had owned his business, he had gone from a tall, thin man with a bushy head of hair to a balding, forty-three-year-old with a bulging waist. Opulent living and little exercise had made him an unhealthy man.

His business was in trouble, but he had just received a proposal over the telephone that might just save him. The sliver of hope for remaining solvent gave him great pleasure. There was a chance for him to get out from under his debts and save his factory.

After the Jew, Itzhak Weiss, had been deported to the east, Lavell had approached the German occupiers and offered to collaborate. His company received a contract to manufacture boots for the German Army and the rest of the war had been very profitable for him.

Louis had given little thought to the fate of the Weiss family. He didn't believe there was any deity or any accountability after death, so concepts like honesty and morality were stupid in the extreme. What was the point in obeying rules promulgated by the followers of a make-believe God? All of mankind was just animals fighting each other for survival on a rock hurtling through space. All that mattered to Louis was his personal comfort and pleasure. If he had very likely caused the deaths of the Weiss family, it was just too bad. Everyone had to die sometime. He didn't stop to consider the fallacy of these beliefs. Just because he chose to believe there wasn't a God didn't necessarily mean that there wasn't one.

Problems in his business had surfaced in the immediate aftermath of the war. Lavell was denounced as a collaborator and traitor. He responded that he had to make boots for the Germans because they threatened him with death if he didn't. In the end, he had to pay a huge bribe to a high official in the new French government to get out from under the charges. For a long time, Louis had been concerned that Itzhak Weiss would survive the war somehow, return to Paris and contest his ownership of the company. When Lavell heard nothing by the end of 1946, he relaxed.

Madame LeClerc had visited him shortly after the liberation. She demanded an explanation of Lavell's ownership of the company and was still suspicious when he explained the circumstances. She also demanded her share of the profits since 1940. Lavell hadn't paid her during the war. Louis was forced to pay up and continued to pay thirty percent of the factory's profit to the old hag.

Then Inspector Maurice Bretan had shown up at Lavell's office. He was the policeman Lavell had bribed to arrest the Weiss family. Bretan had threatened to expose to the government how Louis had obtained his business. Every year since, Lavell had also paid Bretan twenty percent of the revenue of the shoe factory.

Between Le Clerc and Bretan, Louis paid out half of his profits. Even with this, he could have survived but he lived too well. His family had a spacious apartment in Paris and a beautiful country home thirty kilometers outside the city. His wife was fashion conscious and insisted on wearing the latest designer clothing. Lavel's daughter had attended a succession of exclusive schools. The one where she was boarded now in Switzerland was enormously expensive. To add to his expenses, Louis kept a mistress named Monique in an apartment he paid for in the Sixth Arrondissement. In short, he took too much money out of his business and put none back into it.

When things started to get tight, Lavell had looked for ways to cut corners. He used cheaper leather in making his shoes and increased the daily quota for his workers. This ensured that the quality of his product suffered. Factory orders began to decline. Louis played games with his suppliers' payments and began to get a reputation in the French business community as being dishonest.

This morning, before he received the phone call from the American, Louis was looking at bankruptcy. He anticipated he could only go on for another few months.

The American said his name was George Thompson and that he represented the Evelyn Moore chain of department stores. Louis had heard of the stores. There were hundreds of them across the American midwest. Thompson told Louis that he wanted Lavell's company to provide a huge order of shoes to the Evelyn Moore stores. With sweaty palms, Louis agreed. Thompson was due to arrive at ten with a formal proposal and details. In his desperate state, Lavell didn't consider that there was something not quite right with the deal. Why would the Evelyn Moore company select an obscure French manufacturer with a shoddy product for such an arrangement?

Promptly at ten, the American was ushered into Lavell's office. He was younger than expected, in his late twenties, but he wore an expensive, Saville Row suit. He had dark hair and blue eyes that gave him a handsome Celtic appearance. The American stuck out his hand and spoke loudly in American English. Why do Americans always talk so loud? wondreed Louis.

"Mister Lavell? I'm George Thompson and I'm pleased to meet you." Louis noted that Thompson's handshake was firm and dry and he made direct eye contact.

"Ah, Monsieur Thompson, my pleasure." Lavell's English was poor and his words carried a heavy accent.

Thompson sat down across from Lavell's desk and produced a proposal, written in English and handed it to Louis.

"Our initial order will be for fifty-thousand pairs of shoes based on styles sold by LE CHAUSSURES PAR NATALIE, a company operating in Paris in the thirties. We are trying to start a revival fashion trend featuring that era. We had in mind paying you five dollars per pair."

Five dollars per pair? That was two hundred fifty thousand American dollars! Louis mentally converted the sum into French francs. That was eight and three quarter million francs! Lavell almost wet himself with excitement. He would end up with a profit of over one hundred thousand American dollars. He could pay his debts and have plenty left over.

For the next half hour, the two men discussed the arrangement. Thompson said the proposal still had to be approved by the board of directors at Evelyn Moore Inc. but, with his favorable recommendation, that shouldn't be a problem.

"Now that we have agreed on doing business, I have a personal request," said Thompson.

"Anything, anything at all, Mr. Thompson," replied Louis.

"I have never been to Paris before. I was wondering if you could show me the sights. Maybe we could find some female companionship, maybe something exotic?"

"I think that could be arranged. I will come for you at your hotel, say around seven? Where are you staying?"

"The Ritz."

"Fine, until seven then." The two men shook hands and Thompson left.

When the door closed, Lavell was on the phone immediately with his mistress, Monique. "Exotic French sex!" Monique had echoed. She would do it if it was normal sex but "exotic French sex? She had visions of whips and chains and being suspended from the ceiling naked. She utterly refused.

Louis called his wife, who was still good looking, although a little old. For this one time she agreed with Monique. She was not having exotic French sex with Louis let alone an unknown foreigner.

Lavell thought about the problem. He would have to find a prostitute who wouldn't give the American venereal diseases to take back with him to America.

Louis picked Thompson up at the Ritz and took him to a ridiculously expensive restaurant for dinner. After that, he drove the American to the Pigalle district. There were plenty of prostitutes in the district's numerous cafes and bars.

They had drinks in several bars. Louis repeatedly pointed out seductively dressed women and raised his eyebrows. Thompson shook his head, no, to each, frustrating Louis. Late in the evening, they were walking down a particularly dingy street with little foot traffic when Thompson pointed to a red light bulb outside a seedy hotel down the street. They started walking toward it. As they passed the mouth of a dark alley, the American suddenly grabbed Lavell's shoulders and forced him into the gloom of the alley. Thompson was very strong. Louis tried to resist but he couldn't. He was backed up against a brick wall and felt a sharp object being pressed to his throat.

'Monsieur Thompson, why are you doing this," asked Louis, with naked fear in his voice. The American's face was very close. The American replied in perfect Parisian French.

"My name is not Thompson. It is Weiss. On 21 January 1943, you bribed a French policeman to arrest my family. We ended up in a death camp called Sobibor. My grandfather, parents and little sister were murdered there. What was the policeman's name that you bribed that day.?"

"His name is Maurice Bretan. Please don't hurt me. I will give the factory back to you. I never meant for your family to die," croaked Louis. There was a sudden stench. Lavell's bowels had emptied.

Weiss removed the sharp point from his neck and Lavell breathed a sigh of relief. A second later he felt a sharp pain in his left ear. This was followed by an exploding white light and then darkness.

So Louis Lavell went off to discover the answers to two questions that have puzzled mankind for millennia: Is there a God? And, if there is, are we accountable to him?

CHAPTER
FORTY-FIVE

COMMISSARIAT DE POLICE DU 9 ARRONDISSEMENT
14 BIS RUE CHAUCHAT
PARIS, FRANCE
19 SEPTEMBRE ,1956

T he police station for the 9th Arrondissement of Paris resembled most police stations around the world. It was run down and shabby, badly in need of maintenance. Built at the turn of the century, its battered wood paneling showed numerous impact marks and dents where heads had been slammed against it over the years by over-zealous policemen. The furniture was also worn and scarred. Poor lighting contributed to the dilapidated look. Everyone smoked, so a blue haze suffused the room. The water closets and washroom were in another building out in the back garden where the privies had once stood. Because the jurisdiction of the station included part of the Pigalle Quarter, a steady stream of prostitutes, pimps, and pickpockets, as well as their naïve victims, could be found there at all hours.

The office of the station commander was less shabby but by no means posh. It was six meters square with dark wood paneling on the walls. There was a wooden desk, an executive chair behind it and two hard wooden chairs in front.

Inspecteure Principal Maurice Bretan leaned back in the executive chair with his feet on the corner of the desk and his ankles crossed. A thick file was open on his lap and Maurice was studying it intently.

He was a tall man and big boned. He had the natural strength that people of his build possessed without having to exercise with weights. Though in his late forties, he looked much younger. His coarse black hair and mustache were still holding their own against the grey invasion. He perpetually wore the skeptical, world-weary expression of the veteran police detective.

Inspecteur Bretan commanded the Surete police force in the 9th Arrondissement of Paris. His men went by the formal title of Keepers of the Peace. To the Paris public, including the criminal element, they were the "Flics." They patrolled the streets, directed traffic and conducted minor criminal investigations. The file Maurice was studying was concerning the murder investigation of Louis Lavell.

On the morning of 3 September, one of his men had discovered the body of a man in an alley just off the Boulevard de Clichy in the Pigalle Quarter. Maurice was called to the scene. The finding of a body in the Pigalle quarter was in itself not that unusual. The district was the center of the vice trade in Paris and where you had vice, bodies had a way of turning up. They were usually dope addicts who had overdosed or prostitutes who had unfortunately angered their pimps, but this body was different.

A well-dressed man was sprawled face down on the pavement in the midst of bits of broken glass, cigarette butts and used condoms. The body stank of shit. It was hard to tell but there didn't seem to be any sign of a struggle in the immediate area of the body. A police photographer was called and he photographed the body from many angles in the position it was found. Bretan and one of his men then turned the body over so they could see the face.

Maurice Bretan was so surprised he lost his balance and landed on his backside in the midst of the broken glass and other litter. It was Louis Lavell! He got to his feet in the most dignified way possible and stood over the body of his benefactor of twelve years. Bretan went down on one knee again and minutely examined what used to be Louis Lavell. He appeared to be unmarked except that his tie was askew and there was a tiny drop of blood in his left ear. More photographs were taken and the body was hauled off to the Medical Examiner's office. Depending on the cause of death, Bretan's station would either keep the case or he would hand it over to the Police Judiciaire.

Bretan had returned to his office deep in thought and closed the door. He sat and mulled over what Lavell's death meant. The loss of the yearly blackmail payment from Louis Lavell would be a blow. Maurice didn't consider himself a corrupt man, but Surete pensions were notoriously small and it was prudent for a man to build up a cushion to provide for himself and his family in their old age. Prostitution was still illegal in France. Bretan, as the commander of police in the 9th Arrondissement, received a small gift every month from each establishment in his district that engaged in the sex and narcotic trades. This wasn't new. It had probably gone on since the Paris police were organized in 1812. These gifts weren't large but, taken together, they added up.

Breton's arrangement with Lavell stemmed from a darker place. When the Germans had conquered France in six weeks, the citizens of France, including its police, were dispirited and shocked. They thought that the Germans wcrc unstoppable and would conquer the world. Seeing no alternative, the French cooperated with their new masters. The French police were ordered to enforce the Nazi racial laws in France and they complied with enthusiasm, trying to impress their new masters. Bretan, an ordinary gendarme then, routinely participated in numerous roundups of Jews and Gypsies. Trainloads of them were shipped east. It wasn't until late in the war when the Germans were shown to be far from invincible that the French police began to grow a backbone and temper their cooperation in the Nazi's persecution of the Jews. After the war, this cooperation with the Germans was a huge embarrassment. All records of French police collaboration with the Nazis were locked away and no one ever talked about it.

Louis Lavell had walked up to Maurice on a Paris street in 1943. He said that he knew where some unregistered Jews were hiding. Lavell then offered Bretan a thousand francs to arrest them. It was a simple matter to gather a small squad of fellow policeman and raid the Jews' apartment. There were five of them, an older man, a younger man and his wife and two children. Bretan overheard the conversation between Lavell and the younger man. He figured out pretty quick what was going on. Lavell wanted them out of the way so he could steal their business. The Jews were taken to the Drancy internment camp and then shipped east.

After the liberation, when the Third Reich was dying, news began to surface about what the Germans had done with the Jews the French had rounded up. Bretan had felt terrible. He thought about the two children in the family Lavell had bribed him to arrest. Maurice had a daughter of his own. He decided to make life hard for Louis Lavell and at the same time help himself. He squeezed twenty percent of the profits from the stolen business, payable on a yearly basis, out of Louis Lavelle. The arrangement had proven very profitable for Maurice Bretan.

Who would want to murder Louis? Bretan's policeman's instinct told him that it was a murder. Louis was a sneaky little crook. It was possible that he had cheated the wrong people and gotten killed for it. But over the years Bretan had developed a finely tuned sense of self-preservation. Now alarm bells were going off in his head. He was sure the murder could mean personal danger to him.

Three days later, the medical examiner's report arrived. He said Lavell had died from the thrust of a long, thin object into his brain through his left ear. It was definitely murder. Bretan notified the Regionale de la Police Judiciaire de Paris and they took over the case.

They were the agency charged with investigating murders. Maurice asked them to send copies of their reports to him.

This morning a copy of the case file had arrived from the Judicial Police. The day of the murder Louis had met with an American who presented him with a business proposal, supposedly from a large American department store chain. The American had said his name was George Thompson. Both Lavell's wife and mistress said that he and Thompson were going out together that night to have sex with prostitutes. The Judicial Police contacted the president of the department store chain in America. He said he never heard of George Thompson.

So the American was the murderer. The Judicial police got a good description of him from Lavell's secretary. He was a little taller than average, in his late twenties with dark hair and blue eyes. He appeared very athletic and wore an expensive suit. The description and the method in which the murder was carried out spoke of a very capable assassin.

Bretan thought about the weapon. The medical examiner said that it was incredibly thin, less than one cm in diameter, and 24 cm long. Maurice thought about that. What weapon fit that description? Then, out of the blue, it hit him. An icepick! It was a brilliant choice. Available everywhere and untraceable. The thought of it gave Maurice an involuntary shudder.

In the file, the Judicial police included a copy of the spurious proposal that the killer gave Lavell in the hours before the murder. Maurice read through it. He stopped when he saw the name, Le Chaussures Par Natalie. Why did the killer pick that name?

Bretan picked up his telephone and called a clerk he had dealt with before in the bureau that was in charge of business regulation in Paris. After waiting for ten minutes, the bureaucrat came back on the phone and told him that Le Chaussures Par Natalie, was a high-end shoe store that opened for business in 1926. The original owner was listed as Erhard Weiss. The store was still in business but with a different owner.

Maurice put down the telephone and concentrated. What was the name of the family Lavell had bribed him to round up? At first, he drew a blank, it was all so long ago. Then he remembered a conversation he had had with Lavell three years ago. Louis had been bragging about production at his factory and had said, "This is better than that Jew Itzhak Weiss ever did."

Bretan now knew that Lavell's death was a revenge attack. But the killer had tried to be too cute. In using the name of the Weiss family business, he had given the game away. Maurice now had to assume that he was also a target. It was frustrating that he could tell no one about his deductions. To do so would necessitate admitting he had been bribed to send a Jewish family to their deaths. And how would he explain taking money from Lavell all those years? If that came to light, he could end up in prison. No, he couldn't tell anyone.

Maurice Bretan, in spite of his years as a policeman and all the suspects he had confronted, was frightened. He could be the target of a very clever assassin.

§

The policeman was actually in no danger. The killer of Louis Lavell wasn't anywhere near Paris. In fact, he wasn't even in France. At the same time Bretan was figuring out the motive for Louis Lavell's assassination, Adrien Weiss was in Bad Arolsen, Germany. He was standing at the reception counter of the International

Tracing Service. He had an appointment with Frau Dressler.

The International Tracing Service was established as the war in Europe drew to a close. Under a charter signed by all of the Allied powers except the Russians, the service's mission was to reunite families and friends after the dislocations of World War Two. At first headquartered in Munich, the service had moved to Bad Arolsen in 1955. Ironically, its new location was a former Nazi SS barracks.

The morning after he killed Louis Lavell, Adrien boarded a train in the huge Gare Du Nord station in Paris. His destination was Kassel Germany. Weiss was perfectly groomed, wore an expensive suit, and traveled first class. The charade cost a lot of money, but police and border guards gave less scrutiny to wealthy, well-dressed people. They were afraid to discomfort them. The rich bastards might complain to the policemen's superiors and cause all kinds of trouble.

In the station, Adrien bought a copy of Le Monde. Wearing cloth gloves and using his penknife, he cut out an article describing the strange case of a Paris businessman found dead in the Pigalle quarter. He poked a tiny hole in the cutout article, put it in an envelope he obtained from the concierge desk and sent it to Maurice Bretan at his home. Obtaining his address had been easy. He was listed in the Paris Telephone directory. The clipping was meant to terrorize Bretan and make his life miserable.

Adrien had no intention of ever physically going near the police inspector. He had something else in mind. Bretan was only a corrupt policeman and played but a small part in the chain of events set in motion by Louis Lavell. If he had not accepted Lavell's bribe, the dishonest bastard would only have found another who would. In short, Bretan was not worth the risks involved in killing him.

Not that Maurice Bretan was without guilt. He stole Adrien's grandfather's gold and he had treated Gabbi shamefully, shouting at her and making her cry. Adrien just wanted Bretan to experience some of the terror and uncertainty his family had experienced when he raided the Weiss apartment in Paris.

He left France because it would have been stupid not to. A killer who remained at the scene of his crime deserved to be caught. The Paris police would all have an artist's rendering of his face by now and would be comparing it to people they met on their rounds.

He got off the train in Kassel and booked himself into the Schlosshotel Bad Willhelmshone Hotel, the best in town, though shabby by Paris standards. He was using the identity of Peter Mays, an Englishman. After settling in, he rented a small car, a Volkswagon, and drove to a local bank, the Suden-Bank Hessen. He transferred twenty thousand dollars from his Swiss account. The fifteen thousand he had originally kept out was almost depleted.

Adrien drove around Kassel. After a while, he found what he was looking for, a used clothing shop. He bought a coat, shirt, trousers and a pair of sturdy shoes. All the items were showing signs of wear but were clean. Once Adrien donned the items, he would appear to be a lower class German working man. He asked the proprietor to bundle up the items. Weiss carried the bundle back to the hotel. He dined on sauerbraten in the hotel dining room and went to bed early.

The next morning, 5 September, Weiss left the hotel and drove his rented Volkswagon out of Kassel and to the northeast. He was headed to Bad Arolsen, thirty kilometers away. During the trip, he pulled off the road onto a farm track and into a copse of trees. Adrien exchanged his expensive suit for the secondhand work clothes he had bought the day before. He soiled his hands with dirt, working the soil under his fingernails, then wiped them off on his trouser legs.

Weiss entered the offices of the International Tracing Service and was given a smile and handshake from the receptionist behind the counter. She was a slim blonde woman and rather plain. She asked Adrien in German how she could be of service. Weiss introduced himself in the Russian accented German, he had been practicing for weeks.

"Ja, help me bitte, Need find cousin from Ukraine."

"Please be seated. I will summon someone to help you."

About five minutes later, a short, stout woman in her forties emerged from a door behind the counter and asked Weiss to follow her. They walked down a long hallway with many closed doors leading off it. At the one open door, the woman entered and seated herself behind a desk. With a gesture, she invited Adrien to sit.

"I am Frau Dressler. How may I help you?"

"Ja, Bitte. Must find cousin. Konstantiyn Yovenko from Kiev."

Frau Dressler wrote the name onto a pad.

"What is your name?"

"Mykhaylo Kostachuk."

Adrien had thought long and hard about how to answer this question. At first, he had planned to make up a name. But then he thought, what if they contact Yovenko and tell him who is looking to find him? If they give him a name he doesn't recognize, he might get suspicious and bolt. Then Weiss would never find him.

On the other hand, giving a name that Yovenko knew, Mykhalo Kostachuk, presented its own problem. Yovenko might have heard that Kostachuk had been executed by the Russians. He might figure out someone was stalking him and surely disappear for good. After long consideration, Weiss decided to give the name of Yovenko's friend.

"When did you last see Herr Yovenko?" asked Frau Dressler.

"In Poland, 1944. We run away. He get lost."

"Can you give me his height, weight, and age?"

"180 cm tall 80 kilo, thirty year."

"Very well. It should take less than two weeks to find out about Herr Yovenko. Is there an address or telephone number where you can be reached?"

"No, no. I come back two weeks. "

"Fine, I will see you back here on 19 September."

Frau Dressler showed him out and he returned to Kassel to wait.

Adrien had two weeks to kill. Kassel was where his family had come from originally, before moving to Paris. He decided to tour the town and maybe ask if anyone remembered his grandfather there. He drove to the town center and parked his car. The buildings were all fairly new and were built in a boxy, ugly, modern style. Weiss learned from a man in an apothecary that the town had been almost totally destroyed by American bombers in 1943. Ten thousand people had died. The way the man said it, made it sound like he wanted sympathy for the dead. Adrien had no sympathy, not for Germans.

Later, he asked an elderly man on the street where the Jewish quarter was. The old man scowled and spat a reply before stalking off.

"There are no filthy Jews in Kassel, not anymore."

Adrien walked the streets. The people were standoffish. He saw no sign of a Jewish presence in the city. Then on his fifth day in Kassel, he came to a section of street that looked like it had been torn up and hastily resurfaced. Weiss looked down and noticed that the street had been resurfaced using Jewish tombstones. Some looked recent, their Hebrew writing sharp. Others were very old. He walked back to his car and returned to the hotel. He didn't venture out again.

§

Frau Dressler appeared and greeted Adrien.

"Herr Kostchuk, I have some results for you. Please follow me."

Once again seated in her office, Dressler slid two photographs across the blotter to him.

"I have discovered two people with the name you gave me. Is either one of the men in the photographs your cousin?"

Adrien looked at the photographs. The one on the right was his target, the man who had beaten his mother to death. He picked up the picture and handed it to Frau Dressler.

"This my cousin," said Adrien, and Dressler smiled.

"Your cousin emigrated to the United States in 1951. The American immigration authorities list his city of residence as Detroit, Michigan."

CHAPTER FORTY-SIX

21195 VERNE AVENUE
DETROIT, MICHIGAN
10 OCTOBER 1956

Konstantyn Yovenko was a bully. Most bullies are the way they are because they were themselves bullied as a child. A kind of weird transference takes place in which they emulate what had been done to them when they were young, weak and helpless. This wasn't the reason Yovenko was a bully. Konstantyn Yovenko was a bully because he was an evil bastard.

He terrorized his wife Lenya and his two pre-teen daughters. If his meals were not cooked to his liking, the Ukrainian would throw his plate of food against the wall and explode in a fit of rage. To him, his wife and daughters only existed to be his drudges. They continually went about with fat lips, swollen eyes and bruises from his thrashings. Konstantyn was also rude and surly to his neighbors, having no friends on the block. To a person, his neighbors considered the Ukrainian to be a "class A asshole."

He worked at the General Motors Cadillac assembly plant on Clark Street in Detroit.

There, he was the leader of a cabal of racists and malcontents who harassed and mocked their fellow workers who happened to be Jewish or black. He seemed to be getting away with it. Numerous complaints to management had gone unheeded.

Konstantyn made forty-eight dollars and fifty cents a week at the plant. It was enough to pay the rent on the tiny house he shared with his wife and daughters and buy food and gas for his ten-year-old car and the two six-packs of Pabst Blue Ribbon Beer he consumed every night.

§

After the Sobibor revolt and escape, Konstatyn had helped the Germans round up the remaining Jews in the camp, who were shot down without mercy. He then tramped through the woods in the area for the next week as part of a Jew-hunting party. They found a few and shot them.

Then Konstantyn and the other Ukrainian guards were put to work alongside numerous Poles from the surrounding villages to dismantle the camp. They tore down the buildings and other structures and the debris was hauled away on trucks. When the land was cleared, they planted trees on the grounds Sondercommando Sobibor had occupied to try to cover up what had been done there.

Konstantyn was transferred to Auschwitz where he worked as a perimeter guard until the Russian Army drew close. On 17 January 1945, Heinrich Himmler ordered Auschwitz to be evacuated. Fifty-eight thousand emaciated prisoners stumbled west, guarded by the SS and Ukrainian guards, one of whom was Yoshenko. Twenty-thousand made it to their destination at the Bergen-Belsen concentration camp in Germany. Along the way when Konstantyn saw a prisoner falter, he would beat him to death with an iron bar.

He enjoyed the way the bar crushed their skulls.

On 27 April 1945, Yoshenko deserted his post, threw away his uniform and joined the throngs of refugees choking the western German roads. A month later he surfaced in the Ukranian DP camp at Regensburg where he stayed for five years. During his stay in the camp, he was reunited with his wife and young daughters after they experienced a harrowing journey.

When the Soviets reoccupied the Ukraine, Lenya Yoshenko was sent packing by her neighbors and she fled west. It turned out her hostile neighbors did her a favor. If she had waited for the political police to arrive, she would have been shot or swallowed up by the gulag system, never to be seen again. The trip west was long and arduous and she had to sell her body on several occasions in exchange for food.

When she arrived in the American Zone, she made the biggest mistake of her life. She signed up with the International Tracing Service to find Konstantyn. She had regretted her decision every day since.

In June 1950, Konstantyn applied for political asylum in the United States. He said he was an anti-communist Ukrainian and would face persecution in his home country if he returned. He made no mention of his activities during the war. In April 1951, Konstantyn and his family were granted asylum in the United States and they settled in Detroit Michigan.

§

Konstantyn Yoshenko sat on the couch in his living room. He was watching Dragnet on the flickering black and white television set. He didn't allow his wife and daughters in the room when he watched television. They had to stand in the kitchen and watch through the pass-through window without making any noise.

Physically, he was a squat man with muscular shoulders. His job at the plant was to swing heavy tires up onto axles and the muscles of his arms bulged. He had a square Slavic face with brown hair, cropped short into a crew cut style. Konstantyn had just finished his eighth bottle of beer of the evening. He set the empty bottle down on the floor and contemplated going to the refrigerator to get another. Maybe in a while, he thought, after I belch.

Konstantyn scoffed at the show he was watching. Why did American cops worry so much about rights? In the SS they knew how to handle criminals--beat the shit out of them until they confessed and then shoot them. Americans were too soft. They let the niggers and the Jews get by with too much. The American police were not feared as the SS had been. That was the secret, fear. It was the only way to keep people in line. His disdain for American society didn't mean he wasn't glad to be in America. This was better than a KGB prison or a bullet in the back of the neck.

Konstantyn's thoughts were interrupted by a loud thump on the side of the house. He decided to go outside and check his car. The neighborhood had been experiencing a few car burglaries lately. He would dearly love to catch some nigger breaking into his car. It would give him the excuse to cave in another head. Getting up from the sagging couch, he caught sight of his wife and daughters standing in the kitchen, their frightened eyes staring at him.

"You bitches go to bed," he snarled, and they ran to their bedrooms.

Yoshenko walked out of his kitchen door and went to stand by his 1946 Ford sedan. It looked okay. He was turning to go back in the house when he felt a blow on the back of his head. A bright light exploded in his brain and then there was only darkness.

He awoke in what he assumed to be the trunk of a moving car.

His wrists were shackled behind his back. He gingerly explored with his fingers and discovered he was in handcuffs. His ankles were also shackled with a bigger version of the cuffs on his hands. The chains of the handcuffs and leg shackles were connected by a length of rough rope that was knotted too tight for Yoshenko's blunt fingers to untie. He was effectively immobilized.

He wondered who was behind this. Was he under arrest and in the trunk of a police car? He dismissed the notion. The police were pussies and didn't operate this way. This was more like what gangsters did to their victims. Konstantyn racked his brain, trying to think of how he might have inadvertently offended a gangster.

The car went over a series of bumps and what Yoshenko thought were some railroad tracks. Next came a bumpy dirt road and he could hear weeds brushing against the underside of the car. Then the car came to a stop. Konstantyn heard the driver's door open and close and the sound of a key being inserted in the trunk lock. The trunk lid swung up.

The Ukrainian looked up at a man in his twenties with neatly combed blonde hair and blue eyes standing over him. The stranger was wearing gray slacks and a black leather jacket. Over the top of his clothes, his kidnapper was wearing a cheap plastic raincoat.

Konstantyn tried to bully his way out of his situation.

"What the fuck are you doing to me? When I get loose, I am going to beat the shit out of you."

The blond man only smiled and grabbed Yoshenko by his ears and began dragging him out of the trunk. It hurt so bad that the Ukrainian helped him by leaning forward and rolling out of the trunk onto the ground.

Yoshenko looked around. They appeared to be in a deserted warehouse district. There was no sign of anyone else around. The blonde man bent down and grabbed the chain on Yoshenko's leg irons. He dragged the bound man toward the open door of a building ten meters away. As he was being dragged past the car he had been locked inside, Konstantyn realized it was his own car! After dragging the Ukrainian through a steel door, the man swung it shut behind them. When they reached a concrete pad under a chain hoist, the man stopped.

The blonde man pulled a chain down from overhead and hooked it to the chain of the handcuffs. A second later, Konstantyn felt himself being hoisted in the air. The lifting stopped when his feet were about one meter off the ground. Yoshenko writhed and grunted with the pain. If he hadn't been so muscular, his shoulder joints would have dislocated. The blonde man stepped back and spoke.

"Konstantyn Yoshenko? Formerly of the Ukrainian SS auxiliaries?"

"Oh, fuck. You have the wrong man. I was a carpenter in Kiev."

The blonde man switched to German.

"Stop the lying. It will do you no good. My name is Adrien Weiss. On seven April 1943, I was a thirteen-year-old boy. I stood on the railroad platform at Sobibor and watched you beat my mother to death with an iron bar. You beat her until she wasn't recognizable as a human being. She was a kind woman who never did anything bad to anyone. I am here to avenge her death. You will die in the same way as she did."

Yoshenko looked into Adrien's cold blue eyes and knew that he was serious. He was starting to panic. He had enjoyed killing Jews during the war and loved to inflict pain, but the thought of his own pain terrified him.

"It was the Germans. They ordered me to do it. I didn't want to." Yoshenko's voice rose to a shout.

"I saw your face as you beat my mother. You were enjoying it."

Adrien walked behind the hanging man and came back with a meter-long piece of rebar reinforcing steel. When Konstantyn saw it, his eyes widened and he begged for his life.

"Oh, please, no, don't kill me. I am so sorry for what I did. I have a wife and daughters, please."

"You made a mistake Yoshenko. You allowed yourself to be listed in the Detroit telephone directory under your real name. I would still have found you, but you made it easy."

Adrien swung the steel bar in a forceful arc and it hit Yoshenko's right shin. There was a sharp crack as the bone was shattered. Konstantyn Yoshenko started to scream, but there was no one around to hear him, except Adrien Weiss and the ghosts of his many victims.

§

Lieutenant Jim Parker, Detroit Homicide Bureau, drove down the lonely dirt road near the river. Through the fog, he saw the flashing lights of the police cruiser parked off to the side. He drove up and got out. A uniformed policeman approached him. Beyond the police ca, there was another vehicle with the trunk lid standing open.

"Hi, Lieutenant. Got a messy one for you. My partner and I were patrolling and saw this car parked here where it shouldn't be. We checked it out and saw blood on the trunk lid.

It was unlocked so we raised the lid and found a dead guy. Someone must have been really mad at him. It looks like the suspect broke every bone in his body. He's like a bag of sticks."

"Let me go check it out."

"Lieutenant, do you think it's a mob hit?"

"I dunno, maybe."

CHAPTER FORTY–SEVEN

12 RUE ETIENNE DOLET
PARIS, FRANCE
2 NOVEMBRE 1956

T he clock on the mantle was the only sound in the room. Maurice Bretan sat in his study staring down at an unopened letter on the top of his desk. He was a wreck of a man. He had lost so much weight that his clothes hung on him like a drape. His hair, coal black forty-two days ago was now flecked with gray. His sagging facial skin had also turned an unhealthy shade of gray and his hands shook. All of this due to worry.

§

On 19 September, he had arrived home in an upbeat mood. On the ride home, he had convinced himself that he was overestimating his personal danger from the killer of Louis Lavell. After all, the killer had no way of knowing his name unless Louis had told him. The chances of that were small.

His well-being was shattered after dinner. His wife walked into his study as he was settling in his favorite chair and reaching for his pipe. She was carrying a letter in her hand.

"Maurice, this letter came for you on the fifth of September. I put it on the hall table. The maid was dusting that day and it must have been swept over the edge and fallen behind the table. I'm sorry. I hope it isn't anything important."

Bretan took the letter from her hand and smiled up at her.

"I'm sure it is nothing, Lucie. Don't worry about it."

After his wife walked away, Maurice absently tore off the end of the envelope, reached in with two fingers, and retrieved what was inside. It was a newspaper clipping. He unfolded it and his heart almost stopped. The color left his face. It was an account of Louis Lavell's death and there was a hole punched in it, presumably with an icepick. This was the beginning of Maurice Bretan's descent into madness.

There was no doubt now. He was being stalked by a deadly killer. What could he do? He couldn't tell his police colleagues without ruining his career and shaming his family. His jaw set. He decided to carry his gun wherever he went and be very vigilant. Maurice changed his daily routine. He went nowhere except the police station and his home. Walking to his car, he would cringe at the thought of an assassin sneaking up behind him and stabbing him between the shoulder blades with an ice pick. His work suffered. In front of his policemen, he would lose his temper over trivial things, then profusely apologize for his conduct. He closed and bolted his office door when he was inside, something he had never done before.

He slept very little and went around in a daze most of the time. At night, any creaking of the old building where he had his apartment would send him bounding out of bed with gun in hand. Bretan's wife became alarmed by the change in him. She repeatedly asked him what was wrong. His response was to shut her out and refuse to reveal anything.

One day there exploded in his sleep-deprived brain the idea that Louis Lavell's murder might have been an Israeli government operation. What if there was more than one assassin? What if there were a whole army of Jews waiting for an unguarded moment to kill him? Bretan's blood pressure shot up even more. If that was the case, anyone could be an assassin, especially every Jew. Maurice began to look askance at one of his policemen, Claude Zimmermann. Maurice watched the poor man like a hawk and never turned his back to him.

An incident in late October brought Bretan's bizarre behavior to the attention of his superiors. There was a fist fight in the Metro station off the Rue La Fayette. One of the participants was injured fairly badly and Maurice was called to the scene. He had just arrived and was talking to one of his policemen when out of the corner of his eye he detected movement beside him,. A well dressed, middle-aged woman was running past where Maurice was standing, intent on catching a train before the doors closed. Thinking the woman was an Israeli assassin, Maurice drew his gun, stuck it in her face and forced her to lie down face first among the cigarette butts and other litter on the floor. A minute later the woman was helped to her feet and Maurice groveled in apology, but she complained to the Commissioner of the Paris Police.

The Commissioner wasn't pleased. Today he had sent his assistant to see Maurice in his office. He was to take some time off. His face was not to be seen in Paris for at least a month or until the furor died down. Bretan went home.

When he walked in the door to his apartment he saw a letter resting on the hall table. It was addressed to him and was postmarked in New York City last week. Maurice carried it into his study, placed it on top of his desk and stared at it.

§

He finally summoned the courage to open the envelope. He tore open the end and took out the folded piece of paper with shaking fingers. His palms began to sweat as he unfolded the note. One word was handwritten on it. "BIENTOT" (SOON) and there was a small hole punched in the letter N.

Maurice jumped up and ran to get his wife. He told her they were going to Nice for a holiday. She was bewildered but went to pack their bags. They caught the afternoon train and were in Nice before nightfall. Mrs. Bretan was thankful that her daughter was away at school and couldn't see the way her father was acting. They checked in to a moderately priced hotel. The rate was reasonable because it wasn't the main tourist season.

Maurice refused to leave the room for two days, only stirring from a chair to go look out the window. Finally, his wife could take it no more. She pushed him out the door and told him to take a walk. A warm spell had set in and the sun was bright. Maurice walked along the Promenade des Anglais amid a sparse crowd of mostly foreign tourists, enjoying the glorious sunshine. Maurice was vigilant, his head swiveled from side to side and he made frequent erratic movements to try to spot the Israeli assassins he was sure were following him.

His behavior caught the eye of a young plainclothes detective. Recently promoted from uniform patrol, he was working the pickpocket detail. Foreign tourists, particularly Americans, were easy marks for pickpockets. He studied Bretan for a moment and then approached him.

Maurice caught sight of the young man walking purposefully toward him and started. Finally the Jews were making their move, he thought. Maurice didn't wait to be approached. He bolted and the young policeman gave chase. They ran away from the beach along narrow streets past gawking tourists. After a few blocks, Maurice was blowing like a twenty-year-old horse. He had to stop. He frantically pulled out his gun and whirled to face the Israeli assassin. The policeman saw the gun and pulled his own. The two men blazed away at each other at twenty meters until they both ran out of ammunition. No one was hit. Neither one of them was a very good shot.

When the uniformed policeman shoved him in the back of a police van, Maurice was wild-eyed and shouting about Israeli assassins. The policeman just shook his head sadly.

An hour later the Paris Commissioner of Police received a call from his counterpart in Nice. It was decided that the incident would be covered up for the good of the reputation of the police. Maurice Bretan was temporarily stripped of his rank and committed to a mental hospital in Lyon for treatment. While there, he attacked his attending psychiatrist when he found out he was a Jew. Yelling that the unfortunate doctor was an Israeli assassin, his hands had to be pried from the doctor's neck. The psychiatrist got his revenge though. He discovered that Maurice was suffering from all sorts of dangerous, undiscovered mental illness. He wasn't released from the mental hospital until 1960.

CHAPTER
FORTY-EIGHT

DR. WURZBERGERSTRASSE 12
BAYREUTH, DEUTSCHLAND
13 FEBRUAR 1957

A fire blazed in the fireplace as the wind howled outside. Little pellets of ice made tiny tapping noises on the windows. Erich Wolf was perfectly comfortable. The central heating system in his home kept the temperature at precisely 21 degrees Celsius. A recording of Mozart was playing softly in the background. He was in his study in the master wing of his home. Erich was sitting in his favorite overstuffed chair wearing a robe over his pajamas. It was late and he was alone in the house. The servants had retired to their quarters in a separate building behind the main house. Mina had taken Addie on an overnight trip to Munich. They were going to attend a fashion show tomorrow. Addie had been a whirlwind of excitement when she had kissed Erich goodbye earlier in the day.

He was reading a legal brief and frowning. Between 1951 and 1953, the West German Bundestag had passed several compensation bills meant to pay the victims of the Nazis for their suffering. Erich didn't learn until 1954 that the bills were written in such a way as to severely limit the number of people eligible for compensation. Recompense was limited to victims of racial, religious and political persecution who had lived in Germany prior to the war.

The millions of people forcibly brought to Germany as slave laborers and residents of other countries who were murdered were excluded. People who had been starved and beaten to keep up war production were owed nothing. Erich had been outraged. He had recruited a group of young, hungry, aggressive lawyers and started a law firm in Munich. So far they had over three hundred clients, former slave laborers, suing the West German government. Despite the government being awash in money thanks to the post-war economic boom, they were taking a hard line with his clients about compensation.

Erich was suspicious about the German economic "miracle". He suspected that it had been largely fueled by the gold and other valuables that were looted from Jews and other victims of the Nazis. When Erich had worked at the SS Main Economic Office, he had seen firsthand the tons of gold, jewels and foreign currency that poured into the SS coffers during the war. Much of this wealth had not been accounted for.

Erich had joined the All German Peoples party last year. The party was very vocal in their opposition to racial and religious intolerance. They were also pacifist, opposing rearmament of the West German State. Favoring an arrangement with the east, they suggested that the western part of Germany become a non-threatening state on the model of Switzerland.

Erich shared these sentiments and contributed generously to the party. The tensions between the Americans and the Russians were rising. He didn't want Germany involved in another war, so soon after the carnage of World War Two. The American occupation troops had left in 1952, to be replaced by American combat formations arrayed against the Soviets. All it would take was an incident, some hothead pulling a trigger, for another world war to start.

Erich was not unaware that all his recent efforts to do the right thing--his charitable foundation, the law firm and his political turnaround, were an attempt to assuage his guilt for his part in the Nazi crimes. In spite of everything he had done, all his efforts, he still carried a huge weight of guilt.

His life was good. He had a loving wife, a beautiful, energetic daughter, and wealth that most men only dreamed of. Did he deserve to have all this after what he had done? His answer to himself was no. In his quest for peace from his demons, he had even tried going back to the church.

The priest who heard his confession was old, in his seventies. While younger priests in the German Catholic Church now wore black suits, this priest, Father Schmidt, still wore the long cassock.

In the confessional, Erich had poured out his sins. He had been a Nazi. He had killed the Brown Shirt officer and his wife. He murdered the Jewish businessman on Krystalnacht. He had stood by and approved as eight hundred Jews, including women and children, were shot. He had murdered a little girl and an old man at Sobibor and ordered the beating death of two more. He had participated in a vast conspiracy to steal the wealth of the people the Nazis murdered. When he was through, Erich was wringing wet with sweat. He would never forget the priest's response.

"I grant you absolution, my son. In wars, men do terrible things. Things they wouldn't dream of doing in normal times. What you were doing, you were ordered to do by your superiors, so don't let it trouble you so much. As for the Jews, they are under God's curse, for denying the true faith and crucifying our Lord."

As he sat back in the confession booth, stunned, Erich couldn't believe what he had just heard. The priest was saying that the Jews deserved to be killed for not becoming Christians and killing Jesus two thousand years ago! He felt like he was going to vomit. He fled the church and vowed never to return.

Erich heard a small metallic sound behind him. Suddenly sensing he wasn't alone in the room, he jumped up and whirled around. He saw a man standing four meters away from the back of the chair he had just left.

"Who are you, and what do you want?"

As he asked the question Wolf looked at the intruder. He was not so very big but appeared to be extremely fit. He had blonde hair and blue eyes and was wearing a gray overcoat over a blue suit and striped tie and was slowly screwing a long tube onto the muzzle of a small, ugly black pistol. If he is here to rob me, maybe he will accept what cash I have on hand, thought Erich.

"I will open the safe. There is a lot of money there. Take it and go."

'I am not here for your money," said the man with the gun in German with a Hessian accent.

"Then, what do you want?"

"Herr Wolf, I want to tell you a story. I am a Jew. My name is Adrien Weiss. On seven April 1943, the deportation train in which I and my family were confined arrived at the Nazi death camp, Sobibor. Ukrainian SS auxiliaries bullied us off the train and made my family and our fellow Jews form lines on the platform."

"An SS officer in a splendidly tailored uniform approached my family and ordered us to follow him. He took us to the edge of the platform and ordered us to stand in front of another group of Jews, who had been picked as workers in the camp. The other Jews, the other passengers from the train, were marched off into the camp to be gassed."

"The SS officer came and took the hand of my little sister, whose name was Gabbi, by the way, not quite three years old, and led her out in front of the group. The officer asked her if she wanted a sweet. Gabbi nodded her head. He told her to close her eyes and open her mouth. She was a friendly child who loved most everyone and she did what the officer asked. The SS man, without emotion, then shot her through the mouth."

"Imagine for a moment, Herr Wolf, how Gabbi must have felt in that split second before the blackness overcame her. Do you think she felt betrayed? Do you think her young brain was able to comprehend that trusting a German had just gotten her killed?"

As the stranger talked, Erich Wolf seemed to deflate. His mouth hung open and his skin took on the color of old parchment. An overwhelming feeling of dread and fear crept up his spine. He began to visibly shake.

"My mother and father rushed to Gabbi's aid and were met by two Ukrainians with iron bars who beat them until they were no longer recognizable as human beings. I, too, would have rushed forward but my grandfather grabbed my shoulders and told me to hide among the group of Jews behind us while he distracted the officer. My grandfather shouted insults at the SS officer. He walked toward him and was shot. I ended up working in the camp. I escaped in the Sobibor revolt and was a partisan in the forest. After the war, I escaped to Israel. I survived."

"While my parents were being beaten to death, my grandfather made me promise to perform a mission, on behalf of our family. I was to survive by any means, grow up, and one day hunt down the people who murdered our family and exact vengeance."

"When I first arrived in Israel, I lived on a kibbutz. I hated farm work and was bored. For something to do, I read books to educate myself. One of the books was the bible.

From it, I learned a lot about my heritage. In the early days of the nation of Israel after Joshua led them into the land of Canaan, they were ruled by judges. There were no police forces to control crime. If a man was murdered, a member of the victim's family would take it upon himself to hunt down his relative's killer and exact justice. The bible called these men, 'avengers of blood'. I am the avenger of blood for my murdered family."

"Hauptsturmfuhrer Erich Wolf, you are going to die for the innocent blood you spilled on that railroad platform at Sobibor. The two Ukrainians who beat my parents to death are already dead. One was executed by the Russians for treason and the other died by my hand last month in America."

Erich stared at Weiss. He looked in his eyes and saw only resolution there, no pity. They were the flat dead eyes of a killer. Erich suddenly, desperately wanted to live. He thought about rushing the blonde man and trying to overpower him but knew instinctively that he was no match for this man, so he remained still. Instead, he began to plead for his life.

"Oh please, Herr Weiss. I have a wife and daughter. I want to live to see my daughter married, with children of her own. I acknowledge my guilt. I deserve punishment for what I have done. Take my money. Take all of it. Spend it to help other Jews."

"My parents wanted to live to see their children grown up and married too. Their lives were cut short because they were Jews and, therefore, could be killed on a whim," said Adrien. Throughout the entire conversation, his voice had maintained a matter of fact calmness. It was as if he was ordering a meal from a waiter.

Erich took a different tack.

"You are alive today because of me. If I hadn't pulled your family out of the lines, you all would have been gassed a half hour later. You survived because of me. And what about the rest of the SS men at Sobibor? They killed thousands of Jews. I was only responsible for four deaths."

"My survival is of little consequence and the three deaths you speak of were my family. You stole something very precious from my family. You deprived them of the ability to breathe the foul air of Sobibor for thirty minutes more, to feel the breeze on their faces for thirty minutes more, for all of us to be together when the gas chamber doors closed. You deprived my family of thirty minutes more of life. As for the other monsters of Sobibor, let the family members of those they murdered come after them."

Erich desperately tried to come up with an argument that would convince Weiss to spare his life.

"I am not the same man today as I was when I did those terrible things. I have changed. I deeply regret the killing of your family. I have established a charitable foundation to help the poor. I underwrite the expense of an orphanage in Israel. I founded a law firm to fight for the rights of former slave laborers of the SS. To kill me now would not be fair."

Adrien looked around the room, then shook his head.

"Fair? Would it be fair for you to live on in opulence while my family's ashes are scattered on the ground at Sobibor? You don't understand. The things you say you have done with your money to help people are good, even noble deeds. But they don't cancel out your debt. Someone has to pay for the blood of my family. All the good deeds in the world will not cancel out the debt. It can only be paid in blood. Maybe the arguments you make would appeal to a normal man, even to me if I had been allowed to live out my life in Paris with my family. But you see, I am not a normal man. You Nazis have seen to that. I'm a killer, but one of your own making. You created me on that railroad platform at Sobibor."

Erich opened his mouth to answer and saw the muzzle of the gun erupt in a flash. Simultaneously, he felt a sharp pain at the back of his throat. Then a curtain of profound darkness descended on him never to lift. The small, forty grain .22 caliber bullet had entered his mouth, pierced the back of his throat and bored through to shatter the nerve center of his brain. He was dead before his body hit the floor.

§

Adrien searched around on the carpeted floor until he found the tiny .22 caliber shell casing and put it in his pocket. Quietly, he let himself out of the tall front door of the house and walked calmly through the blowing snow toward the street and his rented car. The gun he carried would be disassembled and the pieces tossed in the first river or lake he came to. Adrien Weiss looked up into the cloudy, snowy sky and whispered.

"Grandfather, I don't know if you can hear me, but I have kept my promise. Our family has been avenged."

EPILOGUE

SOBIBOR POMNIK
SOBIBOR, POLSKA
7 KWIECIEN, 2011

The rented Volvo sedan drove into the parking lot and stopped. Adrien Weiss was the first to emerge. He got out on the passenger side. He was eighty-two years old now with blown out knees, so he had to walk with a cane. He held on to the roof of the car to steady himself. His middle-aged son Erhard got out from the driver's door. The three women in the back seat were busy talking and not moving so Adrien had to prompt them testily to get out of the car.

"Raus aus dem auto."

Adrien's two daughters Natalie and Rachel smiled at their father and did what he wanted. The last person out was Aleska. As she emerged, she looked at her husband. The two exchanged a look of affection and intimacy that only those who had spent a lifetime together can manage.

The group set out toward the Sobibor memorial, Adrien walking in front with Erhard and the three women following behind.

In late February 1957, Adrien had returned home from Europe and married Aleska. They had wanted children right away but Aleska didn't get pregnant. They both fretted about this for the next three years. Then in 1960, it was like the turning on of a tap. A son, Erhard, was born. The next year brought a daughter, Natalie. A year after that the baby of the family, Rachel, was born. Natalie was now married to an Israeli businessman named Bloom. Adrien had tried very hard, but he didn't like him. Rachel was married to a Gentile American named Clark and lived in New York. Adrien liked Tim Clark very much. Erhard, though in middle age, had yet to marry. Altogether, Adrien had six grandchildren. He loved them dearly but didn't want them along on this trip.

Adrien had never told his children about what had happened to him and Aleska in World War Two. When they were little they would sometimes ask about grandparents. He would tell them that he would talk about it later. The children finally stopped asking. There were a lot of kids in Israel at that time without grandparents. Now, Adrien felt it was finally time. All three of his children were mystified as to why he had brought them to the ass end of Poland in such secrecy.

In 1960, when Erhard was born, Weiss had quit Mossad. He walked in one day and resigned. He said he had had enough of killing. For the next six-and-a-half years the agency tried to entice him back, but he refused. He took some of the money his grandfather had left him and bought a florist shop in Tel Aviv. Aleska helped him run the shop. They had seen so much ugliness in their lives, it was good to be surrounded by beauty. They both looked back at that time as the happiest of their marriage. Aleska went back to school at night and earned a Bachelor's degree in history in 1963.

Then in the run-up to the Six Day War, Mossad was finally able to convince him that he was desperately needed. The survival of Israel was on the line. For the next thirty-two years, Adrien was an agent, control agent, and spymaster, participating in many harrowing operations and momentous world events.

As the years went by, he warmed up to the fact that he was Jewish. He came to look at his fellow Jews as his big family. They were an argumentative and contentious people. If ten Jews got together, it was said that you would have twenty opinions on every subject. Finally, Adrien said, what the hell. As his grandfather would say, you may choose your friends but not your family.

The first part of the monument they encountered was a tall stone wall with "SOBIBOR" spelled across the upper part in big metal letters. Below the letters were eight bronze plaques. They all told the same story in different languages, that between 28 April 1942 and 14 October 1943, Sobibor was an SS-run extermination camp where approximately two hundred and fifty-thousand Jews met their death. In the end, the Jews revolted killed their SS tormentors and escaped into the forest.

A little further along there was a large, crude statue of a mother holding her child and crying out in anguish. Beyond that down a path was a huge pile of ashes and bone fragments surrounded by a low stone wall. When they saw this, the women began to cry. These ashes and bones had once been living, breathing human beings, killed for their misfortune of being born Jewish.

Adrien looked around. He was trying to spot the railroad platform. He reached in his inside pocket, retrieved his glasses, and put them on. He looked around again and saw what he was looking for. He led the group to a flat spot of cracked and broken pavement beside some rusty railroad tracks.

Standing on the spot of his family's murder, he began to tell his story. He told them about growing up in Paris and about their great-grandmother, who loved her family with a fierceness beyond description. He told them about a little girl who loved and trusted everybody. She had a ready smile and a rosy outlook throughout her short life. She didn't live to see her third birthday. He told them about the little girl's parents, whose last act on earth was to go to the aid of their child. He told them about the little girl's grandfather who willingly sacrificed himself that another child might have a chance to live.

Adrien told his children about life in the camp and the daily horrors he witnessed. He told them about his escape and living in the forest like a hunted animal. He told them about meeting their future mother there, who had been by his side since. He told them about the trek to the American zone and the DP camp. He told them about the immigrant ship and arriving in Palestine.

Lastly, Adrien told them about the promise he made to his grandfather and his hunt for his family's killers. He held nothing back. He told them he wasn't proud of what he had done. It was a duty performed and wasn't morally clean and tidy, but justice seldom is. He had avenged his family. The killers had not been allowed to go on living and think they had gotten away with murder. Adrien felt drained when he finished talking. He bowed his head and looked at the remnants of cracked pavement at his feet.

Aleska and the children were all weeping, even his middle-aged son, Erhard. They gathered around Adrien Weiss and put their arms around him. The group stayed that way for a good long time. Finally, emotions spent, the family began to make their way back to the car.

Suddenly, Adrien stopped and pulled Erhard aside. He waited until the women were out of earshot and with an intense gaze he looked into his son's eyes.

"My grandfather exacted a promise from me on this spot in 1943. Now I am going to ask you to make a promise to me. The clouds of danger are gathering. I can feel it in my old bones. Perilous times are ahead for Israel and the Jews. I have seen it all before. Promise me, Erhard! DON'T LET WHAT THE NAZIS DID TO THE JEWS HERE EVER HAPPEN AGAIN!"

Sgan Aluf Erhard Weiss, the newly appointed Commander of 106 "Raptor" squadron, Israeli Air Force, returned his gaze with hard as steel eyes.

"I promise, father. I'll do what I can, but I can tell you one thing for sure, the bastards won't find it quite so easy to do the next time."

THE END.

AUTHOR'S NOTE

Thank you for reading my book. If you enjoyed it, won't you please take a moment to leave me a review at your favorite retailer?

Thanks!

D. W. Drake

Sign up for email updates and receive free advance reading copies, updates on new releases, special offers and bonus content. You can contact me directly by email: dwdrake@savanatpress.com

You may also sign up at: www.savanatpress.com

www.ingramcontent.com/pod-product-compliance
Lightning Source LLC
Chambersburg PA
CBHW072121250626
47159CB00007B/2526